DAVID GILMAN

MASTER OF WAR

CROSS OF FIRE

HEAD of ZEUS

First published in the UK in 2020 by Head of Zeus Ltd

9 7 5 3 1 2 4 6 8

A catalogue record for this book is available from the British Library.

ISBN (HB): 9781788544948
ISBN (XTPB): 9781788544955
ISBN (E): 9781788544931

Printed and bound in Great Britain by CPI Group (UK) Ltd, Croydon CRO 4YY

Head of Zeus Ltd
First Floor East
5–8 Hardwick Street
London EC1R 4RG

WWW.HEADOFZEUS.COM

For Suzy

CHARACTER LIST

*Sir Thomas Blackstone
*Henry: Blackstone's son

Thomas Blackstone's men

*Sir Gilbert Killbere
*Meulon: Norman captain
*John Jacob: captain
*Renfred: German man-at-arms and captain
*Will Longdon: veteran archer and centenar
*Jack Halfpenny: archer and ventenar
*Ralph Tait: man-at-arms
*Richard Quenell: archer and ventenar
*Beyard: Gascon captain
*Othon: man-at-arms
*Aicart: Gascon man-at-arms
*Loys: Gascon man-at-arms
*Gabriel LaFargue
*Meuric Kynith: Welsh archer
*Tom Woodbrook, Robert d'Ardenne, William Audley, Thomas Berford: men-at-arms
*William Ashford: King Edward's sergeant

Welsh mercenary

*Gruffydd ap Madoc

ITALIAN CLERIC

*Niccolò Torellini: Florentine priest

BRETON NOBILITY AND SERVANTS

*Lady Cateline Babeneaux de Pontivy
*Lord Mael Babeneaux de Pontivy
*Jocard, Lady Cateline's son
*Jehanne, Lady Cateline's daughter
*Judikael: lord and ally of Babeneaux
*Gwenneg: lord and ally of Babeneaux
*Roparzh: captain
*Melita: servant woman
John de Montfort: English-backed claimant to the Duchy of Brittany
Charles de Blois: French-backed claimant to the Duchy of Brittany
Jean de Beaumanoir: lord and ally of Charles de Blois

FRENCH CLERICS, OFFICIALS, MERCENARIES AND VILLAGERS

Pope Innocent VI
Guillaume de Grimoard, Pope Urban V
Simon Bucy, counsellor to the French King
Bertucat d'Albret: mercenary leader
Garciot du Châtel: mercenary leader
*Roland de Souillac, physician
*Alphonse: Count de Foix's steward
*Master Gregory: Count de Foix's bailiff
*Raymond Villon: Mayor of Sarlat
*Guiscard the Lame: woodcutter

FRENCH NOBLEMEN AND MEN-AT-ARMS

Henry, Count de Vaudémont, Royal Lieutenant of Champagne

Gisbert de Dome, Lord of Vitrac
Gaillard de Miremont, Lord of Sauignac
Gaston Phoebus, Count de Foix et Béarn
Viscounts of Cardona, Pallars and Castelbou: allies and vassals of Gaston Phoebus
Marshal of the Army, Arnoul d'Audrehem
Jean, Count d'Armagnac
Monlezun, Frezensaguet, d'Aure, Jean de la Barthe, Terride, Falga, Aspet, Count de Comminges, Lords of Albret, lords of Pardhala: feudal lords and allies of d'Armagnac
Jean de Grailly, Captal de Buch: Gascon lord

French royalty

King John II (the Good) of France
The Dauphin Charles: the French King's son and heir
Charles, King of Navarre: claimant to the French throne

English royalty

Edward of Woodstock, Prince of Wales and Aquitaine
Joan, Princess of Wales

English knights and noblemen

Thomas de Beauchamp, Earl of Warwick
Sir John Chandos: English commander
Sir William Felton: Seneschal of Poitou

Teutonic Order

*Rudolf von Burchard: knight
*Walter von Ranke: knight
*Andreas von Suchenwirt: knight
*Wolfram von Plauen: knight

*Gunther von Schwerin: knight
*Sibrand von Ansbach: knight
*Albert Meinhard: half-brother
*Johannes Hartmann: half-brother

*Indicates fictional characters

1362

BLACKSTONE'S ROUTE

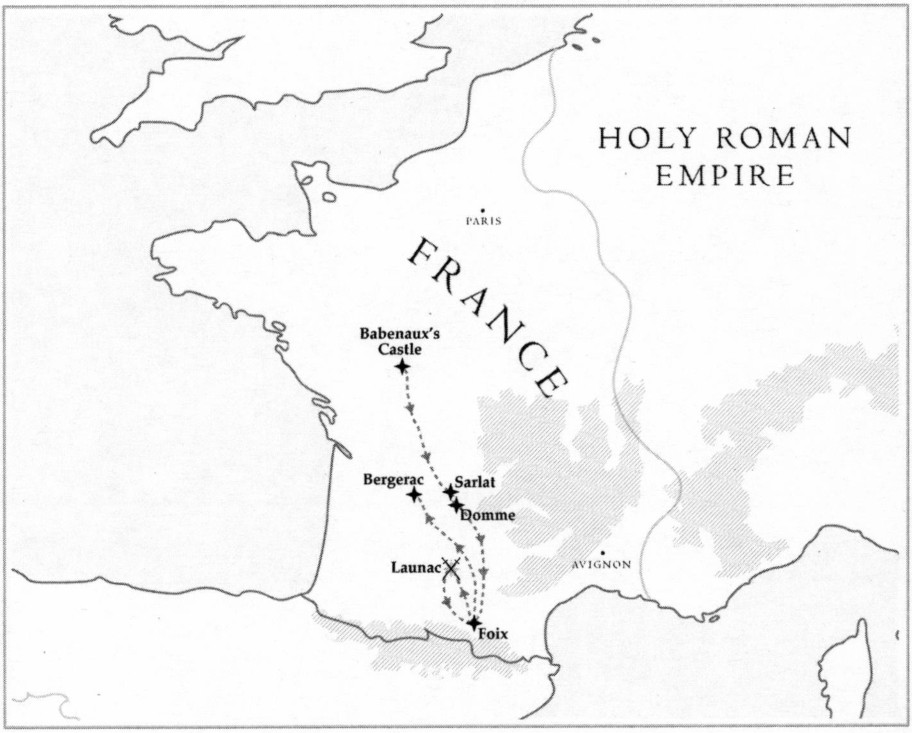

BLACKSTONE'S ROUTE

And power was given unto them over the fourth part of the earth, to kill with sword and with hunger and with death and with the beasts of the earth.

Revelation of St John the Divine 6:8

PART ONE

SWORN ENEMY

CHAPTER ONE

Here is the corpse of Thomas Blackstone enemy of France declared a sign hanging from the scar-faced man's broken neck.

Thirteen bodies dangled lifeless from gibbets outside the town's walls, the dead men left as carrion. Sir Gilbert Killbere swallowed hard when he saw the sign. The taste of death clung to the back of his throat as the hollow sockets stared at him. Killbere and the ten-man scouting party eased their horses past the bodies, whose lower limbs had been gnawed to the bone by wolf and wild boar. It was too dangerous to stop in case those who had done the killing were still behind the walls. Killbere and the men rode in single file, shields raised against any sudden onslaught of crossbow quarrels from the low parapet. Saint-Ouen could barely be called a town; it was more of a hamlet, a settlement for hundreds of years since the Romans had first encircled their camp with a balustrade followed by an earth embankment and then built a low stone wall. That stonework had crumbled and fallen into disrepair but was of sufficient height for determined men to defend. The entrance was through two wooden gates, nine feet high, spiked poles bound to each other with iron brackets, which told the cautious riders that a blacksmith had once plied his trade in the town and might well have used his skills to fashion weapons for his fellow citizens.

Hunchback crows hopped across the parapet fighting noisily for the flesh dangling from the ropes. The bodies were less than a week old but their putrefaction assailed the men's nostrils. They needed no words of command as Killbere kneed his mount towards the open gates; the men formed a protective shield behind him. Two others rode alongside the veteran knight: Renfred, the German captain, and Ralph Tait, both veterans of battles against mercenaries and Bretons at the behest of King Edward's negotiator in France, Sir John Chandos.

The town was a ramshackle place and must have been abandoned a long time ago. Wattle and mud dwellings had succumbed to time and weather, sod-covered roofs had collapsed and there was no sign of feral dogs or loose-running fowl. There was no smell of smoke-soaked thatch. Fires had not burned in the bleak compound for years. Nothing lived. Only the scavengers.

Killbere and the two hobelars weaved their horses through the deserted hamlet but still nothing stirred. He led them around the walls until they returned to the open gates. A column of riders emerged from the treeline beyond the meadow that surrounded the town. Killbere waited and blew snot from his nostrils, wiping his hands on his jupon.

'There's only the stench here. Nothing more,' he said to the approaching men. He gestured towards the bodies swaying gently in the stiffening breeze. 'Just as well we didn't announce ourselves when whoever did this lurked behind the walls. Looks as though someone's been telling the world he's you.'

Blackstone grinned. 'And he doesn't even look like me.'

Killbere cleared his throat, spat, and then spurred his horse. 'No one's that ugly, Thomas.'

When King Edward had summoned Thomas Blackstone to Calais after the Battle of Brignais in April of that year the scar-faced knight thought he would be arrested. Instead, he was honoured and made Master of War to serve the King and the Prince of Wales in securing the newly gained territory held by mercenaries and those who fought against the English King's choice in Brittany. The proxy war was being fought between Edward's ward and favourite John de Montfort and the French-backed Charles de Blois. Blackstone was tasked with clearing towns and territory ceded to Edward in the peace treaty with France and securing the loyalty of wayward Gascon lords in the Duchy of Aquitaine, ready for the Prince's arrival, already delayed by months. The treaty with the French King Jean le Bon was worth only as much as each monarch ascribed to it. Territorial disputes had not been settled and because of that the English King had not renounced his claim to the French throne. Much of France was held by English, French and German routier captains, who commanded their mercenaries with ruthless efficiency. No sooner had Blackstone and his men defeated one band and forced them to release their towns for King Edward than the routiers rejoined others. And so the fight went on. Belligerent Frenchmen still thirsted for Blackstone's blood and it was obvious outside the walls of Saint-Ouen that one foolhardy routier had thought to claim the legendary mantle and force those behind the walls to surrender their weapons and women. He had failed.

'At least thirty men were inside the walls, Thomas,' said Killbere as they rode south through the Breton march. 'There was enough churned ground for maybe more.'

'Either Bretons or skinners,' said Blackstone's squire, John Jacob. 'Little to choose between the two.'

'We have a quarrel with both,' said Blackstone as he searched the open countryside beyond the town. There was no sign of campfire smoke rising in the cool autumn air over the treetops. It suggested that whoever had slain the men masquerading as Blackstone's had come upon the abandoned town as a resting place. It had been the thirteen dead men's misfortune that they had tried to frighten those they thought to be helpless townspeople. The horsemen's tracks had petered out along a riverbank and as Blackstone's men skirted the shallows, it became obvious that the riders had melted into the forest on the opposite bank.

Meulon's bearded hulk nudged his horse forward. The throat-cutter had ridden in from the flanks. 'No sign of them beyond the riverbank, Sir Thomas. They're still travelling. Back home perhaps. If their lord's domain is near, then they'll keep going until they're safely behind his walls. If they're skinners, then they might be holding out against the French.'

'Whose domain is this?' said Killbere. 'Has it been ceded to Edward?'

Blackstone shook his head. 'I don't know. Sir John made no mention of this place.'

'If Chandos doesn't want it for the King, then let's be on our way,' said Killbere. 'No point in picking a fight just to keep warm. We have enough to do before the Prince sets foot in Bordeaux.'

Blackstone settled his gaze across the sweeping forest that swallowed the river as it curved; somewhere in there was an enemy who had claimed his death. 'The Prince is still at his estate in Cornwall. He won't set sail until next summer. There's time enough for us to do his bidding.'

Killbere yanked his horse's reins as it dipped its head to the sweet grass. 'Near enough a year since they wed and he still can't wean himself away. Like a child on the teat. Mind you, I am told they are tits a man would happily suffocate himself in.' He leered. 'If I had married Joan, the *Fair Maid of Kent*,' he said, emphasizing the sobriquet given to the sensuous countess, 'I'd spend the winter under the covers as well.'

The twice-married widow of Sir Thomas Holland, the Countess of Kent was a woman who enjoyed the freedom afforded by her privileged status. Music, jewellery and parties were a passion, and it was a common belief it was her sensuality that had snared the Prince. Blackstone wasn't so sure. She was already the mother of five children and the Prince could have had his pick of any young woman across Europe.

'He married for love, Gilbert. Even against his father's wishes. I like him the more for it.'

Killbere leaned across his pommel. 'Love, Thomas, is for children.'

'And I was little more than Henry's age now when I fell in love with Christiana.'

Killbere looked to where Henry Blackstone waited behind John Jacob, ready to do the squire's bidding as would any page. The lad was what, fifteen, sixteen? Killbere wasn't sure and doubted that even Blackstone would remember birthdays. It took a woman to count her child's summers but Blackstone's wife was dead, murdered, these past four years. 'You were already a fighting man by then. God's blood, Thomas, sentimentality is not for the likes for us. How did we get onto this morbid subject?'

'You were thinking about sex.'

Killbere's eyes lit up. 'So I was.'

Blackstone heeled his horse towards the river ford. 'And if you can't remember that then you're becoming a senile old bastard that will soon need a nurse to tend to you.'

'As long as she's young and wide-hipped.' He grinned. 'Thomas! Why are we riding this way?'

'To see who wants me dead,' answered Blackstone.

Killbere sighed and shook his head as he heeled his mount. 'That would be most of France,' he muttered.

CHAPTER TWO

The streets of Paris seethed. Shopkeepers barracked passers-by. Butchers and fishmongers swept flies from the tables bearing their wares as they hacked bone and cut muscle or gutted fish caught that morning. The noise from those jostling the criss-crossing streets and alleys sought escape from the narrow confines where half-timbered houses' cantilevered floors blocked out much of the light to those in the passageways below. The pungent smell of human waste mingled with the sweet aroma of freshly baked bread and sweet cakes. Beasts of burden were whipped and cajoled and urged to give way as the eight men on horseback made their way towards the Grand Pont and the royal palace on the Île de la Cité. These knights did not move aside for man or beast. Each knight led a spare horse bearing his armour and supplies; men used to travelling great distances in pursuit of their goal knew the value of having an extra horse. Some of these knights had visited other cities like Prague, Berlin, Cölln and Rothenburg. Wolfram von Plauen, who led them along the Grand'Rue, had survived the Rothenburg earthquake in '56 that had destroyed Staufer Castle, his mentor's stronghold. It had been a lesson in humility. No matter how strong a man's belief in God, if the Almighty deemed it time to deal man's pride a blow there was no force on earth to stop it. And the French had suffered a devastating blow to their pride when the English slaughtered thousands of their finest at Crécy and Poitiers. Now the humbled French King had crawled back to

Paris on his knees, riddled with debt and shame. And as von Plauen gazed in wonder at the grandeur that was Paris, called by some the most beautiful city in Christendom, he knew it was centuries of men's pride and greed that had built it. His stern countenance betrayed no sense of his wonder. A hundred thousand souls lived behind its walls and in its suburbs and they had withstood the war brought on them by the English King. God had smiled on the venal Parisians. Wolfram von Plauen did not.

Iron-rimmed wheels trundled past the German knights as handcarts bore the fruit of bow-backed peasants' labour on the way to market. An idiot dressed in an undershirt danced barefoot on the cobbles at the end of a rope. Perhaps it was the ragged-looking man's father who urged the demented soul to jig like a monkey while he held out his cap for any meagre offering. Destitution and starvation lurked ever present like the evil in men's souls. And yet, von Plauen acknowledged to himself, the Basilica of Saint-Denis and the Notre-Dame were testament to the glorification of the divine.

They reached the Grand Pont and gazed across the Seine where barge traffic unloaded their cargo on the riverside bank. Men hurried back and forth from warehouses to vessel, bowed under the weight of sacks of grain. Scurrying ants who laboured day and night to keep the city fed. Von Plauen gazed across the bridge to where the royal household's banners and pennants curled from the river's chill breeze. The once mighty French King and his son the Dauphin as trapped in their island palace as surely as in any grand prison.

'It is a place of corruption, Wolfram,' said one of the men riding with him. 'Money changers and goldsmiths pave the way across the bridge to the palace. These French are creatures who cherish wealth and possessions.' Walter von Ranke was a younger man recently accepted into the brotherhood of the

Teutonic Order. The vicissitudes of the world had not yet tempered his zeal for righteous justice.

Wolfram pointed to Notre-Dame's twin towers. 'It takes money to build such a magnificent edifice to God, Walter. Let us be generous with our thoughts towards them.' He heeled his horse across the bridge. 'We need them to tell us where the man we seek hides from our justice.'

The Dauphin was irritable and had retired to his chambers. When the King of France was held hostage in England his absence from Paris had allowed the Dauphin Charles the right to rule. No longer. Now the Dauphin's life hovered between France and purgatory. His tongue had lashed the King's counsellor Simon Bucy all morning. And now it looked as though Bucy's day would get worse. Beneath the tumbling clouds that threatened rain he watched the horsemen approach along the Grand'Rue from his office high in the palace. Their route led directly from the city's north walls through the heart of Paris to the Grand Pont. Teutonic Knights were not ambassadors of goodwill, or pilgrims making their way on the Via Francigena, the route to Rome. They were troublemakers. Of that he was convinced. These stern, unsmiling brethren believed the Almighty guided their swords for justice and retribution. Bucy turned to warm his hands at the fireplace, seeking a modicum of comfort from what would surely be some kind of demand. The Germans would be admitted and relinquish their swords; the captain of the guard would escort them to the chamberlain who would soon knock on Bucy's door because it was Simon Bucy who had the ear of the King – and of the Dauphin. During the King's captivity in England, Bucy, who had once led the Parlement, had been a key adviser to the Dauphin Charles.

The knock on the door came sooner than he expected. Bucy followed the chamberlain to the grand entrance. Behind the massive carved oak doors stood pillared arches bedecked with banners from France's history: past glories soon to be regained if only the Dauphin could convince the King to act more assertively in the face of English demands and to cease his irrational behaviour. Wolfram von Plauen and his companions bowed as Bucy entered the hall. The chamberlain would already have given them a courteous welcome. There was no need for Bucy to extend any further goodwill.

'I am Simon Bucy, adviser to the King.'

'My lord, I am Wolfram von Plauen and I seek an audience with your gracious King, may God keep him safe in these troubled times.'

May God keep us all safe, thought Bucy, without a flicker of irritation. After the French army's defeat at Brignais against the routiers in April the King had made the extraordinary decision to travel to the Pope in Avignon and seek permission to marry the Countess Joanna, Queen of Naples. A vain attempt to strengthen the Crown by taking possession of Provence, which she ruled. His ransom still unpaid, hostages still held in England, defeat still burning in French souls, routiers flaying the land and King John had gone to the Pope. At such a time! If he could not secure the marriage, he would take the cross and raise a crusade. What madness had possessed him? It had been this final act that had swung the loyal Bucy to support the Dauphin's dream of reclaiming France against the English.

'The King is in Avignon. He has gone to…' He hesitated. The least said about the monarch's behaviour the better. Best to keep these hospitallers believing John II to be the most Christian king. '… to raise a crusade against the infidel.'

The Germans looked suitably impressed. 'Such a righteous desire augurs well for our own quest, my lord.' Wolfram's blue eyes settled on the older man. 'For justice.'

Ever the diplomat, Bucy graciously bowed his head despite the anxiety he felt about having Teutonic Knights in the city. Revenge was on their minds, but against whom? 'We will extend our help wherever possible. Continue.'

'Henry, Count of Vaudémont, the King's Royal Lieutenant in Champagne, waged a private war against German princes beyond your eastern frontier. The Duke of Lorraine and the Count of Bar and their people suffered grievous harm at his hands and the routiers he employed.'

Bucy stoically showed no sign of his discomfort. De Vaudémont had caused vexing problems for the Crown. When his private war ended the routiers had swept back into France, some seizing strongholds south of Paris as they raided along the Loire.

'We have undertaken to admonish the Count of Vaudémont,' said Bucy, even though no action had been decided by the absent King.

'My lord, the routiers were Bretons, Gascons and Navarrese led by Gruffydd ap Madoc, a Welshman. Their torture, rape and slaughter must not go unpunished. We seek him,' said von Plauen.

Bucy's keen lawyer mind snapped taut as a crossbow cord. Ap Madoc had led the mercenaries that saved Blackstone at Brignais. These Teutonic Knights were God's gift. Perhaps He favoured them after all. They were better than any paid assassin. Planting a lie now could yield great benefit. 'The man you seek, this Welshman, another led him – an Englishman, Thomas Blackstone. Blackstone and ap Madoc are the men who wreaked such indiscriminate violence against the innocent. Find the Englishman and you will find his friend.'

Wolfram von Plauen looked at the other knights. This was news they had not expected. 'Our thanks, my lord. Where can we find this Thomas Blackstone?'

Where indeed? Bucy raised a hand, a gesture to buy time for thought. This was too good an opportunity to miss. Now that the treaty was in place and Blackstone was the English monarch's Master of War, the French could not act against him; however, if Germans killed the man, no blame could be laid at the Crown's door. Where *was* Blackstone? How could Bucy enable these zealots to find – and kill – him?

And then he knew. Bucy suppressed the excitement that surged in his chest. His day had improved beyond his best expectations. The clouds parted. The sun bathed the palace in its warmth.

'The English King's emissary, an Italian, Father Niccolò Torellini, is travelling under safe conduct with an escort across France to Avignon. He will go via Chartres. If anyone knows where Thomas Blackstone is, he will.'

CHAPTER THREE

Blackstone led the men into the forest, avoiding the direction of the other horsemen's tracks, and made camp. Twenty-five mounted archers, the most valuable men of any fighting company, settled in the camp's centre under the command of the veteran archer Will Longdon, who would normally be centenar of a hundred bowmen. It was through choice that Blackstone kept his column lightly armed and ready to traverse quickly across the wasted land that was France. Those archers and an equal number of men-at-arms were easier to feed and equip and served Blackstone well as a raiding party that could move across distances quickly, strike where necessary and move on. Once they'd conquered a town they left the garrisoning of it to others under the local seneschal's command. Blackstone's chosen were worth more in fighting skills and experience than brigands three or four times their number. If the French or Bretons rose in force, then Blackstone's rallying call would bring men from far and wide to do his bidding and swell his ranks.

Meulon and Renfred set their men on the perimeter as a protective shield around the camp. Horses were hobbled and picketed and beyond the ring of armed men they set listening posts to challenge anyone probing their defences and alert the camp. Fear of night creatures, demons and dispossessed souls would keep most superstition-racked men at bay but if a bold commander struck, as Blackstone had done in the past, then death might visit the band beneath the cloak of darkness.

Will Longdon beckoned to his ventenar, Jack Halfpenny. 'We have meat enough for another two days,' he told the young archer, 'but if Thomas is planning to take us further afield then we need more. There'll be boar and deer in these woods. We'll make our way to the river and find where they come to drink at dusk.'

Killbere bit into an apple. 'Will, you get lost in these woods and we'll ride on without you. Jack, you tie a piece of rope to him and keep him in sight, you hear?' he growled through the apple's pulp.

'Sir Gilbert, when we come back with venison you will be grateful you have such good hunting men to ride with you,' Longdon answered.

'Scab-arsed poachers more like. Don't go shooting a tough old buck – bring us tender meat, you hear?'

Killbere and Will Longdon were veterans who had served together longer than any of the men under Blackstone's command, since before Killbere had even taken the young Blackstone to war.

'Best keep a night light burning, Sir Gilbert. Shall I rouse you when we return to give you the comfort of knowing we have made our way back safely?'

Killbere tossed the apple core at them. 'Get your arse moving, you insolent bastard – and don't go shooting blindly; Thomas is out there.'

Late sunlight flooded the glade where Blackstone's tethered horse bowed its misshapen head into the sweet grass shaded from the sun. It had been a hot summer that burned the grass and the warmth had lingered into the autumn that now settled on Blackstone as he perched on a log considering whether he should pursue the routier who had claimed to have killed him at Saint-Ouen. They were already late for an agreed rendezvous with the Seneschal of Poitou, Sir William Felton. There was no love lost between him and Blackstone. It gave Blackstone some comfort to know that despite Felton being awarded the victory Blackstone had orchestrated against the Bretons at le Garet earlier that year, before defeating the French at Brignais, the King and Sir John Chandos knew the truth of the matter and had privately acknowledged it. The honour of Master of War bestowed on him by King Edward could be a blessing or a curse. The Prince of Wales and Aquitaine would be a difficult master to serve. Honour could turn to disgrace with an unguarded word or action and he was under no illusion that the recently married Prince would not be even more demanding with a wife at his side.

Blackstone's meandering thoughts were suddenly interrupted. The bastard horse raised its head; its muscles quivered. Blackstone knew the warning signs. He quickly climbed into the saddle and waited, eyes searching the treeline. They were downwind but he heard nothing more than the breeze rustling the treetops and the hardening leaves whispering their impending fall to earth. The horse quivered again and pawed the ground, its great strength yanking the reins as it tossed its head towards the breeze.

'All right,' Blackstone muttered. 'Let's see what it is.' He eased the horse across the glade. If there was danger lurking, then being in the open meant he would not be caught unawares by any sudden attack. As they reached the far side he looked through the trees, picking first one to focus on, then further ahead another, until his gaze penetrated a hundred yards into the forest. There was no sign of threat. He picked out an animal track and guided the bastard horse forward. A sound like a bird cry rose faintly on the breeze. Pushing further through the trees he caught the soft gurgling of the river tumbling over boulders. He could feel his horse's tension beneath him. As they emerged from the edge of the forest, he saw the river curved left then right. Downstream was devoid of any threat but the horse was insisting on moving upstream. They were still downwind and he concentrated on trying to make out anything untoward over the shallow water dashing across the pebble riverbed. And then he heard it again. An animal cry. High–pitched, thrown into the breeze. As they rounded the bend he saw movement on the opposite bank.

He nudged the horse back into the safety of the trees; the bastard horse's cinder-burnt mottled coat that made men believe the belligerent beast had been sired in hell camouflaged any movement as Blackstone weaved through the shadows between shafts of sunlight. A magpie snickered, a flash of blue and white causing men's faces to look upward. A dozen of them on the far bank. More men, perhaps, further back in the trees where Blackstone couldn't see them. A sudden bellow of laughter and shouting. A taunt. A sharp, flat crack travelled on the breeze. A man's open hand slapped a figure being pushed this way and that. A circle of men. Two of them tormenting a raven-haired woman, cloak half ripped from her chemise, blood-red velvet on the ground leaving her nothing but her torn dress. The men laughed as they tossed a bundle of clothing between them as the woman tried to reach it. It was a rag doll. Flaxen-haired, limp. A child. The men were tormenting the woman by throwing it back and forth.

A distant memory caught Blackstone unawares: when he had fought across the river crossing at Blanchetaque before the Battle of Crécy to find a girl who had been abandoned in the forest. The girl would become his wife but the sixteen-year-old archer did not know that at the time when he rode into the forest and skirted the French and Bohemian knights who hunted for her. Her rescue and his final swim back with her against a turning tide had brought both praise and criticism but it defined the young Blackstone's daring and courage. Now he weaved quietly between the trees watching another woman fearful for her life and that of her child.

The bastard horse was eager to press on but Blackstone restrained it and guided it into the shallows. When they reached the middle of the river he brought it to a halt. Its ears were up. One twitched left and right listening for any other threat, but its eyes, like Blackstone's, stayed rigidly fixed on the men. The belligerent beast stood four-square. Blackstone knew that if he gave it its head and charged into the men, then the woman would probably be the first to die and then the child – if it was still alive. And a dozen men, like a pack of wolves, could bring him down. He would draw them in. Blackstone hoisted his shield onto his arm and drew Wolf Sword from its scabbard.

And waited.

One man on the far side of the tormenting circle tilted back his head as he raised a wineskin to his mouth. It was then that he saw the lone knight waiting in the middle of the river. Dappled light caught the water and reflected the eyes of a wild-looking horse that pawed the shallows. He spluttered wine and then said something that made the others turn and stare. Moments later three of them broke away and mounted their horses tethered in the trees. They spurred their mounts as their comrades shouted encouragement. Shouts carried across the water: voices bellowing that they would kill the interloper. Laughter. It was going to be easy.

Blackstone waited and then pressed his left leg into the bastard horse's side, kicking his right behind the girth. The war horse needed no further command. It suddenly swung its hindquarters left and struck the first of the oncoming horses, forcing it to veer. The horseman swayed in the saddle, struck blindly, but his blade only met Blackstone's shield as Wolf Sword swept in a perfectly aimed arc at the exposed man's throat below his helmet's chinstrap. There was no need to wait and see the man die: Blackstone heard the splash and was already swerving to strike the second attacker. The man raised himself in the stirrups to gain an advantage over Blackstone's height. His intended killing blow whispered across Blackstone's head and gave him no chance of recovery as the momentum of horse and body forced his groin onto Wolf Sword's point. The blade ran through him out and of the small of his back. His scream startled a coven of crows that voiced their alarm as they flapped wildly from the canopy. Wolf Sword's blood knot bit into Blackstone's wrist, keeping it secure in his fist.

The third man tried to steer his horse away from the snarling scar-faced knight but Blackstone's next blow severed the man's sword arm and bit into his rib cage. The killing had taken less time than the men on the riverbank took to reach their horses. One of them shouted commands. They cuffed the woman to the ground; she lay unmoving, as did the rag-doll child. The horsemen bellowed with wine-fuelled courage as they urged their horses towards the riverbank. Nine against one. Blackstone spurred his horse. It surged into the approaching men as they splashed into the shallows, their horses suddenly uncertain of the riverbed beneath their hooves. The bastard horse barged into the two leading horses before they or Blackstone delivered a blow, forcing them past Blackstone with their riders fighting to regain control and turn them back. The ragtag formation that followed were too scattered to attack Blackstone en masse. The nearest fell as Blackstone's sword swept across the horse's flanks. The wounded and terrified animal balked; the blade took the man's leg below the knee. Horse and rider went down in a spurt of blood. The bastard horse turned without command, as aggressive as its master as it fought the bit and bared its yellow teeth. The wide-eyed horse it confronted reared as its rider cursed, savagely yanking the reins. The vital seconds he took to steady his mount cost him his life. The rim of Blackstone's shield struck beneath the man's chin and the crack of jaw bone and spine flopped him backwards into the water. River boulders caused another attacking horse to stumble, throwing its rider into the water and then rolling on top of him. The horse recovered but the man lay unmoving, face down. Two more riders challenged Blackstone. Seeing he would be vulnerable if they attacked both sides at once they came hard at him. It was a mistake. Their action blocked their companions from smothering Blackstone completely. Blackstone spurred his horse to force them apart. His shield took the blow from one rider but the strength behind the strike forced Blackstone back from its impact, giving the second man the opening he needed to swing his flanged mace at Blackstone's open helm. Momentarily stunned, Blackstone slumped as his horse's momentum took him past his attacker and the other men wheeled their mounts around.

Blackstone recovered, shaking his head to clear his blurred vision. He was boxed in. There were now four men behind him and two in front. He urged his horse towards the riverbank and killed the nearest man to his front; then the bastard horse was on firm ground. Blackstone freed himself from the stirrups and planted his feet on the riverbank. He needed an advantage and fighting on foot gave it to him. Not only did the horsemen have to expose their horses as they clambered up the low bank but they would have to bend low to strike him. Blackstone's agility avoided the first horse whose rider was already sweeping down his sword, but Blackstone was no longer in the same place. Half-turning he spun around before the horse reached him and struck the man's blind side, thrusting the point of his sword into the man's buttocks as he leaned forward. The screaming man twisted and fell. A horse's shoulder caught Blackstone. It threw him to the ground. He rolled, struck upwards and found the beast's soft belly. It bellowed, stumbled and fell, trapping its rider's leg. Blackstone ducked from the thrashing hooves and plunged the point of his sword into the man's throat.

He wiped an arm across his face to clear the sweat and blood from his eyes. The bastard horse was kicking its hind legs at one horse whose rider was trying to kill the devil's offspring. The hooves kept the man's blade at a safe distance and when they connected Blackstone heard the man cry out in pain as they broke his leg. He dropped his sword. His horse veered clear of the thrashing hooves. Despite his pain, rage gave its rider courage and he pulled a fighting axe from his belt.

The three surviving men steadied their mounts in the river. The man they sought to kill had slain six of their number. They hesitated and then, three abreast, spurred their horses towards him. Blackstone raised his face to the breeze. It cooled him. A sound like a fluttering bird's wing rippled the air. Blackstone knew it well. It was the sound of goose fletchings travelling fast through the air. Barely a breath separated the two men falling with a yard-long bodkin-tipped arrow shaft through their chests. Two figures on the far bank were already nocking arrows but the surviving horseman yanked his reins and fled. Blackstone raised his sword arm amid the carnage to salute his archers.

Will Longdon's laughter echoed across the water.

CHAPTER FOUR

The two archers carried the unconscious woman and child back to Blackstone's camp.

Killbere looked from the survivors to Blackstone, who was now free of his mail as Henry took his jupon and undershirt to dry in the final rays that streaked through the forest. John Jacob attended to honing Wolf Sword. Its hardened steel blade was still sharp enough to sever a man's arm but even such a blade forged by German master sword makers in Passau needed attention when it had cut into helmets and mail.

'You couldn't just ride away, I suppose,' said Killbere as he passed a wineskin.

'Would you?' said Blackstone before drinking thirstily. Henry brought a length of rough cloth for Blackstone to wipe the sweat from his torso.

Killbere sighed. 'Women who need rescuing bring trouble into a man's life, Thomas. There's a reason they need rescuing. And that reason can rear up like an adder and bite a man in the balls. Would it have been so difficult to just come back and get help or leave her to her fate?' He raised a hand to stop Blackstone from answering. 'I know. You did what you thought was right. God's blood, how many times has that caused us grief? Whoever those men were you've given them a thrashing, so it's unlikely any more of their friends will come at us tonight. I'll have Meulon double the pickets just in case.' He fingered the torn blazon Blackstone had taken from one of the dead men. A boar's head against a faded yellow background was smeared with dark-stained blood. 'They weren't routiers. They're a lord's men but I don't know this device.'

'Nor I,' said Blackstone and pulled on a clean shirt. 'I'm hoping she will when she comes around.' He nodded to the woman, who now lay on a bed of cut ferns and moss, attended by Will Longdon, who supported her head and trickled potion between her lips.

'She's no serving girl, that's for certain. Look at her clothes. That's a fine embroidered linen shift. And that cloak wasn't bought at a marketplace. She belongs to someone. A man can become agitated if you take his horse or woman.' He tossed the blazon back to Blackstone. 'Though a horse has more value.'

The violence against the woman and child cast them into a fitful slumber. Their fever intensified during the night but Blackstone instructed Henry to lie close to them both and to bathe their foreheads with a soaked cloth. He had a fire built and river stones brought to contain the deep embers. When the woman shivered uncontrollably, they lifted stones with sacking and placed them against her back for warmth. Henry Blackstone attended to his duties without respite unaware that his father, who lay wrapped in his blankets twenty feet away, kept a watchful eye on him.

When the men awoke as the first light penetrated the forest Blackstone was already checking the camp with John Jacob at his side. His captains Renfred and Meulon had stayed as alert as their pickets throughout the night but neither man showed any sign of tiredness. The years spent with Blackstone had taught them to overcome weariness, especially when it was tempered by duty, and they were as caring for their hobelars as Will Longdon and Jack Halfpenny were for their archers.

When the woman's fever broke she awoke to see a scar-faced man kneeling next to her. She recoiled. Henry pressed his hand on hers.

'My lady, this is my father, Sir Thomas Blackstone, who saved you from those men at the river.'

Hearing Blackstone's name caused the woman to be more fearful. Bewildered, she squirmed away from the blankets covering her until her back pushed up against a tree. Looking around at her unfamiliar surroundings she saw ghostly figures of rough-looking men moving silently through the dappled light and campfire smoke. Henry's look of consternation did nothing to calm her. She crossed herself; her lips muttered a prayer. Eyes wide, she searched for her child.

'My daughter. Where is she?'

'She is alive,' said Blackstone, his gentle voice belying his rough demeanour. 'One of my men is with her. We have a potion of herbs that will give her strength. She is safe. Be calm. You are not in danger here.'

Blackstone nodded to where a crude woodland shelter had been constructed a few feet away. The child lay on a soft bed of vegetation. A figure crouched over her. His leather skull cap and the brace on his forearm told her he was a bowman.

'I beg you – do not harm my daughter. Do what you must with me but do not harm her.'

'We did not rescue you to cause you further harm or distress. The men who held you are dead,' said Blackstone.

The woman clambered to her feet, forcing Henry to move quickly aside as she went to her child. Will Longdon was kneeling next to the unconscious girl but saw Blackstone's gesture telling him to move away so the mother could reach her.

She scooped her into her arms and paced this way and that, looking desperately for a means of escape. Men stood watching her. She was trapped. Any of these men could stride forward and snatch her.

One man stood eating an apple, one hand resting on the sword hilt in his belt. 'Calm yourself, woman, for pity's sake,' said Killbere. 'You were saved. Get down on your knees and thank God that it was by an Englishman. That scab-ridden archer tended your child as if she were a newborn lamb. We are fighting men but we have some understanding of herbs and medicines. A woman not unlike yourself gave us the knowledge.' Killbere took a pace and half-turned as if giving her a clear path. 'Run if you like, but the men who attacked you will have companions. We saw their tracks. If you run your girl will die.'

She was frozen with fear and uncertainty. No one had made any attempt to reach her, or stop her. They stood back respectfully.

She raised a dirt-ingrained hand to wipe tears from her face; then she tenderly lifted the sweat-soaked hair from her daughter's forehead.

She saw the archer's stubbled face crease as he smiled at her and pointed to the shelter. 'Had one of the lads build it for her. Keep the dew and the smoke off the child. Gives a bit of warmth on these chill nights and that's my own horse blanket I put over her so there're no lice to cause her distress. You'd best think of y'self an' daughter, my lady. Thomas Blackstone is a good man who fought hard to rescue you, and me and Jack Halfpenny, we killed two of them ourselves. They died slow with a broadhead-tipped hunting arrow tearing their chests apart.' Longdon frowned as if he had spoken out of turn. 'Thought knowing that might give you some comfort.'

'Stay with her until you are both strong enough to go where it is you want,' said Killbere. He nodded towards Henry. 'The lad there has food ready for you. We'll give you what we have, then you can be on your way.'

She was less fearful as she faced the man who had saved her. 'We were on our way south and we were resting in an abandoned village. Men came to the gates and demanded those inside surrender. One declared himself to be the Englishman Thomas Blackstone.' She fixed her gaze on Blackstone.

'He was an imposter,' said Blackstone.

'And how do I know you are not?'

'How well did the man fight?' asked Killbere.

'Badly,' she told him.

'There's your answer,' Killbere said, tossing aside the apple core as he stepped closer to her. Her courage had returned, and she did not flinch. Killbere brushed a hand across his jupon as if it would have made a difference to the grime that covered the stitched image of its blazon. 'This declares who he is. Given by a royal prince, honoured by a king and feared by their enemies.'

She looked at Blackstone. 'He has my son,' she answered.

'Who?' said Blackstone.

'Lord Mael Babeneaux de Pontivy. When the brigand declared himself Lord Mael said he had sworn to kill you. They broke every bone in the man's body and then hanged him so that he strangled to death. If you are who you say you are,' she said, 'then Lord Mael would be aggrieved to know that you are still alive.'

'And who are you to this Breton lord?' said Blackstone.

'I am his wife, Lady Cateline Babeneaux.'

CHAPTER FIVE

In the hours it took for the feverish child to recover Blackstone and a handful of his men backtracked to where the churned earth showed the Breton lord's ride for home from the abandoned village. They followed the meandering river that snaked in and out of the forest from the point where they had avoided the tracks to where the scarred ground led them through a broad path on the far reaches of the woodland. The ground broadened into an undulating expanse of meadows, a forest copse and a distant village. Sheep were penned near the muddy track and the low walls of the rough stone-built houses supported a pitched roof whose moss-laden thatch spoke of a wet and cold prevailing westerly wind. A single door allowed man and beast to share the same quarters. Blackstone knew only too well the stench inside such a hut. He and his men had kicked down many a leather-hinged door to root out an enemy. A tanned goatskin covered a window opening but even that would keep the inside oppressively gloomy. Blackstone knew the thatch would be hard to torch if they needed to attack and destroy the village, but the dry hay and straw kept in the loft for the animals would burn quickly enough and that would engulf the crucked timbers. Then the smoke from the smouldering thatch could blind and choke enemy soldiers. Everything needed to be considered when facing determined men who wanted your head on a pole.

A narrow stream, no wider than a man's stride and as deep as his calf, curled this way and that from the riverbed: water that would supply the village. The beginning of winter would be upon the villeins in another few weeks and if they were fortunate enough to keep enough mutton, then the meat would supplement the mounds of turnips piled outside one of the barns. The faint sound of chickens being disturbed reached the men, and then a woman's voice carried on the wind. The breeze flattened the angry voice of an old crone waving a stick who came around one of the huts to chase a girl moving swiftly away with a haltered goat. It was a scene re-enacted a dozen times a week in any village. A goat breaks free, eats a neighbour's cabbages and the youngest girl in the family is sent to retrieve the miscreant. No other threat appeared to lurk in the huddled village; the threat lay further afield on a turret that rose above the distant forest. The flag wavering in the stiff breeze displayed a boar's head.

Killbere scratched his beard. 'Thomas, that castle is not part of the King's treaty. We have no need to strike at it or this bastard Breton lord. The man who survived the fight will have warned him of us, and it's a domestic affair anyway. Let's get about our business.'

'Did I say anything?'

'Your thoughts are louder than a village preacher's voice condemning the damned and I reckon that is what we will be if you try to take that castle. If we can see the tower over those trees you can be certain it will have broad walls and high parapets as well.'

Blackstone grunted by way of an answer, but kept his eyes on the landscape.

'Burn the village, use its smoke,' said Gilbert. 'Is that it?'

Blackstone smiled.

'You see! God's tears! You can draw the bastard out and we can kill them but for what reason? The man hates you. That's not reason enough. I swear there were times over the years when I could have done more than kick your arse myself.'

'Gilbert, he threw his wife and child to his men.'

Killbere sighed. 'It's not our business. When a Lord of a manor turns his wife over to his men, then she's been rutting with others or he's got himself a mistress. I'll wager she was not meant to survive the assault in the forest. Perhaps the man's blazon tells us all we need to know. He's got his snout in some other woman's trough.'

'Why keep the son and not the daughter?' said Blackstone, gauging the shifting breeze, not wanting it to carry their scent towards the village from where they sat in the shadows. A villein had a keen a nose as a feral dog alert for danger and if they were loyal peasants, then a messenger might already be running to warn of Blackstone's party and gain favour with Lord Mael.

'Girls need a lot of attention, Thomas. Nurses and a governess, someone to dress and feed them. They can put boys to work, give them rough clothing and teach them something useful like how to fight.'

'But in time a girl would have value. Such a man could arrange a marriage, buy himself status or a treaty with an enemy,' Blackstone answered.

'A son will inherit his father's estates one day and carry on his name. A man's name is worth more than a dowry for a girl.'

Blackstone didn't answer. He was studying the ground. If they moved closer to the distant forest and were caught in the open by any of Lord Mael's men returning from patrol, then they needed to use the terrain to their advantage.

Killbere read his mind. 'You're not thinking of riding over there, are you? We'd be as exposed as a mastiff's bollocks. Why are we even here? If Babeneaux has sworn to kill you, then you have probably slain someone he knows. I'll wager he has bastards running over half of France, Thomas, and you're bound to have despatched one of them to meet the devil.'

Blackstone turned in the saddle and looked at the men waiting. Richard Quenell, like Jack Halfpenny, was both archer and ventenar to the few bowmen under his command. He had fought well against the Bretons earlier that year when he joined Blackstone's men. Blackstone knew he had spent time in Brittany and the Limousin where the Breton lords held sway over vast tracts of land.

'Quenell,' Blackstone called.

The archer drew his horse alongside Blackstone. 'My lord?'

'This Babeneaux, did you come across him?'

Quenell shook his head. 'Heard the name but never had the pleasure of putting a yard of ash into his chest. I saw his banner when we fought at le Garet.'

'Then we didn't kill him when we had the chance,' said Killbere. 'More's the pity. We'd have less to concern ourselves with now and we could be on our way.'

'There was a family further north. A sister married to a Breton knight,' said Quenell.

'What name?' said Blackstone.

Quenell searched his memory. 'It was an unusual name to my ear... It was... Regard or Beauregard... No, it was Sagard, Rolf de Sagard. Aye, that was it.

'Merciful Christ,' said Killbere. 'The past haunts us like forest ghosts. De Sagard. How long ago was that, Thomas? Five, six years back?'

Blackstone nodded. It had been the time when the French monarch had set the Savage Priest against him. Blackstone's family had come close to death, his young squire, Guillaume Bourdin, had been brutally tortured and slain, and they'd set a trap for Blackstone's friend, the Norman lord William de Fossat. De Fossat had been lured to the Breton march and held in de Sagard's castle where de Fossat was flayed alive by the Savage Priest. Blackstone had put his friend out of his misery and then killed Rolf de Sagard for allowing the atrocity.

'And de Sagard's widow is Babeneaux's sister,' said Killbere. 'Thomas, we have no business here. It's obvious why he wants to kill you. You threw his sister to the wolves of poverty without a man to protect her and her children. He's probably had to raise his rents on those poor bastards in the village just to keep her fed all these years.'

'I have no quarrel with him, Gilbert. He has the quarrel with me.'

'Thomas, see it as a piece of grit in your boot. It irritates, it might pinch, but it can be ignored.'

'Babeneaux has the same poison in him. He tortures and kills and does it slowly like he did to that man we found hanging. And he gave his wife and daughter to his men,' Blackstone answered. 'Grit can be shaken from a boot.' He turned the bastard horse back to where they had come.

Killbere nudged his horse to follow. He glared at Quenell. 'You have a big mouth. There are times it's best to plead ignorance and not try so hard to remember.'

Blackstone stood before mother and child and felt the barbed point of memory of his own dead wife and daughter. The child's name was Jehanne. She was five years old. Her body was bruised from the soldiers' rough handling and a blow to her head had rendered her unconscious during the assault but now the blue-eyed girl stared up at him as her mother cradled her.

'She has recovered,' said Cateline. 'Thanks to your son and these men.'

'They were shown how to heal by a woman versed in such skills.'

'Then my thanks and prayers must go to her.'

'Prayers will do her more good.'

The explanation was plain enough. She nodded. 'What will you do with us?'

'I have discovered why your husband wishes me dead but I want to know why he has taken your son.'

'Hatred for me and a female child. I was widowed with a young son. He married me because I had land and title in my own right. I could not give him a son of his own. My son Jocard will inherit when he comes of age and with me dead Mael will act for the boy.'

'And you tried to escape?'

'Yes. We were going south to first seek protection from the English seneschal at Poitiers, Sir William Felton, and then ask for an escort to Avignon where I will place my son in the care of tutors until he is of age.'

'You know Sir William Felton?' said Killbere.

'By name and reputation.'

'Reputation?' Killbere said, barely able to keep the sarcasm from his voice.

She nodded. 'He defeated the Bretons months ago. He is favoured by the English King.'

Killbere bent at the waist and glared at her. 'Madame, it was Sir Thomas Blackstone who defeated the Bretons. Why would Sir William look favourably on you? You're Breton. Your son is Breton. Your land is in the march.'

Cateline Babeneaux stood, unafraid of the threatening veteran knight. 'Do not presume to lecture me. I am no fool. My domain lies close to the lands of John de Montfort. If my husband controls it then he can strike out against those favoured by the English. The French King would like nothing better than to have a viper squirming in the heart of the English King's ambition.'

Blackstone looked at Killbere. It was now obvious that removing Mael Babeneaux from his stronghold would help Edward's chosen ward, the young de Montfort, to one day secure Brittany.

'Thomas,' Killbere said. 'This woman will wreak destruction on us. I feel it.'

'Gilbert, I'm charged by the King to secure his territory.'

Killbere growled his displeasure. He half turned to return to the men and then swung back to face Cateline Babeneaux again. 'Thomas, ask yourself why this woman was abandoned now. Eh? A daughter of five years and no other offspring since. Why did her husband cast her out? Why not when the girl was born instead of the son he expected? Why now? He could have had her domain years ago.'

'There was no dispute years ago,' Cateline insisted.

'The Bretons have been at each other's throats for generations,' Killbere answered her. 'She's hiding something, Thomas. You mark my words. It's more than she's telling us.'

Blackstone sensed the woman's unease and knew Killbere had drawn a deeply buried secret close to the surface.

'Why hand you over to his men? Why not cut your throat and throw you in the river?' he asked.

'Because he is cruel and saw me as sport for his men,' she said. 'And since the birth of my daughter he thought he could win me around – that I would grant him my lands.'

The answer was too glib. Blackstone stared at her. The danger in his eyes would cause a battle-hardened soldier to hesitate.

'Why now?' she said wearily and then lifted her chin defiantly. 'One of his lieutenants helped us escape. When Lord Mael caught us on the road, he butchered him. That man was my lover.'

CHAPTER SIX

Henry Blackstone earned a sharp rebuke from John Jacob. The boy had questioned his father's decision to leave him in the forest under Killbere's command while Blackstone and his squire rode out to find Babeneaux's castle.

'Know your place, boy. I serve your father and you serve me. Time will come when you will earn the right to be given responsibilities beyond those you now bear.'

There was no question of Blackstone reprimanding John Jacob. The squire had saved Henry's life in the past and his tutelage of Blackstone's son as a page was at the express command of the boy's father.

'You'll obey your squire, Henry. There's nothing more to be said on the matter,' Blackstone told him, secretly yearning to soften his harsh tone. The unwritten law of a boy serving his apprenticeship with an experienced knight or fighting man demanded no favour be shown.

'I understand, my lord,' Henry said with a bow of his head and turned back into the forest.

Blackstone and John Jacob shared a glance. 'He's like a hunting dog straining at the leash, Sir Thomas,' he said and smiled.

'And a defiant streak as wide as my shield,' Blackstone answered.

'I wonder where he got that from,' Killbere said as he stood next to the belligerent horse before Blackstone led the scouting party away. 'Thomas, I fear this woman and her desires distract us. She may wear fine clothes but a whore is a whore no matter what they cloak themselves in.'

'Gilbert, the woman followed her heart and tried to save her son and his inheritance. Nothing more.'

'Had an itch between her legs is more like.' Killbere sighed. 'All I am saying is that if we are to die in a fight, let it be for the right reason.'

Blackstone tightened the reins. 'We will defeat Babeneaux and hold the woman's domain in Edward's name. It fits well with his support for John de Montfort. We'll fight the Bretons soon enough and we will defeat them. Then with Edward's alliance with de Montfort he'll have the territory north of Aquitaine and a stronghold from the coast to Anjou and Maine. It's strategic, Gilbert, and little to do with the woman's lovers.'

Killbere shrugged, cleared his throat and spat. 'And you leave me here to wet-nurse the woman and child. Get a damned move on and stop chattering like a washerwoman.' He knew defeat when he saw it and Blackstone's plan had merit. Though he had no desire to admit it.

Blackstone and John Jacob reconnoitred Babeneaux's castle. The German captain Renfred and Quenell along with six men accompanied them. Blackstone wanted another archer's eye to confirm accurately the distance between the forest and what was certain to be the open ground leading to the castle walls. They found what high ground there was beyond Babeneaux's village where woodcutters' tracks meandered this way and that. Riding cautiously, they neither saw sign of villagers nor tasted acrid woodsmoke from charcoal-making kilns. No cur barked or wary goose cackled in alarm as the men moved silently through the forest skirting the village. The trees closed in on the rutted ground and then, sensing the sweet smell of cut meadow grass, Blackstone chose a track that eventually opened into broad fields where stacked wood lay in piles ready to be hauled by cart to the lord's castle.

A mile beyond the open ground the castle rose up, its walls embedded in the granite escarpment.

'Mercy,' said John Jacob. 'That's a damned fine castle.'

'One of the best we've seen,' said Blackstone. 'Unfortunately.'

The men drew up alongside Blackstone, each man's eyes gauging the difficulty of scaling the rock face and then the walls. Blackstone studied every line of defence that lay before him. A broad slope swept up to the north wall, a natural defence that exposed any attack. The broken ground made it difficult for men on horses to approach and any attacker on foot would be exhausted before they reached the rock face. An approach road, wide enough for a cart or two or three horses abreast, snaked its way towards the main gate across the uneven ground, the route forcing riders to jostle shoulder to shoulder and making them easy targets for crossbowmen or archers on the walls. On the flank of the castle walls quarried stone lay in mounds: gritty limestone rich in iron oxide and sand that was easy to cut and gave the castle a ruddy hue. There was evidence of ongoing building and fortification.

John Jacob grunted in appreciation and gestured towards the three-cornered defence that jutted out from each end of the walls, which would give defenders an enfilade against exposed attackers.

'I see them,' said Blackstone.

The outer defences were several hundred feet long and boasted four half-cylindrical bastions. Three spur-shaped bastions completed the reinforcements around the south-east and an entrance gate where the portcullis would snap shut its jaws. From where they stood Blackstone could see that if they could breach the outer wall another parallel curtain wall inside awaited anyone who survived the initial assault. Behind this wall additional towers were being built. Wooden scaffolding rose where masons hauled rope pulleys hauling aloft baskets loaded with cut stone.

The more Blackstone studied the castle the greater his respect for the men who had built it and the more he realized that the castle could not be taken without siege engines. Well protected behind the curtain walls, five levels of a baronial hall loomed beyond the keep; each level's upper window openings were braced with rows of columns of white limestone. This was home to the Lord of the manor and perhaps other seigneurial families. The keep was ninety feet high, accessed only by steps rising to an iron-studded double door entrance twenty feet up which would no doubt open onto a large vaulted chamber.

'Quenell? Two hundred paces and more across the face of the wall? Between those bastions.'

'Another fifty, my lord.'

Blackstone nodded. He had been testing the archer; Quenell's answer confirmed his own estimate. To assault anywhere along the outer wall would mean certain slaughter for the men on the ground.

'They didn't spare a sou on that,' said John Jacob. 'Have we ever seen anything that grand? There's no way in, Sir Thomas. Our best chance is to find any underground rooms used for storage. They would be accessed from the courtyard.'

Blackstone looked at the men. They all knew it was impregnable but if Blackstone ordered an assault, then they would not question his command.

'It can't be done,' he said to the men. 'We'll find another way. John, Renfred, take the men and find us a place to fight in the open. We can't get inside that fortress but I'll find a way to draw them out.'

CHAPTER SEVEN

On his return to the forest camp Blackstone called together his captains and their sergeants. He explained how the castle could not be seized and that his plan was to draw out Mael Babeneaux and fight him in the open.

'We could send word to Sir William in Poitiers and with his men lay siege against Babeneaux,' said one of the sergeants.

'It would take an army,' said Blackstone. 'We would need siege machines and enough food to see us through winter. Besides, we are not to linger here. We must get to Poitiers.'

'If the man who survived the river has reached home, then Babeneaux will know you're alive,' said Killbere.

'If he recognized my blazon then Babeneaux will be all the more determined to find me. He won't fall for a simple trap,' said Blackstone. 'That's what we must use to our advantage.'

'Yet he sends no patrols back into the forest,' Will Longdon said.

'So we don't know if he is aware of you, Sir Thomas,' said Jack Halfpenny. 'If that man never returned then his lord will think you dead.'

'Aye, he'll believe that vagabond back at the hamlet he tortured and hanged was you,' said Meulon the throat-cutter.

Cateline sat outside the circle of men cradling her daughter. Henry Blackstone stood by her side. 'May I speak?' she asked.

The men raised their heads and turned to look at her. She did not wait for permission. 'Sir Thomas, you are right not to consider laying siege against him. My Lord Babeneaux had thirty men when he caught me. There are another forty behind his walls. He has grain and salt stores and winter fodder for his horses and enough food for another hundred men. He is a wealthy and powerful man who controls a dozen villages and towns, every one of which will betray you to him if they see you.'

'Then we use that to our advantage. Let them see a few of us and that will be reported,' said Killbere.

'He would believe you had paid the villein to lie,' said Cateline. 'He would torture the man to confess. Under such pain any villager would admit anything, and then he would kill him.'

Meulon pushed his bulk forward through the men, forcing Will Longdon aside. 'Sir Thomas, I will go into the fortress and act as a beggar and tell him I have seen you and that you have only a few men with you.'

'You a beggar?' chided Will Longdon. 'You're too well fed, you oaf. You look as though you've eaten a hog for breakfast. Your arms are as thick as a man's legs and stop you scratching that lice-ridden beard of yours.'

The men laughed and jeered at Meulon, whose face darkened in anger. 'At least I am no hunchbacked archer,' he answered. 'Bending to your bow deforms you.'

'Aye, with sinew and muscle to pull a draw weight that few men can conquer,' Will Longdon answered.

Before Meulon's temper led him to begin taunting Longdon again, Blackstone raised a hand and silenced everyone. 'Meulon has a good idea.'

'Just not the right one,' added Killbere. 'We should send Will Longdon's scrawny arse in there. He stinks like a beggar most days.'

'I lay no scent to scare the animals I hunt,' Will Longdon answered. He looked up at Meulon. 'You want fresh meat, a man needs to smell of the forest.'

'Out of his own mouth. He stinks!' said Meulon happy to continue his duel with the archer.

'Enough!' Blackstone's irritation silenced the bickering. He turned to Cateline. 'What can you tell us?'

Cateline hesitated. 'Beggars are not tolerated. They are beaten if they present themselves at his door. But if you could get someone inside there is a postern gate in the outside wall. They use it for supplies from the village; it's wide enough for only one man at a time to enter. It leads into a storage courtyard.'

'Then unless you have another lover to get a message to and open the gate we can abandon any hope of breaching the walls,' said Killbere.

'There is a way,' she said, brushing a wisp of hair away from Jehanne's forehead, ignoring his jibe. 'Lord Mael would never turn away a pilgrim.'

'He beats a beggar but feeds a pilgrim?' said Killbere.

She nodded. 'Several years ago some Englishmen caught Lord Mael's daughter when she was travelling home from Chartres. It was before the great battle at Poitiers. Lord Mael fought at King John's side. He thought his family safe behind his walls but she had gone to pray at Chartres Cathedral at the feet of the Madonna. You English were a plague that swept the countryside. They killed her servants, but she gave the men the slip and reached the Abbaye de la Sainte-Trinité de Tiron, which gave her sanctuary.' The men remained silent as Cateline's gentle voice lulled them. 'The abbot stood firm and defied those who gave chase. It was a miracle they did not murder the monks and take her. Thereafter Lord Mael vowed he would give safe passage to anyone who makes a holy pilgrimage from the abbey.'

Blackstone got to his feet from where he squatted on the ground with the men. 'Daughter, you say? I thought he was childless until you gave him the girl you cradle.'

'The pestilence took his wife, his daughter and his young son. I was already widowed. I sensed no threat from him when we were introduced. As I told you, I hold title in my own right.'

'So you were seduced by him?' said Killbere; an unmistakable hint of sarcasm laced his question.

She stared back at him unflinchingly. 'I was,' she said with no trace of regret or shame. 'Your wars kill husbands and leave us women abandoned. We seek protection and comfort from those we hope will not degrade us.' She gathered up the child and faced the men before she turned to where the makeshift shelter nestled in the undergrowth. 'Lord Mael changed. Desire for wealth and property is greater than an honest desire for a woman. If you want to get inside his fortress find someone among you to be a pilgrim and pray his story is convincing. If it is not then his screams will haunt you forever.'

CHAPTER EIGHT

Killbere sat cross-legged in his linen shirt and breeches ignoring the chill breeze that whispered through the forest. He was in a small clearing softened by ferns, away from the other men. Killbere's jupon, mail, helmet, arm and leg armour rested on a low bough of a tree. His personal weapons were neatly laid out on his blanket spread before him; all had been cleaned and oiled. The chain of his 'holy water sprinkle' flail was laid in a gentle curl between its spiked ball and leather-bound shaft. His sword lay free of his scabbard. Next to it a misericord, the mercy knife, gleamed dully, its pitted steel as old as the man who wielded it in anger. Its thin blade was used by archers to despatch wounded enemy knights by forcing it through a helmet's narrow visor. Killbere kept it as a secondary knife, his first preference being his rondel dagger. He spat on his whetstone and lovingly stroked it along the length of the twelve-inch blade. When enemies closed in during those final desperate moments of close-quarter battle and a man's survival lay in his ability to bring down his opponent, the tried and tested rondel was often his last chance to kill his enemy. The weapon's rounded hand guard and pommel offered a firm grip for a fighting man to plunge its tapered point between armour and mail. The veteran knight's eyes shone with something akin to love for his weapons as he turned the gleaming blade to meet the stone with a tenderness few would ever observe. Killbere's attention did not waver from the task at hand.

'How much longer are you going to stand there, boy?'

The crunch of a footfall behind him signalled Henry Blackstone's startled reaction. The boy had been standing as quietly as he could fifteen feet away from Killbere, waiting for the appropriate moment to approach him. He had remained silent, his breathing controlled, but still the old fighter had known he was there. 'Sir Gilbert, may I speak to you?'

'When have I ever denied you?' Killbere answered.

Henry Blackstone moved around Killbere and stood watching the veteran fighter attend to his task at hand. He said nothing for a few moments and then, 'You have always sharpened and cleaned your own weapons, Sir Gilbert.'

'That's because we belong to each other. They fit my hand and they know exactly what it is I expect of them.' He laid down the dagger and looked at the nervous boy. 'I have a duty towards them. I honour them because they are my salvation. They deny me meeting God.'

Henry nodded. 'I understand, Sir Gilbert.'

'You do?'

'When John Jacob instructs me to sharpen and clean Wolf Sword, then I... I feel... I don't know... It whispers to me.'

Killbere gazed at the earnest young Blackstone. It was no time to deride what the boy was stumbling to express. What a fighting man felt for a weapon was something seldom shared. He smiled. 'What you feel, Henry... it is a gift.' He paused and wiped his hands on a well-used piece of torn linen. 'Your father has already decided.' He looked at the dumbfounded boy. 'I know what you want and you cannot have it.'

Henry's startled look betrayed him.

Killbere got to his feet. 'You want to know who is to go into Lord Babeneaux's stronghold. Who takes his life in his hands and convinces them to ride out. You wanted to go – is that it? And for me to speak to your father on your behalf. You're too late. LaFargue. Gabriel LaFargue. He's going.'

Henry saw the chosen man's face in his mind's eyes. Five years more than Henry's fifteen. One of Meulon's spearmen. Strong. Tested and chosen by Meulon and accepted by Henry's father. His mind flitted across the chosen man's features. Not as tall as most. Sturdy and broad-shouldered with strength to stand his ground and face a charging enemy. Aggressive too. Not known to back down in an argument.

'He can read and write and he's got the heart for it,' Killbere said, clambering to his feet and pulling on his jupon.

Henry regained his composure. 'I am the better choice, Sir Gilbert. It is a mistake not to choose the one who is better suited to a task.'

'Oh? You think you have more courage?'

'No. Gabriel is a good fighter. But he is not convincing as a pilgrim. He will argue and not take the taunts that a man such as Lord Mael will surely throw at him. I speak, read and write Latin. I can play the role with more conviction. Besides, Gabriel's arms are the size of a man's thigh and his calloused hands speak of a fighting man.'

'Or a man used to using a scythe on late summer grass, or laying hedgerows. A peasant seeking salvation.'

'I would be in your debt, Sir Gilbert, if you would speak to my father and tell him what I have said.'

Killbere gathered his weapons. 'You think you are man enough for such an adventure?'

Henry nodded.

'Then tell him yourself.'

The men's horses were tied onto a line of rope stretched between trees. They kept the bastard horse separate from the others. Blackstone stroked the horse's back, feeling the ripple of its muscles beneath his hand. He had always thought, as the years passed, that the brute might warm to him but even now as his calloused palm caressed its withers it tried to twist its head, yellow teeth snapping. The rope halter restrained it and Blackstone, knowing the beast's habits, stepped quickly aside as an iron-shod hoof lashed back.

Despite its animosity Blackstone knew they were well suited, and he had desired no other horse. They were as scarred and belligerent as each other. Having heeded the warning, he moved forward and laid his palm onto the horse's cheek. 'I will not give you the satisfaction of denying me my own sense of comfort,' he whispered. 'I care as much for you as I do my men and now I must risk sending one into harm's way.'

The beast remained docile for a few subversive moments and then headbutted Blackstone's chest. He stumbled back a couple of strides and grinned. 'If I had the strength, I would do the same to you.'

In an instant the beast's head twitched, its ears perked, a wary eye looking past Blackstone, whose self-same survival instinct had turned him on his heel, knife quickly drawn. Half-crouching, he sidestepped ready to strike whoever had made the near-silent footfall he and the bastard horse had felt rather than heard.

Henry Blackstone was still ten paces away on the animal track. There had been no rustle of fern or fallen leaf beneath his foot. He had approached slowly, uncertain whether his father would welcome the intrusion. He was as startled as he had been minutes before with Killbere. The two men's sixth sense was as honed as their blades.

Blackstone let his guard drop when he saw his son. 'Henry. God's blood, lad. You must never sneak up on me like that.'

'I was not sneaking, Father. I did not wish to disturb you.'

The horse snorted, dipping its head.

'May I approach, Father?'

'Of course, boy, of course.' Blackstone sheathed his knife as his son skirted the horse and then laid the palm of his hand against its nose. Its lips caressed his hand. Henry pulled free a piece of cut turnip and offered it. The yellow teeth bared and quickly crunched the dry offering. Henry smiled, looked at his father and stroked the horse's face.

'He likes a treat. I always bring him one. He remembers.'

'I swear you are the only person who can get that close and not lose your fingers.'

'I don't fear him and he trusts me.'

'Aye, well, I trust him with my life but the beast would take a piece of my flesh if he had the chance.' Blackstone laid a hand on the boy's shoulder. 'What is it, son?'

'Father, you have entrusted me to John Jacob's care, and he has taught me well, but I am old enough now to be of more use to you.'

'You serve John and me well enough. What more would you wish? I won't have you stand shoulder to shoulder with the men in a fight. You are not yet trained for that. Your life is too precious to me.'

'You will not let me fight and you will not let me go to university to further my studies.'

'You were sought out by French assassins when you were in Florence. They tried to kill you.'

'Then let me go to Avignon. There are teachers of law there. Fine scholars. I want to learn – they will feed my craving.'

'And when they discover your name someone would betray you to a killer for hire.'

'I would use Mother's name – de Sainteny.'

'No. You stay here and serve your time as a page to John Jacob. When the time is right and when you are sufficiently skilled, then you might fight.'

'I am the same age as when you fought at Crécy.'

'Nearly the same age. And where I came close to dying of my wounds. No man has skill enough to avoid Fate. It awaits him at every turn.'

'Then my fate is already decided.'

'It is destined but a man's decisions can take him left or right at any crossroad and that can make the difference between life and death. We all die in the end, Henry, but we try to avoid the Reaper. We do what we can to avoid unnecessary danger. If we cannot then we summon more violence than our opponent and send them into death's embrace.'

Henry thought for a moment. 'When I was in Florence under the guidance of Fra Pietro, he told me a story about death waiting to claim a man.'

'A story is just that.'

'No, Father, it was exactly what you are saying.'

Blackstone sat on a fallen tree and indulged his son. 'All right. Let me hear this fairy tale spun by a man of God.'

'A devout man had a vision when he was praying,' said Henry. 'The angel of death visited him and told him it would take him the following day before the church bell in his town rang out for prime. He gathered what possessions he could and rode hard to the next town safe in the belief that he had avoided his own death foretold. When Death arrived at his village, disguised as a travelling monk, he asked the burghers if they knew the man's whereabouts and was told he had left for another town. Death smiled and said that was good because he had an appointment there with him later that night.' Henry paused for breath and waited for a response.

'And this means exactly what I told you,' Blackstone said.

'It means, Father, that whatever turn you take you cannot avoid that meeting with Death.'

'Henry, I do not see the point of this conversation and my stomach tells me it is time to eat.'

'Gabriel is the wrong man to send. I should go,' he blurted out.

Blackstone looked at his son, weighing up what to say. He shook his head. 'No. Gabriel was my choice.'

'Father, he is a fighting man and he will not take kindly to any taunt that would test his resolve. He does not have the heart of an educated man.'

'Henry!' Blackstone interrupted. 'You are no better than any man here because you have been protected and given the opportunity to further your knowledge. I allowed that to appease your mother's wishes. Gabriel was raised by devout grandparents after his own died in the pestilence. He can answer any question put to him by Lord Mael about serving in a monastery. He is my chosen man. Let that be an end to it.'

Blackstone turned his back on his son. His reprimand masked the desire to protect the boy and keep him out of harm's way while in his heart he knew the boy spoke the truth. But Gabriel knew enough scripture to convince Babeneaux.

'Father!'

Blackstone turned. He expected to see anger flushed on his son's face. Instead, he saw contrition.

'I beg you then to let me sit with Gabriel and Lady Cateline when she explains everything he must learn about the castle. And then I will also help him with a few Latin words that a novice would know which would stand a pilgrim in good stead.'

Blackstone studied his son, searching for any hint of artifice, but the offer was heartfelt. 'Very well. Help tutor him. It will serve you both well. He will gain a better understanding and you will learn humility.'

CHAPTER NINE

Henry Blackstone and the men waited patiently, ready to move as soon as word came of where they would ambush Lord Mael's men. Horses saddled, arms and equipment readied, they remained alert should anyone be foolish enough to attempt an attack through the dense forest. Henry had sat with Gabriel LaFargue as he listened to Lady Cateline describe the inner wards of the castle in detail. If her son was anywhere, he would be in the keep, and once Lord Mael took the bait, he would still leave twenty men to guard the walls and gate. If LaFargue were to reach the postern gate undetected to allow Blackstone and his men to enter, it would need to be before nightfall.

'We must time everything carefully,' said Blackstone. 'Does Lord Mael adhere to the times of prayer?'

Cateline nodded. 'But only prime and vespers.'

'Then dawn and evening is when we must plan. Gabriel, you will seek refuge soon after vespers. With luck, Lord Mael will ride out soon after morning prayers and hope to catch us sleeping. Once he is beaten then we will take the castle.'

'And if I reach the postern gate I need to signal you that all is well,' said Gabriel.

'We must time everything B I need to signal you that all is well,' said Gabriel.

'My lady?' said Blackstone.

'The stables are on the far side of the courtyard. Winter feed is stacked there, under cover. Burn that and you will see the smoke.'

'And it will draw men from the walls to put out the blaze,' said Blackstone. 'Then that is the signal we will wait for. Until we see the smoke, we will not attempt to reach the postern gate.'

'Understood, my lord,' said Gabriel.

'My woman servant still serves Lord Mael in his private quarters. I beg you, see that she comes to no harm.'

'We are not here to kill women,' said Blackstone and turned away.

'Her name is Melita,' Cateline called. 'Please, tell your men.'

Blackstone nodded and strode to where Meulon and the others waited. 'Sir Thomas. John Jacob has returned,' said Meulon.

Blackstone grinned, slapped Gabriel on the shoulder. 'I hope you have learnt your lines well; our success depends on you.'

'You can depend on me, Sir Thomas,' said the eager volunteer.

Blackstone strode towards John Jacob and the waiting men. 'Make ready,' he commanded.

Gabriel LaFargue whispered to Henry. 'Master Henry, I cannot remember the Latin you told me. It's the one thing that worries me.'

Henry gave a reassuring smile. 'Ride by my side. Between here and where we fight, I will instruct you.' He had been right to think the brave fighter would be vulnerable.

John Jacob and Renfred had found a good site to lure Mael towards. It was an open meadow of rising ground already scythed for winter silage. The top of the gently sloping land levelled out and then dipped slightly, dead ground that unsuspecting men might think gave them cover out of sight when they camped from an approaching enemy. Two hundred paces either side of the meadow the forest buttressed the open ground where a ditch crossed horizontally. The approach from the castle would lead naturally to the bottom of the meadow and it would take an overcautious man to hold back an attack when he saw how few men were encamped there. And Lord Mael Babeneaux was a warrior who, by all accounts, did not hold back.

Blackstone studied the flat area. 'Build three fires here. Four men with me. Meulon, pick your men for your position. John Jacob and I stay here in the centre.' He beckoned Will Longdon. 'Will, you and Halfpenny place your archers as I told you. Make your marks on the open ground. Know your shooting distance or we'll fall under your arrows. We'll draw him in and snap shut the trap. Gilbert, choose your ground.'

Killbere drew his sword and struck it into the ground. 'This is where I will be when they come.' He pointed to one of the mounted men, Ralph Tait. 'Get the horses to the flank for those of us acting as bait. Keep them saddled. Post three men to guard them.'

'Aye, Sir Gilbert.'

'And a dozen men to gather wood. Dry wood and green fern. We need to dampen the fires so they smoulder till first light and fool the bastards.'

Within minutes they had deployed the men. Blackstone, Killbere, John Jacob and four other men would huddle around the fires soon to be lit while the archers and the rest of the men would spend a chill night huddled in their positions waiting for the expected dawn attack.

'Gabriel!' Blackstone called, beckoning the spearmen to him. The young man quickly dismounted.

'You know what you have to do,' said Blackstone.

'I do, my lord.'

'Take only a blanket roll and a small sack of provisions. Strip off your mail, weapons and jupon and wear that cloak

Henry found for you. It's threadbare enough to belong to a humble pilgrim.'

'I have not seen Henry since we arrived here, my lord. I have no cloak.'

Blackstone looked among the men as they moved into position. His heart lurched. 'Henry!' he called. There was no response. Blackstone strode away from LaFargue. 'Henry!' he bellowed again.

Meulon reined in his horse. 'Sir Thomas, he dismounted and went into the trees. Said he had to relieve himself.'

'He's not pissing up against a tree, I'll wager that,' Killbere muttered, barely able to hide his grin. 'God's tears, he's taken Gabriel's place.'

Blackstone cursed. 'John, find him! Go left.'

John Jacob spurred his horse.

'Meulon, search the track at the bottom of the meadow. See if he's turned back on himself. He knows we'll follow him so he'll lay a false trail. He's wily enough to do that.' Blackstone turned to Killbere. 'I'll thrash him, Gilbert. I swear I will. I'll lock the disobedient whelp in a monastery and throw away the key.'

Killbere snorted. 'Aye, and end up with a sodomized scribe with snot permanently dripping as he wastes his life hunched over a manuscript. No, Thomas. The lad has courage. And if he survives, then we should let him fight at our side. It's time for that.'

Blackstone fought the anger at his son's disobedience. He felt the pulse in his neck slow. 'If he survives,' he murmured.

Henry Blackstone ran hard. He had several miles to cover before the bell rang for evening prayer. Cateline had described the castle in fine detail and he knew Babeneaux had a chapel within the walls and a priest to lead prayers and administer the sacraments. Henry's blanket roll was tied with rope across his back and he carried a small sack of provisions, as would any pilgrim. He pushed through the undergrowth; a low branch caught his face and he felt its cat's claw scratch across his cheek. That too would serve its purpose when he was questioned. Animal tracks criss-crossed through fern and bramble and he chose a narrow path not wide enough for forest boar and trusted his knowledge of forest lore which told him he was heading south and east. Lichen clung to one side of the trees and low light filtered through the branches over his shoulder. He stopped, gathered his breath and listened past the thud of his heart in his ears. He half turned his head, closed his eyes and let the woodland sounds settle in his mind's eye. Far behind to one side was the unmistakable sound of a horse crashing through the undergrowth. It was moving away from him. Had he run directly east then the rider would have already been on him but he had traversed in a wide loop, deliberately heading in the wrong direction. His breathing settled, he crouched, looked through the trees in the fading light and let his eyes focus on the trees twenty paces ahead; then he shifted his gaze another twenty, and another, and so on until his eyes penetrated the forest more than a hundred paces ahead. The way was clear. The animal track would take him beyond the trees where he hoped to find a cart track. The villagers must have a route from the cut meadow to their hamlet and from there he would be close to the castle.

All he had to do was find it.

CHAPTER TEN

The sun was low in the sky as Henry turned his face to the breeze carrying the tang of woodsmoke. He had run tirelessly for miles but now he slowed, his thoughts filled with trepidation as he remembered everything Cateline had explained about the castle. The landscape broadened, curving away from the rutted track he had come upon when leaving the forest hours before. It had taken him longer than he thought because of his desire to stay hidden in the forest, but as he followed the track the first houses came into view and beyond them, rising above the woodland canopy, the crenellated walls of the castle, its boar's head banner curling in the light wind.

'Boy!' a voice challenged.

Henry turned and faced four rough-looking men who, by the tools they carried, were obviously returning from the fields. Before he had a chance to answer them the men advanced. 'You thieving, are you, lad?'

They closed in on him. He was downwind and the tough-looking peasants stank of rancid sweat. Their insular way of life made them suspicious of any stranger. Henry stood his ground and where others might have turned and ran he faced down the men. 'I am a pilgrim and seek sanctuary with my Lord Mael Babeneaux.'

Henry felt a rush of relief when he saw their expressions alter from open hostility to what he perceived as being more welcoming. One of them smiled. 'Then you are a fortunate traveller, young man.' The speaker seemed to be more senior than the others. He addressed his companions. 'You get on home. I'll show this devout lad the way to the castle.' The men nodded their agreement. They muttered good wishes to Henry and wished him well on his journey. 'This way, young man,' said their leader. 'You've travelled far, then?'

'I have,' said Henry not wishing to give away too much in case it incriminated him. 'Tiron.'

The man sized up the youth who strode along silently next to him. 'I see you are not a boy who enjoys the sound of his own voice. I know silence is the rule of the house at the abbey, but, Master Pilgrim, find your tongue when my Lord Mael questions you.' The old man laughed. 'Or he'll cut it out.'

The villager led Henry down the woodland paths and when he stepped out into the open ground he realized why the fortress could not be assaulted. By the time they had wound their way along the stone road towards the broad ramp that led to the main gate, soldiers had appeared on the battlements. 'A pilgrim!' shouted the old man to those above the portcullis. The grinding chains lifted the defence and as soon as it was high enough for a man to enter without bending the elderly villager slapped Henry's back. 'I will pray for you, stranger. My lord does not take kindly to vagrants so choose your words with care. I have seen others who heard of my lord's generosity hanging from the walls with a rope around their neck and their balls cut off. They were liars who sought his shelter and food and drink. And if that be the case with you then I will be rewarded for bringing a charlatan to my lord's door so he may exact his pleasure. As I said, I will pray for you,' He gave a broken-toothed grin and spat. 'I'll pray that you are a lying miscreant.' He turned away into the fading sunlight.

Henry was escorted into the outer ward where twenty men or more lazed beside their quarters. Some sharpened weapons;

others washed clothing; one man hauled a bucket up from a well, spilling water into a trough. Henry took in as much as he could of his surroundings. Men were plentiful. Crossbowmen lined the walls, and soldiers milled about in and out of various buildings. Lady Cateline could not have known just how many men served her husband and from what Henry could see there must be close to a hundred men in this outer ward. Did that mean there were more within? They outnumbered his father more than he could realize. A sentry from the main gate accompanied him until met by a burly man whose surcoat, worn from years of use, still showed the boar's head blazon. He was bareheaded and his unwashed hair touched his shoulders. His beard reached his deep chest, and he was as tall as Henry's father. He reminded Henry of Meulon: a wild-looking man who might have spent a lifetime fighting wars. From the way the men responded to him Henry took him to be a sergeant-at-arms or one of Lord Mael's captains.

'Who's this?' he demanded of the sentry.

'A lad on pilgrimage. They brought in him from the village.'

The big man grunted. He suddenly reached out and grabbed Henry's face in his calloused fist. 'Scratched and bleeding. Wandering lost like an innocent in the forest. Scared, were you, lad?'

Henry had recoiled but instinctively struck out at the arm that held him to knock it away. It was as solid as a tree branch. The man released him. 'No simpering monk in waiting, this one. Where are you from, boy?'

'The Abbaye de la Sainte-Trinité de Tiron.'

The big man studied him a moment longer. 'Take him to the kitchen. Feed him.'

'Aye, my lord.'

Lord Mael Babeneaux laughed, yellow teeth parting his beard. 'Look at his face! He thought me a common soldier.

Kick him in the arse if he speaks out of turn.' With that he strode past towards the soldiers.

The sentry gave the shocked Henry a firm push in his back. 'Move!'

This time Henry restrained his impulse to strike back. This Breton lord was master of a greater territory than most other lords. To feed, clothe and pay so many fighting men and to equip them with horses, which also needed fodder and farriers, meant he had wealth and power.

They took Henry through another gate to the inner ward and he followed the sentry's orders to clamber up the steps towards the great hall in the keep. Henry felt suddenly alone and fearful – and his foolishness in taking Gabriel's place taunted him as he ascended the steps to the keep's main door. At the top platform two sturdy ropes attached through iron eyelets were looped to the final rungs of the wooden steps. If an attack was made against the castle they could be raised to keep invaders away from the keep. His father's assessment had been correct. Lord Mael's castle was prepared for any assault and it would take an army to seize it. He salivated as he caught a whiff of roast meat from the kitchens.

The sentry turned the iron ring handle and put his shoulder against the studded door; then he stepped back. 'Inside, lad. Follow your nose. Tell them Lord Mael said to feed you. In with you!'

Henry stepped into the gloom, his eyes taking time to adjust. They had ushered him into a great hall but no fire burned in the vast fireplace despite the autumnal chill in the room. Faggots and logs lay stacked ready for use but it seemed obvious Lord Mael did not believe in creature comforts or gaily decorated rooms. A dining table and benches sat in the room's middle, bare except for the spiked iron candle holders, the wax columns unlit, half used, rivulets of dried wax furled at their base. Narrow windows high in the wall admitted meagre shafts of light. The reed floor looked freshly laid and the benches around the fireplace were made of heavy chestnut like the beams supporting the floor above. Another staircase rose on the far wall and he guessed that led to where Lady Cateline's son was held. Lord Mael's quarters would be in the baronial hall in the more elegant building beyond the keep.

'Who the fuck are you?' said a gruff voice from the far side of the fireplace where there was obviously a passage leading through to the kitchens. A servant in a grease-covered leather apron looked as though he could have been the castle's blacksmith, so big was his girth. He pointed a wicked-looking carving knife towards the intruder when he asked the question.

'I am a pilgrim,' said Henry. 'Lord Mael said to feed me.'

The man huffed and turned away out of sight. Henry stepped further into the hall. Mael's blazon hung across one stone wall as big as a battle banner. It was grimy and dust-laden, the image of the boar's head blackened by smoke from the fireplace – when lit – making its teeth and tusks look as though the beast had just emerged from a thicket. Henry picked his way along the benches that boxed the space around the fireplace; a slab of planed wood made up the top of a dining table surrounded by several stools. The heat from the kitchen fire wrapped itself around him as he stepped into the room where the sweating, burly cook was basting a pig on a spit over the crimson embers of what had once been a large fire. A cauldron of boiling water steamed suspended from the iron rack across the fires. The evening's gloom had already settled on the kitchen but cresset lamps, their flames spluttering in their oil-filled shallow dishes, gave enough light to those working at the stone slab used for food preparation.

Something lurched in the corner of Henry's vision. A mastiff, as grey as the stone floor, lunged from beneath the cook's table. The dog's slavering jaws issued a rumbling growl. The brute was as high as Henry's waist and he recoiled, slamming back against the wall.

The cook raised a hand. 'No!'

The dog obediently dropped to its belly.

'My lord keeps his hunting dogs in their kennels but this bastard lives in my damned kitchen until it's called to its master's feet at night – in there,' he said with a nod towards the keep's empty hall. 'And if it lives here, it obeys me. I feed it. It does what it's told. There's a lesson there for vagrants like you. Get me?'

'I understand,' said Henry.

'You want food?'

'I would be grateful, sir.'

'Sir, is it? Aye, right enough, you know how to toady up to those you need. Well, Master Pilgrim, no one gets fed here without earning it. Out there in the yard there's a well. Draw water and bring it here. Take that bucket.'

Henry slipped his bedroll from over his shoulders and laid it on the bench along with his meagre food sack; then, obediently, he took the leather bucket and followed the man's gesture to go out of the small doorway at the other end of the kitchen. A rickety ladder leaned against the doorsill; it was steep and felt immediately unstable as Henry put his weight on the first rungs. He wondered whether the cook was having fun at his expense by sending him down this ladder instead of the main stairway into the keep. If that was his intention then Henry was determined not to falter. As he made his way down he realized that they would not allow the kitchen boys to enter through the main entrance and that this was what they had to endure every day.

Henry gazed down into the darkness of the well. The size of the windlass's barrel told him it was a well of great depth and to haul up the water-filled bucket at the bottom would take strength. Grabbing the handle with both hands he put his back into it and wound the handle. His action gave him time to look around the inner yard. Whoever had built the castle had planned carefully. On the far side of the yard were the stables and their proximity to the well meant the horse troughs could be filled quickly. The grain and hay store was at the far end of the stables and abutted the inner curtain wall. If he could light a torch from the kitchen fire, then he could burn the hay and signal his father. He was ahead of himself. First, he had to find the boy and then the postern gate. And even then his father's men would have a fight on their hands within the confines of the castle. By the time he had thought it through the bucket had drawn level with the well's low wall. He grabbed it and spilled the contents into the leather pail. Climbing back up the ladder with the unsteady pail took balance and strength. He was sweating from effort when he reappeared in the kitchen. He delivered the water without thanks from the cook and saw that his bedroll had been undone and his food sack opened. The cook kept his back to him. It was obviously a rite of passage to see whether a pilgrim carried anything of value. The cook glanced at him.

'Over there,' said the cook, nodding to a bench at the table. He ladled pottage from a pan into a wooden bowl and handed it to Henry; then he deftly sliced meat from the boar on the spit and tossed it to the dog. 'He's more important than you. Understand, pilgrim? You eat what we eat; he gets the choice cuts. Him and his lord. Do well to remember your place here. Understand? It's lower than the dog's belly.'

Henry remained silent and spooned the peas, beans and onions. The cook placed a dark loaf of rye bread on the table, sliced it and put the thick piece in front of him. 'That's what you'll get tonight but you'd best get on your knees when the bell tolls in the morning. My lord likes to see prayers being said by them who thinks themselves baptized and saved from Satan's clutches. You got sins, have you, boy?'

'No. No, I don't think so.'

'No?' the cook said, raising his voice. 'Hear that? We've a virgin here.'

Henry was suddenly aware that there was another room behind the kitchen from where sniggering laughter emanated. Two kitchen boys emerged carrying baskets of prepared vegetables. 'If poverty is a virtue, he's a virgin right enough. There were nuthin' in that bedroll.'

Henry thought the two youths looked to be a couple of years younger than him. One of them glared, arms resting on the table. 'You sleep in the corner; we get our backs against the grate, understand?'

Henry nodded, lowering his eyes, not wishing the bully to see the challenge in them. When the time came, he knew that if necessary he would have to kill the two servants, but the cook was a big man and it would take strength to bring him down. He gathered his bedroll and sack and retreated to the shadows in the corner of the kitchen. Between him and the boy he had come to rescue were the three servants and a hungry-looking brute of a dog.

Doubt plagued him: fear of his own inability to kill the servants while they slept.

In cold blood.

CHAPTER ELEVEN

Shadows reached into the courtyards, smothering the buildings and defences as darkness crept across the castle walls. Lanterns were lit and guard-post braziers flared along the parapets. Henry watched as silence fell as quickly as the night. The only sound was the dull clanging of the compline bell from the castle's chapel. Henry watched the yard below but saw no evidence of soldiers or their lord going to pray before retiring for the night. The kitchen boys served Lord Mael's food while the men in the courtyard returned to their quarters and others manned their posts.

The brute dog barked.

'Captain?' said the cook as a man entered his domain from the keep's hall. There was little respect in his voice and he remained seated, slumped on a bench, his back against the wall.

'Keep it back,' said the captain. The cook raised a hand; the dog growled but stayed where he was. Babeneaux's captain looked as tall and broad as his master. His beard had wisps of grey and his hands bore scars that were visible even in the dim light. Henry thought the man would as soon kill the dog as have it made obedient, but that would incense his sworn lord.

'Lord Mael wants it inside.' He glanced at Henry who sat, knees hunched, in the corner. 'And the pilgrim.'

A low whistle came from the hall and the dog bounded forward, nearly knocking the heavyweight man back on his heels as he avoided the dog's salivating jowls.

'Goddamn beast,' the captain muttered and turned back from where he had come.

The cook grabbed Henry's arm as he went to follow the man-at-arms. 'You might see me as a coarse peasant whose only skill is with a ladle, but I am God-fearing. That man is not. Captain Roparzh would eat raw human flesh if our Lord Mael let him. God knows our master is a brutal man, but Roparzh… Well, all I am saying is do not cast your eyes on him because pilgrim or not the moment you step beyond Lord Mael's protection, Roparzh would gouge your eyes out and let you go blindly to meet your maker.'

Henry nodded his thanks and with a thudding heart followed in the killer's footsteps. The fire in the hall had not been lit but extra candles now cast their warm glow around the hall. Babeneaux was stripped to his linen shirt, impervious to the chill air; his sword belt and surcoat were draped across the nearest stool. The pewter plates on the table bore remnants of food, which he tossed to the mastiff. Lord Mael swept a hand across the table, clearing the last crumbs.

'Name?' he asked. The captain stood behind him and Henry felt that one wrong answer might be a signal for the Breton lord to have his captain despatch him where he stood.

'I am Henry de Sainteny,' he answered, using his mother's maiden name.

'Your father?'

'I do not know,' he said. 'My grandfather fought the English, that much I do know.'

Babeneaux sipped from a dark thick glass that obscured the colour of the red wine, making it appear as black as blood. He drank slowly, his voice without threat – almost kindly now that he was out of sight of his soldiers where perhaps he felt the need to behave more coarsely. 'I don't know the name, boy, but I am certain that he honoured his family. Does he still live?'

'No, my lord.'

'The English?

'Yes.'

The Breton's eyes never left Henry's face. 'The abbey? All is well?'

'I stayed only a few weeks, lord. I was put to work to earn my keep but I travel to Avignon and the Pope.'

'The abbot told you to journey there?'

'I never saw the abbot. I stayed with others in the dormitory.'

Lord Mael signalled someone behind him in the darkness: a priest, clothed in black, a moving shadow that flitted quickly to where Henry could make out a sideboard, heavy oak with locked doors. The priest reached in and pulled out a large black book. He returned and handed it to Mael and stood as obediently as the pet mastiff. The priest raised his face to gaze at Henry, a cruel, sallow face that glared at him from beneath the cowl. Henry's stomach tightened. Was this place nothing more than a pit of darkness inhabited by malevolent beings?

'I was given this by the Abbot of Tiron because I serve both the monastery and the memory of my daughter granted shelter there many years ago,' said Lord Mael. He placed the large bible on the table and opened it without caring what page his fingers found. 'You are educated?'

'Some, my lord.'

'You must have been in the scriptorium then? What? Sharpening quills? Mixing the colours?'

Henry's heart thudded. He did not know whether the monastery even had a scriptorium. Skilled monks able to illuminate manuscripts were difficult to find, and many were trained from when young. He glimpsed a page and saw a flash of rich blue and red. A block of colour at the top of the page. It followed then that if the bible had been given to the Breton lord for his patronage and that there was an illuminated page then there must be a scriptorium.

'I have been in it, yes, my lord.'

'Then you will know the colours on the wall. They are not as drab as many would think. What colour, boy?'

Henry's mouth dried. He was desperate not to reveal his ignorance. He shook his head. 'I cannot say, Lord Mael. I could not work with the monks there because I cannot see colour. My world is without it. I see only grey.' He said a silent prayer that the boy he had known when studying in Florence and who claimed to have the same affliction had been truthful.

Babeneaux studied him a moment longer. 'I have heard of this,' said Mael. 'All right, boy. Read for me.'

Henry stepped towards the table and gazed down at the Latin script where the Breton lord's finger rested. They were lines from the Old Testament. Henry faltered. The text was faded. He concentrated and then read. '"And I will draw unto thee to the river Kishon Sisera, the captain of Jabin's army, with his chariots and his multitude; and I will deliver him into thine hand."'

Lord Mael looked to the priest, who nodded. It was obvious that Mael could not read Latin and that his priest was his gatekeeper to its mystery. He gestured Henry to return to where he stood.

'And I will deliver my enemies into the jaws of hell,' said Mael. He let the threat hang. 'You are well taught and your mother must have placed you in the care of monks at an early age. What work did you do at Tiron?'

'I attended to the Lantern of the Dead.' Henry prayed that the information given by Lady Cateline was accurate. Such small domed towers, pierced with narrow openings, emitted the light from a raised lantern that signified a monastery's graveyard. The towers and their light were symbolic, providing guidance for the souls that travelled from earth to heaven.

'And you intend to travel on the Via Francigena?'

'Aye, my lord, once I can find my way safely to Avignon. The route is too far east for me until then.'

'The roads are clear in my domain.'

Henry had deliberately kept silent about his father and men, trusting that when questioned Lord Mael would expose the truth for himself. To do otherwise would have made his story less plausible. 'Not so, my lord. I came across routiers and they chased me. I feared for my life, which is how I came by these cuts on my face. I ran hard through the forest where their horses could not pursue me.'

He saw the information had had its effect.

'How many men?'

'No more than twenty. I stumbled on their camp.'

'You saw their blazon?'

'I think so, lord. Their clothes were dirty but their jupons bore a fist curled around a sword's hilt. The man who led them was big, as tall as you, my lord, and he bore a scar down the side of his face. It was he who ordered his men to chase me. I think he was afraid that I had seen too much of where they camped.'

Lord Mael's demeanour hardened. 'Thomas Blackstone. They were English.' It was not a question but Henry answered anyway.

'They were,' he said. 'English devils,' he added for good measure.

Babeneaux pushed back from the table so urgently the dog yelped. The priest retreated into darkness. Mael turned to his captain. 'Sixty men. Leave before daylight. The boy here will tell you where. Bring Blackstone alive if you cannot bring me his head.'

Henry's heart thumped so hard he feared his pulsing neck would give him away. Babeneaux was not leading the attack. If the lightly armed archers were caught in the open the sixty men-at-arms would overwhelm them. And there were less than half that number of hobelars under his father's command. Even if they triumphed over the ferocious-looking captain the Breton lord was still behind his walls with enough men to fight off any attack. And if any of the captain's men survived and reported back to their sworn lord he would know the pilgrim beneath his roof had lied about the strength of Blackstone's force.

Henry Blackstone was trapped.

CHAPTER TWELVE

Henry slept fitfully. Lord Mael had retired to his chamber but the dog had slunk back to the kitchen where there was warmth. The stench of the dog's farts and the stale sweat of the cook and the servants made the fetid air worse than sleeping rough with his father's men. He eased himself free of the blanket and his threadbare cloak. The autumn chill slithered beneath the outside door and unfurled down the stone walls from the narrow window. The dog raised its head, a low growl in its throat. Henry stepped carefully over the snoring men and cut a slice of meat from the spit. The dog stood and licked its lips. Henry laid two generous cuts on the floor and when the dog bent its head he crept silently from the kitchen.

Only one tallow candle remained flickering on the table, which gave sufficient light for him to cross the room and climb the stairs. At the top a half-landing plunged him into darkness and he regretted not peeling the candle from its split wax and using it. He had been frightened that someone would notice shadows playing on the walls but now he thought it might have been worth the risk. Like a blind man he extended his arms forward, palms pressing against a wooden door. His fingers found the turning handle. It creaked as he tried it but the door was locked. He stood in the darkness, annoyed with himself for not realizing the boy would be held as a prisoner. He would need to be fed and that meant the cook held the key. He pressed his ear against the door and a moment later heard floorboards creak. He held his breath. He was certain someone was mirroring his action on the other side of the door.

'Jocard, are you there? I am a friend.'

Henry heard the intake of breath; a fingernail scratched against the door. 'Yes. I am here. Who are you?'

Henry bit his lip, almost spilling his true identity. 'That doesn't matter. Your mother is safe.'

He heard the intake of breath. 'Can that be true? And my sister?'

'Yes. Both were saved from Lord Mael's men.'

There was a silence and then he heard doubt creep into the boy's voice. 'How do I know you are a friend? You might be one of Lord Mael's men sent to gain my trust.'

'Your sister's name is Jehanne,' Henry whispered.

'That means nothing. Everyone here could know that.'

'Jocard, listen to me. My life is in danger being here. I came to rescue you. There are men beyond the walls who will come for us but I need your help. Where is the postern gate? I couldn't see it when I arrived.'

Again there was silence. And then: 'You're trying to trick me. If I tell you, you will tell Lord Mael and I will be beaten. Show yourself to me when they bring me food tomorrow morning. Only then will I believe you.'

'How can I do that?' said Henry.

'That's your problem. If you are who you say you are, you will find a way.'

Henry's voice hardened. This was no time to try and persuade. 'Listen to me. My father killed men to save your mother and I tended her and your sister throughout the night. My life is forfeit if my identity is revealed. Now, help me. Where is the postern gate?'

He heard the boy's breathing, his face close to the door. 'Across the yard. Past the well.' The voice paused. 'Thank you.'

The floorboards creaked again as the captive boy retreated.

Henry stayed awake until the first signs of light lifted the darkness. It would be a clear day. Mist lay across the low ground, skirting the forests and villages beyond the castle. It would be a good time to launch an attack on the castle if such an assault were possible. He imagined his father and Sir Gilbert suddenly appearing from the mist with an army at their backs, and siege engines and scaling ladders; instead, reality was the chapel bell clanging out. The summons to dawn prayer would attract some of the household but not Lord Mael's captain, who had gathered his men-at-arms in the courtyard below in the darkness an hour or so before. Henry pulled open the kitchen door. The dog snapped up its head but did not growl at the boy who had served him meat the previous night. It stood and shook itself and stretched.

'Boy!' the cook called, roused by the creaking wood. 'You've work to do.'

'Lord Mael said I could attend prayer,' Henry lied, knowing it unlikely the cook would ever dare raise the subject with his master.

Cook grunted. 'Pious little bastard. Get yourself back here when the praying's done.' He didn't wait for an answer but threw aside his blanket and dragged a piss pot from beneath the preparation slab. The dog barked, willing Henry to take him. 'Quiet!' the cook demanded, but the dog persisted. 'Christ's tears, he'll have the household awake. Take him, dammit.'

'He won't be able to get down the ladder.'

'Don't be a damned simpleton. The main door! Tell the sentry I said you were to go that way. Now piss off and take that brute with you.' He raised his head, and sighed as he relieved himself.

Henry wasted no time and beckoned the dog. He swung open the keep's main door and was faced with one of the sentries, who blocked his way. The man stood back when he was told Henry's instructions. The man swore at the dog, who slavered and growled, but Henry went quickly down the steps, the dog at his heels, descending into the dank morning's shadows in the courtyard. He ignored the chill, alert to where men moved as they took up their stations and servants began pitching hay in the stable. The castle was awakening and the bell fell silent. With his new companion at his side, Henry searched for the postern gate. Its narrow passageway would lead from the outer wall into the first courtyard between the curtain walls but Lady Cateline said that it gave access to the inner yard below the keep. Where? The keep's walls curved into the Breton lord's quarters, five floors of private rooms. How many people were inside? Henry had seen armed men wearing a different blazon. If there were seigneurial lords visiting then the private quarters is where they would be housed. There were other areas of the castle grounds restricted to him and for all he knew there were even more of these visiting men-at-arms swelling the castle's ranks.

The dog lowered its nose, sniffed here and there and then cocked its leg. It loped towards a sheltered area where stout poles supported a thatch covering; it was an open-fronted storage area that ran along the wall for thirty long paces. The mastiff sniffed the stacked barrels and timber, cocked its leg again and went on, enticed by the scent of animal and man. The barrels and timber blocked an entrance. Henry quickly got his bearings. The sun was casting a dull glow over his shoulder. The postern gate lay in the west wall. This was it. He quickly checked to see that the awakening soldiers and servants were paying him no attention and then ran to the planked and studded door almost concealed behind the barrels and timber. It would be impossible for him to clear the gate. Despair quickly turned to panic. The sun would soon rise and then his father would be attacked.

And Henry knew in that heart-squeezed moment that he had failed.

CHAPTER THIRTEEN

Roparzh and his men, all veterans of the Breton civil war and – because of Lord Mael's alliance with the French – men who had fought the English, waited patiently for the first glimmer of light to stretch up from the horizon. The riders huddled against the morning chill beneath their cloaks. They had travelled slowly because of the pre-dawn darkness and mist, but knowing the land as they did they rode without torchlight, letting the moon's glow guide them to where they could strike at Blackstone's encampment.

They stood back from the lower slope, obscured by a treeline as they watched the faint wisps of smoke curl from the top of the plateau. Roparzh gazed back into the trees. Woodcutters had thinned them and brambles and thorns entwined themselves around stumps and felled timber.

'They'll be sleeping,' said one man at his side. 'Their horses will catch the scent of ours. Shouldn't we strike at them before it alerts them?'

Roparzh glanced at the smoke. He shook his head. 'The breeze is in our favour. It's blowing left to right across us. Neither their horses nor ours will alert the English.' He took his time looking across the meadow. The trees either side were dense, too choked with undergrowth to make a flanking attack. 'What wolves lurk in those trees, do you think?'

'Wolves?' said the perplexed rider. 'None. Their packs hunt beyond us.'

'Aye, so you say, but I have fought these bastards before and we lost too many riding into such a place. Those trees either side are too dense for horsemen to fight among easily and the way ahead invites us to go forward, but I have seen English archers step out from woodland and slay us where we stood.' He squinted at the sky. 'If they are expecting us, then they mean for us to ride from here on that rising ground.' He tugged his horse's rein and turned to face his men. He spoke quietly. 'Pass the word. We go back and use that woodcutter's track we passed and attack them from above.'

The sun had still not risen by the time the sixty armed men gathered on the top of the hillside. They dismounted fifty paces behind the crest of the hill and, daring to edge forward, gazed down to where twenty bedrolls clustered around three dying fires, men huddled in their blankets seeking to keep the chill from their bones. Roparzh raised and lowered his arm. His men crouched. One of the Englishmen below had thrown off his blanket and groggily stood to relieve himself over the lip of the plateau, his back towards the men waiting for the signal to attack. The man's sword was stuck into the dirt, the breeze catching its blade, making it sway gently, as gently as the old man who rocked slowly side to side as he pissed into the cool morning air. He stretched, turned and climbed back under his blanket. Roparzh grinned. The stupid old bastard was content to sleep until the warmth of the sun reached him. He signalled his men to move down the slope towards the unsuspecting Englishmen.

'They're here,' said Killbere as he climbed back under his blanket and feigned sleep.

'I heard them,' Blackstone answered from one of the bedrolls at the next fire. 'Be ready,' he ordered loud enough for the few men who shared the danger to hear, his voice carried away from the approaching men by the breeze. Despite the distance between Blackstone and the advancing men, the sound of boots finding their grip on a downward slope, of men's breath coming fast as they readied themselves to kill, of creaking leather and of buckles jangling against mail was unmistakable – and it was coming closer. Halfway. Eighty paces. The slope made the Bretons move slowly for fear of slipping and warning the sleeping men below. Blackstone waited. Watching through half-closed eyes. Listening for any attempt to outflank his position. Another fifty paces and he and the men who baited the trap would be overwhelmed. Throwing aside the blanket he leapt to his feet and faced the startled attackers. The half-dozen men with him abandoned their blankets. Blackstone saw the surprise of the attackers when they realized the few men who stood facing them were all that slept there. The other sleeping men were nothing more than mounds of ferns. The shock tore through Lord Mael's men. It was a trap; but where were the other Englishmen? Their momentum stalled. They hesitated as Blackstone raised Wolf Sword above his head. 'Now!' he bellowed.

His voice swept down across the open meadow to the treeline where Roparzh had first stopped; the undergrowth came alive. Fern and grass, forest detritus used for concealment, fell away. Rough-clothed men emerged and quickly formed a line, bent their backs and unleashed a withering storm of yard-long arrows onto the men halfway down the slope above Blackstone's position, arrows that found their targets. Men turned to run, clamouring for the safety of the ground above them. Blackstone saw their leader bellow a threat. The man knew what he was doing. *Attack!* The closer they got to their enemy the less able the archers would be to shoot into them.

Another whispering hail fell, but they struck fewer as the men leapt downward in desperation for their lives and eagerness to kill the man who had trapped them. They took heart. There was only a handful of men below and no more than a couple of dozen archers beyond who would not be able to fight them when they swept through the few defenders. The cry went up. *Kill! Kill!*

Blackstone, Killbere and the others raised their shields, quickly forming a wedge. The attackers emptied their chests of fear, bellowing hatred, driving strength into their legs and raised sword arms. They clashed. The wall held. The attackers' momentum carried them a few yards beyond Blackstone; then, hearing cries of men behind them they turned to face more Englishmen swarming down the hill, led by a bearded giant. Roparzh's sixty were now less than forty but their enemy was still weaker.

'On me!' cried Roparzh and struck out before the descending men could reach them. His men knew how to fight and quickly formed a fighting line. They were safe from the archers now that they were so close to the shield men and those who raced towards them could not hold formation. It was man against man and the Breton knew the tall, muscular knight with the scarred face striding forward to take the attack to him was Thomas Blackstone. Another equally formidable-looking soldier was at Blackstone's side and Roparzh knew these swordsmen needed to be smashed apart. He cried out for those around him to barge through.

The sheer weight of attackers finally pushed John Jacob away from his sworn lord as Roparzh struck down a man in Blackstone's shield wall. Blackstone was barely five strides away but one of Roparzh's men sought to claim the prize by killing Blackstone himself. As the man traded blows with Blackstone another Englishman barged Roparzh aside. Roparzh pressed forward into Blackstone's men who had stumbled their way onto the plateau. There could be no retreat. To turn and run would expose Lord Mael's men to the archers who waited below, and they'd have Blackstone's men at their backs. The archers could only be slain if they killed Blackstone's men first. And then he realized the archers had abandoned their war bows and were running uphill, sword and knife in hand. They wore no mail; their leather jerkins or cloth jupons offered no protection against a sword thrust but they came on. Mad bastards wanting to kill.

'Left flank turn! Turn!' Roparzh bellowed. His men obeyed. Half turned their backs on Blackstone to face the approaching archers. Men were grunting with the effort of killing, a jagged roar of desperate voices as they slithered in gore, fighting, ramming, slashing. Desperate to kill and survive in the close confines of the narrow plateau.

John Jacob blinked the sweat from his eyes. As he fought a hard-arsed Breton who refused to die, he saw Blackstone was being assailed. John Jacob traded blows, twisting this way and that, locking his eyes on the spittle-cursing man as blurred images swirled around him and, beyond, blood-curdling screams from mutilated and dying men dulled his senses. One sight loomed in the background. Quenell the archer clambered up the slope, slit the throat of one man, parried a blow from another but was then suddenly overwhelmed. He heard Quenell's name being called as Ralph Tait turned away from the men on the plateau and barged and cut his way through to the wounded archer. Then he too went down. The surge of hatred gave strength to Jacob's arm, and he struck his opponent with such force across the top of his shoulder that his blade nearly severed the man's head. The Breton fell without a sound. Jacob spun around to reach Blackstone but the cacophony of screaming, cursing, battling men seemed as impenetrable as a locked shield wall. He waded into the fray.

Blackstone was being assailed by three Bretons as Roparzh forced his shield against an Englishmen, throwing him off balance, thrusting his sword tip into his groin and then, as the man squirmed, pulling it free and pressing it into his throat. Blood gushed. The man's legs curled into his stomach in agony as he died. A man in the fracas called out *Othon!* as he tried to reach his fallen comrade but Roparzh spun on his heel and swept his sword in a fast arc that caught the man behind his knees. Hamstrung, he went down, floundering. Roparzh stepped onto his face and felt the man's neck crack beneath his weight. Now there was only one other man between him and the big Englishman.

The sun was not yet fully up but already the bloodstained ground reflected the day's dawning.

Blackstone saw him coming. Gabriel LaFargue was down and one of his Gascon hobelars who had tried to save him went underfoot. The powerful man had strength enough to sweep aside two more of Blackstone's men. Yet another Breton attacked Blackstone, who rammed his shield upwards, felt the man's jaw shatter and saw teeth and blood spew. Reversing Wolf Sword he smashed its pommel into the side of the man's head and then the leader of the Bretons whom Blackstone took to be Lord Mael Babeneaux was on him.

Roparzh's strength and weight gave him impetus, forcing Blackstone to quickly backtrack. He stumbled over a body. His back slammed into the ground. He rolled away from the strike. The Breton's brute strength sliced into the corpse, cleaving chest and arm. Blackstone rolled onto his feet but the next blow smashed into his shield. Blackstone's arm muscle twisted as the force of the blow caught him at an awkward angle. He dropped to one knee, covered himself with his shield and struck Wolf Sword upwards in a killing blow. The Breton swept the blade aside and aimed a kick at Blackstone's face. It connected with his chest. Once again Blackstone was open to a killing blow.

Jack Halfpenny had scrambled into the fray with the archers as they attacked the Bretons. He clambered over bodies, slipped on the bloodied grass, lunged and caught Roparzh's calf with his archer's knife. It split the thick muscle to the bone. The stab was not fatal but the big man faltered for a few vital seconds.

Roparzh turned his strike away from Blackstone, swinging down his blade like a man swats a fly, but the lithe archer had already rolled away. Blackstone threw himself onto the big-chested man, his weight smothering him. Roparzh's wounded leg gave way. Blackstone straddled him; they twisted and rolled. They abandoned shields; their swords were useless in the close-quarter fight. They pitched down the hill, entwined, kneeing and jabbing. Roparzh's sword was lost but Wolf Sword stayed attached by its blood knot and now hampered Blackstone from reaching for his knife. The Breton slashed his dagger into Blackstone's mail. It pierced deep enough to wound his arm but the sudden shock of pain gave Blackstone the energy to beat down on his adversary's face beneath his open helmet. The leather ties snapped. Bloodied, nose broken, Roparzh snorted blood and brought his knee up sharply into Blackstone's groin. Agony tore through him and he was thrown clear, head swirling. The killing blow would come any second. He clambered painfully to his knees. Roparzh reached for an abandoned sword, raised it quickly in a double-handed grip. Blackstone's head cleared as the man's bulk loomed over him. Using his whole body weight the Breton struck: the blow would cleave Blackstone from shoulder to hip. Roparzh's weight bore him forward, bent at the waist. Blackstone rammed Wolf Sword's pommel into the ground and the hardened steel blade went into the Breton's belly beneath his rib cage and out beneath his right shoulder blade. Roparzh uttered an animal grunt and pitched forward onto Blackstone, forcing Blackstone's breath out of him. He lay winded, the stench of the man's foul body stifling him. With a huge effort he pushed the dead man off him. The fight was over. Surviving Bretons ran. They were open targets for the archers who gave chase and brought them down either in the open meadow or on the forest edge where men were caught in bramble and briar. Sixty Bretons lay scattered, their carcasses twisted in death. Several of Blackstone's men lay dead too, some lying with men they had killed and who had in turn killed them in a final deathly embrace.

Blackstone staggered to his feet, caught his breath and spat the bile and phlegm from the back of his throat. He loosened the blood knot that had saved his life by keeping Wolf Sword close to his fist and then made his way towards the gore-splattered figure of Killbere halfway up the hill. The veteran had a gash above his eye that was bleeding onto his cheek and beard.

Killbere grinned. 'God's tears, Thomas. They fell for it. Sweet Jesus, but that was some fight. They almost had us, I can tell you. They fought like the damned.' He laughed, spat blood and stuck two fingers into his mouth to pull out a loosened tooth. 'I thought you were done for.' He spat again. 'It was a hefty kick.' He wiped his arm across his face and turned back up the hill. 'I always knew your balls might be your downfall.'

CHAPTER FOURTEEN

The dull clanging of the bell for morning prayer still echoed around the castle walls. Henry made his way across the inner courtyard and entered the small chapel. The priest stood behind the altar, looking as much the haunted soul as he had the day before. The chapel was lit with sweet-smelling honey-wax candles, which reflected not only the gold and silver reliquaries, a wine goblet and crucifix but also Lord Mael's generosity. The reliquaries alone were worth more than most men would ever see in their lifetime. Henry followed the priest's gesture for him to kneel to one side. There were no benches: the intention was not to provide comfort but display humility before God. The limestone floor slabs, worn smooth, were testimony to a hundred years of prayer. No sooner had Henry knelt and clasped his hands than the heavy footfall of Lord Mael and two other knights entered. They wore only their tabards and Henry realized that the two men following in Babeneaux's footsteps must be the seigneurial lords whose men he'd previously seen. How many extra men were in the castle? Had Lord Mael been generous in sending his captain with sixty men to strike against Henry's father because he knew he had more reinforcements inside the walls to defend the castle should the need arise?

Lord Mael did not glance at the pilgrim boy at the back of the chapel. The three men knelt, bowed their heads, and the priest began to recite the liturgy of the Divine Office in a monotone. Henry looked at the three kneeling men of violence and cruelty, a wave of disgust squirming in his stomach. Was Babeneaux a true believer who honoured the church with his expensive gifts? Or was he bribing God to forgive his sins? Whatever prayers these men of war offered one was certain: that Thomas Blackstone and his men had been slaughtered.

Henry bowed his head and asked that his own sin of disobedience be forgiven and that his father had been the one victorious in the fight.

The kitchen fires flared as fat dripped into the flames. Henry ate the near-burnt dark bread; coarse and dry, it stuck to the roof of his mouth but the tumbler of rough-tasting wine swilled it away.

'Let him take it,' said the cook to the kitchen boy, who had just picked up a tray of food from the table. 'We need more wood. Fetch it.'

The lad pushed the tray towards Henry and then reached for a large iron key on a ring that hung from a nail on the wall.

'Upstairs, pilgrim,' said the cook. 'There's a boy. Feed him and bring down his shit bucket. Make sure you lock the door or you will hang by your cock from the castle walls until the crows peck it away.'

'If they can find it,' the kitchen boy said.

The cook kicked his backside. 'Get your arse moving.' Then he glared at Henry. 'It's not a damned invitation.'

Henry lifted the tray and the key, his heart racing at the unexpected opportunity to reach Lady Cateline's son. He strode across the keep's great hall. The dog followed and loped up the stairs after him.

It took two hands to turn the key in the massive old lock and when he shouldered the heavy door open he saw a dark-haired boy three or four years younger than him pressing himself against the far wall. His fearful pallor told Henry the boy was expecting punishment – or worse.

'It's all right,' Henry whispered. 'I am the one sent by your mother.'

The dog sauntered into the room, tail wagging, and sniffed the young prisoner. After a moment's uncertainty the boy smiled, his relief obvious. He knelt and embraced the slobbering dog. Henry quickly took in the room; he saw the rough-hewn table and stool placed against the wall behind the door and a straw mattress, worn flat from years of use, stretched across a wooden-framed bed. He picked up the tray from where he had placed it on the floor outside, brought it in and closed the door. He handed the tray to the boy.

'Who are you? said the boy.

'If I give you my true name, it could be the death of me. It's enough for you to know me as Henri de Sainteny.'

'Where is my mother?'

'Safe. And my father will bring men here to rescue you.'

'No one can breach these walls. Did you find the postern gate?'

'Yes, but it's blocked.'

Cateline's son grabbed the food from the plate, tore a piece of bread for the dog and studied Henry as he ate hungrily. 'I am fed only once a day. I am kept here and allowed out to walk once around the yard. My mother tried to get us away. Me and my sister. I was going to Avignon to—'

'I know all that,' Henry interrupted. 'There's not much time. I have to find a way to get my father and his men inside the walls. Is there any other gate?'

'There's nothing,' said the hungry boy, crumbs spluttering as he answered.

'Jocard, think hard. You've spent several years here; there must be something. Either for us to get out or my father and his men to get in.'

The boy stared, blinking as he tried to remember anything that might be of use. 'My sister Jehanne and I used to have the run of the castle. I know the walls are high, and they guard every gate. We only managed to escape because my mother's friend helped us.' He paused, the memory of what happened to his mother's lover souring any further taste for food. He tossed the bread to the dog and Henry saw tears sting the boy's eyes.

'This is no time for sadness, Jocard. We must think clearly,' Henry insisted, determined to focus the boy's thoughts. 'I have to get back to the kitchen and unless we can signal to my father and get him inside these walls, you will stay locked in this room until Lord Mael secures your inheritance, and then he will have no further use for you. He'll kill you.'

Jocard nodded. 'I expect an assassin every time they unlock the door.' He stroked the big dog's head. 'His name is Jupiter. He was my dog until I was locked up in here. He would give his life for me.'

'By now men have died for you. Sixty men rode out before first light to attack my father. I know he will have been victorious but I'm sure men whom I count as my friends will lie dead on the battlefield. Think hard so that their death was not in vain.'

Jocard was silent for a moment. Henry thought he had driven him to despair.

'Perhaps there *is* a way.' Jocard's voice was almost too quiet for Henry to hear. The boy raised his head. 'Have you seen the well in the yard?' he said more clearly.

'Yes, I drew water from there. You can't think of using that to escape. It's far too deep and who knows how the well is fed.'

'*I* know,' he answered. 'One day Jehanne and I were playing in the far corner of the castle yard, beyond the stables, past where the grain stores are. We found an overgrown iron grate in the rock face. We were playing hide and seek and she had squeezed between the grate's iron bars and the rock. It took me a long time to find her, and I only did because I heard her crying. She was frightened because she'd slipped a few feet down into a cave. I reached in and pulled her out. I could smell the cold air and I heard water running in the distance far below. I think there's a stream or river underground that feeds the wells in the castle. There are many caves around here and if we could get down into the river perhaps we could find a way out.'

Henry imagined such an escape underground. Rivers could flow with no opening above the rock face and if they dared to risk it the chance of survival was slim.

Jocard's face grimaced. 'But... but it's a fearful place.'

'It's guarded?'

Jocard shook his head. 'Not by the living. It was Lord Mael's father who put the bars across the entrance. One of his sons, Lord Mael's youngest brother... he went down one day and never returned. Tormented demons lie below us. Spirits of the dead that feed on the living. They call the entrance Hell's Gate.'

Henry's throat tightened. There was no doubt the devil kept souls trapped beneath the earth – how else was the gateway to hell guarded? He put on a brave face.

'Superstition. Be ready. We'll go tonight.'

PART TWO

HELL'S GATE

CHAPTER FIFTEEN

The dead grinned their contempt for the living.

Blackstone walked among the slain as his men stripped them of anything worthwhile. They took the corpses of his own men from the field and laid them side by side. Some he had known longer than others, but all were a loss.

'Nine. We were lucky,' said John Jacob as he accompanied Blackstone.

'Another six wounded,' said Blackstone as he gazed at the dead men, calling their names as he passed by them. 'Gabriel LaFargue, Othon... Merciful Christ, John, I didn't know Ralph Tait had gone down.'

'He saw the archers attack and turned to fight the Bretons' flank. They overwhelmed him, but he took four or more with him,' John Jacob said as they stopped next to Quenell's body.

'Damn. We can't afford to lose experienced archers,' Blackstone lamented. He turned as Will Longdon approached. 'Will, I'm sorry you lost Quenell.'

'Aye, he stormed ahead of us when we came up the hill. Got himself isolated. Stupid, brave bastard had fire in his belly and took on God knows how many.' The insult was intended as respect. A few men followed Longdon up the hill. 'Jack and me and a couple of the lads will take what gift he offers. Meulon and Renfred's men will do the same with Ralph Tait and the other men-at-arms.'

Blackstone nodded. Whatever was taken from their own dead served not as booty but as a part of the man to be honoured and remembered. No matter how insignificant the item it served to keep their companionship alive.

The German captain Renfred stood back while Ralph Tait's comrades took what they wanted. Killbere sat on the ground as one of the men spat on his head wound in an attempt to clear the dried blood. The man's dirt- and blood-encrusted hands probed the wound until it trickled blood again.

'Merciful Christ!' snarled Killbere and gave the man a kick. 'Will, get yourself over here and attend to me. Get brandy and your needle and thread.'

Will Longdon stepped away from the ceremony for the dead. 'And have you kick my arse when I stitch your skull, Sir Gilbert? Best you bathe it yourself and let it bleed and then when it hampers your vision you will be grateful for me and my sewing skills.'

'I'll buy you a whore in the next town. Is that not fair payment?

'Before or after you have had her yourself?'

'Damn you, do not test my generosity,' growled the veteran fighter.

Will Longdon grinned and turned away to retrieve his satchel and the implements he needed. 'Thomas,' said Killbere. 'You've seen Babeneaux's men dead on the field. Some wore a different blazon. He has others under his command.'

'I saw them,' said Blackstone. 'More men than we expected. If Henry lived long enough to tell Babeneaux how few we were I thought he wouldn't send so many against us. He has men to spare.'

'Henry will be fine,' Killbere assured him, one hand pressed against the wound. 'But what if Lady Whore has given us false information?'

'Why would she do that?'

'God only knows why women lie, Thomas. It serves their purpose to lay smokescreens. Perhaps she hoped we'd fall under her husband's sword and has plans to barter for herself and her children if we don't return, given she had sent us to our death.'

'I think not,' said Blackstone. 'And I am wondering if the man I fought was Babeneaux. His weapons were not that of a lord.'

'Shall we take his head to Lady Cateline?' asked John Jacob. 'So she can identify him?'

'No, we'll bring her to us.'

John Jacob watched as the men finished taking their mementos from their fallen comrades. 'You need to attend to your own wound, my lord.'

Blackstone glanced at the stab wound on his arm. He had already bound it with torn linen but now it seeped blood. 'Get a fire going, John, and I'll sear it with a hot blade.' John Jacob nodded and went to do his knight's bidding.

Killbere tore a piece from his shirt and made a knot of material to press against his wound while he waited for Will Longdon's ministrations. 'You know, Thomas, if Quenell had not told us that Babeneaux had been at le Garet we would probably have laid the same ambush as we did then. Archers either side and us at the top of the hill. And we'd be the ones lying out there as crow bait.'

Blackstone nodded. 'We all have memories of past battles, Gilbert, and that knowledge has kept us alive. That and hard fighting.'

'We make no progress on this, Thomas. There's still a fight waiting for us inside the castle. We are getting short of arrows and the men need rest. I was wheezing like a damned carthorse back there and all I did was stand my ground and let the bastards come to me.'

Blackstone cocked an eyebrow. 'Are you telling me you're getting too old for a fight?'

'Damn you. I'm saying you've driven the men hard these past months. We've cleared towns and put routiers to flight. We've survived longer than many others doing the King's bidding, but the men and the horses need rest. We should get ourselves to Poitiers and let William Felton fume and fart while he tells us we are late for the rendezvous and the men drink and whore in town.'

Blackstone didn't argue. How could he? Everything Killbere said was true. He had asked more than any other commander from his men and they had not raised a voice in complaint. It was important that Killbere spoke for them. 'If I let them loose in Poitiers, we could have a riot on our hands. Felton takes his duties as seneschal more seriously than an abbot at a monastery.'

'And can make life difficult for us. He lies abed at night knowing you won the fight at le Garet and he took the honour. Let's not make enemies we do not need. Find a way to get Henry out of Babeneaux's castle and let's abandon further thoughts of taking it.'

Blackstone watched John Jacob fanning embers to heat the knife that would soon sear his flesh. It would be painful but not as much as losing his son. 'We have to give him time, Gilbert.' He gave the matter a few moments' further thought. 'But if we can take the castle, then we will.'

Killbere cursed beneath his breath. 'You're an obstinate bastard, Thomas Blackstone.'

'I learnt it from you,' said Blackstone and then raised an arm to summon Meulon and Renfred. The two captains strode to him.

'Sir Thomas?' said Meulon.

'Renfred, choose six men to ride back and bring Lady Cateline and the rest of the men here. Leave your wounded; we'll attend to them. You and Meulon ride close to Lord Mael's castle, stay out of sight, avoid any villagers, see if there's any signal from behind the castle walls tomorrow morning. We'll camp a league behind you. I don't want so many men close to the castle.'

'And if there is smoke?' said Renfred.

'One of you returns here and the other finds a place for us to lie up so we can get through that postern gate tomorrow night.'

Meulon asked the question no one wished to. 'And if there's no smoke?'

'It's finished. We ride on. My son will be dead.'

CHAPTER SIXTEEN

Henry took his time emptying Jocard's latrine bucket. He clambered onto the parapet where the sentries patrolling the walls made way for him, pointing to where he should tip it over the end wall. It gave Henry time to gauge the distance from the forest to the castle walls over the open ground lying in between, and to determine more of the layout of the castle's defences. He returned to the yard and swilled out the bucket, deliberately not returning the bucket to the boy in the keep. No one would question a servant carrying a bucket and going about his chores. Likely he'd earn a cuff around the ear from the belligerent cook for his tardiness but he needed an excuse to get back and speak to Lady Cateline's son later in the day once he had explored the castle grounds further.

The day dragged on. He busied himself with chores in the kitchen, making any excuse he could to get into the castle grounds. Every corner, tower, building and sentry post could play a part in their survival. He made his way past the stables to where a new tower was being built. Masons clambered up wooden poles lashed together, strong timbers of ash and alder that supported platforms of poplar. Men below laboured to haul rocks to them on a pulley once other stonemasons had cut and shaped them. Labourers mixed mortar with hoes and trowels. A blacksmith sharpened tools. A carpenter's pit bore the weight of a heavy beam on trestles being sawed to length by a long two-handed saw. There were men everywhere. Ostlers gaped at the stranger among them as they led out horses from their stalls. A labourer shouted at him to stay clear of the new construction. Even if his father could get inside the castle walls Henry knew the artisans and stable hands would take up arms, be it hammer or pitchfork. The English were the enemy and a man would fight to keep his family safe. He saw no sign of Mael Babeneaux or the other lords staying in the castle. Henry skirted the five-storey building with its palisade. Now and again a shadow moved in the upper colonnade and a glimpse of a tabard and the sound of voices echoed down to him. If it came to a fight, Mael would either be up there in his private quarters or in the keep with the steps drawn up. All the determination in the world would not dislodge him. The attack would fail. It was better for him and the boy to escape and to find his father.

No one hindered Henry from going where he pleased as the dog dutifully followed him around the courtyards and then towards the far end of the castle where old inner curtain walls in a state of long disrepair were being butchered for the new tower. There, boys scrambled into the rubble to load wheelbarrows, back-breaking work in service of the more skilled labourers and masons. These boys assumed the older youth who picked his way through them with a large mastiff at his side had some senior role, so no one raised a challenge, and those that stood in his path bowed to him. Barren ground lay beyond the old wall, with stubs of boulders breaking the earth's hard surface. Perhaps, Henry thought, a generation before, the area had been the place where the first castle fortifications were raised; now, long abandoned, it was a courtyard that lay beyond the other buildings, enclosed by the high castle wall ninety paces or more to his left and the outer wall a hundred or more to his right that was built on top of twenty feet of rock face. Somewhere near that far corner where the brambles grew was the iron grate that covered the possibility of escape. All he and Jocard had to do was stumble their way through the darkness and find it.

Henry was correct in thinking the cook would admonish him on his return. The man's hand across the back of his head made his ears ring, but he hastened away up the steps to return the bucket to Jocard's room.

'I couldn't see the grid but I saw the rock face they built the walls on. I'll come for you when the bell sounds for matins.'

Jocard swallowed nervously, his hands twisting together. 'Yes, that's good, only the night watch will be manning the outer wall. No one gets up in the middle of the night except the priest to read the service once he's rung the bell. It will disguise any sound we make.'

'And neither Lord Mael nor anyone in his household attends the vigil?'

'Never.'

'Good. Then once the prayers are said I'll take the candles from the church to light our way.'

Jocard nodded but was still nervous. 'There's a night lantern by the grain store and a storeroom next to it where they keep reed torches for the night watch.'

'Then I'll forget the candles.'

'No, take them. We pass the chapel first before we get to the store. If the store's locked we'll have wasted too much time and made it even more dangerous. You have a flint?

Henry nodded. 'I'm hoping the clouds will obscure the moon; if they don't then we'll be seen too easily. Tear your mattress and bring a handful of straw. We'll need it to light the candles or torches.'

They fell silent as fear held them. Henry broke the spell and pressed an encouraging hand on the boy's shoulder. 'We are younger than any man here. We have speed on our side and they will not know where to look when they find us gone.'

Jocard shook his head. 'Unless they hear our screams when the demons come for us.'

Henry attended the early evening prayers, as did Lord Mael and the two knights. It was a repetition of the morning service. Henry barely heard a word the priest said as he concentrated on memorizing where the candles were placed so that he could find his way in the darkness six hours later. He waited for Babeneaux to leave, averting his eyes, fearing his thoughts were plain for all to see. God saw everything and so too might Lord Mael. His heart skipped a beat when his name was called.

'Henri,' said the Breton lord. 'Stand, boy.' The barrel-chested man waited with the two knights. Henry lowered his eyes and bowed. 'My men have not returned as I would have expected by now. You swear you told the truth about how many men Blackstone had with him?'

Henry felt God's hand press over him. He stammered, unable to bring himself to lie in the place of worship. And then he felt the devil's cold claw squeeze his heart. 'I swear,' he lied.

For a moment he thought the lie so obvious that they would seize him. Lord Mael Babeneaux, protector of pilgrims, stepped forward and lifted Henry's chin.

'Henri, you are on a pilgrimage. I have given you safety and food; I ask nothing more than an honest answer,' he said gently. 'If you think you were mistaken, say so. No harm will come to you. Captain Roparzh is blood kin. He has a family. A wife and children. He went at my bidding on the information you gave. I would be aggrieved if he came to harm because you were mistaken, but if that were so I would not punish you. You're a boy, you know only the way of the Church. Now, think again. Could you have been mistaken?'

The flickering candlelight caused shadows to cross the man's bearded face as he looked down at Henry. Mael's eyes reflected the candle flame. Had the devil slithered into the man's soul and given him the power to detect the untruth?

'I saw what I saw,' Henry said as determinedly as he could.

Lord Mael locked eyes with Henry, searching his face for any shadow other than those dancing across the walls from spluttering candles. He nodded. 'All right, boy,' he said softly. 'Get to your bed and attend to your duties in the morning. Once my men return with news of Thomas Blackstone's death the way will be safe for you to continue your journey, for a while at least.'

'Thank you, my lord,' said Henry, swallowing hard at the utterance of his father's name, hoping he had been convincing in his lie.

As Lord Mael Babeneaux turned away Henry's hands trembled and, before fear made him lose control of his body, he wrapped his cloak tighter around him and stepped out into the night to find more danger had presented itself. The moon was rising, casting its glow.

Darkness would not befriend them that night.

CHAPTER SEVENTEEN

Henry lay awake listening to the grunting snores of the cook and the servants. The dog snuffled and whimpered, dreaming of the day's smells. Henry's heart beat faster the longer he lay waiting. He had noticed the routine within the castle walls and knew the guard on the walls changed over before the bell rang for matins. Muffled voices reached him from men who had left the warmth of their beds to stand their duty watch on the walls. He half raised himself and looked at the sleeping bodies around him. Fire glow gave enough light for him to see the key on the wall nail. He stood slowly, remaining motionless in case the men or the dog stirred; then he moved forward carefully as his father had taught him, rolling each foot gently to keep the minimum pressure on the ground. The challenge would be to get across the reed floor and reach the staircase.

His heart beat so loudly he thought it likely that the men patrolling the walls would hear it. He concentrated on the dark shape of the distant stairway, key grasped tightly in his hand. The crunching of the reeds beneath his feet must surely raise the alarm but fear of discovery didn't stop him from lengthening his stride. By the time he was at the top of the stairs he had steadied his rapid breathing. If they were to succeed in their escape, he knew he needed to bring his fear under control, so he could remain focused on what he had to do. The grinding lock and the creaking door caused him to hunch, as if that might help him remain undetected. The room was in darkness except for the beam of light through the narrow slit window. The moonbeam revealed Jocard waiting nervously.

'Ready?' said Henry.

The boy shook his head and forced a grin. 'No.'

Henry remembered how afraid he had been when, even younger than Jocard, he had faced danger and violence at his mother's side.

'Just follow me. We'll soon be out of here,' he said reassuringly, despite his own uncertainty.

He led the way downstairs and across the floor to the main door. There would be no sentry there at night. The guard had been at his post only when Lord Mael had been expected in the great hall. As Henry lifted the iron ring to open the door he heard Jocard hiss behind him. He turned. The dog had come out of the kitchen and sat waiting to see what his master was up to.

'Jupiter!' the boy whispered fiercely, sweeping his arm in a gesture for the dog to return to the kitchen. The dog glanced over its shoulder and decided it was more interesting to stay where it was. It whimpered and looked as though it might bark. Jocard was quick-witted enough to bend down and smother the dog's muzzle, embracing its deep chest. In the gloom Henry saw the plaintive look on the boy's face. Henry had unconsciously taken out his knife. He would have to kill the dog before it betrayed them.

Jocard got to his feet and gripped Henry's arm. 'There's rope in the yard. I'll tie him,' he pleaded.

Henry had no desire to cut its throat. He nodded, turned and led boy and dog into the night.

True to his word Jocard found the length of rope and secured the dog's studded collar. Henry ripped a piece of sacking and bound the dog's jaws to stop it barking. The bell for midnight prayers clanged dully around the walls as the two boys pressed themselves against the buildings seeking the shadows. By the time they reached the chapel they knew their way was clear. No one ventured out other than the night watch, on the outer walls, who could not see them. Henry and Jocard hunched between wall and buttress watching glowing candlelight reflect through the chapel window. If the priest attended to his duties diligently, then he would recite the Divine Office word for word. But Henry hoped the lure of his warm bed and the lack of congregation would override his sense of duty, and that he would return early to his room at the back of the chapel. They waited and were soon rewarded by the light growing dim. Candles were being extinguished. Henry concentrated his thoughts on the priest's actions, following him with his mind's eye. He would genuflect before the crucifix, walk to each lit candle, snuff the flame and then walk back to the rear and his room. There, he would close his door, pull the blankets on his cot over him and be ready for more prayers in three hours' time. The light dimmed further, telling Henry that the priest had reached his room and when darkness engulfed the chapel again he got ready to run.

'Wait here,' he told the boy. 'If anything goes wrong, then make your escape without me. Understand?'

Jocard nodded. 'But—'

Henry raised a hand. 'Get through the caves and find a way out. My father and his men are out there somewhere. They are waiting for a signal from me but I cannot give them one, so take any path you find that leads you beyond the direction of the postern gate and they will see you.'

Henry did not wait for an answer. Glancing left and right, he ran across towards the chapel door. Its archway gave him enough shadow to look back and see that no one unexpected had stepped into the courtyard. He lifted the door latch and opened the heavy door wide enough to slip sideways into the dank chill of the place where men unburdened their souls. If disembodied sins could take on ghostly form they would be entombed here in the stone cold walls. For once he was glad of the moonlight; it eased his fear of the imagined spirits and showed him the candles in their silver holders.

The sweet smell of candle wax hung in the air as he loosened a candle from its holder. There were several but he decided that four would suffice. Two for each boy and easier to carry. He laid down the three he had already retrieved and gripped the silver holder that held the biggest candle. It had been rammed firmly into the base. He twisted and pulled and as candle and holder separated a bony hand gripped his shoulder. Instinctively he swirled around, wielding the heavy silver base. It caught the cowled figure who stood behind him with a club in his hand ready to fell the thief. The priest fell heavily, his gnarled wooden club clattering on the stone floor. Henry gaped unbelievingly at what he had just done. Heart thudding, his breath stayed trapped in his lungs. He forced himself to exhale, wondering what to do. Was the man dead? It made no difference. It was too late now. Henry had blood on his hands. He gathered the candles and ran for the door.

The village masons and labourers had returned home when darkness fell so there was no one around the new tower. Jocard led the way to the storeroom where tools and torches were kept but, as he had suspected, it was locked. That meant the foray into the chapel had been a wise move but Henry knew, even if the priest was alive, they would hang him if they captured him. He guided Jocard around the scaffolding and pointed to the far corner of the abandoned yard and the grate. Pushing aside the bushes, ignoring brambles that snatched at them, they slithered down several feet to where the rock face met the ground. The rusted iron grate covered a cave mouth that sprouted plant tendrils through its grid: prisoners of darkness seeking the light. Henry laid down his two candles and heaved on the grate. It gave slightly. All they needed was to widen the gap between the iron frame and the side of the rock.

'Help me,' he whispered.

Jocard grasped the grate and on Henry's signal they pulled. The ground below the grate's base had eroded over time which allowed the rest of the frame some leeway. It creaked. Henry's back muscles ached; his arms felt as though they were being torn from his shoulders. Bracing his legs, he leaned back and yanked. The grate yielded enough for Jocard to do as Henry instructed and squeeze through. Henry pressed his back against the wall, turned his head sideways, pressing his face against the rock face, and forced his way through the narrow gap. Elated, they embraced each other. Jocard pulled out the handful of mattress stuffing. Henry struck his flint and blew on the smouldering lump to entice a flame. They each lit a candle's wick and shielded the flame. The narrow entrance sloped away into what seemed to be an abyss. The sound of water flowed somewhere below. Henry edged forward.

'It's not as steep as it looks,' he said, and went on down, ducking below the low rock ceiling.

Henry guessed that they had slithered downward for a couple of hundred paces. The air felt more humid as the sound of water drew closer and the cave's ceiling became higher, smooth curved rocks gleaming with dripping moisture. The boys shielded their candle flames. Their descent was easier now and the water's noise grew louder the deeper they went until the faint speck of light that was the entrance disappeared. They reached a beach of crushed stone as fine as salt. Shallow, crystal-clear water gurgled, calf-deep, a gentle stream that surely fed the castle's deep well flowing over water-smoothed rocks coated in its own wet sheen. Henry raised his candle higher and looked along a ravine.

'We have no choice but to go down there,' he said, looking towards the gap wide enough for a half-dozen men to stand abreast.

'If the water gets deeper than this… I… I can't swim,' said Jocard nervously.

'Don't be afraid. If it's shallow here, then it will probably be the same depth further along. If it gets deeper, I'll help you. I can swim. But we can't stay here. We have to find a way out.' Without waiting for the boy to answer Henry stepped into the water and led the way into the cavernous underground passage.

The riverbed was soft beneath his feet; lowering the candle he saw small puffs of disturbed silt. There was no sign of life in the clear water. No fish or creature would survive here, no vegetation clung to the rocks, no weed choked the passage of water. Their candles burned lower and their clothes clung to them from the humidity in the air. Henry raised a hand and brought them to a halt. The narrow passage opened into a space like a cathedral with a vaulted ceiling. He heard Jocard gasp in surprise. Henry suspected no man had ever seen this grandeur. Calcified columns hung down from a ceiling that looked to be more than a hundred feet high. Candlelight brought the rocks alive with the glint of a million stars trapped inside the stone. Henry held his breath. He turned to the boy behind him, whose face was filled with wonderment. The water spread before them in a small lake, edging further away to the left where it disappeared beneath low hanging rocks. It was barely a hundred paces wide in front of him. Henry edged forward, its depth reaching his thighs.

'Bring your light here,' he told Jocard.

The boys stood shoulder to shoulder and raised their candles together. The light exposed a sheen of water dribbling down the rock face beyond the shallow lake which led to a dry passage, a path eroded by time and water. It appeared to ascend into more rock formations.

'Up there,' said Henry. 'We might be in luck.'

With renewed hope they waded forward. The darkness closed behind them, the sheer walls suffocating any voices they might have heard were they nearer the entrance.

When the bell for lauds had not rung three hours before dawn its absence raised the alarm. They found the priest alive and able to recount what had happened. And when Lord Mael found the dog with a frayed rope attached around its collar whimpering at the iron grate he quickly understood Henry's betrayal.

They summoned the masons who hammered and chipped into the rock face to loosen the grate. Lord Mael berated them, impatient to send men to pursue the fugitives. His dozen soldiers held back. They knew the legend of the cave. Lord Mael grabbed one by the neck, forcing him closer to where the masons feverishly chiselled at the rocks holding the iron grate. 'You'll lead the men down. Every man has a burning torch. No demon would dare approach a flame.'

'My lord, I beg you. Do not send us through Hell's Gate,' said the unfortunate man, dropping to his knees.

'Get to your feet, you snivelling bastard!'

'I cannot, my lord,' the man begged, arm raised, knowing Babeneaux would beat him.

Lord Mael did not strike him with his fist as the man expected; he unsheathed his knife and slit the man's throat.

As his victim writhed, hands clutching his torn throat, Mael pointed the stained blade at the others. 'You go down or you die here.'

The masons pulled aside the iron stanchions. With trembling hands, the soldiers lit their pitch-soaked torches and hesitantly stepped into the cave.

CHAPTER EIGHTEEN

'That's not Lord Babeneaux,' said Lady Cateline when she looked at the dead Roparzh in the early morning light. 'It's his captain of the guard. You killed a vicious man, Sir Thomas, taught by his master but a less able swordsman.'

Killbere's eyebrows raised but he left his thoughts unspoken. The man had come close to beating Blackstone. But then he took heart, despite his moment of doubt. Close had not been good enough.

'There are others behind your husband's walls who wear a different device,' said Blackstone, thrusting away the memory of the hard-fought contest with Babeneaux's captain. He showed her two bloodied blazons: a black unicorn on the one and four small castles set in a square on the other.

Lady Cateline fingered the torn remnants. 'Allies of his. The unicorn is Lord Judikael, the other Lord Gwenneg. They support Charles of Blois and have the French King's backing. He depends on these men to hold the English and de Montfort at bay in Brittany. If they are in the castle, then they are planning an assault elsewhere to secure more territory.'

Killbere shrugged. 'Thomas, we have stepped into a viper's nest.'

Blackstone looked at Cateline. 'Do you know how many men each lord has with him?'

'Perhaps ten or more as a personal escort.'

'So there could still be more men than we thought behind the walls,' said Killbere. 'I had hoped we had slain enough here to favour us if we ever got inside.'

'We cannot leave Master Henry in there, Sir Gilbert,' said John Jacob. 'We must find a way.'

'There is no way unless your son opens the postern gate and even then I don't know what awaits you on the other side,' said Cateline.

A horseman appeared on the track at the bottom of the meadow. An arm raised. Another rider clung to him behind the saddle.

'Sir Thomas! It's Meulon and Renfred,' Will Longdon called from where he and his archers held the high ground in case there was another attack from forces they had not yet come across.

The two captains reined in. John Jacob reached up and hauled an exhausted Jocard down from behind the throat-cutter. The boy trembled. His face had the pallor of a resurrected man long entombed in a grave.

'Jocard!' his mother cried. She embraced her son. 'Merciful God, you are safe.'

'He needs food and drink is all,' said Renfred. He turned to Blackstone. 'Found him crawling out of a forest on our way back here. There was no smoke signal from behind the castle walls, Sir Thomas, but now we know why. Young Henry got the lad out through an underground river.'

Blackstone turned Jocard away from his mother. 'Boy, where is my son Henry? Is he alive?'

'He saved me,' Jocard answered, lip trembling, tears threatening.

'That's not what I asked.'

'Quickly, son, tell this good knight who fought to save us,' urged Cateline.

The boy controlled his exhaustion. 'We travelled for hours underground and then found a place that had ridges in the rock face. We saw there was light above. But there was no foothold that let us reach it. Henry made me stand on his shoulders so I could reach a handhold. But then he could not get out. He told me to climb out and find his father and to ask forgiveness for his disobedience.'

Henry's image lodged in Blackstone's thoughts. Picturing the boy sacrificing himself to save Cateline's son, he felt a stab of pride that pierced his anger at Henry's disobedience. 'Does Lord Babeneaux know of this tunnel or cave?'

Jocard nodded. 'He will send men after us. It is a place the size of a cathedral. If they are searching, I think they would return before their torches burn too low. No one would want to stay down there in the dark.'

'And my son is still down there?'

A look of guilt clouded the boy's face. He nodded. 'Unless men or unearthly creatures took him. It is called Hell's Gate.'

The place from where the exhausted Jocard had clambered looked like an abandoned quarry, dug deep, smothered with brush and sapling, shaded by the forest canopy. A place perhaps where ancient man had clambered down for protection and shelter.

'Down there?' said Will Longdon. 'God's tears, we're not goats.'

'You smell like one,' said Meulon.

'Aye, well, living alongside you for so many years rubs off,' Longdon answered, more concerned with the dark, gaping abyss that awaited the men than the taunt from his friend.

Blackstone tossed a rock down into the hole. The men listened. It tumbled away, crashing through bushes, bouncing off the rock face, but there was no sound of it reaching the bottom. 'Will, you and Jack won't be going down. If what the lad says is correct your bows will be useless down there. It's too wet.'

'Then what do you want of us?' the centenar asked.

'I'll tell you later,' Blackstone answered. 'Get your men together. Check everything, bow cords and fletchings.'

The archer turned back through the trees where his men waited. Whatever Blackstone expected of them Longdon and his bowmen were to play a key part.

'We still have lamp oil,' said Beyard, the Gascon captain. 'If we're to go down into the devil's arsehole we should light our way.'

'Have torches prepared,' said Blackstone. 'Meulon, Renfred, get what rope we have.'

'They're not long enough to reach down there,' said Meulon.

'I know. We'll climb halfway down. Will and his archers will lower our weapons and armour to us and then we will lower them to the bottom. That way we go down unencumbered. See to it.'

As the men left Killbere spat a globule of phlegm into the void. 'I heard what the boy said, Thomas. Hell's Gate. Fighting the French is a different matter than battling against the devil's imps.'

'Gilbert, it is superstition spread to keep brave men out.'

'Or draw foolish men down.'

'Courage will win the day.'

'But you failed to tell the men.'

'What is not known cannot harm them. I do not expect you to tell them and put fear into their hearts. They will need strength and determination. We must not strip that away – it can leave a man defenceless.'

Killbere scratched his beard. He watched the men go about their business, ready to do Blackstone's bidding. 'Even if you told them, they would follow you.'

'I know. No man would refuse. But they would carry an extra burden if I told them.'

Killbere nodded in agreement. 'Aye, you're right. And the woman and her brats?'

Blackstone laid a hand on his friend's shoulder. 'I thought I would leave them here under your care, Gilbert, seeing you hold her in such affection.'

The veteran ground his teeth. 'One day your jests will burst the veins in my head and drop me like a felled oak.'

'Who said I'm jesting?' said Blackstone.

CHAPTER NINETEEN

The men busied themselves preparing for the descent while Killbere fumed. He knew the climb into the depths would tax him, but to be given nursery duties?

Blackstone attempted to assuage his friend's anger. 'Gilbert, I need you to create a diversion. If you do not, then the men and I will be trapped like rats in a sewer.'

'A diversion? With these few archers? You expect me to stand there with my cock in hand and wave it at the bastards?'

'It is a formidable weapon,' said Blackstone.

'Thomas, for Christ's sake. What is it you want from me? I am no wet-nurse child-minder. Do not demean me.'

'I would never do so. We must make our way into the castle using this underground passage. From what the boy told us it might take us until the sun is past its zenith before we get there. And by now Lord Mael will know of Henry's escape.'

What sounded like a growl rumbled in Killbere's chest. 'Tell me and be done with it, then try not to break your damned neck. You're no youngster yourself.'

'You must return to the meadow that fronts the castle. Look to where the sun is. Three hours after noon. Then you ride out in full view with Will and Jack Halfpenny and their archers. Stand out of crossbow range. Declare yourself a routier and that you found the woman and her children in hiding.'

'I'll need three or four men-at-arms with me to look even half convincing.'

'Meulon and Renfred will give you their best men, and take Beyard with you: he's a good man to have at your back if the tide turns against you. Tell Lord Mael his men lie dead. That you came across the ground where they were slain. Keep him interested. Keep him on the outer walls. Bargain money for Lady Cateline but do not show him the boy. Not until he tells you he has no use for his wife and daughter. Then bring the boy in sight. He will pay to have him back. Is it likely he will ride out himself? No. Would he send a messenger with the ransom?'

'And risk me taking the money, keeping the boy and killing the messenger? No.'

'Exactly. Gilbert, it is you who face the greatest risk. It is your life that might be forfeit before any of us below ground.'

Killbere grunted. 'I see it, Thomas. He will invite me in as Will Longdon and the others hold the boy. He pays me and then barters me back for us to bring in the lad. And for all the good it will do me if you are not inside the castle walls by that time then I might as well wave my cock at them. If I still have one.'

Ignoring the hurt from his seared wound, Blackstone led the first group of men down the rock face, tree roots and rock outcrops giving them purchase. The void was more than a hundred feet deep. When they reached the bottom, the others lowered their weapon bundles. The light filtered down, enough for them to dress and arm themselves. Once all the men were ready flints were struck and half of the torches held aloft. They kept the remainder in reserve. Jocard had told them they might follow the riverbed for hours and no man wanted to be plunged into darkness when the torches spluttered and died. Blackstone raised Arianrhod to his lips and kissed the archer's talisman. Slinging their shields across their backs the men waded behind the torchbearers Blackstone, John Jacob, Meulon and Renfred.

The humid air soon engulfed them as did their wonderment at the underground river and its glinting, towering walls. They waded steadily forward, constrained by the loss of the arcing sun that would tell them how long their journey was taking. Dripping with sweat, they pushed through the water, skirted the small lake, sweeping the torches across their path to deter any malevolent creatures that might lurk in the cloisters of rock. They did not need Blackstone to tell them about the threat of dark places in the bowels of the earth. Ignoring the narrow alleyways of moisture-slicked rock, places where no man or boy could hide or traverse, they reached a narrow channel that funnelled the men closer together. Blackstone raised a hand. The men stopped splashing their way forward. The close air made their breathing laboured. Heads cocked, they listened to the faint sounds that reached them. Eerie sounds of discarnate voices that did not sound human.

They listened. Distorted echoes whispered, twisted and curled through the channels and columns. Blackstone handed his torch to a man behind him. 'Stay here,' he said, then moved slowly forward, the water barely making a sound as he walked into darkness and the unknown. His extended arm guided him along the rock wall, his fingers telling him the rock was curving. Closer to the source of the sound he knew he would face men not demons. Edging around the turn he quickly counted more than a dozen men whose torchlight threw their shadows high onto the roof, giants of the underworld. They were bickering, some pointing from where they had come, another pointing to something at their feet. From what Blackstone could determine they were on a shallow sandbank that surfaced between the pools of water spilling each side of the stream. He heard one demand: 'We go on! That's a footprint. The bastards are here somewhere close. There's reward to be had if we find them.'

'No further,' another cried.

'I'm with him,' a third added his voice to the discontent. 'We have already come too far. We tell him the boys are gone. Taken by creatures.'

Blackstone carefully made his way back to his men as the men argued. 'Twelve men or more. A search party for Henry and the boy. It's too narrow for us all. Six of us will go forward and kill them. The others keep the torches burning here.'

'And if there are more than you think?' said Meulon.

'Then we make the best of it.'

The lead men passed their torches to those behind, unslung their shields and let their eyes settle on the darkness ahead of them. It served no purpose to be blinking away torchlight as they advanced. Blackstone waited, and the men whispered their readiness. Swords were silently drawn.

They stepped forward. Phantoms of destruction.

CHAPTER TWENTY

The sun angled across the pale sky. The cooling breeze rustling the canopy above Killbere's head was already shaking free leaves. Killbere turned to the men behind him who cosseted Lady Cateline and her children in their midst. 'All right, it's time. Will, bring them forward.'

Will Longdon nudged his horse through the fern-covered ground and led Babeneaux's wife to the edge of the forest. Cateline did not meet Killbere's gaze.

'Do not look so suspicious,' said Killbere. 'Thomas Blackstone has taken you under his shield for protection. No harm will come to you. I have explained everything, have I not?'

'And when you go inside and they bargain your life for my son's, then how do I know these men will not turn him over?'

'These men who saved you and your children? These men who have shed their blood for you? You are an ungrateful bitch and I would trade you and your brats for any one of the men we lost.' Killbere reined in his disgust. 'But Thomas's son is trapped somewhere in those caves and I pray his courage was not rewarded with his death. For some reason known only to God and himself my friend has embraced your dilemma. And now I am obliged to give my word they will not harm you. These rancid, arse-scratching, murdering scum archers who slew the greatest host in Christendom are more trustworthy than any Breton lord, French king or crow-black priest.' He glanced at Longdon and the other unkempt bowmen. He sighed. 'Providing there's not a brothel in sight or silver to be stolen. Place your care in their hands and thank the Virgin Mary that Sir Thomas Blackstone stumbled on your misfortune. Now play your part.'

Killbere urged his horse forward into the open, tugging the leading rein of Lady Cateline's horse as if he had her captive. Her daughter stayed back in the trees with Jack Halfpenny. The child cried out. Cateline turned, her anguished look betraying her fear. She heard Jocard calm his sister with soothing words and the straw doll that Jack Halfpenny had made for her.

'She is in good hands, and your loss will be the more convincing,' Killbere told her. Will Longdon took six archers with him and the additional four men-at-arms made them convincing enough to pass as a small group of routiers. Beyard the Gascon and his hobelars, like the archers who rode into the open, had abandoned their jupons bearing Blackstone's insignia.

'They've seen us already,' said Will Longdon. 'Up there on the walls, Sir Gilbert. One of them's turned and called to someone below.'

'I'm not blind,' said Killbere. 'I need your eyes for distance. Pull us up when we are out of crossbow range.'

Will Longdon checked the direction of the breeze and the positioning of the spur-shaped bastions. Bowmen there might gain another fifty yards on the men placed on the walls. 'Here, Sir Gilbert,' said Longdon, pulling the small party up 350 yards from the castle.

'No closer?' said Killbere. 'I'll be bellowing like a rutting stag to be heard from here.'

Will Longdon shrugged. 'They angle their aim upwards and a fifteen-inch quarrel might find your helm, Sir Gilbert. Better a rough throat than a permanent headache.'

Killbere snorted, spat and raised himself in the stirrups as if that might help carry his voice. 'Bring your master to the walls!' he bellowed.

'Sir Gilbert, they could hear you in Poitiers,' said Will Longdon.

'Aye, well, you had better hope that Sir Thomas is where he said he would be by this time,' he said, squinting into the sun. 'If not, and things have gone awry, then you and the lads ready yourselves for this bastard to come and fetch his son once my head is on a pole. When I go in have them hold their position in the trees. If those behind the walls ride, then bring them out and show your strength. Twenty archers with arrows nocked will deter many a man's courage.'

'Identify yourself,' a voice answered moments later from the castle walls.

'Is that him?' said Killbere, turning to Cateline.

She nodded. Her lips parted, but no words came.

'We have no need for names, my lord,' answered Killbere. 'We know who you are. We have information and goods to trade. We are few men in need of money and supplies.'

'And I have men riding in my domain and if they come upon you, then what information and goods you have are of no interest to me. You are whoreson routiers and I would see you as crow bait.'

Killbere saw Lord Mael shield his eyes.

'You have my wife,' Babeneaux called.

'And for a price we will return her to the bosom of your hearth, my lord.'

'And my daughter?'

'I bear sad tidings, Lord Mael. Your daughter succumbed to a fever. She is dead.'

Babeneaux glanced at the two knights by his side. Their movement allowed a brief glimpse of a different blazon.

'The woman is of no use to me,' the Breton lord answered Killbere. 'Do with her as you wish. My daughter's life was short and of no consequence. Now get off my land before my men return.'

'We found sixty men lying dead a few leagues from here. They were butchered by a greater force. We ride to avoid a similar fate. Come, my lord, that information alone is worth some food, surely.'

There was no answer but Killbere and his escort saw Lord Mael's head dip despairingly at the news. Then he raised himself again. 'You have nothing I need,' he called and turned away as if to walk down from the battlements.

'We found a boy!' Killbere shouted, cupping his hands to help his voice carry and arrest the man's departure. The distant figure stopped. 'Found him this morning. He is this woman's son. Is he of interest, my lord?'

'Where is he? Show him!'

Killbere sighed. 'And here the game begins,' he said quietly, and signalled to those in the forest two hundred yards away. Jack Halfpenny rode out leading Jocard. When the horse was level, Killbere reached across, winked at the boy, and raised Jocard's chin so his face might be more easily recognized from that distance. Unnecessary because Babeneaux knew his stepson well enough, but Killbere's act was convincing.

'Bring him to me and I will reward you,' Lord Mael called.

'You think me a simpleton?' Killbere spat aggressively. 'Do not insult us, Lord Mael Babeneaux de Pontivy. This woman has told us of his worth. I will deliver him to Sir William Felton and be paid in gold coin for it. Now do not fuck with me! Send me gold and then take him!'

'And have your men in the trees kill my men so you can steal the boy and the ransom?'

Killbere smiled at the two archers. 'So far so good. He plays the game as Thomas predicted. And now I step into the bear trap.' He raised his voice again. 'Then how to complete our trade?'

'You come inside and I will pay you. Then your men will bring the boy closer and mine will escort you out. Then the exchange will take place.'

'And have a quarrel in my back?' said Killbere.

'My crossbowmen will lay down their arms until the exchange is complete.'

'We would see their weapons placed on the wall without their quarrels,' Killbere answered.

'Agreed,' Lord Mael answered.

Killbere turned in the saddle and looked at Beyard and the three men-at-arms with him. He grinned. 'Well? Do we accept his invitation?'

'And be ready for Sir Thomas,' said the Gascon captain.

'Take a couple of my lads with you,' said Will Longdon. 'With luck, they will bring down some of those men on the wall.'

Killbere shook his head. 'No. It will be a sudden flurry of killing. There will be no time for an arrow to be drawn, let alone loosed in there. We take our chances. You will hear the fight. Bring the lads out of the trees. Shoot onto the walls. It will give us a chance.'

'A slim one, Sir Gilbert,' suggested Halfpenny.

'When has it ever been any different?' said Killbere. He raised an arm in acknowledgement to the Breton lord. 'Open your gates!'

CHAPTER TWENTY-ONE

Lord Mael's men had not overcome their fear of the underworld as they hunted for the two missing boys. They had caged it deep within themselves but when they reached the glistening crystal cave the rock formations and twisted shapes there created the face of a demon in their inflamed imaginations – and they had faltered. Gazing up at the gaping jaw that dribbled saliva, in reality nothing more than the sheen of water on the rocks, and the glinting eyes staring at them with unabated desire, they cowered, argued and, eventually, succumbed to their fear and turned back.

It was too late.

As they peered into the darkness and caught the whiff of burning oil – surely the devil's brimstone? – the void shuddered with movement. The darkness came alive. Terror gripped them. They cried out as Blackstone's men surged forward. Behind them torchlight created looming shadows the size of giants. As Mael's men scrambled to their feet, they fought each other to turn and run. Yet one of them found his courage.

'They are men! Nothing more! Turn and fight,' he demanded, grabbing his comrades and turning them to face what was only a mortal enemy. 'Run and you die! Fight! We have a chance. We outnumber them. Turn!'

It was to their credit that most of the fourteen men found their footing and their backbone and raised their flaming torches, swords and maces ready. Abandoned torches lay spluttering in the wet sand or fell against the narrow rock wall, flames casting their own giants to combat those who attacked.

Babeneaux's men bellowed aggressively, fortifying themselves as they closed on their enemy. They splashed through the water, teeth bared, eyes wide with a desire to kill, mouths gaping, sucking fetid air with lungs bursting. The chamber resonated with a frightening response as Blackstone's men roared their challenge that tore the heart out of an already frightened enemy.

They clashed. Half-darkness enveloping them. Shadow killing shadow. Cries of pain chasing down those who had escaped. Clanging steel, blade on blade, echoed around the chamber. What had been an unspoilt place of fearful beauty became violated with blood and death. Lord Mael's men fought bravely, desperation fuelling their strength. No man wanted to die. No man wanted to die in Hell's Gate, a veil's thickness away from where Satan's imps would reach up and grab their slain bodies. Church and monastery, Bible and Book of Psalms: all had images of being seized and taken. And as each man fell, calling out for mercy, begging to be spared, Blackstone's men hurled them into the arms of the devil.

Blackstone did not slow his attack. They trampled over the fallen, snatched up the longer-burning pitch-soaked torches and gave pursuit to the escaping men. How long had it been since he and his men had descended? How much time had passed since Killbere had placed his survival into Blackstone's hands?

Killbere, Beyard and the three men-at-arms rode slowly beneath the portal. Crossbowmen on the ramparts watched them. None yet aimed at the riders but the weapons were ready for use. The outer yard was stiff with men and horses.

The second gate was already open, inviting them through the inner curtain wall. As they rode, they searched for a place to defend themselves. To fall back and form a small defensive shield wall until Blackstone reached them. Killbere glanced at Beyard. No words were needed. This place was a death trap for so few men.

Lord Mael Babeneaux waited, feet firmly planted on the ground, his wide stance telling these intruders that he was the foundation rock of the castle. Two knights stood by his side. Killbere recognized their blazons. It had been their men who had died in the meadow alongside Lord Mael's captain and soldiers. Killbere pulled up his horse. To be on horseback offered advantage over the men on the ground but when fighting in such a confined space it would be better to dismount and keep the horses between them and the men who stood along the walls.

'You scum think you can come here and bargain?' snarled Lord Mael. He made no move towards the men. He had no need. There was nowhere to run. Behind the Breton lord Killbere saw the scaffolding and the tower. Labourers and masons had stopped work, clearly watching what fate would befall these interlopers. But there was a more grisly sight that seized Killbere's interest. A large man who might have once had hair on his thick arms and back was spreadeagled across a wooden frame. His back had been lashed from a whipping. One of the soldiers threw a bucket of water across the bloodied stripes and the man cried out – so he was still alive. One arm of the scaffolding had been used as a gibbet. Two boys hung by their ankles, stripped of their breeches, shirts falling over their features obscuring their identity. They had been emasculated. Blood had drained down their bodies and pooled in the dirt. Flies fed on their blood and wounds. Killbere's stomach tightened. Either boy could be Henry.

Lord Mael noted the men's attention to the dead. 'You see what happens to those who fail me? Worthless servants.' He nodded his head towards the whipped man. 'He is my cook, so he had value. They did not. A pilgrim came into my castle and slept in the warmth of my kitchen and ate my food. I gave charity and was rewarded with betrayal. Kitchen boys are little more than slaves, but a cook is harder to find. They slept while the viper escaped in the night with the boy you now hold.'

Killbere concealed the sigh of relief that neither of the two dead boys was Henry.

'You have the pilgrim as well?' asked the Breton lord.

'No. Only your stepson.' Killbere's gaze swept across to the ladder leading up to where smoke curled from a chimney and what he thought to be the kitchen. From the top rung of the ladder a mastiff's body swing at the end of a rope. Hanged like a common criminal.

'No one and nothing escapes my wrath,' Lord Mael said.

Killbere spat. This was a vile creature to inflict such punishment on a dumb animal. Killbere's horse shook its head from the flies gathering around its eyes. Its bridle jangled; the bit clattered between its teeth. Killbere held the killer's gaze. 'Where's the money?'

'You think I will pay you?' said Lord Mael. 'An oaf of such stupidity?' He suddenly snatched at the air and then opened his palm to expose a crushed fly. 'Who steps into my web?'

'If you want the boy, pay.' Killbere squinted at the sun now below the castle walls. 'One way or another.'

Lord Mael taunted. 'Senile old man, I do not barter. I take what is rightfully mine.'

'Send men out there and the boy will die,' Beyard said.

'You think mercenary scum would not give him up?' He put out his hand to one of the nearby soldiers, who stepped forward and placed a bag of heavy coin in his palm. 'I pay them. I get the boy. I get the boy – I kill them. Money and boy where they rightfully belong. My men await my command and they have twice as much as this ready to tempt the greediest. How many more men are in the woods?'

'A hundred,' said Killbere quickly, deliberately instilling panic into his voice.

'I'll wager less than fifty. More likely twenty in all. You bear no blazon. You are scavengers. You look like desperate men. Men such as you do not travel in large numbers. You are little more than vagabonds and thieves.' He turned to his men on the walls. 'Anything?'

A voice answered. 'No more men than we saw before, my lord.'

'Send them!' Lord Mael commanded.

Killbere and Beyard turned as the great gates swung open and a dozen men spurred their horses from where they waited between the outer and inner walls. Killbere glimpsed them riding hard towards Will Longdon, Cateline and the boy.

The shadows lengthened; the breeze scurried leaves across the dirt yard. Killbere's horse's ears stiffened. Its head raised. Horses whinnied in the stables. Lord Mael looked around. There was no obvious danger, but the seasoned fighter knew to trust what he saw and something other than his men riding out had alerted the horses. A distant howling crept up from behind them. It was coming from the open cave mouth. A wail that rose and echoed. Men scurried from the scaffolding as the eerie screams reverberated from the bowels of the earth. Some soldiers backed away. A horse bolted from its stable hand, knocking aside baskets of stone. A blood-curdling shriek tore its way from the cave to claw its way down men's spines.

'The devil!' cried a soldier near Lord Mael, who turned rapidly, drew his sword and killed him.

'Stand your ground!' he commanded. The two knights with him also drew their swords, looking nervously around them. A soldier ran screaming from the cave, blood sluicing his face and arms. Confusion and panic gripped Lord Mael's men as a tall, scar-faced knight burst from the entrance. Blood splattered his beard and chest. The devil's ascent, for that is what legend would relate, took less than ten rapid heartbeats. Blackstone pounded on the heels of the wounded man, the sole survivor of those sent into Hell's Gate. A huge bearded man half a pace behind Blackstone cut the survivor down. More men spilled from the cave and swarmed into Lord Mael's soldiers. Killbere released his skittish horse and it bounded into the two knights, knocking one aside. The man tried to rise but Killbere's sword pierced his throat.

'The gates!' Killbere shouted. There was no need for the command: Beyard and his men were already running for the main gate, killing the two men who guarded it as Killbere struck out at Lord Mael, but the men closest to him blocked the veteran knight. As Killbere fought off the three soldiers Lord Mael was running towards Blackstone. The surviving knight called out for his own men to join them and within seconds thirty men ran forward to bolster Lord Mael's ranks.

Blackstone and his men were outnumbered.

CHAPTER TWENTY-TWO

Blackstone blinked away the glare of the late afternoon sun as he emerged from the darkness. His stomach lurched when he saw the castrated bodies hanging upside down. Like Killbere he feared one of them was his son, but there was no time to reflect for a tall, heavy-set man was racing towards him, blocking his view of the mutilated corpses.

The courtyard seethed with men. The sight of the fearsome killers emerging from the underworld caused Lord Mael's men to hesitate – all except those at his shoulder, who hurled themselves forward.

Blackstone saw Killbere out of the corner of his eye, and as he slammed his shield into an attacker he looked beyond the man's battered face to the inner curtain walls. There were no crossbowmen there yet; they would still hold their position on the outer walls. Still expecting an attack from beyond. Within moments Meulon, John Jacob and Renfred formed a broadhead wedge with their shields. The sudden rush against them faltered. Blackstone's men were clear of the cave and formed up behind Blackstone. They shuffled forward, pressing back the desperate defenders. Creating order out of chaos, taking control of the fight, they hacked their way forward one stride at a time. And then the shield wall parted, men broke free, slamming and thrashing three, four determined paces forward. Blackstone struck out towards the Breton lord. Shadows engulfed the yard. The sun edged below the castle walls. The chill soothed the sweating men, giving them renewed vigour. The odds were against Blackstone but their defence had not been broken and their counter-attack had scattered Lord Mael's men. Some of them surrendered.

'Spare them!' Blackstone bellowed over the cacophony. He was too late for some; others clasped hands in prayer awaiting the death blow that never came. These were not untrained militia, they were fighting men, raised and paid for by Lord Mael, men who had fought the English on past battlefields and who now begged for their lives, unable to contest the violence that Blackstone and his men inflicted on them.

A crow cackled at man's folly.

A priest appeared, a bandage around his head, a crucifix raised, a dazed look in his eyes. The fighting faltered and then stopped. An eerie silence suddenly smothered the castle. Men whimpering in pain succumbed to death; others drew their agony into themselves, cradling its ferocious bite, swallowed whole by it.

Lord Mael had backed himself against the tower's scaffolding, bloodied sword in hand. He had killed three of Blackstone's men and now only his sworn enemy faced him. Blackstone's men went quickly among the survivors, stripped them of their weapons, kicked their legs from under them, forcing them face down. The priest stood like a beacon, eyes blinking, clearly believing that his appearance had caused the combatants to cease fighting. Killbere seized his shoulder, forcing him down.

'On your knees where you belong, priest. This isn't your doing. It's his,' he said, pointing his bloodied sword towards Blackstone, who stood ten yards from Lord Mael. Babeneaux had not yielded, and he wanted Blackstone dead.

The knight who had stood at the Breton lord's side throughout, and fought as hard as any man, turned his sword and offered its hilt to Killbere. 'You are no vagabond, sir. I see that now. To whom do I surrender?'

Killbere glanced at Blackstone, who nodded.

'I am Gilbert Killbere. A knight by King Edward's grace.'

The knight bowed his head. 'I am Lord Judikael. You have slain good men who served me loyally.'

'Then when matters are settled here, you can have this priest pray for their souls and I will ransom you. I demand your parole not to raise arms against King Edward or John de Montfort until that ransom is settled. Agreed?

'It is agreed.'

Lord Mael pivoted. 'Traitor!' His blade rammed into his ally's side and tore a gaping hole wide enough for his innards to spill. As he pulled free his sword he paced quickly towards Blackstone.

Killbere was ready to intercept but Blackstone raised his sword. 'No!'

Lord Mael stooped and picked up an abandoned flanged mace. The Breton had no shield to protect him so Blackstone cast aside his own. Lord Mael feinted; it caught Blackstone wrong-footed, and the Breton slammed his shoulder into him, trying to throw him down, but Blackstone took the blow, squared his stance and parried the subsequent sword thrust that would have pierced heart and lungs. Mael tried to smother Blackstone, striking down with the mace, slamming it against the scar-faced knight's helm, but Blackstone spat in his eyes; the man's neck snapped back, forcing him onto his heels. Too close for a sword strike, Blackstone reversed his fist and slammed the pommel towards Mael's face, but the man was quick, turned his head and took the blow on his raised arm, exposing Blackstone's chest for a killing blow. His blade struck upwards, its tip catching Blackstone's mail beneath his jupon, enough to snag for an instant. Blackstone spun on his heel, his body movement forcing the man off balance. Blackstone struck down from the high guard, a blow to sever shoulder from body. Lord Mael sacrificed the mace, gripped his sword blade with his free hand and blocked the strike. Metal clanged, hardened steel shuddering from the strike.

Those who had surrendered dared to stand up when Blackstone fought their master. The dust beneath the two men's feet swirled like a shroud as each sought the advantage, manoeuvring back and forth, wild beasts slamming horns, battering the other until one fell. Now the Breton was quickly side on again, both hands gripping his sword hilt, swinging left and right, high to low, scything the air before him with renewed ferocity, forcing Blackstone back. Men scattered as they shuffled, sidestepped, testing and striking, dancing with death. Blackstone counter-attacked. Sweat stung both men's eyes but their violence continued unabated. And then the watching men gasped. Blackstone was wrong-footed, his blade cut through thin air, his shoulder turned exposing neck and back to the skilled fighter who reacted without a second thought, brought his sword from across his shoulder, committed with all his strength to cleave Blackstone's head from his body. He bellowed. And drawing that breath to spur his strength gave Blackstone the heartbeat moment he needed. He had fooled the master swordsman. Using his own momentum he pivoted on his heels and plunged Wolf Sword's blade beneath the man's armpit, through his shoulder and into his neck. The strike stopped Lord Mael where he stood. A gaping hiss, eyes blinking at Blackstone's face so close to his own. Blackstone ripped free the blade, its edge scraping bone. Lord Mael Babeneaux de Pontivy dropped to his knees, eyes staring upward towards the God he would never meet.

And then fell back.

*

Silence settled. Exhaustion claimed the men. Some sank to their knees to ease weary muscles or favour their wounds. Blackstone took the wineskin from Killbere and drank thirstily, red liquid splashing across his beard, sluicing away the blood. Blackstone's small force had killed thirty-four men behind the walls, another thirteen underground. They had lost seven of their own in the courtyard and two of Beyard's Gascons at the main gate. Eleven of Lord Mael's men lay dead in the meadow, slain without loss by Will Longdon's archers. Lord Mael's crossbowmen on the outer walls surrendered when they realized all was lost and they beckoned those outside the walls within. Lady Cateline stayed at a distance from her slain husband, shielding her young daughter. Her son stared at the carnage. None of the archers spoke when they saw the slaughter. It had been a fearful fight and friends had died.

Blackstone turned to Meulon. 'Question the survivors. Have the men search for Henry,' he said. Meulon nodded and summoned weary men to him.

The priest had not moved, still clutching the crucifix to him as he knelt. Eyes unable to fathom what he had witnessed; lips muttering silent prayers.

'I think his mind has gone, Thomas,' said Killbere. 'The blow to his head must have scrambled his brain.'

'And we will use it to our advantage,' said Blackstone. 'When we leave this place will be abandoned. Have the masons seal the cave's entrance. We close the castle gates, burn down the keep, destroy that new tower and send him on his way to tell what he saw here.'

Blackstone raised the cleric to his feet. 'Priest,' he said gently, 'what did you see here today?'

The priest blinked uncertainly, unable to answer, so

Blackstone helped plant the seed that would flourish ever bigger in the telling. 'Did you see the devil's disciples swarm from beneath the earth and slay these men?'

The priest looked intently at the scar-faced Englishman. His eyes searched for the vision. 'Yes... yes... I saw that... I saw the devil himself rise up...' His finger pointed towards the cave. 'Hell's Gate... yes... So it was true – demons were caged there... and now...' He suddenly stepped back, fear clawing his chest as he gazed at Blackstone. 'The devil is among us. This place is cursed. Haunted by death and evil.'

Blackstone nodded. 'Warn everyone. Preach what you saw.' He turned the priest towards the main gate and watched him shuffle away, crucifix held tightly, to spread word of the terror that lay behind the castle walls. A warning that would see Babeneaux's castle remain unoccupied and condemned.

CHAPTER TWENTY-THREE

As the bodies were dragged across the courtyard a bedraggled Henry Blackstone clambered down the kitchen ladder.

'Thomas,' said Killbere, drawing Blackstone's attention to the boy.

Blackstone watched his son's hesitant approach as he wiped the last of the blood from Wolf Sword's blade. Henry stood off like a wary dog, expecting to be whipped.

'Where were you, boy?' said Blackstone sternly, not yet prepared to show how relieved he was that his disobedient son had survived.

'I found my way back through the caves and hid in plain sight, my lord. In Jocard's room in the keep. A place they would not think of looking. Lord Mael had already slain those who worked in the kitchen. I dared not show myself when you were fighting in case my presence distracted you.'

Killbere turned away from Henry so that he would not hear his whispered words. 'Do not be too harsh with him, Thomas. He showed courage and daring.'

Blackstone returned the generous comment with a dark scowl.

'I'll attend to the men,' said Killbere and left father and son to settle their differences.

'Come closer,' said Blackstone.

Henry did as he was told and stood just beyond arm's reach.

'I do not tolerate disobedience. Men's lives depend on discipline.'

'I understand, my lord, but I thought to save Gabriel because he was uncertain about the Latin I taught him and to hesitate with Lord Mael would have meant his death.'

'Gabriel is dead.'

Henry's face registered shock.

'I am weary and I have my men to attend to. I will decide what to do with you later.'

'May I speak with Lady Cateline's son? I would like to know he is all right after his own ordeal.'

Blackstone shook his head. 'Go to John Jacob and find out what his orders are.'

Henry bowed his head and followed his father's command. Blackstone watched his son walk away. His back as straight as a sword blade, he strode with purpose, undeterred, it seemed, by Blackstone's admonishment. Pride in the boy taunted him, but so too did uncertainty. Henry was strong for his age, had proved his courage, but he had defied his father and his squire, John Jacob. Defiance Blackstone understood. How to harness the boy's intelligence and potential as a fighter? Despair seeped into his heart. Perhaps the boy needed to be sent away again. A university, perhaps: somewhere he could return to his studies. Somewhere safe. Blackstone slipped Wolf Sword into its scabbard. Nowhere offered safety if they discovered you bore the name Blackstone.

John Jacob growled at his page, 'Henry, you are an ill-disciplined wretch, and I shall find you every unpleasant job to instruct you otherwise. Report to Meulon. He attends the dead. You will help strip the enemy corpses of anything of value, and then you will drag the bodies to the pit the survivors are digging. Tell him those are my orders for you. And when you have done that go with the men and bring in the rest of our horses from the forest. Only you have a way with your father's beast. Get to it.'

Henry knew John Jacob's threat and his father's anger meant weeks of punitive duties. It did not matter. He had done what few others could have done. There was satisfaction in entering a beast's lair and surviving, in planning and executing an escape. How many men, no matter how courageous, would have entered Hell's Gate and then saved his charge before saving himself? Punishment was nothing compared to that. He suppressed his self-satisfied grin.

'You laugh at the dead?' said Meulon, who'd caught the lad's indulgence. The broad-chested throat-cutter sat on a barrel, his back resting against the wall, binding a linen bandage over a slash on his arm.

'I do not. I beg your pardon. I am instructed to help strip the bodies and drag them to the pit once it is dug,' Henry said, gazing across the mutilated corpses and the survivors digging a long trench against the far wall.

'Punishment eh?'

'Yes.'

'It was to be expected.'

'It was.'

'Men here respect you, Master Henry. We have watched you grow in courage over the years. Perhaps there are times to be disobedient, perhaps this was one such a time, but you must earn trust, lad. Understand me? You have to be trusted to be where you are supposed to be. We each rely on the other for that. Trust is the key to men's loyalty. Remember that.'

'I will.'

Meulon's teeth flashed for a moment through the dense black beard. 'I never liked listening to lectures either. It will soon be dark, but these men will keep digging until we can bury the stench. Renfred has others digging graves for our own men who fell. Go and find lamp oil or torches.'

'There's a storeroom but it needs to be unlocked or the door broken down.'

Meulon pointed. 'My men are resting by the stables. They'll help.'

'I can do it myself.'

'Then be quick about it.'

'May I ask who among us we lost?'

'Ralph Tait and Quenell at the ambush. Othon as well. Gabriel LaFargue.' Meulon named the others who had not survived the fight. Henry saw their faces. Heard their laughter.

'And here?'

'Tom Woodbrook, Robert d'Ardenne, William Audley, Thomas Berford among others. It has cost us dearly. More than half our men-at-arms all told.'

'And what of Will and Jack?'

'They are alive. They are manning the outer walls while we see to ourselves here.'

'Thank you, Meulon. I'm sorry for those men we lost.'

'It's the price we pay to fight those who hate Sir Thomas. Besides…' He tied off the bandage, flexed his arm and picked up his shield. 'It was their time to die.'

Blackstone went among the men offering encouragement and promised they would share equally whatever Lord Mael had in wealth. The sorrow of losing friends was soothed by the knowledge that there would be more plunder for every man. And that they would soon be in Poitiers to spend their coin on women, wine and ale. Killbere was stripped to the waist, washing himself down with a torn piece of linen. His bruises and welts from the fighting would be eased by the well's cold water.

'Have you seen her?' Blackstone asked.

'Aye. She went up into Babeneaux's quarters. Took her offspring with her.'

'Have we searched the place?'

Killbere nodded. 'There's no one there to cause us trouble. Servants were hiding in the cellars. If there were any guards, they are dead or missing.' Killbere thrust his head into the bucket, then shook himself like a dog. 'Strange she didn't mention the tunnel.'

Blackstone ignored the comment and swept his gaze across the castle. It was secure; the men were safe. No one was out there to cause more harm. 'See that the men have hot food, Gilbert. The cook will have enough life left in him to organize it. Have fresh straw taken from the stables for the men's bedding and set the night watch.'

'And where are you going?'

'To satisfy your curiosity.'

Blackstone made his way to the five-storey building, more elegant than the keep's basic structure. If it was where Babeneaux had his private quarters then it stood to reason that his wife would also have her rooms there. The broad heavy wooden staircase rose from the cut limestone floor. Wall sconces clung like swallows' nests to the wall so that there would be no need to carry candles to light the way in darkness. It told of a man who had a taste for the small luxuries of life. Comfort he would no longer enjoy. Blackstone followed the flickering oil lamps. Guiding. Inviting. He took his time. Weary from fighting for his life, he allowed himself a few moments when there was no need to act with urgency. His spurs clanked; his scabbard tapped each heavy step he took. The first three floors were devoid of life but voices murmured from the top floor. As he reached the next level, he could smell fragrance. He looked along the broad colonnade, and out across the outer walls. Moonlight blanketed the forest and meadow, still plagued with specks of crows that fluttered and cawed, bickering like hunchback priests over the scattered dead. Night creatures would soon join them. Wolf and boar would gorge tonight.

As he reached the top floor he heard women's voices.

'Is she asleep?' said Cateline's voice from one of the chambers.

A woman's respectful voice answered. 'She is, my lady.'

Blackstone rested his hand on the sword hilt so it made no sound as he walked slowly towards the voices.

'Where is my son?'

'I do not know. He said he would look for the boy who saved him.'

'Then when he returns make sure I am not disturbed. I will be sleeping.'

'My lady.'

Silence. The oil lamps spluttered. There was steam in the air. He heard the gentle sound of water splashing. A door closed somewhere in the distance. He reached a heavy door, half ajar, warm light filtering through the gap. He bent forward and peered. A copper bathtub reflected the shimmering light from a handful of candles seated in dribbled wax. Cateline wore only her linen undergarment as she luxuriated in the water. The material clung to her. Sweat speckled her face and her hair was pulled back and held with a comb. Blackstone's throat tightened; he tasted lust on his tongue. Surely his thudding heart would echo down the corridor? Guilt made him glance quickly down the passage but he was alone. He looked back and Cateline was staring directly at him. His head snapped back.

Mother of God. He had been seen. Caught like a teenage boy peering through a brothel window. His heart beat faster. Without thought words of apology stumbled from his lips.

'There is no need, my lord,' said Cateline. 'The door was not locked.'

Her husky voice drew him like a riverbank poacher reeling in his catch. He pushed the door open. She smiled. 'Now close it, my lord.'

He turned and dropped the latch and now that he was in the chamber saw the large bed and its canopy, crisp sheets exposed from laid-back covers. He turned to face her. She stood without shame, the shift clinging to every crevice and rise. Blackstone's mail chafed the nicks and cuts. His boots were leaden. She smiled, reached out her arms. The fragrance. Was it a magical potion that befuddled his thoughts but aroused his body? He unbuckled his sword belt, peeled off his jupon and kicked free his boots. He bent, letting her pull free his mail and the sweat-soaked shirt beneath it. She gazed at his scars and injuries, the raw arm wound, the weals and bruises. Loosening the cord on his breeches she eased them down his hips and they fell to his ankles. As Blackstone stepped into the water she pressed close to him, her musk more enticing than the scent in the water. She raised her arms to let him peel the wet cloth from her, and as it freed her hands she unclipped the comb, letting her hair fall. They settled in the deep bath. She soaped and washed the dried blood from his face and hair, then bathed his wounds and kissed his calloused hands that had wielded a sword in her defence. Their passion was kept in check like a shield wall denying a surging enemy. And when the water cooled and the dirt and tiredness was washed away, he lifted her onto the bed. The chill autumn breeze tingled their skin.

The shield wall yielded.

CHAPTER TWENTY-FOUR

Killbere watched Blackstone stride across the yard towards him. He looked refreshed. And scrubbed.

'You slept?' said Killbere.

'I did.'

'You stink of something. A woman's scent.'

'It will wash off in time.'

'I hope so. If we ride to Poitiers with you smelling like a brothel-keeper's daughter, Sir William might ask you to marry him instead of giving us the supplies and replacement men we need. So? What did she say?'

'Who?'

'God's blood, Thomas. Take your brain out of your balls. You were to ask her why she had not mentioned Hell's Gate.'

'I forgot.'

'I wonder why.'

Blackstone ignored the veteran's sarcasm. 'The men?'

'Ready.'

'Good. Scour every building and send any servant away from here. Empty the grain store. Fill our sacks and distribute the rest. Did he have any horses we can take?'

'Very few. I had the men exchange any poor or lame mount we have for theirs. The others are rounceys, not worth exchanging. I set them loose. They'll find their way to the villages and end up beneath a plough harness or in the pot.'

'Did we find his gold?'

'A chest full of mixed coin, florins, livres, gold and silver, even a bag of Edward's leopards.'

'Then we have enough to pay for men and supplies instead of being dependent on Sir William's favour should he deny us. If he gives us what we want then we have money to engage fresh men-at-arms. How many of Babeneaux's men survived?'

'Eleven. Six died from their wounds in the night. What do we do with the living?'

'Give them enough food for a week's journey. They'll make their way to another Breton lord and offer their services. They will tell what happened here. That we slew the strongest ally of Charles of Blois and the French King.' Blackstone grinned. 'Devils from the underworld. Now, let's get barrels of pitch and burn down the keep and tower.'

Blackstone and the men stood back in the meadow watching the pyres billow black smoke high in the sky. It was a still day but the clouds on the horizon threatened darker days and storms to come. Lord Mael's castle was bereft of life, the gates barred, the keep and tower burnt like the devil's horns. They rode through the nearby villages but the doors stayed closed, and windows covered. Word had already reached the villeins of the slaughter that had taken place. Blackstone's men dropped bags of grain at the crossroads for the villagers but kept the more valuable sacks of salt.

Henry rode in his usual place behind John Jacob. Lady Cateline's son rode alongside his new-found friend. Henry was glad of the companionship because neither his father nor John Jacob had relinquished their displeasure with him. Jocard looked back along the column of men. His mother was caring for his sister as they rode on the supply cart.

'Your father spent the night with my mother. Did you know?' Jocard whispered, not wishing anyone else to hear.

Henry snapped a look at the younger boy. Jocard nodded in confirmation. Neither looked pleased. Henry had never thought of his father being with anyone else other than his mother and the thought tormented him. Surely he still honoured her memory? 'How can you be sure?'

'When I left you in the yard last night I went back to my old room. Jehanne was crying in her sleep so I went to her but Melita was with her. She has been my mother's servant since I was born. Once I saw that Jehanne was settled I said I wanted to see my mother and tell her how many men were killed. But Melita stopped me and said she was sleeping. It was early. My mother would never go to bed so early.'

'She might, having spent a frightening day with the men. And she would have been worried about you before they found you,' Henry said, hoping what he said was true

'I went past her room. I heard them.'

Henry's stomach squirmed. 'You're wrong,' he whispered. 'My father was with the men. I saw him with Sir Gilbert.'

Jocard shook his head. 'Henry, you saved my life. You gave me courage. I am forever in your debt, so I would not tell you this unless I was certain. You are like a brother now.' He hesitated. 'My father and your mother are dead. Do you think—?'

'No!' Henry said too loudly, clenching his teeth to stop the words spilling out for all to hear. His father would never marry Jocard's mother. Never. His own mother and sister had been murdered. His father would never replace them. It was an impossibility.

John Jacob glanced behind him. 'You speak when you are not spoken to, Henry. Is there something you wish to share?'

'No, Master Jacob.'

'Keep it that way,' said the squire. A page needed to be kept in his place. An added discipline that Henry Blackstone had still not learnt. Yet the boy had shown initiative and courage and he hoped the father would soon allow him to be less harsh. His thoughts remained unspoken to Blackstone, however.

It would take three days to reach Poitiers, and by the second night Blackstone had not yet made any approach to Cateline. He had ignored her. As Henry gathered sufficient wood for the night's fire and then attended to Blackstone's horse, Killbere sat on a log by their fire honing his knife blade.

'I've been thinking,' said Killbere.

Blackstone was lost in a reverie, gazing at the flames. Killbere's words prodded him. 'Thinking can be bad for you.'

'Which is what you have been doing since we left the castle. You have barely spoken a word.'

'Idle conversation has never been to my liking.'

'And idle thoughts? What preoccupies you? Poitiers? Sir William's ire at our late arrival? The Prince? No, it is the woman. She gazes like a mooning cow your way, hungry for the bull in the next field to mount her. And you have not uttered a word to her. You have not approached her to ask if she and her youngster are comfortable. You have sat in the saddle and stared beyond the horizon and at night contemplated the flames as you sit and scratch your balls. You should face the facts.'

'I don't need a lecture, Gilbert.'

'You need a kick up the arse. You are bewitched by the woman. See it for what it is. For God's sake, take her into the trees and have her again, and soon the attraction will wear off.' He wiped the oiled blade on his sleeve, satisfied with its sharpness. 'Be careful, Thomas. She seeks a husband.'

Blackstone looked up sharply as Killbere got to his feet.

'And I know you have not yet released Christiana and Agnes from your heart,' Killbere added gently.

Blackstone relented. 'You cannot know how Fate torments me. It holds a mirror to my past. Before you and I fought at Poitiers back in '56, I sent Christiana and Agnes to safety in Avignon. What I have never told you is that Christiana was raped on the journey by one of the King's guards. Henry was only a boy, but he tried to stop it. It was John Jacob who killed the man and took Henry under his wing. I didn't know what had happened until later when the Prince banished me and I fought the Savage Priest. Christiana took the children and left me because I refused to accept her bastard child. I fear the worst if I allow Cateline to draw close.'

Killbere made no reply. He placed a hand on his friend's shoulder. 'I will make no mention of this to anyone. Henry and John will never know you've told me. Let your heart guide you.' He turned away and left his friend alone.

Blackstone felt the blood rush to his head. The pulse in his neck beat from the memory of his wife's ordeal. Killbere's words had found their mark. He stood and made his way through the men to where they had settled Cateline and her servant for the night. The servant woman was preparing food for her mistress in a lean-to shelter a few feet away as Jehanne sat safely behind her playing happily with two small clay dolls retrieved from her room at the castle. Cateline was rubbing oil into her hair; its raven-wing sheen glowed even in the dim light. She reached out a hand to Blackstone, drawing him down to where she sat on a blanket. Blackstone went on one knee.

'Thomas,' she said, still with the huskiness he remembered from their night of passion, and held out the comb. 'Will you help?'

'I am no servant to do your bidding, Cateline. Nor am I a love-struck puppy eager to please.'

Her expression hardened. 'I do not expect to be spoken to like that, Thomas. I thought we... I thought we had drawn close.'

'We were drawn by lust, nothing more. Don't make it out to be anything more.'

'You insult me,' she said, suddenly embarrassed, glancing left and right in case any of the men heard their exchange.

'You have everything you need. Your servant, your daughter is safe, you are now twice widowed and will benefit from Babeneaux's estate once Sir William attends to the legalities. I saved your son. I have nothing more to offer you.'

'That's not true, Thomas. I know what we shared.'

'We coupled because we were lonely and desired one another. You will get nothing more from me.'

'Then I have been used.'

'As you seem to use others. Your husband no sooner cold in the grave than you accept Lord Mael; you despair of him and his desire to control your domain so you take his guard commander as your lover. Every man who shares your bed dies.'

A look of pain crossed her face as she lowered her gaze. 'That is so hurtful,' she said in a whisper. She raised her eyes. 'You say cruel things. I am a woman with no one to protect me. I have children to raise. I have the right to live as I should by my own title – and I fight for that right.'

'Don't look so wounded, Cateline. You will never starve and there will be men you will attract who will not wish to seize what is yours by inheritance and right. But I am not that man. Why didn't you tell me about Hell's Gate?'

The sudden question caught her off guard. She recovered quickly and busied herself putting away her comb and oils.

'It was a place of terror. No one ever ventured into the caves. They barred the way in. I could not have known where it would come out or that they could even enter it.'

'When planning an attack a soldier needs to know everything so it can be considered or discounted.'

'I am not a soldier. I was asked what I knew, and I told you. I didn't *hide* anything from you. My son's life was in danger. Why would I not mention something that might benefit him? Why are you being so harsh?'

Blackstone could barely answer the question for himself. The woman had touched something in him he had not experienced since his wife's death. It confused him and his defence against it was to push her away with barbed comments. He restrained his desire to reach out and pull her to him. The smell of her skin and the memory of her breasts against him were almost irresistible.

Blackstone stood. 'Get your woman to attend to you. And look after your daughter. She needs her mother's affection, not a servant's.'

'So you're turning your back on me,' said Cateline.

It was too late in the year for fireflies and yet Blackstone saw two of them alight from the warmth of the forest's ferns. They glowed and danced and came closer: disembodied spirits caught between heaven and earth. Children's souls, some said; others believed them to be the souls of those cruelly slain, seeking a host body so they could re-enter the world. Ignorant superstition. And yet? He watched them rise and enthral him with their light. So close he could reach out and touch them. Appearing as they did the moment he thought of Christiana and Agnes. Murdered mother and child. Beloved wife and daughter. *Do not forget us*. And then they were gone.

Blackstone looked at Cateline. 'You bear no pain. Your men are dead but you turn your back on them. I carry my grief still. I am not ready to relinquish it. We will be in Poitiers tomorrow and then you will be free from my protection. And harshness.'

Blackstone turned away. Lady Cateline Babeneaux was the keeper of Hell's Gate. The entrance to Blackstone's heart.

CHAPTER TWENTY-FIVE

Poitiers. One of the great political centres in France, built on a series of hills rising above the rivers Boivre and Clain and surrounded by streams on three sides, it was one of the country's key defensive cities. The Gallo-Roman walls still protected the ancient centre. It was a thriving commercial hub with its markets and shops, and mills and tanneries along the Clain. It was also the northernmost city of the Duchy of Aquitaine whose territory was vastly increased now that King Edward had signed the peace treaty. Encompassing a dozen counties including Poitou, Aquitaine covered almost a third of France from the Loire to the Pyrenees. Its furthermost boundary north of the great city struck like an arrowhead into the French King's territory. And his heart. The Seneschal of Poitou, Sir William Felton, governed in the name of the Prince of Wales and Aquitaine. A man gruff in manner as unrelenting as the Northumberland countryside he hailed from.

'You were expected sooner,' he snapped.

Blackstone and Killbere stood in a room with vaulted ceilings where light streamed in from long, high windows. The room overlooked the city towards the river. A dominant view appropriate for the man who could decide a man's fate.

'We took half a day to get through all the damned clerks and lackeys you have scuttling around downstairs,' said Killbere. 'Are we to be kept waiting like beggars at the door?'

'I control the city. It requires officials. A treasury, a night watch, a committee of thirteen citizens and their mayor. Taxes need to be levied and collected, traders to be granted permission. You are treated no differently than any other.'

'Then we damned well should be. You were once a fighting man, I'll grant you that. Slow and stubborn to react but when you got off your arse and bent to the fight, you were a worthy ally,' said Killbere.

The mixture of insult and praise momentarily slowed the Northumbrian's response. Then, recognizing the insult was the more pertinent of the two, he slammed the palm of his hand on the heavy wooden table. 'You will show this office the respect it demands!'

'And you show Sir Thomas Blackstone some damned respect! He is Edward's Master of War who keeps you and your cronies safe in this glorified brothel.'

Blackstone raised a hand to stop the argument escalating. 'Sir William, I need supplies and men. Farriers for our horses. Grain and fodder. We have suffered losses and once this matter is settled Sir Gilbert and I would like to bathe and wash the stench of combat and travel from us. My men need food and drink and a place to rest.'

'I will do what I can.'

'What you can?' spluttered Killbere. 'We are on the King's business. You are obliged to accord Sir Thomas every courtesy.'

'We have limited supplies ourselves. But' – Felton's voice took on a more conciliatory tone – 'I will do everything I can to facilitate your requests.' He subdued his irritation as he occupied himself for a moment fingering through the neatly laid out documents fanned across his desk. 'You have caused problems, Sir Thomas,' he said, brandishing a document.

'That is my purpose. To confound, to contest and to defeat my King's enemies.'

'But not to break a treaty made between the Bretons. A treaty endorsed by our King. A treaty that now threatens to be torn apart.'

'Babeneaux? He was an enemy of John de Montfort. He held an unassailable castle. He captured a child whose mother will declare her territory for de Montfort. Edward can have no complaint about that. Nor should you. We have crushed a powerful Breton lord who held a strategic fortification not four days from here. Now it will remain deserted until someone is brave enough to defy the myth of what happened there. I ask you again: I need food and quarters and physicians for my men. They need women and drink and a place to nurse their wounds, so attend to them. Everyone will be paid for their services. My men have money in their purses.'

'And knives in their belts. Your men are mongrels that would as soon start an alehouse brawl as jump into a bear pit. I'll have no murder committed here.'

Blackstone reached out a restraining hand to stop Killbere taking a fatal step forward. The veteran knight looked as though he was going to strike the seneschal. 'My men have bled for the Prince and given the King a stronghold. They deserve more respect,' Blackstone said, an edge to his voice. 'You were glad of them back in March at le Garet when we defeated the Bretons. You took the honour for that fight but you would have been left face down in the mud were it not for my archers and Sir Gilbert's defence of the hill. You do not command my men. I will bring them into the city and they will take their pleasures where they find them and if any of your men try to stop them they will face me first and it will be on your head if murder is committed.'

For a moment the King's Master of War and the seneschal glared at each other. It felt as though Felton might summon the guard there and then and have Killbere and Blackstone arrested. But he knew better than to instigate such a provocation. The rush of blood to his face cooled. 'Very well. They will not carry their swords into the city. That is the ordinance here. Knights excepted. The constable and the night watch are empowered to arrest.'

Blackstone knew it was not an unreasonable demand. London prohibited the carrying of swords within the city limits. Such a restriction might not stop alehouse brawls but it stopped any escalation. 'Accepted.'

'Then you have my permission and I will send a physician to you but you must pay him. There are quarters in the garrison, but I would urge caution of your men mixing with garrison soldiers.'

'I agree,' said Blackstone. It would not be the first time that men confined to garrison duties felt themselves inferior to fighting men. A challenge made could cause more bloodshed than any tavern fight. 'We'll camp outside the city.'

'Good. Then much of our business is settled. I will arrange what supplies I can for you.' Felton returned his attention to the documents awaiting his attention. It was a dismissal.

Blackstone and Killbere exchanged glances and turned to leave. Before they reached the door, however, Felton said, 'What of the woman who accompanied you? This Lady Cateline Babeneaux? What will you do with her?'

'Do?' said Blackstone. 'Nothing. Her intention was to seek your protection and hand over her domain to the King.'

'And what of her then?'

'She wanted an escort to take her son to Avignon and the Pope.'

'Pope Innocent is dead.'

Neither Killbere nor Blackstone had heard that news. 'Then who's taking his place?' said Killbere. 'Let us hope it's an Italian. Someone more favourable to the English Crown.'

'No, it's a Frenchman,' Felton said. 'A Benedictine monk, Guillaume de Grimoard. I have no intention of giving her an escort to the south. I shall arrange for her to return home. Her son is not my concern.'

'Then that's how it is,' said Blackstone, surprised at his own concern, determined not to show it. His hand reached for the door lever.

'Sir Thomas, your late arrival has caused an inconvenience to another. He's been waiting a week. You'll likely find him in the Église Sainte-Radegonde.' He knew Blackstone would be unfamiliar with the city. 'One of the clerks downstairs will instruct you.' A final jab of authority.

The leaden sky trapped the late autumn humidity. Rain threatened as Blackstone and Killbere trudged along the cobbled streets north towards the river and the Bourg Sainte-Radegonde.

'Too many people in too small a space,' said Killbere as the press of people in the narrow streets parted for the two fearsome knights. Merchants and travellers jostled; shouts and ribald laughter spilled from an alehouse. A man staggered outside, barged unwittingly into another and was promptly thrown aside by a burly citizen. The drunk made no complaint and lay where he fell. 'And rats turn on themselves if you cage them.' Tradesmen at their stalls raised their heads at the two knights, men who looked no different from brigands. The citizens of Poitiers had no choice but to agree to be governed by the English and Killbere saw the resentment in their eyes, which were quickly lowered when his own met theirs. 'We could be ambushed here and Felton would put it down to a robbery. A man would struggle to swing a sword in these streets.'

'You think he would arrange such a thing?' said Blackstone, stepping around a helmet maker who reached out, shouting for the two men to inspect his work.

'I would put nothing past him. You are a thorn in his side. No!' Killbere shouted as a tailor ran out of his shop holding up a tabard. Another barged his competitor aside and brandished a bolt of fine cloth. Killbere's arm swept him aside, leaving the two tradesmen to bicker their way back into their shops. 'Mother of Christ, Thomas, is this what people do here all day? Go from stall to stall and spend their money?'

'What else can city people do?' Blackstone pointed, 'There, Gilbert, the road widens. There's the church.'

The throng of people and stallholders gave way to a square and the church's tower as they skirted the ancient city's inner walls. As they turned into the square four armed men appeared suddenly from around the side of the old abbey and blocked the entrance. They wore mail beneath their surcoats, which were belted with swords. Hard-bitten men with unyielding eyes, they glared at the approaching knights, feet braced, two men forward, two slightly behind. If they were attacked they had already formed an effective defence.

'Trouble,' said Killbere, his hand resting on his sword hilt as they stopped. If the men were hostile they had chosen an open area to attack which meant there could be others waiting in the alleys and side streets to encircle the two Englishmen.

'No,' said Blackstone, 'I don't think so. Look at their blazon.'

Killbere squinted, focusing on their jupons. 'Edward's men,' he said.

'And what are they doing here?' Blackstone called out to the men who had not moved: 'Declare yourselves.'

The man nearest them took a pace forward. They were still forty paces distant. 'We are escort to protect a traveller who prays within.'

'God's tears, Thomas,' Killbere muttered. 'You don't think the Prince of Wales is in there, do you?'

'If he were the square would be filled with servants, and another two hundred armed men with pennants flying. He likes to put on a show.' Blackstone and Killbere strode forward another ten paces. 'I am Thomas Blackstone, sent by Sir William to this place. I will not ask again. Who are you and why do you challenge me?'

The man who seemed to be in charge stepped forward to greet Blackstone, his voice now more deferential. 'Sir Thomas, I am William Ashford, sergeant to the King. You are the man our charge has been waiting for.' It was obvious that he was not prepared to reveal the identity of the man he guarded – or had been ordered not to do so.

'Then take us to him.'

The sergeant turned on his heel and led the way to the church entrance. The three other men bowed their heads respectfully as Blackstone and Killbere passed. Ashford pushed open one of the heavy double doors. They stepped into deep gloom. There was barely enough light to see the threatening grotesque faces of carved creatures on the capitals. More armed men stepped forward from the shadows. Ashford's voice echoed across the high-arched ceiling. 'I am instructed to take only Sir Thomas beyond this point.'

Killbere pulled a face. 'I shiver in this damp, Thomas. I fear God requires a prayer of contrition and I dislike being this close to the Almighty. I'll wait outside.'

Blackstone nodded. The chill air outside was preferable to the stone floors spreading their cold upwards through the sole of his boots. An ancient abbey like this would entomb many souls. He stamped his heel to defeat the superstition. *Keep your ghostly clutches to yourselves.*

'This way,' said Ashford. He halted as they reached steps leading to the choir that rose either side of the entrance to the crypt.

'Up there?' said Blackstone, gazing at the soaring pillars.

Ashford plucked a half-burnt candle from its holder and offered it to Blackstone. 'Down there,' he said, gesturing to the tomb-like crypt.

CHAPTER TWENTY-SIX

Blackstone descended. The dank smell of decay reached up to embrace him. Once in the crypt he saw columns of low arches offering gateways to the darkness deeper within. The candle spluttered in the suffocating air. A raised stone tomb stood in the middle of the floor. He waited and listened. A soft shuffling sound whispered its dull echo deep in the blackness. A shimmering candlelight far back in the depths threw shadows towards him. Blackstone raised his own candle, his sword hand resting on the hilt, ready to draw and strike. A cowled apparition in white merged from the dark, the candle glow serving only to light the way. Blackstone took a pace back, keeping the raised tomb before him and the figure.

'Thomas,' said the voice from beneath the cowl. 'Surely you do not fear old friends?' The elderly priest Fra Niccolò Torellini smiled as he pulled back his hood. The man who had once held Blackstone's mutilated sixteen-year-old body at the Battle of Crécy raised an eyebrow and stepped closer.

Blackstone returned the warmth of the man's greeting. They embraced. 'You float like a ghost from a crypt. It's enough to turn any man's blood to water.'

'Ah, my boy, if only I could float. My knees ache and my hand trembles. And I wear my order's cassock out of respect for the saint who lies entombed here.' He rested a hand on the sarcophagus. 'Time binds you and me together, Thomas. Time and events. Look what this woman achieved. Saint Radegonde founded this abbey church. It is not as grand as others in the city but it reflects her modesty. This crypt has been her resting place for eight hundred years and here we are meeting again in a place of death. She no longer feels the chill, but I do. It would be a kindness if you put my cloak around my shoulders.' Torellini gestured to the shadows behind Blackstone where a fur-collared garment lay on a bench. Blackstone propped the candle onto a pediment and settled the woollen cloak on the old man's shoulders. 'Thank you. You can see how a humble man of God like myself could not wear such finery out of respect. But now I ache with cold so enough of this humility.'

Blackstone suppressed his smile. Torellini served the Florentine Bardi family whose bank sustained the English King's wars. He was the English King's most trusted messenger between Florence and England, and Torellini had connections and spies everywhere.

Torellini lit another two candles from his own and then settled down on the bench. Now that there was sufficient light Blackstone saw that the man who had been a thread throughout his life since he had first gone to war looked no different from the last time he had seen him. 'And why are you waiting in this dank place for me?' said Blackstone.

'This place has no doors, no cracks in the walls for servants to listen against. No spies linger down here. The dead do not pass on information.'

'You came from Florence?'

Torellini shook his head and cupped his hands to his warm breath. 'I travelled from the King at Windsor to Calais, then to Chartres and now here on my way south.'

'The new Pope?'

'Ah, you heard.'

'Sir William told me. So, it's another Frenchman.'

Torellini sighed and gave a characteristic shrug. 'It is out of our hands. Pope Innocent made many mistakes. He was a weak man who reigned for nine years, eight months and twenty-five days. I am obliged to know such trivial information so I can speak with authority when I acclaim his non-existent achievements. The new Pope was not the cardinals' favourite. Bargains were struck. Who knows how long he will last?

'Edward won't be pleased.'

'And that's why I journey to Avignon. He had hoped for an Italian or an English cardinal to be honoured, because the French like to favour their own King; the new Pope must see Edward to be generous in his goodwill towards the appointment. They will name Guillaume Pope Urban V. He is a Benedictine. Perhaps that will make some difference. If he abides by the Rule and lives simply and honestly, then that might curb the excess and affluence of those in Avignon. Simony, usury, prostitution and the life of luxury for the cardinals might soon be curtailed.' Torellini spread his hands. 'He's different. He might succeed. He has even threatened to excommunicate anyone who persecutes the Jews.'

'I think I've heard of him. Before I went to Milan and faced the Visconti an Abbot Grimoard had been there some time before trying to subdue Bernabò Visconti's excesses.'

'The same man. Yes, he failed. Bernabò made him eat the letter he carried, and its wax seal. If he had not, then he would have been killed. But it proves the man has courage.'

'And has the good sense to know when to back down,' said Blackstone. 'What does any of this have to do with me?'

Torellini tugged his cloak's fur-lined collar into his neck. 'King Edward needs to offer reassurances to the Pope. He must gain as much support as he can for the future. The routiers who went to fight in Spain are returning to France. Avignon might once again be threatened. That is bad enough but those who should protect the Pope in the area, the Counts of Armagnac and Foix, are at war. Gaston Phoebus has sworn to destroy Armagnac.'

Blackstone nodded. 'They've been at each other's throats for years.'

'It is not only the newly elected Pope that Edward needs to impress, Thomas. The Prince will arrive in Bordeaux in the next few months and Edward must secure the territory beyond Avignon.'

'The south has already pledged allegiance. The Gascons wanted the Prince there.'

'But now they have made him Prince of Aquitaine they must repeat their pledge. Every lord must come forward and swear allegiance personally. The Prince will travel from Bordeaux to Bergerac then Périgueux, all the cities, until he gets here to Poitiers. The Count of Foix is important not only as a potential ally but as a source of men and equipment to keep the routiers at bay. Edward sees a dual benefit to be gained. Securing loyalty from Gaston Phoebus and giving assurances to the new Pope. It's politics, Thomas, and Edward has ever sought the advantage.' Torellini rested a hand on Blackstone's arm. 'You fought at Gaston Phoebus's side at Meaux against the Jacquerie.'

Blackstone had a questioning look on his face. 'What? You think I should help the Count of Foix? He has always supported the French King.'

'Ask yourself this. Who has been Gaston Phoebus's most bitter enemy? Over generations it has always been the Count of Armagnac. They made Armagnac the French King's Lieutenant of Languedoc and then adviser to his successor. He used that power and authority to undermine his old rival Phoebus. King John has made a tactical error, Thomas. He has thrown his weight and support behind Armagnac. And that has enraged the Count of Foix. It is a betrayal of his loyalty to the French Crown. Both men are recruiting mercenaries. Armagnac has the upper hand. If Gaston Phoebus does not raise enough men, cannot find the money to pay them, he will lose. And so now Edward sees the chance to bring him over to his side. Help him defeat Armagnac and then drive a wedge between the routiers who threaten Avignon.' He tugged free a folded document and held it in front of Blackstone's face. The red wax bore the unmistakable privy seal. 'For you. By royal decree. You take whatever you need from whoever you need to take it from.'

Blackstone felt the parchment between his fingers. He nodded. There was no choice to do anything else but to follow his King's orders. 'My men need rest. Then I'll go south. But I have a favour to ask in return. A titled woman needs safe conduct to Avignon for herself, her daughter and her son. She wishes him to be educated there, and she seeks sanctuary. She's a Breton and they will return to their conflict no matter what talk there is of a truce.'

'My escort is well chosen; they'll offer her protection. It is fortuitous that the boy goes there. The new Pope has pledged to increase education. He plans more schools and universities across France and the Holy Roman Empire. There is to be a flowering of knowledge, Thomas. I have recommended scholars from Florence to teach there.'

'More spies, Father?'

'Let us say, educated men who have a keen eye for what goes on.' Torellini got to his feet. 'Let's get into the fresh air. We'll dine now I have attended to the essential business in private.' He reached the steps and looked up towards the light and the King's escort who waited for him. 'There is one matter I must share with you, Thomas,' he said, hesitating. 'You killed the Bohemian knight at Crécy whose sword you now carry; you slew his kin at Meaux. You haven't been killing any more Germans, have you?'

'Not that I know.'

'Ah.'

'Why do you ask?'

'When I was at Chartres some Teutonic Knights approached me. Eight or nine of them. Two more travelled with them: half-brothers – I saw they wore grey livery beneath the black cross and were armed with crossbows, each trailing a horse carrying supplies. I suppose they serve the knights and hunt for fresh food. But all these men looked as though they had travelled a long way. They asked if I knew where you were.'

'Why would they think you knew where I was?'

'I am close to your King, and he has honoured you. They seek you out. They looked to be angry men. I denied all knowledge of where you might be.'

'If they came through Paris, then that's where they got the information about you. The King and the Dauphin will never miss a chance to see me killed.'

Father Niccolò Torellini bent into the stairs and stepped towards the light. 'Be careful, Thomas. They will be somewhere on the road ahead.'

CHAPTER TWENTY-SEVEN

Killbere stood with one foot in a bucket of water and the other, already washed, on a piece of sacking. He wore only his breeches and a linen shirt that would have welcomed a scrubbing. They had camped with the men outside the city limits. The tents were in no particular order: the haphazard way of how they were pitched would give little help to an enemy should an unsuspecting attack take place. Killbere and Blackstone shared the same quarters, which did not differ from any of the others. They had set aside a secure area for the men to leave their swords before being allowed into the city. An older man wended his way through the tents; a younger man trailed behind, bearing a heavy leather satchel on his back.

'He's no tinker,' said Killbere.

'It's the physician,' Blackstone said.

The man reached the two knights, pulled free his skull cap and wiped a sleeve across his sweating brow. 'They have sent me to speak to Sir Thomas Blackstone. I am Roland de Souillac, physician.'

'I'm Thomas Blackstone. You're too late, Master Roland.'

The man's anguished look was more a concern at losing his fee than losing a patient. 'They have died from their wounds?'

'They have gone into the city. I bound their wounds and the drink will ease their pain. Come back tomorrow – your skills will be in greater demand after tonight's drinking.'

'Tomorrow?'

'Aye,' said Killbere. 'And bring herbs and ointments and a sharp needle for stitching.'

The ageing doctor nodded and turned on his heel, the faithful bearer following in his footsteps.

'If he survives the climb up the hill, I'll wager his hand will tremble too much to stitch even a tear in my breeches,' said Killbere. 'Which reminds me: I'm leaving my dirty clothes with the washerwomen in the town square so don't let me forget to collect them because when I leave the tavern my mind will be on other matters.'

Blackstone sat on an upturned wooden bucket, tapping the King of England's letter on his fingertips. 'Don't give the washerwomen your braies, by now they must be as deadly as the pestilence.'

Killbere scowled, wobbled free of the bucket and stamped his wet foot onto the sack. 'You worry too much about what women think of you, Thomas. If I did not give these women dirty clothing they would have no work. They would not have a sou to feed the children. I am doing them a kindness. And a pair of arse-stained braies is nothing compared to what Edward has handed you in that letter.' Killbere rubbed his foot dry and tugged on his boots. 'He casts us into the shit pit. The Count of Foix is as difficult a nobleman as you would wish. He will not take kindly to any interference from us. And I do not relish the thought of riding to the foothills of the Pyrenees this close to winter.'

Blackstone unfolded the letter for the hundredth time and gazed at the scribe's neat hand and the seal's impression at the bottom of the text. 'Edward demands a lot, but we must honour it and see it's done before the Prince arrives next summer.'

Killbere finished dressing and tightened the broad leather belt around his waist. 'The Count of Foix, the Prince of Wales and Sir William Felton. I'd rather take on those Teutonic Knights.'

'Not if they seek some kind of retribution. They have influence and can call on their brothers-in-arms if we cause them trouble. And who knows what comfort the new Pope will offer them. If he sides with them, then I have already set him against me. And if he is against me he is against the King.'

Killbere tugged and fussed his clothing, straightening his jupon. 'That's true. I pray to God that whoever these Teutonic Knights are that they don't have their heads up their arses blinking in the light as they peer out their own backsides like every other damned fanatic. I have served on crusade with them and I have no wish to take on that particular brotherhood.' Killbere dragged his fingers through his beard, untangling the congealed hair. 'They kill in the name of God, which as far as I'm concerned offers no benefit if you're their victim. We must take care on the road and see where it leads us.' Killbere rubbed a finger over his teeth, swilled his mouth with wine and swallowed. A final act of preparation. Eyebrows raised, he looked at Blackstone, the unspoken question seeking confirmation as to his readiness.

Blackstone cast a critical gaze over his friend's attire. Killbere quickly stopped any comment. It was bound to be barbed. 'Never mind,' he sighed.

The evening gloaming settled across the hills. Sentries stalked the city walls as the sound of fiddle and drum from the alehouses escaped over the high parapets. 'I owe Will Longdon a woman. I will honour my promise.' Killbere bundled up his dirty clothes for the washerwomen. 'Are we to be graced with your presence? Or are you seeing the husband-hunting woman tonight?'

'I dine with Father Torellini and then I'll find you. Tell the men again that Sir William's night watch have the power to arrest and if they resist, then it will go more badly for them. I want us out of this place as soon as we find replacements.'

'Don't worry, Thomas. I'll be with them.'

'Now I really am worried.'

Killbere's wolfish grin needed no further comment.

Blackstone watched his closest friend make his way towards the city gates. The camp was quiet, other than the sound of pots clanging together and a blade being sharpened. He went towards the sound. John Jacob sat on an upturned bucket outside his tent, his sword blade singing from the whetstone; a piece of meat cooked slowly over the low fire before him.

'John.'

The squire made to rise but Thomas rested a hand on his shoulder. 'Are you for the alehouses and taverns tonight?'

'I think not. I prefer some hours of quiet. And where alehouse whores are concerned there's always trouble.' He lifted a wineskin. 'Lord Babeneaux had good wine in his cellar. It would be a pity for it to go to waste.' He handed the skin to Blackstone, who swallowed some of the warm liquid. Wiping his mouth, he nodded his agreement as to its quality and handed it back. The taste of the wine and the smell of the juicy meat made him feel nostalgic for simple times and simple pleasures. No burden of command. Time spent travelling with Christiana, sleeping under the stars and lovemaking in the scented pine forests. South. Near Avignon. Before her death. He shook his head to rid himself of the dark part of the memory and the horror of her murder.

'Is Henry behaving?'

'He's chastised. I am less strict with him now. I... we... must not crush his spirit – if you'll forgive me for saying so.'

'You have always spoken freely. I depend on it. And I agree. But I am torn.'

'He was speaking to the Breton lad on the ride here. There's a friendship between them. I know he talks of more learning.' John Jacob turned the meat. 'Or... it's time he took his place in the line with the men. He has the strength and his skills improve. But he does not yet have the ability to focus the rage it takes to kill. And, if I'm honest, Sir Thomas, without that he will go down in a mêlée.'

The steady clank of rattling pots made their way through the clustered tents. Henry Blackstone had been down to the bottom of the hill and the river. He glanced up, saw his father and his squire and lifted his chin, determined not to be seen crestfallen at the menial tasks he had to perform.

'My lord, Master Jacob.' Henry maintained the formality when speaking to his father in another's company. 'I met the physician on the way. He told me the men have already gone into the city.'

'Your work is done?' said Blackstone.

'It is.'

'I am dining with Fra Torellini. Would you care to meet him again tomorrow once we have dealt with what needs to be discussed privately?'

The boy seemed uninterested despite the affection he felt for the Florentine priest. 'Perhaps another time, my lord.'

Henry's answer caught Blackstone by surprise. Normally any promise of being in Torellini's company would have the boy's enthusiasm spilling over. 'He has tutors going to Avignon. There's a new Pope.'

John Jacob glanced up at the news. Blackstone nodded in confirmation. And it caught the boy's attention. 'Perhaps there's a teacher who might offer you guidance into law or medicine. It's what you want, isn't it?'

'You would let me go to Avignon?'

'I would consider it if that was your earnest wish.'

Henry looked at John Jacob and then back to his father. Why the hesitation? A tent flap caught by a swirl of the night breeze beat like a wing. The pungent smell of the horses tethered on their picket line reached him. 'I am happy here. I want to fight with these men. And with you and Master Jacob. I have tried to prove myself to you but you don't give me a chance. That's why I went into the castle.'

Blackstone listened to the unemotional words. Simple facts. A desire to be with the men – easily understood. 'Henry, no one among these men doubts your courage. Time and again you have proved it to them. And to me. I could not be more proud of you and John holds you close to him. You know that. Much has passed between the three of us. It binds us.'

Henry waited. There was more. 'But?' he said.

'But you are not ready to fight in the line with the men.'

'You cannot know that.'

'We do. You are skilled. You are intelligent. You have contained your fear and known the closeness of a violent death, but that is not standing in a wet field with rain dribbling down your neck facing charging men on horseback who must carve you apart if they are to survive themselves. That brings fear of a totally different kind. Another year perhaps. But now... I want you to attend to your studies. You may find there is a better life to be had.'

'Then you wish to banish me to Avignon?'

'No, I want you to find the truth in yourself. And if it is to become more learned, to have the privilege of furthering your education so that your life is enriched and enables you to help others without a sword in your hand, then it is an offer you should consider.'

'Or stay here and serve as a page?'

'Yes.'

Blackstone saw the dark cloud of anger rise. The boy contained it. 'May I speak freely?'

Blackstone nodded.

'Are you keeping Lady Cateline at your side?'

The implication was obvious. Henry knew about them sharing a bed.

'No. She is to go to Avignon with her son. Father Torellini has an escort. He'll take them. If you go then you will use your mother's name, de Sainteny. There must be no association between us or your life is forfeit.'

Henry's voice dropped to barely a whisper. 'Let me fight. I beg you.'

'No.'

Blackstone's son nodded his understanding. He looked at the pot he still held in his hand. 'I'll go to Avignon, then.'

CHAPTER TWENTY-EIGHT

It was, as John Jacob predicted, a fight over an alehouse whore. Though not at first. An argument broke out when Will Longdon questioned the quality of the wine being served. In England an alehouse and tavern would have their cellar doors open so that the marks on the barrels could be inspected if someone made any complaint against the quality. The French owner thought it would be a personal insult to allow any inspection from a wine-soaked savage Englishman who, with other bastards, had seized his King and defeated his countrymen on the field at Poitiers years before. His wife wagged a finger and spat enough curses to flay a cat. A drunken Jack Halfpenny bent his back, raised his arm and showed how a bowman had slaughtered the French that day and others. It was the whore who really started it. She smashed the earthen cup across his head and the woman resting comfortably on Will Longdon's lap lunged and hit her because what she'd done might stop the Englishmen paying for their pleasures. The two women fought like alley cats. Blood flowed, hair was lost and screams and grunts filled the tallow-lit room. Men bet which woman would win. When the betting started to involve personal insults against the less attractive whore, the men who supported her took exception. Will Longdon hit a Gascon, Meulon felled two Hainaulters, and by the time the women lay exhausted on the ale-sluiced floor, the fight had spilled out onto the alley.

Killbere had dined at a tavern and was turning down the alley with a woman on his arm when he stepped into a mêlée of ten men being attacked by twice their number. He edged along a wall, keeping the woman close, and cursed at the aggressors. But when a Spaniard spat in his face and said something he did not understand, Killbere hit him. Only once, but the man tumbled into the dirt. Two attackers snatched away the woman on Killbere's arm, pressed her against the wall and lifted her skirts. Jack Halfpenny, seeing Killbere tussling with them, pulled one of them away. The man suddenly had a knife in his hand and slashed out at Halfpenny. The blade swept beneath his raised arm, sliced into his jupon and scored a mark across his ribs. Killbere wrenched the man aside, heard the sickening crack as his arm broke and then threw the whining assailant to the ground. Women screamed; men spat blood, grunted and – perhaps following that intangible instinct known to a fighting brotherhood – sought strength by forming a defensive line across the street. By some quirk of movement it was Killbere who headed the assault as more men spilled out from another alehouse, bargemen, merchants and slaughterhouse workers whose leather aprons were stained with animal blood. The odds against Blackstone's men had increased threefold. The slaughtermen gave no thought to the law, their only desire, fuelled by drink, was to kill Englishmen who took their women and had money to spare from their thieving ways. Tanners with their unmistakable stench produced wicked-looking curved blades used for scraping the flesh off hides. The packed alley surged; Meulon held a bench in front of him and pressed the first line of attackers back. They cursed and spat, sweeping their arms forward to slash him. Will Longdon and the others drew their archers' knives as Killbere jabbed his sword into men's thighs, disabling them without killing them. Strong arms that could hold a bull and slit its throat were rendered lame. Slaughtermen screamed as their tendons were severed. They fell squirming, those behind stumbling over them, blocked from pressing home the attack. Killbere bellowed an order.

'Forward!'

Years of discipline made every man take a stride forward. Forward, slash, and forward again. Knives deadly in their hands. They trampled over the fallen, heel-kicked gaping mouths, broke teeth and jaws. Necks snapped. The haze of drink lifted; now it was blood lust that gave them strength to press on relentlessly. Those who'd sought to punish Blackstone's men turned and ran. Killbere halted the assault. A dozen attackers lay sprawled in the bloodstained dirt; at least two of them were dead, their heads twisted at an awkward angle. Others attempted to raise themselves, hands clutching at wounds.

Further down the narrow streets torchlight shimmered against the walls.

'It's the night watch, lads,' said Killbere. He looked around at the men; his woman had gone, but one whore screamed at them from the alehouse door, cursing them for not paying. Killbere threw a handful of coins at her feet. She scrambled for them.

Will Longdon wiped his sleeve across his bloodied nose. 'I favoured that one, Sir Gilbert, but her friend took exception to Englishmen.'

'I might have known you'd started this.'

Longdon spat blood. 'Lucky for us you came along and finished it, Sir Gilbert.'

Shouts of alarm reached them. Their beaten adversaries had stumbled into the night watch. 'And I kept my bargain.

I paid your whore.' Without another word Killbere led the men away from the approaching watch. The twisting narrow streets swallowed them.

The guest quarters for visiting dignitaries stood close to the palace's great hall. Father Niccolò Torellini, the English King's emissary and representative of the Florentine banker Rodolfo Bardi, was one such honoured guest. Blackstone looked out of Torellini's tower window. Lights twinkled in the darkened alleys as torchbearers moved towards the dimly lit alehouses. The distant unseen clamour had reached this place of safety and comfort.

'Thomas?' said Torellini.

'It's nothing. A street fight somewhere.' In his heart he knew there was a likelihood that his men were involved. He turned back to where the Florentine priest sat at the table, the scraps of food pushed to one side on their platters. Torellini poured another glass of wine for them.

'You could leave Henry here. There are a dozen grammar schools. You have the money to pay for a good education and Sir William would offer him protection.'

'No. He either stays with me or hides in safety using his mother's name. He has a fine mind and I know he is torn. He will make a strong fighter one day but if his thirst for knowledge exceeds his desire to fight, then he will have a future that neither his mother nor I could have imagined.'

'Thomas, you cannot rip the tendrils from someone's heart. They go as deep as any oak tree's roots. He will defy you if the urge to fight is in him. How many times must he prove himself to you?'

'I cannot lose him, Father. I cannot. It would be too hard.'

'And from what you have told me he has already disobeyed you and placed himself in mortal danger. Don't forget, Thomas, when he was with me in Florence we thought it likely that it was the French who tried to kill him. And after you saved him at Brignais, you swore to hold him close.'

'He will not stay at the Bardi house in Avignon; he will rent a room like any other scholar. All I ask of you is that you secure him and the Jocard lad a good tutor in a school that will test him. Henry needs to be challenged. If no one knows who he is, then he is no different to any other boy given the privilege of a good education. If he does well, he can attend university in Prague or somewhere else.'

'Then you are not asking for a Knight of the Tau to be his shadow?'

'No. There is less risk if he stays anonymous.'

The priest spread his hands. 'So be it.'

The agreement was made. Blackstone bade farewell to the loyal emissary. Lighting a lantern he made his way down the spiral staircase where he saw Lady Cateline's woman servant curled in the doorway of a room three floors below Father Torellini's quarters. Most servants slept where they could, ready to be summoned at any time. Indentured since childhood, women like her knew no different life. She was frail from poor nourishment, a sparrow of a woman, and the threadbare blanket that covered her as she lay on the stone floor would barely keep a feral dog warm. He thought of the woman who slept behind the door. Imagined the heavy rise and fall of her breasts as she slept. The quilts and blankets pushed aside because of their warmth. He fought the urge to push open the door and take a blanket from her bed for the servant. Such an act of compassion would simply make her employer accuse the woman of theft. And besides, if he went into the room Cateline's scent would draw him ever closer until his lust forced aside any pretence of not desiring her.

He stepped over the servant. Legendary knight and humble servant: perhaps they were both slaves to the Lady Cateline.

PART THREE

THE RAVEN AND THE CROSS

CHAPTER TWENTY-NINE

The alehouse fight resulted in minor wounds, some of which the men attended to themselves, but there were a few who needed the physician's attention from the previous conflict against Babeneaux. The old man plied his skills happily; he would earn more in the few hours' work here than he would in a week attending to the burghers of Poitiers. Killbere made his way through the men towards Blackstone who stood talking to Henry.

'It's been agreed, Henry. I have spoken to Father Torellini. It would be a courtesy to visit him this morning and see what he requires of you.'

'He requires my obedience, Father.'

'Aye, well, that might cause a change in the weather should that ever happen. You don't need to fight me, Henry. I am not your enemy.'

'You don't trust me, though.'

'I would trust you with my life, as did your mother and sister.'

'I couldn't save them.'

Henry had misunderstood Blackstone's words. Taken them as a criticism. Four years before Henry had defended his mother and sister, had killed to save them, but a hidden assassin had defeated the best of men and slain them anyway. 'No one could have saved them. How many times must I tell you that their death is not on your shoulders? They are on mine. Another year and you will be of an age when you can fight. Now strengthen your heart and sharpen your mind. You carry my love with you and the memory of your beloved mother and sister. You are a man, Henry. Behave like one.'

Killbere slowed his pace, observing father and son. It was difficult for a boy desperate to live up to a legendary father. Killbere wished Blackstone would keep the lad close and between them bring on his fighting skills. Henry glanced his way, said something to his father and walked towards the city. Killbere timed his arrival so that the boy was out of earshot. 'He looks as though he's just been tasked with cleaning out a latrine with his bare hands.'

'He's going to Avignon. Now he must pay his respects to Father Torellini.'

Across the field where the horses were tethered, ostlers attended to the men's mounts. Grain and fodder had been delivered. Farriers had shod them. He looked to where the men were being treated. 'How many were hurt last night?'

'No more than those who attacked us.'

'For Christ's sake, Gilbert, I am already short of men and must scour the streets looking for archers and men-at-arms,' he said testily. The combination of a recalcitrant son and suppressed desire had shortened his temper.

Killbere had no wish to make it worse but the news he brought was going to create more anger. 'Several of the men are wounded. The physician knows what he's doing – I'll give him that. Better than the damned barber-surgeons. Some wounds from when we fought at Lord Mael's castle are festering. If the physician draws out the pus and treats them, they'll be ready to fight again in a few days.'

Blackstone eyed the veteran fighter. His report had been given too easily. 'And?'

Killbere shrugged and sighed. 'Jack Halfpenny is missing.'

'For God's sake. He was with the men, wasn't he?'

Killbere nodded. 'After the brawl we ran for home when the watchmen got close. Jack took a knife cut, but it wasn't a mortal wound. The alleys are narrow and as black as a cat's arse so he might have taken a wrong turn or stumbled on the cobbles. Will Longdon and a couple of the lads have gone back into the city to search for him. He might be lying in a doorway. The men drank enough to keep ordinary men pissed for a week.'

'We'll join the search. Take Beyard with you – he can speak to any Gascons. I'll take John Jacob and Renfred should we find Germans to question. Meulon stays in charge of the camp. I'll not lose Jack Halfpenny, Gilbert. Search every tavern and alehouse. Brothels as well. With luck, he is bedded with a whore.'

The city awoke slowly. Farmers brought in their daily supplies of fresh food and set up their stalls while the merchants laid out their wares in their shop fronts. Few people clogged the streets this early in the day but those who needed to be about their business moved aside as the tall, scar-faced knight and his companions forged their way through them. The twisting narrow streets led Blackstone and his companions around the ancient walls. The German captain and John Jacob went into every church they came across in case Halfpenny had crawled inside to sleep off the excesses of his drinking. The bells for the third hour of prayer rang out, bringing the faithful and the fearful into God's place of worship, keeping the streets empty enough for the three men to continue to make their way unhindered by crowds. Renfred led them to where the fight had taken place. Smears of dark blood had dried. The gutter in the middle of the street still held small pools of gore. The alehouse was closed but John Jacob beat his fist against the door until a window opened above. A sour-faced woman gazed down at them.

'There was a fight here last night,' John Jacob said. 'We're looking for any of the men involved.'

'You're no watchmen,' she said. 'Revenge, is it? Men died outside here and we don't want more trouble. You soldiers have caused enough. Now move your arse before I empty my piss pot over your heads.' She disappeared for a moment but then quickly reappeared and flung the contents of her bedpan down anyway. The three men danced back.

'Bitch takes the men's money, waters down the ale and wine and then complains that it's Englishmen paying her. Her husband is the one who provoked the fight,' said Renfred, 'and then the other alehouse over there emptied onto the street. The sooner we get back into open countryside the better, Sir Thomas. The French will never forgive us for winning the war.'

'Or for giving Aquitaine back to the Prince,' said John Jacob.

'I don't have time to go begging at every door,' said Blackstone. 'Stay here.' He took three long strides and kicked in the alehouse door. This time the woman's husband peered out of the window.

'You bastards will pay for that! I'll send for the provost and...'

His curse was cut short by the woman's scream as Blackstone yanked the alehouse owner out of sight. Cries for mercy echoed down the alley. John Jacob and Renfred looked left and right in case any concerned citizens dared venture out of their houses at the commotion. Blackstone quickly returned.

'The provost's watchmen took John. He's rotting in a cell.'

'If men died here last night, then they mean to make an example of him and hang him,' said John Jacob.

The disturbance in the corridor outside his office caused Sir William Felton to bellow for his chief clerk. The door swung open revealing Blackstone and a gaggle of robed clerks fussing at the intrusion. One of them stumbled over an apology but Felton waved him aside and told him to close the door.

'You do not behave in this manner, Sir Thomas. It is not acceptable.'

'I made an urgent plea to see you but some arsewipe downstairs insisted I make an appointment. You're holding one of my men.'

Felton's irritation was immediately soothed. Once again he held sway over Blackstone. 'The archer? Yes. He killed three men. The magistrate has already declared his guilt.'

'I want him back. He's my ventenar. My men were not blameless but even Sir Gilbert will testify that armed men from the slaughterhouse and tannery attacked them. It was self-defence.'

'Not according to witnesses.'

'Since when do you take a Frenchman's word over an Englishman's?'

'I am the seneschal, charged with governing, in the Prince's name, a ceded city of burghers, mayor, council, magistrate and court. A city where I must keep good order and appease those who have been wronged – those who, if denied, would rise up on the streets. More than that, I govern beyond the city. Aquitaine is the jewel that must be held in trust for the Prince's crown.'

'I'll pay reparation.'

'No, Blackstone, they want to see an Englishman hang. I have signed the warrant given by the provost and magistrate who found him guilty.'

'It's barely past terce. The bells are still echoing around the damned streets. No court will have convened yet.'

Felton lifted a document from the desk. 'The provost brought him in after curfew. They roused the magistrate from his bed. And then I had to confirm the sentence. You bring trouble to my door. I want you and your scum gone from my city. Imagine the ill feeling that will greet the Prince when he arrives if I do not carry out the sentence. Innocent or not, I will sacrifice him for the sake of peace.'

Blackstone lunged forward, slamming his fist onto the desk. Felton involuntarily stepped back, despite the broad-planked top forming a barrier between the two men. 'I have my own damned piece of paper and it's signed by a higher authority than you.' He tossed the King's letter in front of Felton. Felton looked down at the seal and carefully unfolded the parchment. His eyes scanned the King's command that Blackstone be given whatever he needed. After a moment he refolded the letter and tossed it back.

'It does not usurp criminal justice. You cannot have him. He'll hang from the old city walls tomorrow in the marketplace.'

The pulse in Blackstone's neck throbbed. The table might have been made of solid chestnut and take four men to lift it but in that moment he had the strength to hurl it through the window. Instead, he calmed his breathing. 'Let me see him. You cannot deny me that.'

'I can,' said Felton and then, after a deliberate pause: 'But I will not.'

*

Blackstone met up with Killbere and Will Longdon and they made their way to the castle. Their accompanying guard gave the jailer permission to allow the two knights inside. The squashed-face jailer nodded his understanding. Perhaps he was mute, Blackstone thought, because his grunted acknowledgement did not resemble speech. Lifting a lantern, he led the way along a stone-walled corridor and then down a spiral stairwell, the turns so tight there was no chance of a fighting man wielding a sword. The lower they descended the heavier the smell of damp. Water trickled down the walls. A dirt-floor corridor led to a cage. The jailer lit a second lantern and handed it without a word to Blackstone, then turned and made his way back the way he had come. Blackstone raised the flame and saw the crumpled figure lying on the cold floor.

'Jack?' he called.

Halfpenny stirred at the sound of his name. Turning to face the light, he raised a hand. 'Sir Thomas? Is that you?' he said, his dry throat croaking.

'There's no water here,' said Killbere. 'The bastards mean him to suffer.'

Halfpenny crawled to the cage bars. His face was swollen from a beating and a dried line of encrusted blood scored his jupon. 'I fell in the alley, Sir Thomas. The night watch found me. They say I killed three men – I swear to you I did not. We fought a mob determined to see us die. We acquitted ourselves well, did we not, Sir Gilbert?'

'That we did, lad.'

'Jack, they're going to hang you in the morning,' said Blackstone.

Halfpenny's head dropped to his chest for a moment, absorbing Blackstone's words. Then he raised his face and pressed close to the cage. 'Can you do anything to save me?'

he asked quietly. 'I'd rather die with my father's bow in my hand than at the end of a Frenchy's rope.'

'I will do everything I can to save you, but if I fail, you must make your peace and be ready.'

Jack Halfpenny smiled bravely. 'Then my life is in your hands, Sir Thomas, and if you ask me to give it, I will do so gladly.'

Blackstone and Killbere trudged back up the dark steps to the prison entrance, glad to be free of the fetid conditions in the cells. A few deniers pressed into the jailer's hand ensured Halfpenny would receive food and water, and if the financial inducement wasn't enough, the threat given with it ensured Blackstone would be obeyed.

'We should speak to the Italian,' said Killbere. 'He has influence.'

Blackstone shook his head. 'We cannot. Sir William's reasoning is correct. The city needs to see what they believe to be justice done. There's too much at stake for the Prince. Once a city's blood-lust is aroused it has to be quenched.'

'We can't let Jack hang, Thomas. Merciful Christ, our own men will tear this city apart.'

'And you and I would lead them. I know, old friend, it's a sacrifice too far. But we have to give Felton what he demands.'

Killbere grabbed his arm. 'You're going to let them hang him?'

'I'm going to do what needs to be done.'

CHAPTER THIRTY

Blackstone made his way through the narrow streets. The deeper he went into the heart of the old city the narrower the alleyways became. He knew exactly what he was looking for. The gloom-laden passages yielded little but the noise and stench of people living in cramped conditions. He heard the screams before he saw the sign declaring the occupant's profession. Pushing through the door, he saw a man being restrained in a chair by a barber-surgeon's two assistants, who were pushing broken bones back into place in his patient's arm. They glanced up from their labours as the man passed out from the pain; the barber-surgeon quickly bound the arm tightly with a wet bandage and wound a strip of leather thong over it to keep bone and bandage in place. He turned to Blackstone.

'My lord,' he said, knowing the man who stood before him must be a man of some authority. 'How can I help you?'

'You serve the people in the poorest part of the city.'

'I do, as you can see from this wretch. He was injured by masonry falling from a poorly built wall.'

The two assistants were slapping the man's face to rouse him. As he came around, they lifted him to his feet and took him back onto the street.

'Who among the people you know have lost all hope?'

'Of life or the chance to rise above their destitution?'

'Either.'

'Begging is forbidden, so look down any alley rank with the stench of piss and you'll find them. They come to the city hoping to find work. They would be better staying in the countryside where at least they can grow their own food. Here, without work, they starve. Then they get ill when disease sweeps through their hovels. The children die first and then the men and women.'

'I'm looking for paupers I can help. A woman close to the edge of despair whose children are starving, whose husband lies rotting away with some disease.'

'There are many such people, my lord.'

Blackstone fingered a florin from his purse and presented it to the barber-surgeon. 'Then take me to them.'

The fifth hovel Blackstone visited yielded what he searched for. The stench of the place caught in his throat. The man inside was racked with disease; he coughed blood continuously. The woman held an infant to a withered breast as three others with little more than a year separating them clung to her skirts. Did such outcasts ever dream of salvation? Blackstone wondered. Such conditions condemned them and their children to poverty for the rest of their miserable lives. The hollow-eyed man listened carefully to what Blackstone told him. Then he gathered what possessions they owned – nothing more than a cooking pot and a few threadbare blankets – and followed Blackstone and the barber-surgeon back through the twisting passageways to a boarding house known to the barber. The owner agreed to offer the paupers a room to sleep in and a place to cook. Money changed hands along with the dire threat that if anything happened to the destitute family then Blackstone would return and kill everyone under the boarding-house roof before setting it ablaze so that the whole street burned down. Blackstone took the woman across the yard and settled her children onto the one narrow bed. Her husband stood in the doorway like a beaten dog, head down. Raising his eyes to her, he nodded in farewell and then followed Blackstone back to the city. No tears were shed. They had none left. The woman pressed the infant closer to her, tightly clutching the purse Blackstone had given her.

'You cannot do this,' said Sir William Felton.

'It's done. Paid for and agreed in full. The man is near death. He will take Jack Halfpenny's place dressed in his jupon.'

'You would hang an innocent man to save an archer?'

'I would hang you to save an archer,' Blackstone told him with no hint of humour. 'I gave his family money and a place to live. His children will survive now. He is of no use to them. He knows that. His death gives them life and gives me back a valued bowman.'

Felton's mouth tugged down – in displeasure or disgust, Blackstone couldn't tell. And he didn't care.

'And you get to keep the peace,' he added. 'I'll take him down to the cells and make the exchange.' He paused, granting Felton a moment of ill-deserved respect to pamper his vanity. 'With your permission, Sir William.'

Felton's silence was all the permission Blackstone needed. Once outside he led the man across to the jailer, who was paid more ale money.

'Sir Thomas,' said Jack Halfpenny. 'Are you here to help me?'

'Give this man your jupon, and your belt. Dress him. His hands tremble too much.' Blackstone turned to the jailer. 'The seneschal will send the provost for this man tomorrow morning. See he is fed and given wine. As much as he can eat and drink. There is no need for him to be sober when the sun rises.'

The jailer nodded, knowing where his good fortune lay.

Halfpenny finished tightening his belt around the man and placed a hand on the man's shoulder. 'God be with you.' He faced Blackstone. 'And with you, Sir Thomas, for saving me.'

CHAPTER THIRTY-ONE

Blackstone led his men out of Poitiers the next morning. Torellini and his escort with Lady Cateline and her children were placed in the middle of the column. As they followed the road along the river they heard the roar of the crowd as the unfortunate was hanged. A few of the men turned in the saddle. Blackstone did not look back.

'Poor bastard,' said John Jacob and crossed himself.

'Money well spent,' said Killbere.

'We are still too few,' said Meulon. 'There were few men of quality in Poitiers to replace those we lost, Sir Thomas.'

'We would not want Felton's cast-offs,' Killbere told him. 'Our problems begin when we part company with the Italian's escort. They're the kind of men we need to go with us to smooth the Count of Foix's peacock feathers.'

'You think we should ride with them as far as Avignon?' said Renfred. 'They travel through English-held territory. Safe enough for a few days until we find reinforcements.'

'Several days of arse-aching misery to the Count of Foix is enough, ten or more to Avignon could bring a man to embrace the Church,' said Killbere. 'Thomas?'

Blackstone turned in the saddle and looked at the column snaking behind him. The rising towers of Poitiers were already shrouded in low cloud. 'We need to strike out and pick up the pace. Today we follow the river; tomorrow we turn east. There's a monastery where we can stay for another night and then Father Torellini and those with him will find sanctuary in towns held by the English and any other religious house that lies on their route. Renfred, you and Meulon scout far enough forward for us to make camp tonight. Take three men apiece. There are Teutonic Knights searching for us.'

The news brought a look of surprise. 'They're a long way from home,' said Renfred. 'Are they seeking trouble?'

'Perhaps,' said Blackstone.

'Miserable bastards, they are,' said Will Longdon, who was riding further back. 'Half-shaved heads and a dislike for whoring. They think they're some kind of holy warrior. You don't want them as an enemy is all I know.'

'All you know is what it costs for a whore and how to pull a bow,' said Meulon.

'And you men-at-arms should seek a priest every day and offer prayers that our aim is true and our bow arms stay strong. And everyone knows whores prefer us archers. It's not only our bows that have the length.'

Meulon snorted and spat. 'I hear your quick shooting is what pleases them.'

'If I want to hear bickering I'll ride with the Lady Cateline,' said Killbere. 'Get about your business, Meulon, and leave Will to scratch his balls.'

Meulon and Renfred veered away, rode down the column and called out the men to join them.

'Trouble is, Thomas,' said Killbere, 'Teutonic Knights swoop like falcons, talons bared. They could strike in our centre, ride through, and be gone until the next ambush. Once we get across open country, we should put outriders on our flanks.'

'No need, Gilbert. They won't strike at us.'

'Oh, and what prophets have you been listening to? Does Torellini have God's ear?'

'No. I intend to find them before they find us.'

They made good progress along a well-travelled road. Late in the day Blackstone changed direction, leading them across rolling meadows offering sweet grass for their horses and chestnut forests which gave shelter for the night. If anyone wishing them harm saw their fires they would have to travel across the open ground. Not even belligerent Teutonic Knights would attempt an attack across such terrain in darkness. But Blackstone never trusted the obvious and had outposts sited so that any ghostly attempt to get close would be seen before someone inflicted violence.

'Father?' said Henry as he crept closer to where Blackstone lay next to his campfire, careful not to approach too close in case his father was asleep. A rude awakening could mean a lunge with a knife before identifying his son.

'I'm awake,' said Blackstone.

Killbere snorted and turned in his sleep.

Henry trod carefully around the sleeping veteran. 'I heard Renfred say that there might be German knights on the road ahead.'

'What of it?'

'Jocard told me that days before Lady Cateline tried to escape from the castle there were men he had never seen before at the gates. He says they spoke with a heavy accent and wore blazons of a black cross. They rode sturdy coursers and looked as though they had travelled a long way.'

Blackstone knew that if they were the same men who had questioned Father Torellini at Chartres, then it was possible that priests or monks further west towards the monastery that had once given Babeneaux's daughter sanctuary had directed them. From there it would not be difficult for them to seek the man renowned for giving sanctuary to pilgrims. And it seemed possible that by design or good fortune they were following Blackstone's route or had bypassed Poitiers and were ahead.

'That's valuable information, Henry. Thank you.'

The firelight's shadows caught the boy's face. Blackstone saw his uncertainty.

'Will says they are terrible men. Fearsome fighters,' Henry said. 'And that they are hunting you.'

'Will Longdon is gossiping like a washerwoman. Don't listen to him. And he's only half right. Most of the Teutonic Knights are noblemen. They take the monastic vows and another to devote themselves to serving the sick. Courage, prowess and honour guide them. They wear no gold or jewels, own nothing of value except their armour and their horses, but they are indeed fearsome fighters. They're known for their pride and their tyranny. They can be as cruel as any routier. They have tortured and massacred prisoners, even destroyed churches. No great order of chivalry ever survives untouched by human weakness.' He smiled at his son, who sat as attentive as any student. 'Some things such as this they don't teach at school. And Jocard's observation was accurate. Teutonic Knights wear white surcoats that bear a black cross.'

'Then it sounds as though they might be close,' said Henry.

'We'll see. You've heard what Father Torellini has said about Avignon? That you will have no shadow from the Tau knights as you did when you travelled from Florence last time?'

Henry nodded.

'And Jocard?'

Henry shrugged.

'He is a danger to you. He knows your true identity.'

'He's sworn to secrecy. I saved his life, and you saved his mother and sister. He's a brave boy, Father, and he knows the importance of keeping my name secret. And besides, he will not be in the same school or lodging. Avignon is a big place. I doubt we will even see each other that often.' He studied his father for a moment. 'But you must have considered the risk before sending me there.'

'You cannot live a full life without risk, Henry. I considered it. I wanted to find out if you had.'

They fell silent. Henry got to his feet. 'Goodnight, Father.'

'Goodnight, my son. You have my blessings.'

'Thank you, Father.'

As the boy turned Blackstone could not resist asking the question that itched like an old battle scar. 'The boy's mother. Lady Cateline is well? She is not fearful of the journey?'

Henry faced his father. 'She has expressed no misgivings. I think Father Torellini's escort has given her confidence.' He hesitated. 'But she is not as brave or as strong as Mother,' he said, unable to stop himself.

'No one could ever replace her or her courage,' said Blackstone.

Blackstone's gentle reply brought a brief smile of gratitude from his son. Henry made his way back through the sleeping men.

Killbere turned in his blanket, pushing his back towards the flames. 'Yet still the widow squeezes your heart and stirs your cock,' he said, without opening his eyes.

The following day's journey was uneventful. Blackstone used the pretence of going back in the column to speak to

Father Torellini. The priest did not know the monastery that Blackstone had chosen for the night's stay.

'I used to raid this far south,' Blackstone assured him. 'One year we beat off a band of routiers who threatened the monks. They'll give us sanctuary and food.'

'Is there anywhere in France that you don't know?'

'There are many places I haven't visited,' said Blackstone.

'And few you have not fought at,' Torellini answered. 'Depending where we travel there will be people who embrace you or fear you. I would be frightened for my life if any of those who harbour resentment discovered I was the priest who cradled you at Crécy. I wonder if our good Lord gave me a blessing or a burden that day.'

'Only you can decide that,' said Blackstone.

'I'm teasing you, Thomas. To ride in the shadow of a legend gives more warmth than basking in the Tuscan sun. I wish you were riding with us as far as Avignon but I know you are on the King's business.'

'You'll be safe enough. The English hold the road and towns and the routiers are scavenging further east. And your escort are the kind of men I wish I could recruit.'

'Once they deliver us to the new Pope, they are still the King's men and would obey any order given from you. You're Edward's Master of War. Speak to them. You have my blessing.' He smiled and laid a hand on Blackstone's arm. 'As always.'

Blackstone reined in the bastard horse and let the column move past him. When Cateline drew level, cradling her daughter, Blackstone eased the belligerent beast next to her. 'You are managing the child, my lady?'

'You care?' she answered, keeping her eyes on the way ahead.

'Your welfare is my responsibility until I leave.'

Cateline eased the sleeping girl into a more comfortable position. 'You needn't concern yourself. You made your opinion of me very clear.'

'I spoke harshly and I apologize.'

'Is there anything else you wish to say, Sir Thomas? I don't want to wake Jehanne.'

Blackstone accepted her dismissal and heeled the horse forward to retake his place at the head of the column alongside Killbere.

'Everything all right back there?' Killbere taunted gently. 'Our Italian not complaining? The weather not too hot or cold?'

'I was discussing the men who ride with him.'

'And the husband-huntress? She is in good humour, is she?'

'Mind your own business.'

'Ah. Well, Thomas, when a woman uses her wiles to draw you back to her and then beats you over the head with a mace to show she controls you, then it is something a man should recognize and turn his back on.'

'Gilbert, you talk like a court fool. She has not used her wiles on me. I went to see that she and her child were all right.'

Killbere gave him a disbelieving look.

'After I spoke to Father Torellini,' Blackstone added quickly.

'Thomas, I trust your instincts in battle but when it comes to women, you are as helpless as a sack full of blind kittens being thrown down a well. Of course she wants you. God's blood, man, she tells her son about the visitors at the castle; he tells Henry; Henry comes creeping through the night to tell you. She meant for you to go to her last night. To go and question her. To find out what she saw. What she knows. It was a message, you dullard, to draw you into her bed. Why do you think her tent was some distance from the men?' He sighed. 'A pity your wits are not as sharp as your sword when it comes to women. She has thrown grappling irons to scale the walls of your resistance. Good riddance to her, Thomas. Know the game she plays. If she breaks through your defences, you are lost.'

CHAPTER THIRTY-TWO

Wolfram von Plauen led his men across the unfamiliar countryside. Certainty had been his lifelong companion but this foreign land tested him. He was not used to self-doubt; it had never entered his thoughts when fighting in the crusade against marauding Samogitians in Prussia. They were a pagan enemy like the Lithuanians and the brethren had brought both to God by killing them. Like cauterizing a wound on the body, dying beneath a Teutonic Knight's sword seared the infection in a heathen's soul, releasing it in the final moments of agony to the care of the Almighty.

Von Plauen and his companions had tracked down some routiers who had fled from the eastern border and were now raiding along the Loire and into Brittany. These men had served with Gruffydd ap Madoc and knew of Thomas Blackstone but none had admitted that the Englishman had been on the eastern border with the Welshman and the Count de Vaudémont. Von Plauen and his brethren had killed nine routiers so far and given alms to the peasants who had suffered from their depredations, but the mercenary scourge had now outrun them, leaving the Germans to find only burnt-out villages and massacred civilians. He and the knights with him slept in Dominican abbeys yet no information was forthcoming from the monks either, despite the Teutonic hospitallers' close association with the religious order. Von Plauen knew that was because the monks often paid *patis* to the routiers for protection – they could not deny hospitality but they could remain silent.

Horse tracks went this way and that across the meadows. They had been following fresh signs but now those tracks had separated into two groups. How was he ever to find the Englishman and his raiding companion ap Madoc? In truth, he told himself, they were lost.

'Brother Wolfram,' Rudolf von Burchard called, urging his horse forward. 'We have passed this place before. Without stars or sun in a clear sky to guide us we are making poor progress.' The broad-shouldered knight wiped the sweat from his eyes. He was not laying blame. 'I saw signs of woodcutters at that forest we passed. One of them might be willing to guide us towards those who came this way. It's worth a few livres, surely? Criss-crossing the land like this, hoping to find the Englishman is taking too long.'

Von Plauen nodded. 'If Blackstone is ahead of us, then we must discover his route. We are close to him – I feel it.' He tightened the reins in his hands and tugged his spare horse with him. 'As the Frenchman said in Paris: we find Blackstone, we find the murdering ap Madoc. And from what we have since learnt about this Englishman there will be honour in killing him also.' He gestured one of the two half-brethren forward. The man's grey mantle beneath the black cross denoted his status as a sergeant-at-arms. 'Hartmann, ride into the forest. Find a guide among the woodcutters. Bring him to me with the promise of payment. We will wait here.'

The half-brother wheeled his horse.

'Have Brother Gunther bring up the horses. Secure them until Hartmann returns. We'll rest and pray here. We must stay on our guard, Rudolf. We are few and the enemy are many.'

Von Burchard smiled. 'And when has that ever been different?'

*

Guiscard the Lame seldom left the woodcutters' village. His leg was crooked – had been ever since the day he had helped his father rope some felled timber onto his cart twenty-six years before. The holding knot had slipped, tumbling the heavy oak logs onto the boy's leg. The limb eventually healed, but remained bent in a misshapen bow that caused him no trouble as he cut timber for charcoal burning, following his father's trade. The local lord's domain spread far and wide but Guiscard's world extended no further than the forests and the town a day's journey away. He paid half a mark for the licence to cut the woodland and produce his charcoal. Twice a year he took the results of his labours to the town to be sent north to the furnaces for forging weapons, and the lord's reeve paid him. For years, ever since the war against the English, men had skirted the forest. Few ventured into its gloomy depths – fear of woodland spirits and wolves kept them out. Guiscard and his neighbours knew how to deal with those ravening beasts by setting traps and skinning the victims. Wolfskins hung from poles was the time-honoured way of keeping the wolves at bay: the villagers believed it warned the packs of man's superiority – a short-lived comfort in their harsh existence. They barely had enough food to feed themselves; they trapped birds and grew meagre ground crops. But the dark of the forest that protected them from outsiders inflicted its own cruelty. Children died of disease. The damp, sodden ground rotted crops. There was no food for those who could not work and the elderly among them struggled when no longer able to cut, heft and split the logs. They existed by stripping the inner bark from lime trees for rope making, and when too infirm even to manage that, they were sent into the forest to await death from wild beasts.

What frightened the villagers most was armed men, even though routiers who rode past the forest hamlet of twenty-seven souls usually caused no trouble. The villeins had nothing to steal, and their women, dirt-caked from grubbing root vegetables and stinking from charcoal burning, were not worth raping.

Guiscard had not yet lit his kiln. The rider appeared in the clearing as he was laying the cut seasoned logs into a circle, building it with an expertise born of a lifetime's practice. The stranger was not one of the men Guiscard and his friends had seen riding past their forest two days before and who were now camped a few miles away. Those men looked like brigands; this rider looked as though he might be a man of importance. The black cross on his grey mantle denoted authority. A priest? Guiscard's crippled leg would not allow him to go down on his knee. He bowed as deeply as he could.

'My lord?'

Hartmann looked around the clearing. The kiln's sod roof retained the acrid smell of burnt wood from previous fires. There was no one else in sight. Caution made him circle his horse around the bent man. A lone man-at-arms in a dark forest could be brought down from his horse and slaughtered by a pack of villeins for the value of his weapons and horse. Satisfied that there were only the two of them in the clearing, he halted his horse before the subservient peasant.

'Stand up.'

Guiscard raised his head but kept his eyes averted from the horseman's face. To gaze directly at a man of such importance could provoke a beating. If he was a priest why was he travelling alone? And no monk or priest Guiscard had ever seen bore arms. He tried to clear his muddled thoughts. A knight then.

'My companions await my safe return. If there are any in your hovels who would seek to cause me harm, you would fall under my comrades' blades. Understood?'

Guiscard nodded. Arrogant bastard. But he accepted it. Why would anyone show a villein respect? 'We are but few, my lord. We work the forest. Trap, hunt. Burn wood for—'

'Quiet. Your life is of no importance,' Hartmann interrupted. 'We are seeking Englishmen. Men who might have passed this way. Who has come through the forest?'

'None, lord.'

'There are tracks around its edge.'

'Aye, lord, but they did not come through, they went around.'

'And they are close?'

Guiscard shrugged. He dragged a sleeve across his dribbling nose. Information was always worth something.

Hartmann was under orders to bring a guide to his companions so there was no point in berating the woodcutter. He spilled out a few deniers from his purse and threw them at the man's feet. As Guiscard scrabbled in the dirt, Hartmann tugged his reins. 'My comrades are waiting. You can walk unaided?' he said, pointing to the bowed leg.

Guiscard's grin revealed gums stubbed with blackened teeth. 'Lord, for money I can run.'

CHAPTER THIRTY-THREE

The monastery nestled close to a broad river. Forests surrounded the warm-coloured stone buildings and the thickets and hedgerows had grown since Blackstone had instructed the monks to let nature act as a deterrent to brigands. The winding road allowed no more than two men abreast to approach. As Blackstone led the column towards the monastery gates, he glanced at the graveyard.

'More in the ground than the last time I was here,' he said.

'Pestilence?' said Killbere. 'Should we find out if the place is safe? It carries on the wind, Thomas. And they say even birds can carry it and those crows in the treetops look like harbingers of death.'

'Gilbert, the birds don't carry it. If they did, why don't we see them dead on the ground?'

'There are some things you can't be too careful about. For all we know crows have a special place to go and die.'

'The graves are old like the monks. Men die, Gilbert. Their hearts stop and they die. It is nature's way.'

'Then you knock on their door. And let us pray it is not a Friday because I need meat in my belly tonight and a straw mattress to lie on. I'm no monk to be offered fish soup and a plank bed and one of the droning brethren reciting a lesson while I eat. That's enough to make any man's heart stop. What these monks need for a long life, Thomas, is more meat and wine and a nun in a feather bed to share their nights. It's the damned hardship that kills them.'

'I'll see if there's more than pottage and stale rye bread on offer and I'll try and get you a bed of your own so you don't have to share with any visiting leper.'

The Rule of St Benedict exhorted that all travellers be offered lodging and food. Father Torellini was the more honoured guest among them and would be housed with the abbot. They would give Lady Cateline and her children rooms in the modest guesthouse reserved for travellers.

'You will stay inside the walls?' Torellini asked Blackstone as the gatekeeper escorted them to the abbot. John Jacob followed them with Lady Cateline and her children.

'Sir Gilbert has ambitions for a meal and a bed. I'll stay with the men in the outer courtyard and stables.'

'Thomas, the abbot will invite any knight and those of the nobility to eat with him. They would see it as a mark of disrespect to ignore such an invitation.'

'Father, I saved this monastery. The abbot would never consider my actions disrespectful.'

They reached the abbot's door. Monks, heads bowed, hands clasped beneath their habit's sleeves, shuffled past them as the bell for vespers sounded. Torellini gestured towards the silent monks. 'You should join us for prayer. It eases us from the troubles of the day into the calm of evening. How long has it been since you knelt in humility before the cross and asked God to ease your heart's burden?'

Blackstone smiled and lifted the Silver Wheel Goddess Arianrhod on the chain around his neck.

'An archer's talisman does not hear your anguish, Thomas, nor offer the balm our souls need in this harsh world.'

'I find her good enough company for me, Father.'

Torellini pointed his finger at the talisman's chain. 'And yet you still wear the crucifix that belonged to your wife. You're only half pagan, Thomas.'

Blackstone pressed Torellini's satchel into the arms of the waiting monk who served the abbot's lodging. 'Then you can pray for that half of me, Father.'

He turned back towards the gate that led to the stables and outer courtyard. John Jacob had delivered Lady Cateline and her children to the guesthouse and stood waiting for him.

'Is she settled?' he asked his squire.

John Jacob nodded. 'Her boy asked where Henry was sleeping. His mother said he could stay with him if he wanted.'

'The lad serves a purpose more than being my son's friend, John,' Blackstone said.

For a moment his squire did not understand, but then Blackstone's smile gave him the explanation.

'Well, Sir Thomas, she's an attractive woman and if she yearns for you and wants to know your plans then sending her boy to be close is a good enough ploy.'

'I am already too involved. We have trouble waiting for us on the road ahead, John. She will not distract me.'

They reached the stables. It could accommodate only a dozen horses; the others were hobbled and tethered in the yard where the men would sleep. Blackstone and John Jacob stepped into the humid warmth of the stalls. Torellini's mount and those of his escort had priority but the bastard horse needed its own stall away from the others. Henry had cleared a corner storage area and tethered a leading rein from its bridle to an iron ring in the wall and was turning straw for the horse's bedding. As Blackstone cautiously approached, the brute lashed out with an iron-shod hind hoof that would cripple a man if it struck.

'God's tears, Sir Thomas, I don't know how the lad manages to be in the same stall,' said John Jacob.

'My horse permits it for some reason. If it was me, it would take a piece of flesh with those damned yellow teeth.'

He skirted the rear of the stall. 'Henry, make sure you put a restraining pole across the back of the stall. I don't want an innocent monk being sent to the infirmary or to heaven.'

'Aye, my lord. I had planned to do just that,' Henry answered, without stopping.

John Jacob lowered his voice. 'He knows his duty, Sir Thomas. He thinks it through.'

'I know. John, find us a place to sleep. The men will have to feed themselves. If I am to avoid the abbot's table Sir Gilbert and I will be obliged to eat in the refectory. And acquaint yourself with William Ashford, the sergeant in charge of Father Torellini's escort. Not that many years ago I came across you in a monastery like this when you were escorting our Italian friend to Avignon.'

John Jacob looked grim at Blackstone's reminder. 'The days of the Savage Priest and a time that still weighs heavily on me.'

'No, John, what happened to Christiana was fate. It could not be avoided. But now history puts another in charge of taking Father Torellini and a woman and her two children to Avignon. Does it not strike you that the stars are aligning in the same manner?'

'You're concerned about the woman?'

Blackstone hesitated. Was ill fortune tempting that bitch Fate? 'I don't know, John. Do events mirror themselves so closely? I pray not.'

'Perhaps we should bend the knee in the church and ask for their safe delivery.'

Blackstone placed a hand on his squire's shoulder. 'You have served me well since those days and if William Ashford and his men are like you then I would welcome them to ride with us. We need to know the character of the man and those under his command.'

'A friendly conversation, then, with a man whose duty I once undertook.'

'Yes.'

John Jacob turned back into the courtyard as Blackstone watched his son rub down the bastard horse with handfuls of dry straw. It snorted, dipped its head and swung it towards the boy at his shoulder. Instead of snapping at him it snickered, a sound that might be thought of as contentment.

'I know, I know,' Henry whispered gently, absorbed in his care for the war horse.

The boy's impending absence already tugged at Blackstone's heart.

As did the thought Cateline Babeneaux might face the same terror as Christiana on her journey to Avignon.

CHAPTER THIRTY-FOUR

The gentle rain settled like a fine mist over man and horse. The men had pressed themselves close to the monastery's wall seeking protection from the elements like any soldier used to sleeping rough. By morning their blankets would be wet and their beards speckled with dew-like droplets. Horses stood, heads bowed, eyes closed, half asleep, hobbled close together in the courtyard. One shifted its weight, its hoof catching a stone, the muted crack of iron against rock barely audible but enough to wake Blackstone. Senses alerted, he half raised himself, hand already on his knife hilt. Despite the yard being in darkness there was enough night light to see the sleeping figures next to him. Gossamer shrouds cobwebbed Killbere's beard. Blackstone freed himself from his blanket. Something more than the horseshoe strike had woken him: a sound that had intruded into his unconsciousness.

'What?' whispered Killbere, opening one eye, staying hunched in his blanket.

'Nothing.' Blackstone picked up his belt and scabbard and stepped away from the sleeping men through the tethered horses. Crossing the yard to the stables he peered into the gloom. The outlines of the horses loomed in the darkness. Beyond the stables the gatekeeper's room showed no light. The gates were firmly closed. No sound of intruders reached him. The horses would have whinnied if they had caught the scent of men they were unused to. Raising his face to the soft rain he dragged a hand through his hair. The bell for compline had long since rung – the last prayer of the day where men could examine their consciences and offer their actions of the day to God – which meant monks would not be roused from sleep until the call to night prayer at matins. Blackstone walked towards the cloisters. The abbot's quarters were unlit, like the rest of the monastery. So that faint, almost imperceptible sound had not come from there. It was probably nothing, he decided. Most likely a monk making his way to the latrines. He walked across the inner courtyard, past the herb garden and the subtle aroma of marjoram and thyme. His mind searched for the image created by the sound he had heard. He gazed at the church door. The heavy latch. It could have been the sound of metal meeting metal as the iron lever was carefully laid to rest. As he stepped to one side, he saw the faintest change in the door frame. A sliver of light, only a hair's thickness, momentarily caught the gap between frame and door. At this time of night any monk wishing to pray would be on his knees on the cold stone floor next to his cot. No need to stumble through rain and darkness when they could wait until matins sounded and lanterns were lit.

He went to the door, gauged the lever's weight in his hand and raised it slowly. The monks had greased the hinges so that those already praying would not be disturbed by a late arrival and a creaking door. He stepped inside and saw the dim light beyond the pillars towards the altar. There was a movement. A shadow from a candle's flame. The open space was cold. Congregations prayed standing; the chapel did not afford even the infirm the luxury of a bench. Going onto your knees was the most relief a supplicant could hope for. Blackstone angled himself across the floor and at the transept saw the huddled figure in a cape, back pressed against the pillar, a half-burnt candle set in its spilt wax at her side. Lady Cateline's hood obscured her face; her head was bent, her shoulders rocking gently from silent tears. Her hands were clasped in prayer, pressed against her lips. Blackstone's chest tightened. A wave of pity washed through him. He stopped himself from instinctively reaching for her. It was too late to retract all he had said. Too late to reverse his decision to deny his desire for her. This was no time for regret. As silently as he had approached he turned on his heel and stepped away. He had taken four strides when her voice whispered across the cold stone floor.

'Don't go.'

He stopped and faced her. She had turned her head and looked around the column, the hood slipping free from her face.

'Please.'

When the bell for night prayer rang the monks who shuffled in to pray saw only the puddle of melted wax next to the column. Long before they had arrived Blackstone had lifted Cateline from the stone floor and carried her along the darkened cloisters to her room. The modest quarters housed her daughter in a bed encased in a cubbyhole. The second mattress belonging to her son was empty. To one side there was a prayer niche for those who wished to kneel and ask forgiveness for any transgressions. Neither Blackstone nor Cateline had any such regret. She had quickly closed the curtain separating the sleeping chambers. With silent urgency they stripped each other. Blackstone lifted her onto the mattress. He never felt the hot wax that spluttered from the bedside candle onto his shoulder. Her fingers curled into the hair on the nape of his neck urging him closer, her legs wrapping around him, demanding him. His weight smothered her, adding to her passion. By the time the ghostly shuffling of monks returning from prayer passed the window they lay embraced, spent from their lust. Unrepentant in the holy place.

Fear had driven her to the altar. Night terrors had loomed out of the darkness in the monastery's eerie silence to claw at her. She had begged for the Almighty's help. Prostrated herself. But the merciful Lord had turned His back on her. He had remained silent. Her transgressions – her lust – had cut the wick that had once burned bright with belief.

The statue of the Lady Mary, Mother of the Church, cradling her infant had gazed pitifully down at her. Mary, Mother of God. She knew the torment. She of all people understood what it meant to have a child's life endangered. Yet there was still nothing, no blessed understanding, no solace for Cateline's heart. The burden of protecting her daughter and of ensuring her son lived long enough to claim his inheritance almost overwhelmed her. Now she had declared for the English King in the Breton civil war her reputation was tainted; her betrayal of the Bretons would not be forgotten and there would be those who sought revenge. If they killed her and her children her domain would become a battleground. She should have inherited Babeneaux's castle and lands but she had forfeited that right when she broke for freedom with her lover.

Now there was another man in her bed. And despite his desire for her she knew he distrusted her. But if she did not yield to desire how else could she secure a man's strength to protect her and her children? Blackstone stirred beside her as she gazed unsleeping into the darkness. A glimmer of light from the dying candle caught the hilt of Blackstone's sword propped against the wall. The pommel bore two half-coins pressed together. Although she didn't know what it meant, instinct told her it had something to do with his dead wife. How could she bring this man's heart to her own? Her son had formed a genuine bond with Henry Blackstone, but that was not enough to bind Blackstone to her. And desire could be as fleeting as clouds passing across the moon. Her mind twisted and turned. She might not know the answer now but even if Blackstone rode on without her, she would find it in the end. She knew Thomas Blackstone would prove to be her salvation.

Her daughter whimpered in the next room. A dream. A fearful one. Her anxiety as a mother redoubled. She and her children must survive. Then she gasped at the thought that reared unbidden from her mind. Would she go that far? She shook her head at her own question. She laid a hand on the broad muscled back of the man who lay sleeping beside her. Yes, she convinced herself. She would go that far. If she had no other choice. She would betray him.

CHAPTER THIRTY-FIVE

By the time the men awoke Blackstone was washing in the water trough, ignoring the chill breeze that swirled across the courtyard. The drizzling rain had passed in the night. Killbere hawked and spat and swallowed a mouthful of wine.

'You slept well?' he said as he splashed water on his face.

Blackstone glanced at him. The meaning was clear. His absence in the night had not gone unnoticed.

Killbere grimaced. 'I had a stone under my hip. And then the damned bells. Monks shuffling like ghosts in the night. It's enough to make a man want to sleep with wild beasts in the forest. And today we lead the Italian and Henry to make their way south.' He dragged his fingers through his hair. 'And Babeneaux's widow,' he added innocently. 'Did she sleep well?'

'I'm not beholden to you, Gilbert. I spend the night as I please. And she goes her own way,' Blackstone answered as he pulled on his shirt.

'And we go ours. The problem of recruiting men-at-arms and archers still faces us, Thomas. We cannot arrive at the Count of Foix with a handful of men. It would be like a eunuch visiting a whorehouse. A waste of time.'

Blackstone finished dressing. 'We will find the men we need.' He buckled his sword belt. 'Or we won't.' With that he strode off to rouse the captains and ready the men.

Killbere glanced towards the woman's sleeping quarters. Cateline came out of her room and fussed with her daughter.

There was no sign of her son. Killbere looked idly around the courtyard. Horses were being saddled; archers were wiping any moisture from their waxed bags: despite their bows' protective cover they were ever mindful of how damp could stretch their hemp cords. They fussed like the woman with her child. Killbere allowed her a moment's leeway. An archer's life – and those of others – depended on them protecting their bows. What she was doing was no different. Safeguard the children and they had a life. Henry Blackstone led the belligerent horse out of the stable. It was already saddled. Jocard walked with him. Everything Killbere saw that chill morning told him that bonds of trust were being formed. Lives were being entwined. The danger was obvious. A snake curled around a limb could bury its fangs at any time. And once its poison disabled its victim death would follow.

Lady Cateline caught him staring in her direction. Defiance flared in her eyes before she quickly turned away. There was no doubt in Killbere's mind. Blackstone and the woman might be going their separate ways but she already had her claws in him.

They rode east, soon to separate into two groups. Blackstone rode at the head of the column with Killbere at his side, and the others behind in the established order of travel. Killbere frowned and peered behind him. Settling back to face the way ahead, he realized what was amiss. 'Where is Beyard? And Aicart?' He turned again. 'And Beyard's other man, Loys? Thomas, have they deserted us in the night?'

'I sent them south at first light to raise men. The Gascons wanted the Prince so they need to fight for him.'

'Aye, but most of these men are loyal to their own lords. There's no love lost between the Count of Foix and Beyard's lord, Jean de Grailly, even though they're cousins. He has his own domains to defend.'

'He isn't in the lowlands, he's up in the Pyrenees. Beyard carries my authority. Jean de Grailly will hear of it. He can either stay where he is or join us. But he has problems of his own against the French. We don't need him.'

'And who else do we ask?'

'Ask, Gilbert? We don't ask, we demand. And when we side with Foix then that's another domain secure for the Prince.'

Killbere shrugged. 'I don't care who comes and stands at our side as long as they fight hard.'

Blackstone remained silent, and that aroused Killbere's curiosity. 'I see what's going on, Thomas. You demand fealty from those who have to give it but there are still not enough men to fight off Armagnac. He has an army at his back. He has the French Crown supplying him. The truce between England and France is something separate. Edward and King John use others, like us, to do their dirty work. Now, how do we defeat Armagnac? There are those who would not side with us without payment.'

Blackstone smiled. 'Then we pay them.'

'Sweet Jesus on the Cross. You intend to bring in skinners? Damn their souls, Thomas, they are mostly scum and undeserving of your favour or trust.'

'I give them neither. I will pay those who will fight with us – if they live. That gives a man extra strength in his sword arm.'

'There're won't be many of them, though. Most are still down in Spain or making their way back. Time is short. And where do we get archers?'

Blackstone shrugged.

Killbere sighed. 'You know, Thomas, if we get enough men and bring in local lords for the fight, it could be a glorious sight. Like the old days. Banners waving, drums pounding, trumpets blaring. Something to stir the blood. Put the fear of Christ into the French bastards again.' He bellowed with laughter. 'Thomas, it will be the best of times again.'

'I'm glad the thought of battle cheers you, Gilbert.'

'My God, yes. Age will take me down before any damned French blade, I guarantee that. And when that time comes I will crawl from my cot and bare my arse at them.'

'A pretty picture. I'll try to put it out of my mind.'

Killbere was more cheerful than Blackstone had seen him for some time. Even the fight at Babeneaux's castle had not raised his spirits as much as the prospect of fighting the French again.

'Come on, Thomas, let's press on. Make your peace with Henry and embrace the husband-huntress one last time, then we bid farewell to the Italian and go our separate ways. We need some distance on the road today and a good place to camp for the night.'

CHAPTER THIRTY-SIX

Guiscard the Lame felt as small as an ant as the looming figure of the German knight stared disdainfully down at him from the saddle. The horse alone dwarfed the woodcutter but the man in the saddle with the black cross on his mantle looked like an overpowering deity. Hartmann had brought the charcoal burner to the group of men who waited in the open meadow so they could see any surprise attack that might come from the copse.

'How are you known?' said von Plauen.

'Guiscard the Lame, lord.'

'Are you able to travel on that bent leg?'

'I am, lord. Have done all my life. I scurry faster than a rat chased by a cur dog.'

'I have already paid you to give us information,' said Wolfram. 'You will be rewarded by taking us to where any of these riders are encamped.'

Guiscard smelt money in the air. 'As you can see, my lord, there are tracks everywhere.'

'And if you do not know which are the most recent, then you are no use to me.'

'Lord, some men rode close by two days ago. I did not count how many but we are cautious in our village and I sent one of the children to follow them. There was only a handful. As few as you. We fear armed men like them.' He dared to raise his eyes to the stern-looking rider. 'And like you, lord.'

'You need not fear any harm from us, woodcutter. We do the Lord's work and bring miscreants to justice. The Almighty will reward you with his benevolence for aiding us.'

'And God's blessing be upon you as well, sir knight. But it takes more than God's kindly gaze upon our dirt-poor community to keep us alive through winter.' Guiscard's meaning was clear.

Wolfram nodded to the other half-brother. 'Sigmund, give him silver, enough to keep a man and his family fed for a month.' He saw the look of surprise on the man's face, etched with lines of hardship and grime. 'My generosity must be rewarded. If it is not or you lead us into a trap with the expectation of stealing from us, then I shall kill you.'

Guiscard nodded furiously, slipping the coins into a pouch on his belt. 'It is a day's ride, my lord. And I can only go so fast.'

'Be tireless, and we will pay you more.'

Guiscard's swaying gait belied his strength. The horsemen followed at a distance, horses at the trot. The silence of the countryside was pierced only by the screech of a passing buzzard and the rhythmic jangling of the knights' armour on the reserve horses. Wolfram von Plauen's keen anticipation of finally coming across Sir Thomas Blackstone and the possibility that Gruffydd ap Madoc might be with him had whetted his appetite to press on at speed. Patience, he told himself, was not one of the virtues in his armoury. He watched with bemused disbelief as the peasant Guiscard sped across the rolling land. His leg kept him at an awkward angle but, like any animal injured in a hunt or by a predator, the base creature had healed and adjusted. Curtains of rain swept across the land ahead of them. That was good. Men would camp and shelter from it, heads low, hunched over a smoking fire as rain dribbled down their necks. He would attack as soon as they were sighted. Did they need armour? he wondered. Mail would protect him and his men, and their mantle announced who they were. No, he decided, honour would best be served if they attacked in full armour. That way their might would provoke fear in their enemy. They would not attempt to conceal themselves. Honour dictated that they show themselves and then charge for the kill. If what the woodcutter had said was accurate, then Wolfram's men would have no trouble fighting so few opponents, even if there were another half-dozen riders.

Guiscard stopped by a stream, dropped to his knees and lapped thirstily. The knights caught up with him.

'He drinks like a dog,' said Rudolf von Burchard. 'He does not even cup water in his hands. These people are animals.'

The knights waited until Guiscard raised his head. 'How much further?' Wolfram asked.

'Before dusk,' said Guiscard, ribs heaving from exertion. He drank some more and without another word set off again.

'Let him run ahead,' said Walter von Ranke, loosening the reins and allowing his horse to drink. He leaned back in the saddle and quaffed from a wineskin. 'I'll wager these mercenary scum we seek are little different from that creature.' He wiped a hand across his face. 'This weather is like a wet blanket. The rain deadens the land and men's minds. There is no biting air to fill a man's lungs. Not like the Baltic. There at least the wind punctures like daggers and sharpens a man's wits.'

Gunther von Schwerin drank from his wine flask. 'Routiers' blades will hone your wits,' he said. He was older than his companions; his hair, closely cut above his ears, showed grey stubble. He had fought a crusade against the Baltic pagans for over ten years and knew nothing should be taken for granted when readying to kill. This land had been raped and pillaged over the years by the English and routiers. Its desolate appearance suggested it had nothing left to offer. Such austerity could make a man think that those they sought were little more than vagabonds, scratching what they could from a pauper's bowl. Men of low birth unwilling to fight hard. But to think that way was a mistake.

'If it is the Welshman he will be vicious. Ap Madoc committed widespread slaughter in the east. He has no fear of retribution. From what we have learnt of Blackstone' – he corked the flask – 'he is a different matter. He will try to outmanoeuvre us. He has the skill. He is no blunt instrument.' He turned to the man who led them. 'Wolfram, I urge you to proceed with caution. Righteousness will not save us if there are more than we know about. When we come upon these men, let us watch and observe them first and then attack.'

'Gunther, we have not travelled across France to sit in the wet grass and watch our enemy. We are here to kill.'

Von Schwerin pulled his mail cowl from his close-cropped head. 'Or be killed. We should be cautious.'

Guiscard was true to his word. He led them to a gentle slope where wild hedgerows and scrub grew and then urged them to dismount. The two half-brethren held the horses as Wolfram and the others crouched low and clambered behind their guide. Guiscard crouched like a begging dog. Wolfram, satisfied that the peasant had done as promised, nodded to Hartmann to pay him. No sooner were the coins in his hand than the woodcutter scurried away. Lying flat the knights peered over the rim of the rising ground. A dozen men were camped several hundred yards away. They had protected themselves from any rain-bearing wind behind them by settling into the curved bowl on the lee of the hill. A small stream coursed downhill: fresh water for cooking and drinking. It flowed into little more than a ditch at the hill's base and then twisted away. The routiers had a clear view across the ground to their front. A sentry sat on the brow of the hill.

'There's a gully two hundred paces in front of them,' said von Burchard. 'The scrubland and bushes obscures a good part of it on the right flank. If we made our way to those trees and wait until darkness we could leave the horses and conceal ourselves there. Then we attack on foot at first light. They would not hear our approach because the wind favours us.'

The others studied the ground. 'Better we should ride hard and take them at first light on horseback. It is God's will,' said Walter von Ranke enthusiastically, eager to fulfil his duty. 'If there are more routiers nearby, then we would be exposed on foot.'

'Brother Walter is right,' said Wolfram. 'There is no dignity in scurrying like rats in a ditch. We show them our strength. Strike them hard and fast. We ride through them to the crest of that hill and then turn and finish them.'

Gunther von Schwerin looked at his comrades. 'We don't know what's on the other side of that hill. If ap Madoc or Thomas Blackstone are in that group they will not run – they will stand their ground.' He pleaded with the man with whom he had shared years of friendship and danger. 'Wolfram, let us take another day and encircle their camp. We should know what lies behind them on the other side of that hill. There might be more men camped there.' He looked across to the youngest and most eager of them. 'Walter, it is not God's will that we throw our lives away needlessly.'

'If they had more men, they would be with those we can see,' said von Burchard.

Gunther could not keep the frustration out of his voice. 'Are you blinded by pride? Look to their left – there is a forest not two hundred yards away. Would you not have men posted there to protect your flank? If these men are greater in number even by six or seven – perhaps more – over the crest of the hill, then we risk being overcome. There are only a few of us. These are not peasants; they are fighting men. And we are not on crusade with hundreds more at our side. We seek retribution, and if they kill us before we find the Welshman or Blackstone, then our journey has been in vain.'

The men fell silent, but they all looked to Wolfram to decide. Finally, he said, 'We will attack on horseback at first light.'

Walter and the others smiled, but Gunther showed no such enthusiasm. 'I will withdraw to a quiet place and spend the night in prayer asking God for his deliverance. My instincts tell me we will die tomorrow.'

CHAPTER THIRTY-SEVEN

The first grey light of dawn had not yet filtered across the landscape. Wolfram von Plauen and his companions, Rudolf von Burchard, Walter von Ranke, Andreas von Suchenwirt, Gunther von Schwerin and Sibrand von Ansbach, adhered to the Teutonic Knights' rule that they could not arm themselves or mount unless commanded to do so. It was the Grand Master who would usually issue such a command before engaging in battle, but as the knights were far from home, it was von Plauen's duty to instruct the men. Once again Gunther had asked their leader to reconsider his decision. To wear armour would slow them down. They were not attacking a great body of men where many blows would be struck against the knights. This attack needed to be swift and deadly. Mail and mantle was enough. Von Plauen insisted that the knights show themselves in full battle armour. Gunther had no choice but to accept the decision.

The men had knelt in prayer and then the half-brethren, Hartmann and Meinhard, attended them. The knights were armoured in order of rank and seniority. Wolfram, because he was deemed their leader, was attended to first. He pulled on a tightly fitting arming doublet – a stuffed cotton and linen jacket with mail sleeves to resist chafing from the armour – and then the half-brethren bent to their task. Their years of practice prepared von Plauen quickly. They strapped sabatons to his shins and then the greaves. A cuirass was secured with ties and a mail skirt belted around his waist. Wolfram von Plauen remained poleaxe straight, letting the two men twist and tug to ensure the fittings were correct. Once the breastplate was attached they strapped a plackart over it to protect his lower stomach. Von Plauen breathed in, testing the strapping.

'Tighter,' he whispered, wary of his voice carrying to the enemy despite the wind being in his favour.

By the time they reached the pauldrons on his upper arms he was ready for his helm and gauntlets. Gunther von Schwerin was next and then one by one the men followed. The youngest and most eager among them, Walter von Ranke, barely kept his impatience under control. But he wished to impress the experienced knights so remained stoically impervious to the half-brethren's fussing.

Dawn light streaked the low clouds as they were assisted onto their mounts. The wind had picked up but had shifted to their left flank. It should still offer them the advantage of not being heard on their approach until it was too late.

'Wolfram, their lookout on the ridge exposes us. Let us put two men on the flank in case there are others in that forest,' said von Schwerin.

'Divide our force?' Wolfram gathered his reins and pulled free his sword from its scabbard. 'Why would some camp in the open and others in the trees? No, Gunther, it is plain to see where our enemy is. God is with us.'

'God is with us,' the others murmured. All, that is, except Gunther.

The horses tore across the divide. There was no sign of anyone stirring in the camp ahead. Blankets still covered the men; a whisper of smoke curled from a fire, the breeze pushing the damp smell of woodsmoke towards the attackers. Three hundred yards from the sleeping men and they saw the first throw back his blanket. At two hundred yards two more rose from the ground. They looked half asleep. Backs turned to the galloping horses. Gunther slammed down his visor. Was it possible the men had not heard their approach? The earth shuddered. Gunther's heart lurched. All the men were on their feet. They turned and raised lances. The pretence of sleep had been a trap, waiting until their attackers could not avert the charge. A line of horseman spurring their mounts broke the skyline on the hill. Wolfram's men would have nowhere to turn. The treeline on the flank shuddered as other men broke cover. Ten or more horseman bore down on them. It was an ambush. Gunther saw Wolfram charge straight ahead, the others only strides behind him. They would attempt to carve a path through the overwhelming odds, perhaps to escape over the crest of the hill as their horses laboured under their weight. Gunther pulled his mount away to blunt the attack from the forest. At least he would die buying the others time.

Gunther heard distant screams, dulled by his helmet, as the charging knights clashed with the horsemen's downhill impetus. The sickening thud of horses barging into each other and their plaintive whinnying heralded the death of man and horse. But there was no time to think of the others now; Gunther raised his shield, angled his horse into the more lightly armed routiers and struck fiercely left and right. Two men immediately fell from the saddle; four more had already spurred ahead of him but his own mount was stronger and more swift and he cut another two routiers down before they had a chance to defend themselves. Those attacking from the forest must have seen their comrades were overwhelming the Germans and swung their horses back to encircle Gunther. He heeled his horse, swept the blade high, caught a routier below his chinstrap and then plunged his sword down into the man's horse. It rolled its eyes, bellowed in pain and went down, which is exactly what Gunther wanted. The flailing beast and its dead rider blocked the immediate attack from others closing in. Blades struck Gunther's armour, and he was thankful Wolfram had been insistent on it being worn. His strength surged: he battered his attackers, taking their strikes against his shield and armour. His blows were precise and controlled, unlike the abandoned ferocity of the routiers. He grunted, sucking air, holding breath in his chest and forcing it out to give more power to his arm. The swirling mass of men made it difficult to see where the next blow might come from but with rein and heel he turned his horse this way and that, using its weight to push others aside and expose their riders' vulnerability. He had slain several men and fatally wounded more but now they were smothering him, making it impossible for him to fight his way clear. At least, he thought, he had drawn these men to him and given the others a chance to escape.

A heavy blow from a mace on the back of his neck threw him forward over his mount's withers. The routiers boxed him in and, unable to find a weakness in his armour, went about killing his horse. It fell, throwing him clear. He hit the ground with such force his breath was driven out of him. Through the narrow slit of his visor he saw his comrades being hauled from their saddles; some were already being dragged away like slaughtered carcasses. His vision blurred as his attackers bellowed a warning, momentarily taking their attention away from him. He turned his head and saw the two half-brethren at the charge, shield and sword raised in a vain attempt to rescue the knights they served and adhere to the vow they had taken. They gave a good account of themselves but were soon hacked to death. Gunther's cumbersome armour made it impossible for him to get to his feet quickly enough to continue fighting. He half raised himself, reached for his sword and saw the dark shadow of a man above him whose snarling face spat a curse as he swung his mace hard and fast, sending Gunther into the black abyss of unconsciousness.

CHAPTER THIRTY-EIGHT

Blackstone's horse suddenly pulled its head back and stopped as if an invisible hand had restrained it. There was no apparent danger ahead. The open rolling meadows cut a swathe through forests of varying sizes, none too close to allow an ambush. Killbere's horse shied at the bastard horse's sudden halt. Horses behind had to swerve. The bastard horse was as fixed as a boulder in the landscape, ears raised, nostrils flared. A shiver ran down its withers.

'God's tears, Thomas, horses are skittish creatures at the best of times but that mongrel beast has a disposition fit only for the damned slaughterhouse. I doubt it would be docile if it was gutted and hung on a meat hook.'

Blackstone raised a hand to silence his friend and quieten the muted curses from the others behind him as they jostled to avoid colliding with each other. He listened but heard nothing. Blackstone kept his eyes trained on the changing landscape. The meadows offered no threat, nor – as far as he could see – did the copse of trees. No crows fluttered cawing into the sky. He looked at the bare top of the tree canopy. The breeze shifted this way and that, more noticeable at that height than on the ground.

Blackstone spoke quietly, eyes still sweeping the way ahead for anything untoward. 'Gilbert, this wretched beast is precious to me. I prefer its belligerence to the world about it. It suits my own temperament, but it has never failed to warn me of danger. I trust the goddess Arianrhod I wear at my throat, you and my men at my side and this devil-spawned, war-mongering, black-hearted creature to keep me safe.'

A distant cry reached them. Gilbert raised a hand to shield his eyes against the brightness of the clouds.

'There,' said Jack Halfpenny. 'High in the sky ahead.'

Blackstone and Killbere looked to where the sharp-eyed archer pointed. After a moment's concentration the speck showed itself a half-mile ahead. A buzzard soared in spiral flight. It keened again. The wind whipped the raptor's cry around the sky.

'Only a buzzard, Thomas,' said Killbere.

Blackstone stayed vigilant. 'No, Gilbert. It's more than that.' He pointed to where they had first seen the buzzard and then to left and right. The clouds had separated: darker below; lighter, higher clouds above; and the swirling black specks became more than the one raptor. 'Crows on the wind. They're settling.' He patted the horse's neck and loosened the reins. The horse walked on but Blackstone felt its tension beneath him. Its ears stayed upright. And then it snorted and insisted on veering to one side. Blackstone did not fight it, and after forty yards it turned again so that the breeze now blew directly into the men's faces. Another high-pitched keening reached them. Clearer this time. No raptor's call. A man's scream.

Blackstone ran at the crouch around the edge of the low hillside. Had he and the men travelled four or five hundred yards from the other direction they would have seen the tracks made by the Teutonic Knights. The King's sergeant, William Ashford, had quickly secured his men in the copse of trees and surrounded his charge, Father Torellini. Henry attended to his father's horse and Jocard helped hold the others to the rear of where Blackstone and the men waited. Lady Cateline and her daughter sat huddled with Torellini. Ashford had followed Blackstone's instructions without question. If there was trouble his defensive position would buy him and his men time until Blackstone returned.

'There!' said Killbere. There was no need for him to point out the twenty or so routiers and their grazing horses. The men were on foot, gathered haphazardly around a fire pit that had been stoked for some hours and reduced to a deep bed of embers. The heat would be intense and the man who dangled over the pit had his wrists bound above his head to a makeshift pole and trestle.

'The bastards are cooking him alive,' said Meulon.

The tortured knight was still in his suit of armour and as he fell in and out of consciousness his gasping breath became an agonizing scream. The routiers were laughing. Another four men stripped to their underclothes were bound to a length of pole. They did not escape punishment either. Two of the routiers kicked and punched them in between swigging from a wineskin. The burning man's chilling screams increased.

'Whoever those men are they need help,' said John Jacob.

'They outnumber us but John's right,' said Killbere. 'Thomas?'

Blackstone nodded. Quickly surveying the ground ahead, he turned to Will Longdon. 'Will, you and the lads get into that gully. Stay low and get as far along it as you can.'

Longdon and his archers had already freed their bows from their bags and nocked their hemp cords. 'We can't kill those skinners easily, Thomas. Those prisoners are right in their midst.'

'I know. When I give the word kill the man over the pit. Your bodkins will get through his armour. We can't let him die like a spitted pig.'

Will Longdon's grim countenance and nod of acceptance was enough. The suffering man would soon be out of his misery. The centenar turned to Halfpenny. 'Jack, you and me both. We loose together. It's a long shot.'

The archers crabbed their way towards the ditch. Blackstone and the others backed away. 'Gilbert, ride across their flank, cut them off if they try to escape. Their horses are untethered. With luck, they'll scatter before they have time to mount. Meulon, take your men to the right. We box these bastards in. Renfred, go straight at the prisoners. Protect them. John, you and I will take the centre.'

John Jacob understood. He and Blackstone were going into the heart of the beast. They would be in the most danger. A broad grin creased his face. 'We kill them all?'

'We kill them all,' said Blackstone.

Within minutes Blackstone's men were mounted. Swords drawn, shields up. The gap between the edge of the forest and the hillside was a narrow strip of land that would obscure their attack for the first fifty yards. Will Longdon and his archers crouched in the chest-high ditch. He addressed his archers, who each waited a yard apart from the next man. 'Jack and me will shoot first. You lads pick a target that's nowhere near them prisoners as soon as Sir Thomas makes his ride across the field.'

The centenar and Jack Halfpenny looked towards the tortured man. His head was free of a helm but even at that distance they could see his bared teeth. An animal screaming in pain. A man begging for mercy. Voices drifted on the breeze. Laughter taunting the suffering man. They would give no mercy, one voice bellowed, drunk with the visceral pleasure of inflicting agony.

'No mercy for you either, you skinner bastard,' said Jack Halfpenny. 'Will? Two hundred and twenty-five yards?'

Will Longdon gauged the distance. The breeze was light. And it now brought the smell of burning flesh. 'I see it as two hundred and ten, perhaps a few strides more beyond that.'

Halfpenny squinted at the target and nodded. Longdon and Halfpenny did as the other archers and nocked a yard-long, inch-thick ash arrow onto their bow cords. Staying crouched, they peered along the line of bowmen to where Blackstone moved his war horse into view. Blackstone turned to face his archers, raised his sword to order the death of the tortured man and spurred his horse.

The two veteran archers stood, bent their backs, their target fixed in their mind's eye. Before the first horse broke cover, the two arrows whispered through the air. A half-dozen heartbeats later they saw them strike. Will Longdon's arrow killed the man instantly, striking through his forehead. Halfpenny, a breath later, punctured his chest. In the time it took for a routier to stumble back, gazing upwards in disbelief, horses thundered across the open meadow. The skinners panicked, wildly grabbing weapons, running for their mounts, some of which had bolted. By the time Blackstone's men swept across the field two more flights of arrows had punctured routiers and horses. Those mercenaries who broke to the flanks fell from the archers' rapid shooting further down the line. Will Longdon saw they could loose no more arrows without hitting their own men. He ordered his archers to clamber out of the ditch, run forward and pick whatever target presented itself. Two escaping routiers swerved their mounts through Blackstone's horsemen and galloped towards the vulnerable bowmen. They fell, each punctured by arrows in their chests less than eighty paces from where the ragged line of archers stood their ground.

Blackstone and John Jacob punched a gap through the routiers who had quickly formed a defence. The impact of shields and the crushing weight of their horses buckled the first group of mercenaries. The gap opened wide enough for Renfred and his men to sweep aside the light resistance offered and quickly secure the prisoners. Renfred shouted his orders over the screams and shouts of the mêlée: 'Stay with them! Cut them free!'

He wheeled his horse. Blackstone and John Jacob were being attacked by more men on horseback and those on foot who had gathered their wits and their weapons as soon as the surge of horseman swept down upon them. Renfred trampled one routier and then slashed down and back with his sword to take another from chin to scalp. His horse barged aside a third and then it was the three of them fighting side by side, turning this way and that in practised discipline and unbridled ferocity. The routiers broke, crying surrender. Those immediately in front of Blackstone went down on one knee, turning their swords to offer the hilt to Blackstone. Blackstone slew them.

The released prisoners took the risk of running through the edge of the skirmish line to lower their comrade from above the pit. The nauseating stench of their friend's flesh assailed them and they could not sever the rope ties quickly enough to stop his scorched body from being burned further.

Blackstone spurred the bastard horse into the two horsemen who stood between him and the prisoners. The beast turned to a quick leg and rein command, swung its head like a battering ram, forcing the opponent's horse to rear up. Blackstone rammed Wolf Sword's point into the flailing rider's face. The bastard horse bunched its hindquarters; Blackstone tugged the reins. It fought the bit but did as commanded, crashing its weight against the poles that held the suspended knight. He fell free from the fire pit.

Blackstone, John Jacob and Renfred were suddenly alone. Bodies lay strewn around them, as though they were farmers amid a field of scythed wheat. Meulon picked off stragglers on the flanks: he speared and gutted them while his men chased down those few who had broken free and they too went under the sword. Will Longdon had brought his men within fifty yards of the fighting, his extended line of archers ready to shoot into any target that presented itself. The men-at-arms gave them no such sport. Killbere and the men with him had rooted out those who had scurried into the fern-deep forest. As Killbere spurred his horse back towards Blackstone, Longdon raised his bow. 'All right, lads. Finish off any of these scum with the knife. See what booty they yield.'

The archers ran forward, eager to claim anything of value before the horsemen dismounted and sought their share from the slaughter.

Killbere, sprayed with blood on his chest and legs, reached Blackstone. 'Too easy, Thomas! Good sport though. Killing vermin has its pleasures.' He checked the equally blood-splattered Blackstone and his companions. 'Outnumbered be damned. It's better that way. Gives a man a greater will to live. How many do you think? Thirty or so?'

'Forty-five by a quick count, Sir Gilbert,' said John Jacob.

'Fewer than that,' said Renfred.

Killbere drank thirstily; then he swilled the specks of blood from his beard. 'Renfred, do not spoil a man's pleasure at his achievements. Why do you Germans have to be so exact about everything? Forty-five it is.'

One of the prisoners who had helped drag free their comrade faced Blackstone. His back was straight, fists clenched at his side. Dried blood streaked his face and beard. The routiers had beaten him as hard as they had his companions, all of whom sported bruises and wounds.

'You bear the blazon of Thomas Blackstone. Are you he?' said Wolfram von Plauen.

Blackstone looked down. 'I am.'

The tall, muscular man raised his chin. 'I am Wolfram von Plauen. I came here to kill you,' he said, his tone of voice a formal declaration.

'Then I suggest you put some clothes on,' said Blackstone.

Blackstone's men's laughter pricked the Teutonic Knight's pride. His skin flushed. He quickly recovered. 'It is no laughing matter!'

'You're not sitting where I am,' said Blackstone.

Ignoring the man's suppressed anger he wheeled the horse away, Killbere at his side.

'Mother of God,' sighed Killbere. 'We found the damned Teutonic Knights and they are as far up their own arses as I remember.'

CHAPTER THIRTY-NINE

They left the fallen routiers where they lay, scattered across the open field. The Teutonic Knights pulled on their breeches and a linen shirt, giving them sufficient dignity to drag their own dead close together. They laid the two half-brethren next to young Walter von Ranke. They did not try to free him from his armour. His flesh would be too badly seared. Then the Germans, ignoring their own wounds, attended to digging graves for their comrades. They found a place near a rocky outcrop and dug four pits. Andreas von Suchenwirt had also fallen. He had seen a figure running free from the routiers' camp: a crouching Guiscard, crabbing his way across the field, safe from the attack. Andreas had fought through the men who opposed him but as he pursued the crippled peasant a crossbow bolt struck him. He managed to ride down and kill the woodcutter who had betrayed them before, weakened by his mortal injury, he turned to throw himself into the fray, smashing through horsemen that surrounded von Plauen and Rudolph von Burchard. He had been dragged down from the saddle and put to death.

The knights laboured despite their injuries until the graves were deep enough to dissuade any wild creature from digging up the bodies. They left no marker for fear of brigands disinterring their friends thinking there might be weapons or money buried with them. They scattered the excess dirt and flattened the burial mounds with rocks until it looked no different from the surrounding area.

Blackstone and the men had withdrawn to the forest where William Ashdown had kept the rearguard, frustrated by the duty of protection that kept him from the fight. Blackstone's men had minor wounds and knew they had been lucky not to lose anyone in the skirmish. Blackstone ordered the men to camp for the night and treat their injuries. The captains placed the pickets; cooking fires were lit and horses fed. Blackstone and Killbere went among the men and assessed their injuries, ensuring every man washed their wounds, bound them with clean dressings and made good use of the potions and herbs they carried to stop infections. 'You took a cut on your back and side,' said Killbere. 'You've bled down into your britches.'

'My shirt sticks and seals it. Once the men and horses are seen to, I'll attend to it.' Blackstone looked to where the Teutonic Knights knelt in prayer at their comrades' graveside. 'They honour their dead with a deep fervour, Gilbert. They've been on their knees for a long time.'

'I'm grateful they didn't try to scrape the poor bastard out of his armour. Be worse than trying to clean out an old cooking pot.'

'You think he's serious about wanting to fight me?'

Killbere stripped off his mail and swabbed a flesh wound on his arm. 'They're mad bastards, Thomas, and when they get caught up in religious fervour, they think they can rule the world. Challenging you to a fight is like a Will Longdon fart. An unpleasant experience to be endured or quickly avoided. Whatever the reason, the German's convinced himself that he has to kill you.'

Blackstone sighed. 'All right, if that's what he wants.'

'He'll be one of those highly efficient swordsmen, Thomas. He'll fight the way he trained. By the book, but not always predictable.'

'I've fought Germans before,' said Blackstone.

Killbere rung out the wet cloth. 'I fought alongside them on crusade against the Lithuanians. They use something called *Kampffechten*. It's a skill they learn for armoured combat on foot. It's effective. You be careful. They sacrifice the strength of a strike – makes you think they have weakened, but then they make a fast, deceptive cut. It can catch you unawares.'

'And you think I can't deal with that?'

'You understand *Meisterhauwen*, Thomas? Their master-cuts? They're predictable but they use a sudden change of tactics to throw an opponent. Five controlled strikes. They call them the secret cuts.' Killbere braced and used the edge of his hand to demonstrate what he knew of the German sword-fighting discipline. 'They close off a line of attack, like so.' He swept his hand across Blackstone's body line. 'But it's a feint. You think they have moved into a defensive stance, like this' – he quickly shifted his weight – 'but it's their first move to counter-attack. It closes off your line of attack. Draws you in, deceives you, and then that stance they've taken…' He squared up to Thomas to impress on him how the German would likely turn what appeared to be a solid defensive position into a sudden killing strike. 'It changes this quickly, Thomas.' He cut the air with the edge of his hand, so rapidly that Blackstone took an involuntary step backwards. 'A single cut or thrust with an immediate follow-up blow.'

'I was taught by my own master, Gilbert.' After being badly wounded at Crécy, sixteen-year-old Blackstone had been taken into Jean de Harcourt's home and taught the way of the sword. It was a debt that could never be fully repaid and the skills instilled in him had saved his life on many occasions. 'I fight the man, not his sword.'

'Thomas, remember one thing: whatever position you adopt they have a counter-strike already in place.' He held Blackstone's attention. 'Defence into attack. They gauge the weight of your blade against their own. If you feel theirs yield beneath your own, it's a deception. Be ready for their killing thrust.'

Blackstone considered everything Killbere had shared. 'Thank you, old friend. I'll remember.'

'When the time comes, finish him quickly,' said Killbere. 'We need to move on and these knights don't let go of a grudge. We don't want them shadowing us, looking for an opportunity to strike. Or him at least.'

'We've just saved their lives, for God's sake.'

'And they will see that God sent you so they can complete their vendetta against you. It is part of their deformed logic. It will make perfect sense to them. Attend to your wound, Thomas. You will need your strength and skill against this man.'

Henry Blackstone stood next to his father's horse, its legs hobbled and its great neck secured with rope. Henry had stripped off its saddle and boiled leather breastplate. A sliver of a wound, a hand's width, ran across its flank.

Cateline's son Jocard was at Henry's shoulder, fascinated by and wary of the great beast that snorted and rolled its eyes in their direction.

'He will try to kill you,' said Henry. 'Even my father has suffered injuries from his bite and kick. The men think the devil spawned him but he lets me handle him.'

'Perhaps you are spawned by the devil as well then,' Jocard blurted out, and then, seeing Henry's flash of anger, quickly stuttered a retraction. 'Forgive me. I meant no offence. I just meant that... well, if he lets you attend to him... I'm sorry. The words were all wrong.'

Henry stroked the horse's neck. 'Don't ever say anything like that again, Jocard.'

The boy bowed his head, acknowledging the censure. Henry's rebuke was spoken so coldly that the stern warning frightened him. Henry Blackstone had saved his life and such courage was something he knew he did not possess. However, Henry seemed to let the insult go and concentrated on treating the horse.

'There are things you should learn about wounds, Jocard. There are not always barber-surgeons or physicians around to help us and a man must look after his horse.'

'I don't intend getting into a fight, Henry, and I don't have a horse of my own.'

Henry took a deep breath and suppressed the urge to berate the boy. Henry knew he would soon be in a place of learning where he would not be the brightest pupil and humiliation would invariably be heaped upon him. Jocard's dullness was a good testing ground to exercise restraint.

'When you have been schooled at Avignon you will return to your domain,' he said patiently. 'They will expect you to govern your people. The day will come when you will be obliged to fight. There are so many things that are asked of us, Jocard, and knowing how to treat a wound is only a small one, but remember even a light wound can become poisoned. My father once saved an apothecary, and she repaid the debt with her life, but not before she passed on her knowledge to him and the men.'

'I understand,' said Jocard, looking puzzled.

'This wound is not deep enough to stitch so we sprinkle this powder into it. It's ground yarrow. It will clot the bleeding and stop any infection getting in,' Henry instructed him.

'Then I must learn about herbs?'

'Yes, and that is something I can teach you.'

'And fighting?'

'That too. Now, take the powder and spread it evenly into his cut, then press your fingers into the wound so the grains soak the blood.'

Jocard's face creased with disgust but he did as instructed. Anything was worth doing if it brought praise from the older boy. And a part of his heart yearned for a father like Blackstone and an older brother like Henry. Perhaps, he mused, when Sir Thomas Blackstone's journey was over he would return and marry his mother.

Wolfram von Plauen and the surviving Teutonic Knights gathered their weapons and armour, recovered their horses and led them to the forest. They kept away from Blackstone's men, who were scattered in the trees and who barely cast a glance in their direction as they treated each other's injuries. The archers had suffered no wounds so they built fires and prepared food for the rest.

Blackstone made his way through the camp to where William Ashford had stayed with his men surrounding Torellini and Cateline and her daughter.

'Sir Thomas,' said the King's sergeant in greeting.

'William. All was well here?'

'Other than me trying to keep my men from joining in, yes.'

'You had a more precious duty. The woman?' he added, lowering his voice.

'Aye, she's no trouble. She was as keen as a flower girl at a tournament to see the fight. I kept pulling her back from the treeline in case she attracted anyone we didn't know about out there.'

'I had planned to go our separate ways tomorrow but you're going to need a bigger escort for your charge. There's a man at Sarlat who will give you additional escort.'

'A Frenchman?'

'Yes.'

'Not so sure that gives us much safety, Sir Thomas.'

'He will be paid enough, don't worry, and his men will give you and Father Torellini additional protection to Avignon. '

'As you wish then, my lord.'

'Stay alert after dark. Scavengers will come in the night for the dead. Wolves and boar. They should stay clear of us here, especially if we keep fires burning, but if they get the taste for flesh and pick up our scent, then we must be on our guard.'

Ashford nodded. 'Aye. I've been in a forest camp when boars came through. They tried to snatch a man, savaged his damned arm. We'll be vigilant.'

'Build a hammock off the ground for Lady Cateline's child. Boars would easily take her.'

Blackstone went deeper into the trees. They had made Father Torellini comfortable. Blankets and cut ferns created a passable bed and his saddle a place to rest his head. A fire of slow-burning ash and oak gave off warmth in the damp forest air. One of Ashford's men was close by preparing food for the priest. Blackstone knelt and recounted what he had told the sergeant about using an additional French escort.

Torellini nodded. 'Yes, that seems wise. I will ensure his men will be amply rewarded when we reach Avignon. The incentive will keep their eyes and swords sharp for any other routiers in our path.' Torellini rested a hand on Blackstone's shoulder. 'Thomas, you and your men fought hard. It was a fight you could have avoided.'

Blackstone shook his head. 'They were burning a man to death. No one deserves to die like that and those who commit such an atrocity have no right to live.'

Torellini looked affectionately at Blackstone. 'You're hurting. Your wound is bleeding.'

'It's not serious. One of the men will attend to it. I have a Teutonic Knight who wishes to kill me.'

Torellini's eyebrows raised. 'One of those men?' he said, looking to where the Germans camped.

'Yes. I don't know why.' Blackstone shrugged. 'But if a man is intent on doing something the reason why doesn't matter.'

'They are the same men who approached me at Chartres. Let me speak to him on your behalf. I'm certain there is a misunderstanding.'

Blackstone got to his feet. 'Thank you, Father, but the day is almost done, and this matter needs to be settled. Besides, he doesn't seem to be a man who would listen.' He put a hand to the blood-soaked shirt, testing the wound's severity. 'And as much as I miss my wife and daughter I will not join them tonight except in my dreams. The German can embrace his own loved ones in heaven.'

CHAPTER FORTY

The Teutonic Knights stood in the clearing beyond the trees. They had dressed in mail and surcoat. Wolfram von Plauen stood at the head of his men, none of whom seemed the worse for wear after their ordeal, other than the visible signs of bruising and cuts from the attack and their beating at the hands of the routiers. Killbere and Renfred accompanied Blackstone as he strode across to meet them. Blackstone's men edged forward from the forest to watch the contest. Blackstone's wound had been treated and bound but the cut aggravated him.

'There is no reason for this, Thomas,' said Killbere in hushed tones. 'We saved their lives so they are in our debt. What we do with them is up to us. Let's kill them and get back to our supper.'

'No, Gilbert, this needs to be done.' He called out to the group of men. 'I wish to know what harm I have caused you and why your repay your lives being saved by challenging me.'

Von Plauen waited, legs astride, hands resting on his sword hilt, its blade point in the ground. Blackstone watched him, sizing up the man's confidence. Von Plauen said something in German to one of the others.

'Renfred?' said Blackstone.

'He has told another knight called Gunther to speak on his behalf, and in English so we don't misunderstand him,' said Renfred. Then added, 'Arrogant shit.'

The knight stepped forward, a streak of blood encrusted in his hair and beard from the blow he had suffered in the fight. 'I am Gunther von Schwerin. We were told that you and the routier Gruffydd ap Madoc fought together. There was great slaughter against one of our princes on the eastern border. Atrocities were committed. We seek retribution and justice in their name. You will admit your guilt, tell us where to find the Welshman and face my comrade Wolfram von Plauen in mortal combat. God will bless the righteous in this matter.'

'They like their speeches,' said Killbere. 'Let me handle this, Thomas.' Before Blackstone could object Killbere took a couple of paces forward. 'Who told you these lies?' he demanded.

'The dead and the mutilated do not lie,' Gunther answered. 'The evidence is known. The French court acknowledges the wrongdoing and use of routiers by Henry, Count of Vaudémont, the King's Royal Lieutenant in Champagne.'

Killbere cleared his throat and spat. 'Ah, so the French in Paris told you this, did they? Whatever language you care to speak, they are liars.'

Gunther listened with a puzzled look on his face. 'I speak four languages. The court in Paris speaks the *langue d'oïl*. I understood perfectly.'

Killbere half turned to Blackstone. 'God's tears, these are idiot bastards. They take my words to the letter.' He faced them and tried again. 'They seek only to destroy Sir Thomas Blackstone by any means. They are our sworn enemy. They squirm like rats in a barrel, these Frenchman. The King or the Dauphin. It makes no difference. They are worthless wretches and liars.'

'Are we to believe the word of a man who stands next to a murderer against that of the French royal court?' said Gunther.

'You have the word of an English knight, you damned

ungrateful arse-clenching cross-bearing monk,' Killbere fumed.

Blackstone stepped forward. 'Thank you, Gilbert. You have expressed your feelings in your usual forthright manner,' he said with a hint of weary sarcasm. 'I don't think they have any intention of believing us and they're looking for a fight.'

'Damned pity they didn't all end up on the roasting spit if you ask me,' said Gilbert as Blackstone beckoned Renfred to his side.

'Renfred, let there be no misunderstanding. Tell them this in their own language. We did not fight on the eastern border. Gruffydd ap Madoc sought us out and betrayed us. We hunted him but he eluded us. Gruffydd ap Madoc then raised an army of routiers and saved us at Brignais. If I knew where he was I would not tell you. I owe him my life and that of my son and those men who served me.'

Blackstone nodded for Renfred to translate into German. The Teutonic Knights at first appeared surprised that one of Blackstone's men spoke their language. When Renfred had conveyed Blackstone's message Gunther turned to von Plauen. 'I believe them. Thomas Blackstone is not the man responsible. We have no quarrel with him. We owe him and his men our lives. We should not dishonour ourselves.'

Von Plauen glared at his comrade. 'They fought together. You heard him!' he said, berating his companion. 'You would dishonour me?' Before Gunther could disagree von Plauen brought the sword to his lips, kissed the blade and raised it in a two-handed grip at the high guard. 'Defend yourself!' he called and strode forward. Blackstone did not hesitate. He rushed the German. The intensity of his attack took von Plauen by surprise. He had expected Blackstone to stand his ground and trade blows. He recovered, altered his balance, blocked the hamstringing strike aimed at his leg and half twisted, altering the grip on his sword, and struck with such force that Blackstone felt the shudder through his hands and arms. Blackstone twisted his own blade, turned on his heel and swung with a cross strike that if not defended would cut into the man's side and at least break ribs with its force. Von Plauen braced, traversed on his right foot, sword high behind his right shoulder, a solid turn that attacked Blackstone's unguarded side – which was quickly defended. The sword strokes were so rapid, blade against blade, that the steel chimed like a church bell calling the faithful to prayer. Blackstone and von Plauen were already at the God of War's altar.

The German's footwork was faultless; pressing backwards with his left foot and pivoting to the right, he altered his line of attack. Every practised step the German made was to attack a right-handed opponent. Blackstone saw it coming, parried and quickly changed his own position. His body twisted; his wound burned, making him drop his hip slightly, putting him at an immediate disadvantage. Von Plauen threw his weight forward; the blades clashed. Blackstone faltered, regained his balance and used his strength to force the man back. The German's determined strikes had Blackstone on the defensive. And that was exactly what Blackstone wanted. He was testing his opponent. Seeing how he fought. Waiting for any attack that was not so rigid in its execution. None came. The man's expertise was second to none. But he was no street fighter, and he had already revealed the five main mastercuts. A lesser opponent who did not have Blackstone's battle experience would already be dead.

Blackstone attacked, his eyes never leaving the knight's body movement, watching his eyes, seeing where a feint might come. Von Plauen was too obvious. Too rigid in his killing technique. Blackstone knew that the German was waiting to deceive him with a feint. Blackstone turned on his heel, pressed forward with the flat of his foot, rose up on the ball of his right foot and hammered down a blow that broke the German's stance. He staggered back, yielding for a moment, preparing to feint. Blackstone pressed ahead a stride, only one stride, one long pace, wanting the man to think he was off balance, that the length of his sword blade was all that he had to worry about. Von Plauen snarled in victory, believing Blackstone had stepped into his trap. He cross-cut. Now would come the parry and that gave von Plauen the exact moment in the fight he wanted. The tip of Blackstone's blade would be flicked away and the point of his own blade thrust into Blackstone's chest or throat.

Blackstone felt the man's grip yield, barely noticeable, but enough for a swordsman to feel the give, to make him think he suddenly had the advantage, just as Killbere had warned. Wolf Sword broke von Plauen's block, its blade sliding down and away, steel against steel, a movement that would force Blackstone onto his toes, making him fall forward unbalanced. The German bared his teeth: the fight was won. He used the feint and his opponent's weakness to deliver the killing blow. But Blackstone was no longer the right-handed adversary he had been throughout the fight. He had twisted his hands, right over left, striking von Plauen's sword with Wolf Sword's guard, moving forward with a lot of power behind it, throwing his attack onto his wounded side, letting the pain befriend his strength. Von Plauen's blade was forced down. Blackstone stepped in, smothered any recovery with his body and smashed Wolf Sword's pommel beneath the man's chin. Dazed and shocked, von Plauen staggered, spitting blood, choking, desperate for breath, trying to raise his sword arm, but Blackstone grabbed his belt and threw him to the ground.

A cheer rose from Blackstone's men.

Wolf Sword's tip hovered at the squirming man's throat, a foot pressed hard into his chest. Von Plauen snatched at his throat strap to release his helmet and try to breathe. He spat blood, eyes glaring at the man who was about to kill him.

'Spare him!' Gunther cried.

Blackstone ignored the cry for clemency and gently pressed the tip of his blade into the fleshy part of von Plauen's neck. A small rivulet of blood trickled.

Von Plauen gasped. 'I yield.'

Blackstone did not release the pressure. 'This is the second time today I have spared your life. You are in my debt. You will honour that debt.'

Von Plauen dared not risk nodding his head lest Blackstone's sword press further into his throat. 'I will honour it. I swear it. My comrades bear witness,' he spluttered through his bloodied mouth.

Blackstone glanced at the other Teutonic Knights who, hands on sword hilts, looked ready to attack were it not for Gunther's extended arm stopping them.

'We bear witness,' said Gunther von Schwerin.

Blackstone hesitated a moment longer and then stepped back. 'You will guard the Lady Cateline and her children until she releases you from your duty.'

Von Plauen's men went forward to help the beaten man to his feet as Blackstone slid Wolf Sword into its scabbard, pulled free his helm and walked to where Killbere stood waiting to offer him a beaker of wine. Blackstone drank thirstily.

'You see, Thomas. Listen to me and you won't go wrong.' Killbere beamed and placed a hand on his friend's shoulder. 'But there were a couple of moves you didn't get right.'

Blackstone's sweat-streaked face scowled as wine spilled down his chin.

'I'll explain later,' muttered Killbere. 'When your belligerence has cooled.' He raised a finger in admonishment. 'But I still think you should have killed him.'

'He is beholden,' said Blackstone, wiping an arm across his mouth. 'And now he will serve her.'

Killbere shook his head. 'Death is preferable to a wounded pride. Now he is twice as dangerous.'

CHAPTER FORTY-ONE

Blackstone's journey south to meet Gaston Phoebus, Count de Foix et Béarn, was taking longer than planned. He had not counted on being guardian to a woman and her children, a woman whose emotions cleaved to him like an infant to a breast. Her hold on him had not yet been released. The battle and then the fight against the Teutonic nobleman had given Lady Cateline no opportunity to approach him. And Blackstone had avoided her. His wounds and bruises made him feel like a flagellant monk but the pain was nothing compared to his desire for her. And it was not mere lust. It was a desire to lie against her soft, fragrant skin and experience a long-lost tenderness. But it was not to be. He had reasoned it all out. Once in Avignon she would find a rich merchant to marry. Someone who provided gold, silk or spices to an indulgent priestly class. A wealthy man, older by some years, who would buy her beauty and satiate himself each night in her bed and turn over, grunting from feeble exertion, leaving her unsatisfied. Blackstone wondered if she would turn to a physician to deal with the unfulfilled gratification or take another lover. He told himself he didn't care.

Having the Teutonic Knights riding with him was an added complication – and one he had mixed feelings about. They were honour-bound to him now and that at least gave him some assurance they would not attempt to assassinate him in the night. The Germans had lined up and then knelt in front of him, each man giving his name and pledge of obedience.

Rudolf von Buchard, Gunther von Schwerin, Sibrand von Ansbach and von Plauen himself. Blackstone had let them kneel long enough for them to understand that it was he who demanded their obedience. The second man, von Schwerin, met his gaze squarely. His blue eyes did not reflect defiance but rather an understanding. Was it a sign of respect or was he searching Blackstone's scarred face for a deeper clue to his character? It made no difference, Blackstone decided. That they were now obliged to protect Lady Cateline meant they stood between him and his unwanted desire for her.

Blackstone had thought Father Torellini's journey would be safe from attack as he and his escort were travelling through English-held territory, but it appeared that Sir William Felton's authority did not yet extend into all the areas he administered: Blackstone needed to find more safeguards for their journey. He was stripped to the waist as Killbere wrapped a clean bandage on his wounds.

'Sarlat changed hands so many times I don't know who commands it now,' said Killbere. 'French or English? Routiers or regulars?'

'Gisbert de Dome, Lord of Vitrac.'

'I thought him sworn to the French King.'

'He was, but when he was nominated as Seneschal of Périgord the regional consuls and citizens of Sarlat denied his confirmation. He tried to take the city by force but his attempt failed so he started raiding in the area. He's greedy for power and money.'

'What damned nobleman isn't,' said Killbere.

'And he has a vindictive temperament. I can turn him to suit our needs,' said Blackstone. 'He brought routiers down from the hills and tore apart the countryside. Seize enough of a city's harvest and decisions can be quickly overturned. He became seneschal after all.'

'Then we can't trust him.'

'Chandos bought his loyalty when we were reclaiming towns last year. Gisbert de Dome will be useful to us, providing he hasn't been strung up in the city square by the merchants and guild members. Privately he declares for the French Crown, publicly he is ours. We must use his letters of authority besides the King's to give Father Torellini and the woman further safe conduct. They must reach Avignon safely. We shall delay sending them south until we've secured more men to ride with them.'

'And Henry.'

Blackstone stood and tugged his shirt on. 'Don't try to convince me otherwise. Henry is going to Avignon, and that's the end of it.'

Killbere threw the blood-dried bandages into the fire. 'Thomas, we are few in number and you now propose we place our lives in the hands of a traitorous Frenchman. And then there's von Plauen. He may have sworn to honour your conditions for saving his life but he will turn like a rabid dog. I know it. And how far can you trust the Lady Cateline? A spurned woman is the most dangerous creature of all.'

Blackstone didn't answer. There was little choice in the matter.

'I've been ambushed before in narrow streets,' said Killbere. 'And there are five or six thousand people in Sarlat. It would be like fighting through reed beds hacking away at so many.'

'When we reach Sarlat you're staying outside the walls. I'm going in with John Jacob.'

'And if they arrest you, how are we supposed to rescue you?'

'You don't. Stay with Torellini as far as you can. John Jacob and I will find a way to rejoin you.'

Killbere watched the blood on the used bandages splutter in the flames. He grunted and kept his thoughts to himself. Thomas Blackstone spent his life walking through fire. This mission, spurred by the orders of the King, might still consume them all.

Two days later Blackstone and the men looked down from the high ground onto the walled city. The standard fluttering over Sarlat-la-Canéda was not that of the English King.

Killbere turned in the saddle to face Blackstone. 'Whose flag is that?'

Blackstone shook his head. 'There's only one way to find out.'

'Thomas. Let us ride on.'

'We need more men with us and he has them. You stay here.' Blackstone gathered the reins. Killbere reached out his hand and gripped Blackstone's arm.

'Thomas, this is foolish. Let William Ashford take the Italian priest and the others south on the main road. There are towns and monasteries along the way who will give them shelter and safety.'

'And let their journey announce their presence to every routier who has not obeyed our King's command to lay down their arms? I thought this area was clear of skinners. Damned if Felton hasn't kept his own domain safe and left the rest to fend for themselves.'

'Then take Henry with you,' Killbere insisted.

'What?'

Killbere pointed towards the abbey's tower. 'Next to the church, you see the cemetery? Take Henry and if anything happens to you and John Jacob, Henry can get along the city walls and into the graveyard. There's a lantern of the dead. He lights that and we know you need help.'

'I said go on without me,' Blackstone insisted.

'Thomas, we will not. Take the lad. He's no threat to the city's watchmen, he can slip into a crowd, he can see how you are received. You can't take someone like Jack Halfpenny or Will Longdon: they might as well carry a sign saying they are English bowmen. Take Henry. Let him be your guardian. And the walls are low enough next to those graves for us to get inside with a scaling ladder.'

Blackstone considered his options and while he thought it through Killbere quietly insisted: 'You are the King's man, Thomas. There is a battle yet to be fought. You need to start thinking about your importance to Edward and what he asks of you. If you are taken, if this Lord of Vitrac is a pig with his snout in the trough of opportunity snuffling for gold then you cannot remain a captive if they seize you. You'll need us.'

Blackstone could not argue.

And Killbere knew it. 'When you were a callow sixteen-year-old stonemason using your muscles instead of your brain and they arrested you along with your brother, you both faced the hangman's noose because they charged him with rape and you were his guardian. Who was it that told you to use your wits and intelligence in your defence?'

Blackstone sighed.

'Exactly. Listen to me and you will avoid the hangman's noose time and again.'

Blackstone wheeled the bastard horse. 'I listened to you and I was sent to war.'

'And I take full credit for your success.'

Blackstone called out: 'John, send Henry to me.'

CHAPTER FORTY-TWO

Blackstone had instructed Meulon to find the most worthless rouncey for Henry to ride. Once again the boy would play the role of a pilgrim but rather than keep up with Blackstone and John Jacob on foot a broken-down horse served its purpose: Henry rode subserviently behind. By the time the city gates hove into sight the cheap saddle and the horse's stumbling gait had the lad wincing.

'I will sell this nag to the nearest butcher,' he complained. 'My arse feels as though it has been scrubbed by a river stone.'

'You remember everything I told you?' said Blackstone. 'Is your brain less bruised than your backside?'

'I know what to do,' Henry replied churlishly, the tone of his voice earning a disapproving look from John Jacob. 'My lord,' Henry added.

'And stay out of trouble,' Blackstone warned him.

Henry made no reply. They had given him barely enough money for a pauper's meal. Any chance to drink in an alehouse and get involved in trouble was beyond his means.

They had descended from the low hills approaching Sarlat's south-western gate. The city rose up before them, the abbey's bell tower peeking above the rooftops to the east. Blackstone turned in the saddle. 'You see it, Henry?'

'Aye, my lord.' The ground fell away as the walls to the south-east dipped and rose along the undulating land. If a breach was to be made they would do it beyond the abbey and the walls that skirted the cemetery.

A gaggle of people pressed at the gates but Blackstone waited until they had been ushered through into the city.

'Market day,' said John Jacob. 'I can hear the cackle of voices from here.'

Blackstone drew the bastard horse to a halt in front of the city walls and main gate. They were beyond crossbow range. If there was to be an unfriendly welcome, they needed a chance to turn and run. Sentries stood on the city walls above the portal and challenged the travellers.

'I am Thomas Blackstone. I serve the King of England.'

'Your business?' one of the sentries called.

'The King's business!' John Jacob bellowed. 'Open the damned gates and bring your captain of the guard.'

There was a hurried discussion between the soldiers. One ducked out of sight.

'You've got to exert authority with the French, it's the only language they understand,' said John Jacob in answer to Blackstone's querulous look. John Jacob shrugged. 'That or a sword point up their arses.'

'Let us hope words are better than blades today,' said Blackstone.

A third man appeared on the walls. 'Sir Thomas, I am the captain of the guard. I beg forgiveness, lord, but the mayor and burghers have instructed us to question armed men who seek entry. Routiers have plagued us since the city yielded to the English.'

'Do you see marauders at my back?' Blackstone answered.

'No, lord, only the boy,' the captain acknowledged.

'He's a pilgrim we found on the road. We offered him our protection. The mayor will receive me and I will disclose my business to him.'

'Aye, my lord, as you wish,' said the captain. The city gates creaked open, manhandled by four men, which showed

Blackstone how heavy they were. Any assault on Sarlat would need a body of men and machines. They rode beneath the archway as the captain came down the steps from the parapet. 'Lord, I will escort you.' He beckoned three of his men to accompany him.

Blackstone and John Jacob followed his lead as the gates closed behind them. They were led into a broader street than many of those that went off to the side. Both men considered the difficulty of having to engage an enemy in the narrow streets that twisted this way and that throughout the city of several thousand. The lanes' pebbled surfaces gave sure footing on a dry day but iron-shod horses would falter on the uneven surface if obliged to move at anything more than a walking pace as they did now. If men were forced to fight in alleyways and streets where four men could barely stand shoulder to shoulder then they risked being easily contained by a determined militia or roused citizens.

The bustling alleyways were pressed with people. The coloured tunics of artisans mingled with housewives in gowns, their hair covered in wimples. The wealth in the city lay with the merchants, those who wore fur-trimmed coats, who jostled through the crowds like any commoner. Tradesmen carried baskets of their wares, crying out impatiently to those shuffling more leisurely as they stopped to examine a stallholder's goods. Filthy urchins, barefooted and dressed in little more than rags, darted through the crowds, palms extended for a morsel of food. The captain of the guard and his three men shouted their authority and cleared a path for the three horsemen behind them and geese and chickens honked and clucked, wings fluttering as they scuttled away from the horses' hooves. Villeins and merchants alike pressed themselves back as the towering horse and scar-faced rider rode by.

The captain gestured towards a side street where horse dung was being swept up by stable lads in accordance with the city ordinance forbidding horses fouling the streets. 'There are stables here for your mounts.' He whistled and called a couple of names and two grubby lads ran into view from the stable yard. The bastard horse raised its ears and stopped. Blackstone knew it would be useless to spur him on. It would likely lash out and kill one of the frail-looking boys.

'The pilgrim will repay our kindness by stabling my horse. Show him where to keep the beast away from other mounts. Understand?' said Blackstone, quietly thankful that he had brought Henry into the city walls. His presence now served a double purpose.

The captain nodded as John Jacob and Blackstone dismounted. Henry's horse drooped its head as docile as a beaten dog and he handed the reins to one of the stable hands, then stepped quickly to where Blackstone avoided a sudden snap of yellow teeth from his own horse. Blackstone swore under his breath. The captain looked uncertain. 'He takes a dislike to some. Not all,' he explained as Henry took hold of the reins and let the big beast snuffle his hand. It shook its great misshapen head and allowed Henry to walk it forward into the yard as the urchin boys followed, tugging the other two horses.

'This way,' said the captain.

'Where are you taking us? Blackstone demanded.

'The guildhall, my lord. On the main square. It's not far,' the captain answered, not realizing that Blackstone had elicited the information for Henry's benefit so he could follow as soon as he and the stable lads had attended to the horses.

Blackstone and John Jacob could see that the deeper they went into the labyrinth the more dangerous it became. The streets twisted and curled like a nest of vipers and stallholders narrowed the lanes even further. Only when the streets broadened out into the town square was there easier passage. In the centre of the cobbled area three bodies hung from a gibbet. Their clothing was already torn by crows, and what flesh was visible had been stripped by strong, eager beaks and stones hurled by children who competed to see who could strike a hanged man's face.

'Thieves?' said Blackstone.

'No, my lord,' answered the captain without giving further information.

Blackstone and John Jacob exchanged glances. Who else would be hanged in the square if not thieves? Routiers perhaps? It was obvious the dead men had been a threat. No doubt they would soon find out.

CHAPTER FORTY-THREE

The captain of the guard escorted them into Sarlat's guildhall's outer chamber, long and broad enough for thirty or more burghers to await an audience with the mayor and city council. Blackstone and John Jacob were left alone in the corridor once the captain pushed through carved chestnut doors into an inner chamber.

'Step outside and see that Henry is watching,' said Blackstone.

John Jacob turned back for the entrance as Blackstone went to the far end of the antechamber. The half-panelled room had long benches along each wall. If they had walked into trouble, there was no door to allow an escape other than the one opened by their escort. John Jacob's boots scraped the uneven flagged stone floor.

'He's across the way. He looks as wretched as any pilgrim I ever saw.'

'He has a sweet tooth and no money to satisfy it,' said Blackstone. He had deliberately given Henry only enough money to buy bread and, if he bargained hard enough, a hot meal. For a pilgrim to have any more in his purse meant he could fall prey to thieves.

The heavy doors creaked open. The captain of the guard stood aside, allowing Blackstone and John Jacob to enter a large room that was empty except for an ornate chair, and, beyond it, a door on either side. A robed man was seated in the chair with a man-of-arms standing behind him. The bearded knight was stocky with a belly pushing against his broad sword belt. There was no doubt he was a fighter. A scar ran across his forehead and a piece of his scalp was missing, leaving a red welt. His gnarled hands and flattened knuckles showed that he was unafraid to use his fists, and he lacked two fingers on his left hand.

Blackstone knew the man-at-arms would have no role to play in Sarlat's governance. The masters of the various city guilds elected the mayor and his council. It was a contract between the city and the Lord of the domain in which the city fell and knights and clergy were excluded from serving. The merchants needed people allied with their own interests on such councils. There were charters in place that guaranteed freedom from feudal obligations, allowing cities to raise their own taxes and operate courts of justice. Blackstone realized Gisbert de Dome must have fallen foul of someone or he would have been there to greet them.

'I am squire to my lord, Sir Thomas Blackstone, who is here on the King's business,' said John Jacob, bowing his head in deference to the dignitary's office.

'Sir Thomas,' said the seated official, 'I am Raymond Villon, elected councilman.' He raised a hand without turning. 'This is Sir Gaillard de Miremont, Lord of Sauignac, whose service to this city is gratefully acknowledged.'

'Sarlat has declared for the English Crown but you have a French knight standing with you. I see no evidence of the Seneschal Gisbert de Dome,' said Blackstone.

'Who, since the declaration, threw in his lot with English brigands,' said Villon. 'They raided Cahors, seized churches and wreaked havoc across vast tracts of land. He was dismissed from his position. Three of his lieutenants were hanged; two were drowned.'

'Where is he?' demanded Blackstone. Gisbert de Dome was not only responsible for holding the city for the English King but Blackstone had counted on his help to escort Torellini and Cateline.

'What is your business with him?' said the French knight.

'It does not concern you,' Blackstone answered dismissively. 'This city is no longer held by the French Crown. You have no place here.'

'He serves to protect us where the English cannot,' said the mayor.

'I will determine who protects this city,' said Blackstone. 'Is he alive?'

'Imprisoned,' said de Miremont. 'Awaiting confirmation that he is to be either pardoned or sentenced.'

'Take me to him,' said Blackstone.

'You must surrender your arms,' said the French knight.

'I will disarm you if you make that demand again,' Blackstone threatened.

De Miremont bristled from the insult but the Mayor raised his hand to stop the altercation. 'Sir Thomas will see him. Arrange it,' he instructed.

The French knight strode from the room. Blackstone heard him summon the captain of the guard. 'Was there an assault against the city? Did you have sufficient men?' asked Blackstone, an innocent enough question that would tease out how many armed men were in the city.

'There is no need for concern, Sir Thomas, and no need to send word to Sir William Felton. There was no attack here and we have the militia and levies, few in number but enough to man the walls, and we have enough food and water. It was Gisbert de Dome's siding with the routiers that led us to arrest him. We wish only for peace,' said the mayor. 'Gisbert de Dome was the instigator of his own downfall.'

'And what of de Miremont's men?'

'Garrisoned in the city. No more than twenty men-at-arms but enough to lead our militia.'

'Then it seems you have done all you could do,' said Blackstone, in a deliberately conciliatory tone to flatter the Mayor.

The door opened and de Miremont beckoned them. 'We will take you to him.'

The Mayor dipped his head in farewell to Blackstone. He and John Jacob turned away. 'If they attack us it won't be here,' said Blackstone. 'It will be once we are in the prison.'

Sir Gaillard de Miremont waited in the outer chamber with the escort. A curt nod indicated Blackstone and his squire should follow him. The escort fell in behind. As they stepped out into the street Blackstone searched for Henry. His back was turned to the guildhall as he gazed down at a pie seller's wares. Blackstone could almost hear the boy's stomach rumbling. If Henry didn't raise his head soon he would miss them.

'Sir Gaillard,' Blackstone called, raising his voice, so that Henry was alerted. 'Is the prison far?'

The belligerent French knight kept walking. 'No.'

Blackstone saw Henry turn, panic written on his face, a mouthful of pie spilling from his lips. Blackstone glared at him. A warning to stay alert.

De Miremont pushed people aside as he strode through the streets. The citizens of Sarlat dared not raise their faces and show their contempt for him but Blackstone and John Jacob saw their resentment towards the nobleman.

'If we got word to Sir Gilbert and William Ashford to bring Torellini and the woman to the gates seeking sanctuary, and have our men riding as escort, we would have all the men we need to seize the walls,' said John Jacob. 'It looks as though de Miremont and his men are unwelcome guests invited by the Mayor.'

'As soon as we see this renegade that Chandos paid off we'll make a move,' Blackstone said.

The Frenchman led them on a circuitous route to the abbey's church, the cathedral of Saint Sacerdos. Blackstone scanned the terrain. To the east lay the monastery's cloisters and vaults. Blackstone knew they were close to the cemetery at the rear of the church and the lantern of the dead by the low wall. Blackstone's demand he be taken to the prisoner had helped guide Henry to where he needed to be in case trouble flared up. De Miremont led them through the vast doors. The dark church smelled damp, and lacked enough light to illuminate the gloom-filled recesses on either side. Their footsteps echoed. 'In the crypt,' said the Frenchman. It was not unusual for a city to keep prisoners awaiting sentencing or execution in a church crypt.

Blackstone looked behind him. Their escort guarded the door. He knew John Jacob shared his unease.

'We're in God's hands now,' said his squire, staring through the half-light towards the altar and crossing himself, following the Frenchman's example by bending his knee. Blackstone gazed up at the column that bore the hewn wooden figure of Christ on the cross. He raised Arianrhod from the leather thong around his neck and kissed the archers' talisman. Despite the darkness, the image glared down at him, brown-painted eyes filled with pain and pity. Blackstone lifted his wife's small crucifix that shared his journey with the Goddess of the Silver Wheel and pressed its cold metal to his lips. There were times a fighting man needed all the blessings he could muster. Beyond the altar a brazier burned to either side of the crypt's steps. De Miremont lifted an oil-soaked torch, held it to the flame and led the way down.

At the bottom of the steps the low ceiling almost touched the top of Blackstone's head; curved supporting arches disappeared into darkness. Centuries ago, a hermit had lived in the crypt and from the sickly odour it seemed as though he was still there. Twenty more paces and the overpowering stench of human waste and the low groan of an injured man reached them. The flickering torch spread a gossamer web of smoke into the curved roof, its light revealing men huddled in chains behind a cage. Fifteen or more at first glance. The Frenchman stood to one side.

Blackstone approached the iron grille. 'Gisbert de Dome? Where are you?'

One figure roused himself with the clank of a chain running through a walled eyelet. 'Who wants to know?' said a defiant voice.

'Thomas Blackstone.'

The mention of his name made the man step more quickly towards the light. He raised a hand to shield his eyes from the unaccustomed brightness. He wore breeches and shirt, both stained with blood and dirt. His matted beard and hair had not seen water for some time.

'Sir Thomas,' said Gisbert de Dome. 'Thank God. You've brought an army with you to hang this wretch who seeks to line his pocket at the city's expense?'

'I'm alone except for my squire.' He was close enough to see the man's brow furrow. His face creased in disappointment.

Blackstone turned to de Miremont. 'I wish to speak to him alone. Give the torch to my squire and leave us.'

The French knight offered no argument, handed the burning torch to John Jacob and made his way back up the steps. 'You betrayed John Chandos and took up with skinners,' said Blackstone.

'I needed money. I have to pay and feed four hundred men in Dome. It's a stronghold that needs a garrison. You know that. It commands the heights on the Dordogne, which is why my men are there and not here. And the English charged me with governing Sarlat. I would have kept my side of the bargain but Villon conspired to withhold taxes. One by one he imprisoned the council.' He turned his head to show the men lying in misery on the cold stone floor. 'Three are dead in their chains. Others soon to follow.'

Blackstone looked more carefully at the chained prisoners and saw that they were all older men. 'These are city merchants? Councilmen?'

'Aye. A gaggle of low-caste men on his payroll voted Villon for mayor. They impart justice in the city. Five of my lieutenants were executed. He cannot kill me yet, not until he is certain news of my death will not reach Sir William's ears. Though I fear the bastard has already poisoned the well as far as Felton and me are concerned.'

'I came from Poitiers. Sir William made no mention of your plight. Had he known he would have told me.'

'Then I am as good as dead. Villon and de Miremont must be parlaying with King John.'

Blackstone studied the man for a moment. 'Don't lie,' he said. 'You could have appealed to the English for help.'

Gisbert de Dome held Blackstone's gaze, and then he smiled sheepishly. 'All right, so I saw a chance to make money. And most of the merchants in the city tried to stop me being promoted to Seneschal of Périgord. I owed them nothing. When Chandos knocked on the gates because Sarlat was to be turned over to the English I saw several opportunities present themselves. The routiers came down from the hills; I went with them.'

'Who?'

'Bertucat d'Albret and Gruffydd ap Madoc were among them.'

'The Welshman rode through here?'

'Yes. South. He'll claim a bounty from any towns, to spare him attacking them. Like I said, money to be made.'

'If I get you out of here, and the merchants with you, you will swear allegiance to me and allow the council to stand again.'

'I will,' said the Lord of Vitrac with sudden hope.

'And I want half your men.'

'Agreed! Do this thing, Sir Thomas, and you will know the safety and hospitality of Dome.'

He extended a grimy hand through the bars. Blackstone took it. A bargain struck. Blackstone turned away. John Jacob raised the light to show the way. Halfway up the steps they saw de Miremont and his men blocking them. There were more than the three-man escort: these were de Miremont's own men-at-arms.

'Surrender your arms, Sir Thomas. There's no escape.'

Blackstone drew Wolf Sword; John Jacob freed his own blade. Both men pressed forward with such aggression that the first rank of men fell back into those behind them. John Jacob swept the torch, forcing those in the front to raise a protective arm. Blackstone maimed and killed four before de Miremont's men could retaliate. John Jacob jabbed low. The men above were at a disadvantage. Hamstrung men fell, floundering in their agony, but their wounds served de Miremont's cause. They tumbled down the steps, writhing bodies hampering Blackstone and his squire. No sooner had Blackstone lost the advantage than de Miremont and his men forced their way down. The two men had no choice but to give way until they once again reached the floor of the crypt. The Frenchman suddenly halted the attack. In less time than it had taken for him to descend the stairs he had lost half a dozen men. Blackstone and John Jacob pressed their backs against the iron bars. Several crossbowmen clattered down the stairs behind de Miremont.

'You're worth a ransom, Blackstone, but I will not hesitate to kill you. Yield or die,' he demanded.

John Jacob bristled. Blackstone sensed he was going to drive forward to give Blackstone a chance to fight his way clear. The distance was too great. They would be dead before they reached halfway.

'No, John. We must live to fight another day,' he said gently, a restraining hand on John Jacob's sword arm. His squire understood and let his blade drop to the floor.

Blackstone threw down Wolf Sword.

De Miremont stepped forward with his men. They stripped Blackstone and John Jacob of their knives. The Frenchman's fist smashed into Blackstone's face as others held blades at John Jacob's throat, rendering him helpless. Blackstone's head whipped aside, his cheek split, but his knees did not buckle.

'I've seen a milkmaid squeeze a cow's teat harder than that,' he said.

Both men took a beating and were then thrown into the cage.

PART FOUR

THE ROAD TO WAR

CHAPTER FORTY-FOUR

Henry had followed his father and John Jacob to the cathedral. Once they'd been escorted inside, he stepped into the gloom but was stopped and turned away by one of the soldiers guarding the door. He waited and minutes later saw the French knight step outside and give an unheard order to one of the escorts. It wasn't long before more than a dozen armed men ran into view. It was obvious from their blazon they served the barrel-chested Frenchman. Fear squirmed in Henry's stomach when he saw several of the men ready their crossbows. When they stormed into the abbey behind their leader Henry got as close as he could to the entrance. Voices raised in anger and pain echoed through the vast church. He peered into the half-light. Figures clustered around the top of the steps to the crypt. It was obvious the confined space was hampering the attackers. And there was no doubt in his mind whom they were attacking. Instinctively he stepped forward to help his father but then realized he was unarmed. Common sense made him falter. If his father and John Jacob lived, then they needed help, and that was the purpose for which they had brought him into the city. A voice commanded those in the street to move aside. It was the provost and his men, running towards the abbey. Henry ducked out of sight behind the nearest building with a clear view of the church entrance. Soldiers dragged bodies clear. Henry felt a wave of relief; these were men his father and John Jacob had killed. Others hobbled from their wounds. The provost ordered the wounded taken to the infirmary and Henry heard the burly Frenchman instruct the provost that the crypt and the church door be manned day and night. He knew his father was alive when he heard the Frenchman tell the provost that the Englishman was worth his weight in gold.

It was still hours until darkness when he could signal Killbere. Reason dictated that he should try to discover the enemy's strength. He forgot his pangs of hunger as he set off to follow the Frenchman who had led the attack against his father. By the time an hour passed he had followed him around the mile-long walls and watched men positioned, braziers prepared and weapons placed ready. His spirits lifted when he saw the quality of the men being posted. The men-at-arms were split up, paired and placed with levies and militia. It was obvious that the men of Sarlat had little experience in fighting and needed those who did to command them. Fear of invaders would make the weakest man defend his city and home, but if an enemy launched a determined attack it needed more courage than many possessed to stand their ground. Professional fighting men would threaten death for any man who deserted his post. Fear always played a part.

Henry made his way back towards the cemetery along a narrow raised path behind the abbey. Below him the graves were laid out neatly behind the church. The path continued past the thirty-foot-high domed structure, a lantern of the dead different in size and shape than any he had ever seen. Henry sat on the low wall and tugged free the remains of the pie from inside his jerkin. He looked no different from any other poor traveller stopping to nourish himself. Henry was more interested in the building than the cold pie. He looked around him. The path was far enough from the city streets not to attract casual passers-by. Cramming the last of the pie into his mouth, he stepped into the building. The chill air made his skin crawl. Death clung to the walls. The circular room was a place of prayer for the dead, built to signal their passing. Did spirits seep from the walls and haunt the graveyard by night? Henry crossed himself. His father and John Jacob were held in darkness barely three hundred yards away below ground in the ancient church's crypt. As good as dead. Buried alive. He checked outside, saw no one, and clambered up the steps counting every tread, the numbers focusing his mind. Forty steps. Narrow. Steep. Up into darkness.

At the upper level slivers of light illuminated the dusty wooden floor. A narrow slit in each of three rectangular bays in the dome faced different directions so that a burning lantern could be seen across the city and beyond the walls to the forested hills. An unlit lantern was placed on each sill. Henry tilted one of them back and forth and heard the oil sloshing inside. His flint would spark the wick and Blackstone's men would bring death into the city. There was nothing more to do except wait for darkness and the terror that would soon follow. He curled up below one of the window slits and fell soundly asleep.

Killbere made his way to the edge of the forest where Meulon and the men waited.

'We fight with you,' said Wolfram von Plauen.

'No, you stay and guard the woman,' Killbere told him. 'That's your sworn duty.'

He could see von Plauen wanted an argument, but the German had been put in his place and he could not go back on his word to Blackstone. The aggrieved knight turned away. His companions watched the exchange.

'We are not obliged by any oath,' said Gunther von Schwerin.

'And your damned white surcoats will flap like bedsheets drying in the wind. When the clouds shift, they'll see you coming in the moonlight before we get halfway. No, you stay.'

'If there is trouble in the city, then it might be because of routiers, and if that is the case then the Welshman we seek might be there,' the German insisted.

'I'm not interested in your revenge.' Killbere turned his back and walked towards Meulon, who stood at the edge of the forest with Renfred and Will Longdon. Clouds obscuring the moon teased apart like stretched silk on a loom, allowing soft light to filter across the city. Braziers burned on the walls at each of the city's four portals, north, south, east and west. The braziers looked to be five hundred paces distance from one to the other and between the portals the walls fell into darkness.

Meulon looked up at the clouds. 'The wind is in our face. It will help.'

Killbere nodded. The flickering light that emanated from the domed tower was the signal they had been waiting for. 'Will, your lads ready?'

'Aye,' said the centenar.

'We take the path down through the orchards as soon as the clouds cover the moon. One man in front of the other so no one stumbles. Renfred, your boys carry the ladder.'

Killbere looked left and right. The moon glow showed him the line of men on the forest's edge waiting for his order. Each one wore a small patch of white linen stitched onto the back of their jupon's collar so that the man behind could follow closely. There was no need for Killbere to give a command when the moon went dark. He stepped forward as Blackstone's men, disciplined in night attack and the use of scaling ladders, peeled off behind him until they became one long line moving silently through the night. The north wind brushed their faces, bringing smells of the city and the silence of a sleeping population. The going was easy through the lanes of trees whose leaves had mostly fallen, cushioning the sound of spurs and creaking leather boots. The wind eased away any rustle of mail or clank of weapons but carried the occasional voice of men at their posts, already weary of standing watch. When the moon was exposed the men crouched, waited for the clouds, and then stood silently and carried on towards the dark shape of the wall. As they reached the lowest point of the city's defences Killbere and Meulon stepped aside, allowing Renfred's men to lean the scaling ladder against the stonework.

Killbere took the lead and scrambled up the ladder to the top of the wall, which was only twenty feet high at that point. He peered carefully along the walkway to see that a sentry lay sleeping with his back against the parapet. A cowled figure in the graveyard below raised a hand and pulled back the hood so that they could see his face and hand in the half-light. Killbere crouched and made his way down to Henry as behind him the rest of the men came over the wall.

'Your father and John Jacob, what's happened to them?' said Killbere.

'They are in the crypt. There was a fight, and I don't know if either of them are injured. They killed half a dozen men.'

Will Longdon and Jack Halfpenny, with their archers, circled the walled graveyard and as the centenar passed by he placed a reassuring hand on Henry's shoulder. This was no time for conversation: that could come later when the killing was finished.

As the men took up defensive positions Henry pointed to the nearest sentry post. 'I went around the walls and saw where they have men posted. There are men-at-arms with the militia at each portal. There are four gates into the city.'

'Aye, I saw their braziers burning.'

'You can approach along the walls, and if you kill the men-at-arms at their posts, I don't think the city's militia would put up much of a fight, but I don't know if there are more armed men somewhere else. There is a French knight who commands the men here.'

'Well done, lad. Now you must take us through the streets so that Will and Jack can get their archers in position. They have sentries on the streets at the gates?'

Henry nodded.

Killbere thought for a moment and beckoned Meulon to him. The big Norman bent his head so he could hear Killbere's quietly spoken command. 'Henry will lead you. At first light kill the men at the gates. Will and Jack will bring down the men on the walls. I'll wait here with Renfred and release Thomas and John Jacob.' He looked towards the church. 'He's in the crypt.'

Meulon nodded his understanding and looked back towards the gathered men. 'How many men to stay with you?'

'Three to watch our back. Henry, you guide Meulon and the men through the streets to the gates, then return here and wait at the lantern of the dead, understood?'

Henry nodded. 'Follow me,' he told Meulon, who signalled his men and the archers.

CHAPTER FORTY-FIVE

Henry ran through the narrow streets that became so dark from the overhanging buildings that at one point he whispered urgently for Meulon to stop. Pressing the back of his hand against the stone wall that ran along the street he heard the men's heavy breathing behind him. Someone stumbled on the cobbles and their whispered curses sounded as loud as a thunderclap. Uncertainty took hold, and he wondered if he had taken a wrong turn. What he had seen in daylight appeared to be different at night. Night shadows contorted the shape of buildings and the curve of the narrow lanes. Meulon whispered an urgent demand. Was he lost?

Henry settled the panic that rose from his chest and pictured the route he had followed when the French knight posted his men. If he was on the right track, then when he turned the next corner and looked up there would be a wind vane showing the bent figure of a blacksmith wielding a hammer against an anvil. Edging forwards, he felt the rough stone scrape the skin on the back of his hand. He ignored it, wanting to keep his palm free of abrasions should he need to grip a knife. He heard the creaking metal of the wind vane before he saw it. The north wind caught the iron blacksmith, nudging him this way and that. Henry's relief spurred him on.

He turned and whispered to Meulon: 'Not far now.'

Memory and instinct took him left and right, skirting merchants' houses and shuttered artisan workshops. A pinched alley led the way to the first portal. Henry pressed an arm back to slow Meulon and then pointed up towards the guard post. Two men stood leaning against the wall, shoulders hunched against the cold damp air, their backs to the city as they gazed blearily across the dark landscape from where any attack was likely to come. Two other men with them paced back and forth. De Miremont's soldiers, who knew the value of staying alert.

Henry pointed and murmured: 'Those two – men-at-arms. The others – citizen militia.' Below the sentry point another two men slept, huddled against the hinges of the sturdy wooden gates. 'Garrison troops,' said Henry. He felt Meulon nod. The men's eyes were accustomed to the darkness now, and they had no trouble identifying their enemy.

Meulon signalled Will Longdon to him. 'Leave Jack and two archers. Kill those two first,' he whispered, pointing out the professional soldiers on the wall. 'I'll leave four men to kill those at the gate and any others if the alarm is raised. Call on the others to surrender. They are not fighters and Sir Thomas would not have us kill needlessly. We need goodwill if he is to secure the city.'

Will Longdon beckoned Jack Halfpenny and pointed at two other archers, meaning they were to come forward. 'Much good it will do us once your knife finds throats to cut,' said Longdon, and stepped away to give his orders.

'The first hour of daybreak will be on us soon, Master Henry,' said Meulon. 'Three more gates. We must move on. Find your way and find it quickly.'

Killbere and the captains had agreed to strike before first light when the bell rang for early morning prayer. The chill of the hour meant men would be stiff and weary from their night watch, and they would be thinking of their warm hearth and a hot bowl of food. It was a cruel time to die but a good time to kill. Killbere edged around the side of the cemetery. The street in front of the church was as deserted as everywhere else. If a night watch patrol turned a corner there was nowhere for Killbere and the others to hide. Renfred lifted the iron latch as quietly as he could but still the metal scraped. He stopped. The men held their breath, listened, but, hearing no movement or challenge, Killbere nodded for him to continue. He and Renfred pressed their shoulder to the heavy door and eased it open. The far end of the church glowed from a brazier either side of the steps leading to the crypt; around them, about a dozen men lay curled in sleep on the stone floor, wrapped in cloaks for their meagre warmth. Killbere led his small party forward, thankful for the cone of light; his companions moved instinctively into position, fanning out so that when blades plunged into unsuspecting bodies, their strike would be as one. They were ten paces from the sleeping men when a cough from the darkness froze them in their tracks. A footfall scuffed the floor as someone approached from the gloom of the side aisle. Killbere and the others silently retreated into the safety of a side chapel's darkness. They watched as a man stepped into the light. From his dress and the sword in his belt he appeared to be one of the provost's men guarding the crypt. He fussed with the ties on his breeches, having obviously been outside to relieve himself. When he reached the sleeping men, he kicked two of them, cursing them for not being awake. They made little protest, got to their feet, yawned, stretched and stood guard. One drank from a wineskin, then passed it to his companion.

Killbere turned, reached for Renfred and pulled him closer, whispering next to his ear. He listened, nodded and then did the same with the first of Meulon's men. The moment every man was briefed Meulon's three men slipped away silently along the side aisle, readying themselves to attack from behind once Killbere and Renfred broke cover. The cold air had seized Killbere's joints and he cursed silently that too many years lying in wet fields on campaign were taking their toll. Ignoring their stiffness, he curled his fist tightly around his sword and slipped its blood knot over his wrist. Renfred was at his shoulder a few paces away. They would need killing room between them. They waited, steadied their breathing, ignoring the anticipation hammering in their chests. Peering into the warm glow, they chose which men would die first. The three men who had skulked through the darkness to attack from the sleeping men's rear were supposed to provide a distraction. Provoke a turn of the head from the sentries that would allow Killbere and Renfred to stride forward.

Somewhere in the background a blade scraped across stone. As the sound echoed the three sentries' response was immediate. They turned, hands reaching for their swords; uncertain seconds that would cost them their lives. Too late, they wheeled back around. Killbere killed the man who had berated the others. Renfred's sword clashed against the other man's blade with a clang of metal as loud as a church bell. The sleeping men rolled out of their cloaks, shook themselves free of sleep and, as the last of the sentries fell in agonizing death throes, launched themselves at Killbere and Renfred. Killbere rooted himself to where he stood, parried, thrust, pivoted and struck with the expertise of a veteran used to fighting so close to his enemy he could smell the rank odour of their bodies and see their snarling lips curl back in hatred. He relished the close-quarter killing.

As he and Renfred were forced back a few paces, moments away from being overwhelmed, their determined attackers were felled from behind. Meulon's three men struck without warning or mercy. Renfred searched the bodies, found a set of keys, tossed them to Killbere and then pressed a torch into the brazier.

'Guard the entrance,' said Killbere to the three silent killers.

Killbere followed Renfred below ground and saw Blackstone and John Jacob, faces pressed against the bars. One of John Jacob's eyes was closed from the beating he'd taken and Blackstone's face bore bruises and swelling. 'You kill them all?' said Blackstone as Killbere fussed with the bunch of keys, trying to find the right one.

'Nine dead, two lying in their gore waiting for the devil to take them,' said Killbere as another key failed in the lock.

'I hope you weren't as slow in the killing as you are with that lock,' said Blackstone.

Killbere kept his eyes on the keys. 'Thomas, I swear the thought rises in my mind of leaving you here. How many more times must I rescue you?'

The lock sprung free. Blackstone grinned. 'As long as we both shall live.'

'That might not be much longer. This damned city is a warren. A half-dozen men could seal our fate in these narrow streets.'

'Where's Henry?'

'With Meulon.'

Blackstone turned to the imprisoned merchants and councilmen. 'You stay chained until we have killed de Miremont and his men. It's the safest place for you. I'll have you free, I swear it.'

The men muttered their thanks. 'God bless you, Sir Thomas,' one of them called.

'You'll need it,' said Killbere as Blackstone freed one of the prisoners. 'Who's he?'

'The man who knows the streets and where the soldiers will be. Gisbert de Dome.'

Blackstone led the way up the steps. 'Where are the men?' he asked, scooping up a sword from one of the dead guards.

'At the city gates until the bell for prime rings.'

'And then?'

'The killing starts.'

CHAPTER FORTY-SIX

Gisbert de Dome shivered as he stepped into the cold night air. The stiff northerly breeze ruffled his linen shirt. He consoled himself that he would soon retrieve his clothing and weapons seized when he had been arrested by de Miremont.

'This way,' he told Blackstone as they went past the men guarding the entrance.

Blackstone caught de Dome's arm. 'Where are you going?'

'The bastard will be in my house sleeping with a whore in my bed. What better place to kill him?'

Blackstone hesitated. 'No, he won't be there. He's a fighting man. He'll expect an assault. He's no fool. I made no mention of my men but he'll know I'd have had them with me and that if I didn't return in good time, then they'd come for me. What he will not expect is that we are already inside the walls. De Miremont will be at the main gate. Take us there.'

The freed nobleman immediately saw the sense in what Blackstone had said and his desire for revenge was as cold as his chilled skin. He nodded. 'This way.' He led them this way and that, as surefooted as any citizen who knew his way blindfolded around his own city, off the main thoroughfares and into the twisting alleyways that would lead to the city walls. By the time he raised his hand to bring them to a halt sweat was trickling down their backs from their fast pace. Blackstone stared at the silhouette of a black storm cloud that was the city wall looming in front. He could see men moving along the wall's walkway. Straining his eyes, he attempted to pick out the figure of de

Miremont. A shadow moved close to them. A startled Gisbert de Dome uttered a cry. Blackstone's hand quickly smothered his mouth. He whispered, 'One of mine.'

Meulon stepped closer. Blackstone released de Dome. 'Sir Thomas, we watched your approach. Thought for a minute you were one of them,' Meulon said quietly, meaning the men on the walls. The throat-cutter's teeth gleamed in the darkness. 'I've got Will here with some of his lads. Master Henry brought us through the streets.'

'He's here?'

'Back in the shadows.'

'Keep him there.'

'We're ready, Sir Thomas. We were going to spare the night watch militia and kill the men-at-arms. Are those your orders?'

'Unless they put up a fight and don't surrender,' said Blackstone.

'Aye. We'll finish them off quickly.'

'How many on the walls and ground?' said Killbere.

'Twenty over the main gate. Not many down here. A handful. I reckon there must be more in the city. There's just not enough men here.'

Blackstone knew that although he could not see Will Longdon and his archers they would be spread along the rear of the buildings in the shadows, ready to loose their arrows and kill those on the walls. Blackstone looked up at the sky. The first glimmer of daylight touched the clouds. The grey light would soon be the last thing many of the men defending the city would see. 'Will and his men will not have time to shoot again. The moment the first men-at-arms fall others will be alerted. Sir Gilbert and John will come with me onto the walls with a few men.' He saw Killbere turn and tap half a dozen men. 'You and the others kill the sentries at the gates and then secure the surrounding area.'

'What about me?' said Gisbert de Dome.

'Stay here. I need you alive.' He glanced down the line of men crouched waiting behind him in the alley. Instinct told him it was time.

Blackstone turned away from Meulon with Killbere and John Jacob at his heels. The steps leading up to the walls were fifteen paces away. A dull clanging of a church bell in the distance denoted it was time for monks to pray and people to leave the warmth of their beds. In the broken silence a whisper of loosed arrows from the unseen bowmen rushed past his head. They struck with deadly accuracy. The first few men fell without a cry, the force of the arrow shafts piercing their chests and strangling any gasp for air. It was their companions who cried out fearfully at the invisible hand that had struck down their comrades, by which time Blackstone was on the walkway with Killbere taking the men left and John Jacob bringing the remaining with him behind Blackstone. The civilian militia threw down their arms and ran. No one at street level could have seen the men-at-arms who had slept with their backs against the parapet. These men did not surrender so easily. They lurched to their feet, swords already drawn. Blackstone killed the first man, who managed to half-raise himself before Blackstone's sword cut into his neck and shoulder. He yanked him aside, his body thudding onto the street below where Meulon's men were quickly killing the sentries. Screams and shouts of alarm echoed through the streets far more urgently than the monotonous ringing of the bell. There was enough room on the wall for three men to fight shoulder to shoulder. Men-at-arms lunged at Blackstone and John Jacob who used the narrowness of the rampart to their advantage. As Blackstone swung and struck, forcing the men back, John Jacob kept his sword low, stabbing upward through their broken defence. They stepped over bodies, or pulled the wounded aside to be killed by Blackstone's men behind them. The clamour of fighting along the wall was evidence of the concerted attack. Killbere, for his part, cursed the men-at-arms who stood their ground and ignored cries for leniency from the wounded. The militia on his section of the wall begged for clemency too as they surrendered and were mostly spared, though in the bloodletting a sword blade often found its mark before its strike could be turned aside.

From every corner a running battle ensued along the walls. Blackstone knew he and his men were now at their most vulnerable. The city had awoken to an assault. Confusion and panic could bring more armed militia onto the streets but Blackstone reasoned that they would not put up any resistance to Meulon and the others who had secured the city gates. Those who fought on the walls would soon be overcome and then it was only the garrison and de Miremont's men who would counter-attack. He needed to find the Frenchman and secure the city.

'I don't see de Miremont,' John Jacob called.

Blackstone looked beyond the dead and the dying. The smoke from the braziers smudged the line of the wall. Then he saw the Frenchman retreating along the walkway towards the next gate. De Miremont ran down a flight of steps into the street. He would soon be in the square to rally and organize the rest of his men. 'John! Secure the wall with Sir Gilbert.' Blackstone ran forward, and then shouted to the men below: 'Meulon!'

The throat-cutter looked up. Blackstone gestured to where de Miremont was turning into the street. Meulon saw him, understood, summoned the men with him and gave chase. Blackstone called out to the hulking Norman spearman: 'Cry *St George*!'

Meulon turned and raised an arm in acknowledgement. The city was King Edward's by treaty and his cry would tell the citizens it was not routiers who had breached their walls. The English were their protection against such brigands and hearing the fighting men declare themselves might restrain them from taking up arms. Meulon and his men raced down a narrow alley. Doors slammed shut at the sound of pounding feet. Anyone foolish enough to step out was shouldered aside and left sprawled in the gutter flowing with sewage.

Blackstone went down the steps three at a time. The monotonous clanging bell now became more vigorous in its urgency. Sounding the alarm. The city was under attack. Will Longdon and his archers stepped forward; Henry Blackstone was with them.

'Will, get your lads on the walls.'

The centenar needed no further command and ran for the steps. Blackstone placed a hand on his son's shoulder. 'Yet again you have proved your courage. Stay with Will.' Blackstone saw the shadow of disappointment. 'I don't want you in this fight. Do as I say.'

Henry knew the urgency of the moment demanded he obey. 'Yes, Father,' he said.

Blackstone spared a moment to watch his son run after the archers and then saw Gisbert de Dome waiting for him, his shirt flecked with blood from the fighting, a sword in one hand, a knife in the other. 'Sir Thomas?'

'We hold and defend the square,' said Blackstone. The enemy he sought bore Wolf Sword on his belt.

The men-at-arms on the walls had fallen under the archer's arrows and Blackstone's fighters had killed the unseen men who slept at each portal. Will Longdon rallied his archers on the walkway once they had secured the gates and sent a runner in each direction to have the others at every gate follow his example. The archers' bows were unwieldy in a close-quarter fight in a town's streets: the bowmen needed space to draw and distance to shoot and their presence on the walls gave Blackstone's men the advantage should de Miremont's men retreat towards the gates. Will Longdon and Jack Halfpenny's archers would cut them down before they reached the portal. Above and below the gates Blackstone's men controlled the way in and out of the city. The confines of the streets might allow their enemy to counter-attack and if that happened Blackstone and the few men with him might need to escape back into the forest. It was up to the archers to cover them.

Longdon scoured the streets, searching across the rooftops for any sign of Meulon and Blackstone. Screams reached him: the clamour of voices raised in panic. He heard men shout. *Saint George! Saint George!* Longdon raised the archers' charm to his lips and prayed that Arianrhod, Goddess of the Silver Wheel, did not abandon Thomas Blackstone now.

Then he yanked bodkin-tipped arrows from the corpses.

CHAPTER FORTY-SEVEN

Blackstone reached the square. All except his archers were gathered together as Meulon and Renfred formed the men into a tight knot of defence. Meulon had spent years fighting in towns and cities throughout France and Italy where the fabric of the buildings could count against men jostling through twisting streets. Buildings often shielded those intent on harm. In Sarlat it was impossible to secure the spider's web of unlit alleyways where de Miremont's troops could wait in ambush. The sun had not broken through the blanket of clouds. Only dull, grey light smothered the city. Better to find open ground and take the brunt of the assault.

Moments after Blackstone reached his men Killbere arrived, gasping for breath. 'Merciful Christ,' he wheezed. 'Since when are we meant to run and fight?' It was a question needing no answer. Killbere had wind enough to draw breath in a close fight; he needed nothing more.

'Where will they attack from?' Blackstone asked Gisbert de Dome.

He shook his head. 'I don't know. De Miremont's men are garrisoned in different parts of the city. Fifteen men in each quarter. He'll have rallied them by now.'

'Why weren't they at the walls?' said Meulon.

'They are kept in reserve to kill anyone who breaches the city defences. Any attack would have come from outside, not within, and an enemy would not know the streets here. De

Miremont's men do. This is where they would win the fight. Your attack caught him by surprise.'

Blackstone knew they were at a disadvantage. Gaillard de Miremont and his men could wreak havoc within the city and Blackstone had insufficient men to root him out. 'It makes no difference,' he said. 'He'll come for us. He wants me dead and the city back under his control. He cannot know there are no more men to reinforce us. There are so few of us he cannot afford to wait. He means to kill us where we stand.'

A woman's cry of alarm alerted them. It came from one of the side streets. Angry shouts followed. When de Miremont's soldiers appeared it was obvious they had been pushing aside men and women as they approached the square. Armed men thronged the narrow alleys; they edged forward cautiously, and paused fifty or sixty paces from where Blackstone's outnumbered men huddled in defence. Word had spread that the scar-faced Englishman was no other than Thomas Blackstone, the sworn enemy of their King and Dauphin. Their caution was a mistake. Had they rushed forward they might have overwhelmed him.

'Bastards have us near enough surrounded, Thomas,' said Killbere. 'Renfred, see to it you cover our flank. Thomas, we must kill these dogs quickly before they swamp us.'

'Let them come to us, Gilbert. We are a wall of steel they must break.'

Killbere glanced at his friend. His concern needed no explanation. He looked at the men and then back to Blackstone. The men were weary. 'As you wish,' said Killbere.

Blackstone walked along the rank of his tired men. The dozen fighters looked strained from the months of conflict that had gone before, but still formidable. Their stubbled and bearded faces, creased from lack of sleep and ingrained with dirt, added to their ferocious look. Their enemies' dried blood stained their jupons and their curled fists that gripped swords and falchions. Blackstone offered words of praise for their action at the gates; he checked that those who had sustained wounds would not be impaired in their ability to fight when the French attacked. His voice carried. 'Your ugly faces are enough to scare an enemy into running for the shit pit before their bowels loosen.'

The men cheered.

One called out: 'And when they see your scarred face, Sir Thomas, they'll shit themselves where they stand.'

The men laughed, their spirits lifting.

Blackstone grinned. 'Aye, that and my blade opening their guts. They gave us sport this morning, lads, they warmed our sword arm from the night's chill. They cannot know each of you is worth three of their fighting men. They ring those bells to summon death. They will hurl themselves from these streets as eager as rats seeking daylight and they will see how we treat vermin.'

The bells suddenly fell silent as if yielding to Blackstone's men's roar of defiance.

Blackstone strode five paces forward and faced the enemy so that every man could see him. John Jacob was four paces to his left, Killbere to his right. Meulon and Renfred stood in front of their men. As a flooding river bursts its banks, streams of men broke free from the confines of the city's passages and poured into the square, fear and the desire to kill spurring them on. Voices bellowed. Blackstone waited, sword raised.

The first men were almost upon him, driven by their ambition to kill the legend who stood alone in front of his men. Killbere and John Jacob took rapid paces forward to stand level with Blackstone so that the attackers now faced three men experienced in close-quarter killing. Their fate sealed, they fell under savage blows.

Behind them de Miremont's men barely faltered. Trampling over their comrades dead or dying at their feet, they pressed home the attack. Blackstone's line still held. After several minutes, he saw through the blur of sweat and mayhem and tumbling bodies how far they were outnumbered. His men were holding their ground, but if the attack kept going as hard as it was Blackstone's ranks would yield under its weight. A wall of seething men were forcing them back. Mouths agape spewing vile curses; spittle flecking beards; eyes wide, some with terror, others with a crazed desire.

Blackstone slashed across three men to his front. The blade caught the first man's throat, the second man's sword arm suddenly hung from sinew and skin and the force of the curved strike cut deeply into the third man's leg. They tumbled aside, opening a gap. Blackstone stepped into it. 'With me!' he bellowed. The time for defence was over.

Blackstone's men's grunting effort forced back de Miremont's fighters. They gave a yard, then three. The enemy wheeled, forced aside, and then they re-formed. As immovable as the city walls. Blackstone knew in that moment his men had thrown every sinew of effort against them and had nothing more to offer. But a small miracle, a blessing from a watching angel, saved Blackstone and his men. The wind turned at their backs, pushing them forward stride by stride. A force of nature giving them added strength, blowing dust into their enemies' eyes. At first the body of men wavered; then they broke. A warning cry rose from the back of their ranks. Men were dying well beyond Blackstone's reach. As they fell, others turned to face a fresh enemy who had attacked their rear. The gap widened. Blackstone saw the four Teutonic Knights, white surcoats emblazoned with black crosses, standing abreast, efficiently killing de Miremont's men. The survivors broke and ran, now too few to win the fight, and too fearful of holy wrath and the Englishmen they had failed to kill.

The clamour fell silent.

Blackstone looked behind him. Two of his men lay dead, others wounded. All stood bloodied, sword or mace in hand. Some bent forward, vomiting from exhaustion. Men sank to their knees, lifted up by a comrade's strong arm, too spent to raise a voice in victory. Blackstone turned to Wolfram von Plauen. 'You disobeyed me. You were to stay with the Lady Cateline.'

'She is in good company with the priest and his bodyguard. She had no need of me. You did.'

Blackstone nodded. 'I did.'

Monks appeared from the abbey, then a priest from the church. They carried water for the men and linen to bind their wounds. It seemed they welcomed Blackstone's victory. The dead lay scattered across the square. Rivulets of blood pooled across the cobbles. Townsmen and -women appeared at the mouths of alleys and streets, gazing at the carnage. A melancholy bell rang slowly. The citizens ventured closer. Serving women came forward bearing wineskins. Men summoned a handcart. And then another. They would strip the dead of clothing, mail and weapons. These were unlikely to be acts of compassion. Death would yield a profit. The citizens of Sarlat were concerned with their own self-preservation. They did not know whether the Englishmen would inflict retribution on them for supporting the rogue Mayor and his henchman de Miremont.

Blackstone saw Killbere leaning on his sword. The man's gaunt stare told Blackstone that he had fought as hard as men half his age. The veteran straightened, then spat contemptuously at his own tiredness and swore at the townspeople approaching Blackstone's fallen men.

Gisbert de Dome lay in a pool of blood. There was a bruise on his temple from the blow of a mace, already turning yellow. Blackstone nudged him with his boot until he came around. 'Get up, you're not wounded,' he said. 'It's not your blood.' He reached down and heaved him to his feet. De Dome staggered and then sat on the steps, needing time for his head to clear.

Henry Blackstone picked his way through the dead. 'My lord,' he said, knowing that he had tempted his father's anger by not staying with Will Longdon on the city walls.

Blackstone wiped a hand across the sweat and blood splatters on his face. 'You have disobeyed me again,' he said. 'Am I to chain you to a tree like a dog?'

'When the fight started I followed the crowd to the square, my lord. They were fearful of who would win. And then I watched the French break and run – those that could.'

'And what purpose does that serve other than to tell me that at least you did not arm yourself and join the battle?'

'I saw de Miremont. He killed two of our men and then he came close to being overwhelmed. He escaped. I saw him.'

Blackstone had lost sight of de Miremont in the mêlée. 'He's in the city?'

'The church, my lord. He went into the side door from the cemetery.' Henry Blackstone waited for the imminent reprimand for his disobedience. His father's commands were not to be disobeyed without retribution.

'You vex me, Henry. You are a feral mongrel running free of constraint. Untamed by discipline.' He smiled. 'There is no doubt you are my son.'

Relief swept over the boy. 'My lord,' he said and bowed his head.

'Now help the wounded.'

Henry turned back into the carnage. Killbere wiped his sword blade. 'Now what? Has the lad brought news of men at the gates?'

'De Miremont is in the church.'

'Ah, the bastard has lost his courage and seeks sanctuary. He is untouchable now.'

'I know. Secure the square, Gilbert. Then we find the rogue Mayor Villon and arrest him. The merchants in the crypt need to be reinstated in their position as councilmen. I'll see to it.'

Killbere knew full well what Blackstone intended. 'Thomas, you cannot kill him. Sanctuary is everything. The city will turn against us.'

'I know,' said Blackstone.

'Let us leave this place in peace and goodwill,' said Killbere.

Blackstone stepped towards the church doors. His men had died in an unnecessary fight. Whether the blame lay solely with Gisbert de Dome for joining routiers to retrieve money lost because Villon had withheld taxes or with the antagonism and aggression of Gaillard de Miremont and his corrupt mayor who had seized the city from him mattered little when good men had died. Blame would not breathe life back into their corpses. What mattered was that Sarlat belonged to the English King. They had broken a treaty. And that was punishable.

By death.

CHAPTER FORTY-EIGHT

The dank chill of the cathedral embraced him, cooling the sweat beneath the shirt that clung to his skin. The braziers were no longer burning near the crypt. Three tall candles flickered next to the altar, another two either side of the transept. They were beeswax candles that gave off a sweet smell, not the cloying tallow scent. A priest must have thought the cost of the more expensive candles worth it to celebrate the victory. Either that or the stench from the crypt had become unbearable.

Blackstone's eyes adjusted to the dull light. De Miremont knelt in prayer at the altar beneath the pitiful gaze of the crucified Christ. A priest was administering the sacrament. He raised his eyes when he saw the tall figure walk without haste across the nave. The concerned priest blessed de Miremont and lifted his face to the waiting Englishman.

'My Lord Gaillard de Miremont has claimed sanctuary. There can be no violation. He has prayed for forgiveness for his sins and prostrates himself before God. Sanctuary is a time-honoured right. And today of all days it permits those in conflict to let tempers cool and to consider reparation.'

'Look at me,' said Blackstone to the Frenchman.

De Miremont got to his feet and turned around.

'You have claimed sanctuary yet you are neither murderer, rapist nor debtor. That we know of.'

'No matter, I have the protection of the Church,' insisted de Miremont.

The priest stepped between them. 'Sir Gaillard will remain here for forty days and then present himself to the court for judgement or go into exile,' he said.

Blackstone ignored the priest and studied the man who had usurped King Edward's authority. 'You still wear my sword.'

De Miremont quickly unbuckled the belt and scabbard, wrapped the belt around it and threw it down towards Blackstone. 'I took it as my right when I imprisoned you.'

Blackstone buckled on Wolf Sword.

'No violence,' the priest insisted quickly. 'To commit murder against a plea for sanctuary will never be forgiven.'

'I give you my word, priest. No further blood will be spilt in God's house. Now release the prisoners. Help those who need it.'

The priest shuffled away, grateful to be out of sight of the scar-faced man whose looming presence frightened him.

'I will remain here,' de Miremont said. 'Gisbert de Dome can reclaim the city.' He lifted his head contemptuously. 'And when our King rids France of the English plague, then it will be your murderous King and his son who will beg sanctuary.'

Blackstone felled him with a punch. He grabbed the man's leg and dragged him towards the door.

'Thomas?' Killbere called as he saw de Miremont's body kicked down the steps. 'Merciful Christ, you haven't killed him?'

'Not yet,' said Blackstone.

The square was clear of the dead now and women with buckets of water were sluicing away the blood. De Miremont's body tumbled into the square as Blackstone's men stepped aside. The released merchants and councilmen staggered out of the church, hands raised to shield their eyes from the unaccustomed light.

'You swore an oath!' the priest shouted. 'Before God Almighty you swore no harm would come to that man.'

De Miremont clawed himself to his knees, not yet clear-headed enough to know what had happened.

Blackstone faced the priest. 'I swore I would spill no blood in there,' he said, pointing to the church. Then he looked at de Miremont. 'That will be done here.'

Townspeople huddled at the edge of the square away from the soldiers. Blackstone's wounded were settled on the side of the church steps attended by servant women. They had summoned a physician, who examined each man. Most told him to look to their comrades, saying their own injuries were not as serious. The Mayor, Villon, was under guard and Meulon and Renfred had put their men in place to keep the querulous Sarladais at a safe distance. The side streets thronged with citizens desperate to know their fate at the hands of the English.

De Miremont was on his feet, looking like a cornered bear in a pit. The ferocious-looking Englishmen showed no sign of caring what happened to him, but he didn't cower from them. Turning to face the crowds, he raised his voice. 'The English seized Sarlat. They claimed it under treaty. I and Mayor Villon gave you back your city.'

A voice carried from one onlooker. 'And kept taxes for yourselves!'

De Miremont lifted his hands to quell the dissent. 'To pay for soldiers. To secure what is rightfully French.'

'Much good they did us,' another cried out, cheered on by those around him.

Gisbert de Dome climbed onto the steps. His bloodied shirt was testament to his involvement in the fight. 'I was forced from this place by Villon and de Miremont.'

'You sold your arse to the English!' one of those in the crowd called out, and he, too, had supporters who jeered de Dome.

'I signed the treaty agreed by our King, our blessed Jean le Bon. His tender heart broke when they placed such heavy demands on him. He did all in his power to save the people here and to hold what is a valued corner of France. His honour demanded we stand by that treaty – that is why I signed. That is why I was placed here. Betrayal comes from these two men,' he said, pointing at Villon and de Miremont. 'We are fortunate that this English knight, Sir Thomas Blackstone, brings no harm to our citizens, seeks no reparation other than for Sarlat to be governed for King Edward.' He let the murmuring crowd settle down. 'He has spared us and released me and our council.'

Killbere blew snot from his nostrils. 'Sweet Merciful Mother of God, this man talks a lot.'

Gisbert de Dome rallied the townspeople. 'I will show you where Mayor Villon and Gaillard de Miremont have hoarded the taxes they collected from you. Taxes I will order returned to you!'

A wave of support swept through the press of people.

'Hang them!' someone called. Then it seemed the whole crowd took up the cry. A chant became a roar. *Hang them! Hang them!*

'Now his big mouth has incited mob rule. We will have more trouble on our hands, Thomas,' Killbere muttered.

Blackstone stood next to the released councillors. 'These men will sit in judgement. Let their decision be recorded. There will be no mob rule here. You will return to the way things were at the signing of the treaty.' He turned to the released men. 'It will be a fair trial or I will come back. Understand?'

They nodded and muttered their assent.

'De Miremont could walk free, Thomas,' said Killbere. 'He still has friends and influence here. You risk him raising men and seizing Sarlat again and next time we would need an army to besiege it.'

Blackstone smiled. 'I know. Don't be concerned, Gilbert, he won't risk the rope.'

De Miremont strode into the middle of the square. 'I will not be tried like a common criminal. I am Gaillard de Miremont, Lord of Sauignac. I took the city back from the English and I will defend my actions.' The Frenchman did not lack courage. His honour would be his downfall, like his fellow knights and noblemen who had fallen in past years at Crécy and Poitiers. Honour was everything. Honour was worth dying for.

Killbere raised an eyebrow. 'You knew he'd never submit to a trial.'

Blackstone shrugged. 'He's an arrogant bastard. What else could he do?' He stepped down to where de Miremont stood glaring at him.

'Arm me and defend yourself, Englishman,' de Miremont said.

'I am the King's Master of War. You broke the treaty. Why shouldn't I hand you over? I don't care how they kill you. A long choking kick at the end of a rope is all you deserve.'

De Miremont turned to the crowd. 'Thomas Blackstone denies me the right to defend myself in combat. I call him a coward and afraid to die at my hands.'

Blackstone remained silent. It was the final act of a desperate man fearful that the court would bow to the will of the mob inflamed by Gisbert de Dome. A knight of any standing would never refuse a challenge by being called a coward.

'*Let him fight! Fight!*' the crowd chanted.

De Miremont turned to face Blackstone. 'I win and you leave Gisbert de Dome for me to deal with. They will release Villon and I will be free to return to my lands.'

'Except you never will,' said Blackstone.

'I give my word.'

'I meant you will never return to your lands because you will be dead.'

They returned the Frenchman's weapons to him. He hefted his shield and circled Blackstone, who turned slowly with him, waiting for him to strike in his eagerness to win his freedom and claim glory for killing the English King's Master of War. When he struck he did it with such force and skill that Blackstone was wrong-footed. De Miremont's rapid attack almost cost Blackstone his arm but Wolf Sword's hardened steel caught the muscle-shuddering strike. Blackstone battered the barrel-chested man with his shield, rained so many rapid blows in return that de Miremont backed quickly, found his footing, steadied himself, and planted his feet as firmly as a rock.

The crowd roared, blood-lust raising their voices to echo around the cobbled square. It would be a trial of strength now that de Miremont's opening gambit had been tried and failed. The hope of using his strength and fury to defeat Blackstone abated into a dogged blow-by-blow contest with the Englishman, who did not waver. Sweat stung both men's eyes; muscles and sinews strained from the force of their blows. Blackstone took a half-step back and pivoted on his heel, enough for the Frenchman to think he had faltered. De Miremont's confidence betrayed him. Instead of shuffling forward and gaining the advantage inch by inch, narrowing the gap that Blackstone had opened, he took too big a stride. As his leading foot went forward so too did his downward strike: an easy blow for Blackstone to avoid, pivoting again and allowing the blade to pass so close to his face and chest he felt the air whisper. The Frenchman's momentum carried him a fatal half-stride past Blackstone. Perhaps a part of de

Miremont's mind told him Blackstone did not have time to reverse his own blade and thrust at him, that in the next few seconds he would half-turn, using his body strength to sweep his blade like a scythe and sever Blackstone's leg at the thigh. It was a perfectly rational thought embedded from years of honed reactions against inferior opponents. What he had not expected was Blackstone's fist curled around Wolf Sword's hilt slamming into his face. His nose and teeth broke. He stumbled as the sudden pain tore into his brain. Had he not overstepped, his fighting spirit would have made him spit out the blood and take the fight back to Blackstone but that fatal over-confident stride had thrown him off balance and he continued falling forward. Before he hit the cobbles Wolf Sword rose and fell behind him and Blackstone's weight forced its blade between his shoulder blades.

Searing pain momentarily blinded Gaillard de Miremont, Lord of Sauignac. He gasped and swallowed blood. He did not feel the impact of his head striking the ground. Face down, his dying gaze took in the cobbles' gleam, and then the feet of those closest to him shuffled back from the sudden gush of blood that spewed from his torn heart and lungs. Despite the crowd's shocked awe, for him there was only silence.

CHAPTER FORTY-NINE

Ignoring the biting wind, Lady Cateline draped her cloak over one of Blackstone's wounded men. Fearing the worst during Blackstone's absence she had told William Ashford and his guard to prepare fires to boil water and cook food for the survivors. Her servant, Melita, had torn strips of linen ready to bind wounds. Blackstone's men had won the fight but it had taken its toll: their exhaustion was clear. Cateline knelt in the dirt and lifted the wounded man's head so she could spoon broth into his mouth. The murmur of men's curses drifted through the trees. Will Longdon and Jack Halfpenny's archers aided their comrades and established sentries around the camp's perimeter.

'You have too many wounded to fight effectively,' said Father Torellini, casting an eye between the bloodied men and Blackstone, who bore his own wounds.

Blackstone drank thirstily, watching his men being attended. No commands were necessary; those who were able tended those who needed help. 'Their wounds will be bound, stitched or cauterized. They'll fight if they have to,' he answered.

'Thomas, they are mortal. All men have a breaking point,' said Torellini reproachfully.

'They are my men,' said Blackstone. 'They do not break or falter unless they are dead.' He swilled his mouth and spat blood. He looked at the Italian priest. 'And they will do what I ask of them.'

'I know that, Thomas, and I know you. You will not ask of them what you will not do yourself. But they are not you.'

'You know me too well, Father. I'll ask no more of them for now. Besides, the horses need rest. We'll ride to Dome before nightfall. You and Sergeant Ashford will come with us. Gisbert promises us two hundred fresh men; I will have fifty added to your escort. I need the others.

'Lady Cateline and her children will also require more comfort than they've had,' said Torellini.

'It's only a few hours' ride and Gisbert is preparing quarters for you and food and care for my men. It will give the woman whatever comfort there is.'

'Do not be so dismissive of her, Thomas. When you and Sir Gilbert went into Sarlat she organized the camp and insisted the Germans follow you into the city. Wolfram von Plauen argued that he was obliged to stay and protect her. She is a forceful woman. It was she who had fires and food prepared.' He pointed to where she attended to his men. 'She abandons her own comfort to aid them.'

Blackstone watched her. There was a streak of blood on her face from where she had pushed back a rogue wisp of hair. Her daughter stood diligently at her side holding a bowl of water for Cateline to dip a linen cloth into and clean a man's wound. Cateline looked less like a woman who held a domain in her own right and more like her servant, who also tended the men.

Blackstone scowled. 'Father, she is an encumbrance to what I have to do. She seems to have impressed you enough to be an amenable travelling companion. She rides with you and Ashford. Be thankful you're a man of the cloth otherwise she might snare you into marriage. We leave before noon.'

*

Blackstone and his men travelled twelve miles south from the woods of Sarlat, passing Vitrac and the fortified Castle de Montfort that guarded the route below a high escarpment. The partially ruined castle had been destroyed in the fighting that had swept across the area during the war. What remained hung perilously on a clifftop. An escort of Gisbert de Dome's men from the castle was waiting to lead them along the narrow track through meadows and fruit orchards, the grass already scythed and stored for winter silage, the fruit trees barren until spring brought its warmth and their blossoms. Oak and chestnut piers supported a bridge across the River Dordogne, wide enough for four horsemen abreast. Blackstone raised his eyes to the heights of Dome as the bastard horse's hooves struck their dull note across the wooden planks. The fortified mountaintop town commanded views across the river as it curved along the vast plain below. There were other strongholds along the river that held strategic positions but it was Dome that would prove one of the most challenging to conquer. From its heights defenders could watch as travellers and armed men made their way along the valley. Yet it was not impregnable. A year after the Battle of Crécy when the young archer Thomas Blackstone lay badly wounded at Harcourt routiers had scaled the sheer cliffs and taken the town. Three years later brigands struck again and scaled the walls on the western slopes. Finally, the lesson was learned, and the burghers strengthened their walls and increased their vigilance.

Blackstone's escort led them in a curving route up the hillside until they reached the fortified gates. Urging their mounts up the sloping street, they saw Gisbert de Dome waiting to greet them. An upheld hand brought the column to a halt. De Dome was no longer bloodstained. His gambeson was stitched with a gold thread, his boots burnished to a dull glow, their quality reinforcing his clothing's lustre, which spoke of a man of authority and, Blackstone guessed, wealth from when he rode with Gruffydd ap Madoc's routiers.

'I have made arrangements for your men over there,' said de Dome, gesturing to the open ground beyond the town's buildings. A copse of bare trees wavered in the wind but the walls would offer Blackstone's men some protection from the elements. 'There are stables beneath the east walls. Enough for all of your mounts.'

Blackstone nodded at Meulon and Renfred, who peeled away with their men. 'Will, have your lads camp beneath the south wall.' Unlike the northern ramparts above sheer cliffs, the south offered ground that was less steep. 'If de Miremont's followers suddenly decide to strike back that's where they'll come – up the southern slopes.'

Will Longdon and Jack Halfpenny's archers urged their horses along the walled escarpment.

'We are safe here,' insisted Gisbert de Dome.

'Nowhere is safe,' said Blackstone, heeling his horse past the man in his debt.

The Teutonic Knights camped away from Blackstone's men. Wolfram von Plauen had to remain close to Lady Cateline Babeneaux. Honour demanded he fulfil his pledge to Blackstone but the duty still rankled.

'We should strike out from here and find the Welshman,' said Sibrand von Ansbach, recognizing his leader's dismay. He was as senior as Gunther von Schwerin and if he could convince his comrade to support him, von Plauen could be swayed.

Gunther cut a piece of salted mutton from the supply sack on his saddle. Since the routiers had slain the two half-brethren the knights fended for themselves. They were no strangers to hardship or self-reliance. 'He has a point,' he said.

Von Plauen looked past their tent to the window where Cateline and her children were billeted. He seemed torn.

'There is no dishonour, Wolfram,' von Ansbach gently insisted. He looked to his comrade von Buchard. 'Rudi? If Gisbert de Dome rode with the Welshman, then he might know where he went. We should question him and strike out. Finding ap Madoc is our sworn duty.'

Von Buchard squatted and fed the fire. He gazed into the flames for a moment. 'Brother Wolfram gave his word and so did we. Our pledge stopped Blackstone from killing him.' He looked for support to Gunther, who shrugged.

'One pledge over another. Which one do we dishonour first? We should bide our time. For all we know Blackstone will lead us to him.'

'Not if we are in Avignon,' said von Ansbach.

Gunther laid a hand on his friend's shoulder. 'No matter where we are we will seek out the Welshman. He must be killed, so that we serve justice. And justice, my brother, requires patience and prayer.'

Wolfram von Plauen laid out his bedroll. 'Gunther is right. We are honour-bound and God will guide us to the Welshman in good time.' He stood and turned towards Cateline's billet. 'I had better check on the woman.' He walked away from his comrades.

Rudolph von Burchard fussed with the fire, poking a stick into the embers, casting a glance from their departing leader to the others. His gaze settled back on the flames. 'How much danger can she be in her bedchamber?' he said.

CHAPTER FIFTY

Lady Cateline Babeneaux eased back into the soft linen sheet lining the copper bath. It caressed her skin as she luxuriated in her first bath for weeks. She tilted her head back so that Melita could pour water over her hair. The servant pressed her hands into her mistress's hair and squeezed free the excess water.

'Did you see to the children?'

'I did, my lady. They are asleep.'

'It has been a difficult time, Melita. They are exhausted.'

'Yes, my lady.'

'You have served us well,' she said kindly, placing a hand on the servant's arm. 'Will you fetch more water and see to my clothes?'

The tireless woman took the wooden pail and bundled up an armful of stained clothing to be washed in the kitchens below. Cateline raised her arms and used a cloth to wash herself. Candlelight spluttered from the steam in the room. The stench of men's blood and sweat had stubbornly refused to leave her but the rosemary in the water soothed away the odours. There was still a long road ahead, but she had a sense that her authority was returning. It had not been difficult to sway the Germans into joining the fight at Sarlat, and after those remaining did as she instructed so that the camp was ready to receive the wounded she'd felt that her status had been reasserted. She needed men for protection and if she could convince them to do her bidding, then her position strengthened further.

Von Plauen stepped unseen into a side passage as the servant left her mistress's chamber, arms full of stained clothing. He had intended to knock on her door and enquire about her wellbeing even though he expected to be dismissed when she saw through his feeble excuse to visit her. The Order strictly enforced his vows as a Teutonic Knight. He, like his brother knights, had sworn an oath of poverty, chastity and obedience. They owned no property. And their vows did not permit expressions of pride in fighting skills, their horses or in their weapons of war. The Order's rules were written in clear, simple language so that there could be no misunderstanding. Knights wore clothes of a priestly hue and covered even that drabness with a white mantle bearing a black cross. And women were to be avoided. They were Satan's gate. Warned against being drawn into the company of women, any knight who fell from grace was severely punished. They could not even embrace their mothers or sisters. The rigid discipline demanded of these men forged them into a fighting brotherhood. Von Plauen knew that to yield to temptation would strip him of his honour and vows and he would face expulsion from the Order.

Melita shuffled past him and once out of sight he turned for the stairs and saw a piece of clothing she had dropped. He bent and felt the soft linen undershift crumple in his hand. Without thinking he raised it to his face and inhaled her scent. His hand shook. He turned guiltily in case he had been seen but the hall and stairs reflected nothing but silence and shadows and the thudding of his heart. His mind searched for a believable reason to be in her presence as his feet carried him to her bedroom door. It was ajar, left open by the encumbered servant. He could not comprehend what compelled him to enter the dimly lit room. Or why he trembled. He stepped towards the open door on the other side of the room and then faltered when he saw her bathing. He fought the desire that drew him to her but the scent of the bath and the sight of her naked aroused him. He cursed Blackstone for making him the woman's guardian. It was a cruel punishment. His resentment was as deep as the desire he felt for this woman. Blackstone had humiliated him by placing him in the devil's embrace. His chest tightened, forcing lust from his pounding heart into his throat and the spittle on his tongue, but he could not tear his gaze from her. He vowed to find the chapel and spend the night in prayer but such pious thoughts were swept away when she stood and half-turned, her breasts dripping with steam, the dark curled patch between her legs moistened with droplets of water. The room's fire burned its heat into the chamber as did his desire into his groin. He gasped. Guilt and shame swept over him.

Footfalls scuffed the stairway as the servant lifted the heavy pail of water. Her laboured step and breath warned him. There was nowhere to hide. He pressed himself into a doorwell. The exhausted servant, head down, went into the bedroom without seeing him. Careful not to be seen or heard, he strode to the end of the passage and stepped outside into the night's chill. He gulped the winter air and vowed to erase his desire for the woman he was honour-bound to protect. The devil always tempted those who held God close in their hearts. He made his way towards the chapel.

The chapel was a place of solemn coldness, dimly lit by a solitary candle. He hurried to the glimmering silver crucifix on the altar. Prostrating himself, he kissed the stone floor, begging forgiveness for his lewdness, and then raised his eyes to the symbol of a sacrificed Christ. Fear gripped him. In that moment the flickering shadows smothered the cross and took the form of a grinning horned Satan whose bloodshot eyes bored into him and whose snake tongue darted between sharpened teeth.

And his heart, which had always been truthful, told him that he was lost and whatever the cost he must have the woman who tormented him.

CHAPTER FIFTY-ONE

Lady Cateline stood by the brazier at the entrance to the stables as Henry Blackstone saddled Blackstone's horse. It swung its head to snap its yellow teeth at Jocard, who stood too close, but Henry had secured the trailing rein to halt its desire to bite. The height of the horse's back and loin made Henry stand on tiptoe. Jocard stepped further back.

'Does your father abandon us now?' he asked.

'He has his duty,' Henry told him. 'We'll ride on tomorrow for Avignon when the weather eases.'

The rain had turned to hail during the night, sprinkling the valley below with a light dusting, but the wind had shifted slightly from the north and now added extra bite from the east.

'My father has arranged additional escort from Lord Gisbert. No one will attempt to assault us now. He has sent word of our journey and we'll have fresh horses along the way. The King's sergeant-at-arms said he'll set a hard pace.' He glanced to where Cateline stood. 'I'm sorry, my lady, perhaps you didn't know?'

'I knew. The sooner we are in Avignon the better. How soon?'

'No more than a week, my lady. If we make good time, four days. Daylight is short and Master Ashford will be concerned to find safe places to rest.'

'I'm certain your father has already advised him.'

The bastard horse whinnied and shook its head, a front hoof pawing the ground.

'It seems the beast is as eager to leave us as your father,' said Jocard.

Before Henry could answer Lady Cateline admonished her son. 'You will not speak so harshly of Sir Thomas. You are an uncouth child. You owe your life to this boy and his father.'

Jocard lowered his head in shame. 'I apologize, Henry. Forgive me. I am unable to do my duty and protect my mother and sister. Such inability makes me say things I should not.'

Henry steered clear of the horse's hind legs. He placed a hand on the younger boy's shoulder. 'Jocard, uncertainty causes fear. It is important to stop it before it spreads. Like putting a hot blade to a wound. Father taught me that knowledge dispels fear and if we know that he has arranged passage and fresh horses with extra men as escort then that should comfort us. We will reach Avignon safely.'

He turned to Lady Cateline so he could assure her but she was no longer there. The look on Jocard's face was enough to know her abrupt departure had added to his guilt. Henry slapped him on the back to cheer him. 'Now, let's saddle John Jacob's horse. You can help. It's not a belligerent beast like my father's and you'll leave the stable with all your fingers and no broken bones.'

Cateline Babeneaux walked across the open ground between the town's walls. Blackstone's men were still camped but after the first two days' rest and hot food, she sensed they were keen to travel on. Now that several days had passed their resilience was becoming apparent – she knew why they were renowned for fighting through the winter months. She glanced over her shoulder. Von Plauen stood in plain sight watching her. He usually followed a few paces behind but when she had ordered him not to shadow her so closely, he meekly did as he was bid. His obedience made her feel powerful, but his respect for her stirred a tenderness within her that had long been buried: a tenderness that would ensure she would not hurt the German knight's pride. She could not know that he was as much a servant to his desire for her as she was to her need for protection. And there was no doubt the accomplished fighter would champion her if she or her children were threatened.

She saw Blackstone with his captains beneath a canvas pavilion. They had returned Gisbert de Dome to preside over his stronghold and his authority had quickly been reaffirmed. Gisbert was tireless, overseeing the needs of Thomas Blackstone and his men as his steward arranged supplies and armaments for the escort. She admitted to herself that Gisbert had charm and that if the circumstances had been less fraught, she would have considered him suitable material as protector and lover. But the town of Dome was too close to the Count d'Armagnac's domain, lying as it did south of the River Dordogne. And d'Armagnac served the French monarch, which meant he would have an eye to her own domains in Brittany, which would be useful in the Breton war. Men like d'Armagnac and de Dome would usurp her right and authority. What influence she had lay in her land and all men were hungry for title and estates: what she would not do was to let another man control her life as Mael Babeneaux had done. She would decide whom to take to her bed and, when the opportunity presented itself, choose the man who could best look after her family. The cold-hearted decision added to her strength. There was no emotion involved, only the stark reality of a woman alone. Self-preservation and that of her family drove her. The wind stung her face but her tears were not from grief. The thought of Lord Mael Babeneaux de Pontivy's slain body left her as cold as the chill that seeped through her cloak. In a few more days a more befitting refuge at Avignon would be welcome. Her son would be safe, his education secure, and she would have men of importance and wealth around her who would help her achieve a future for her son and daughter. Once Sir William Felton confirmed her right to rule her domain, then her influence would increase. She walked across Blackstone's field of vision but he barely glanced at her. She moved away, found a tree stump and sat with her back to the wind. It was time to wait and be patient. Her way ahead was as certain as the river that curved through the valley below.

Blackstone pointed at the map Gisbert de Dome had laid out. His captains studied the route he wanted them to take. 'John Jacob, Sir Gilbert and I will ride east and meet up with Beyard. He has raised men here, here and here,' said Blackstone, pointing out the three places of muster for the troops needed to commit to the Count de Foix, the Pyrenean prince they were to persuade to offer his support to the Prince of Wales.

'And if Beyard hasn't raised enough men?' said Renfred.

'He's a Gascon; this is his land. His sworn lord de Grailly provokes great respect. He'll convince men to reinforce us but Renfred is right, we cannot leave much to chance. Will, you ride with us and test the archers Beyard has recruited. Jack, you'll command our own until we meet up with him.'

'How much do we tell the Italian and his escort?' said Meulon.

'And Gisbert,' added Jack Halfpenny.

'Nothing. Father Torellini is my confidant but we disclose nothing. If anything goes wrong, if someone attacks their column, then we need them to be ignorant. Our Prince needs the Count of Foix and it is our task to draw him to us.'

'Sir Thomas,' said Renfred, 'the Germans are still talking about finding Gruffydd ap Madoc.'

Blackstone rolled the map. 'They will look for him until either he or they are dead but for now they are chained to us by their honour. I'll find ap Madoc. I need his men to fight with us. And if he stands at our side then we will stand against von Plauen and the brethren.'

No more was said. Blackstone and John Jacob bade farewell to the captains.

'Don't insult any Welsh archers you find,' said Meulon to Will Longdon as they left the tent. 'You'll test their patience and your arse will be a target.'

'Unlike your lumbering hulk I can move quickly,' he answered. 'The moment you ride above a hilltop skyline you're a gift to any bowman worth his salt. Bend low in the saddle, Meulon, in case they mistake you for an ogre.' He walked off with Jack Halfpenny.

'Better a man of stature than a dwarf past his best years.' Meulon called out his final insult with a grin.

Henry waited with the tethered bastard horse as Will Longdon and Jack Halfpenny walked across to him. The horse suddenly lashed out with its hind leg.

'Merciful Christ, Henry, the damned beast is possessed,' said Will Longdon, who'd narrowly escaped the belligerent strike. 'I thought you had him tied. He must have eyes in his arse.'

Henry smiled. 'He's not a creature of this world. He sees and hears things that we cannot.'

'The devil spawned him. We all know that.' Will Longdon embraced the boy. 'You and the others go your own way tomorrow, so it's unlikely we will have time to see you again. Came to say goodbye and wish you well. Me and the lads. One and all.'

'Our thoughts and prayers ride with you. We'll miss you,' said Halfpenny.

'And I you, Will, Jack. And the others.'

'Aye, well, I dare say your father knows what he's doing. You're a lad destined for greater things. Education is better than a bag of gold florins,' said Longdon.

'I wanted to stay and fight.'

'Course you did. We all know that. What you did back at that castle took courage but it will take even more courage to be surrounded by scholars and crow-backed priests and peacock cardinals.'

'I like learning, Will, and I know I have to prove myself.'

Will Longdon saw the boy's uncertainty. 'Henry, for someone who has brains you're being very stupid. You have no need to prove yourself to your father or us. Think back on everything you have done. John Jacob, me, the others: we all know what you can do. Not one man here, not even that numbskull Meulon, needs any proof of anything. You're one of us. Don't you see that?'

'Then why does he send me away?'

'Because he gifts you the chance to live a while longer and be more use than a scab-arsed fighter standing in a pool of his own piss as the battle rages. You learn, you come back, you bring words and knowledge that can be more deadly than my trusted bow.' He laid a hand on the boy's shoulder. 'That is why he sends you away. He needs you to come back so we can all benefit. When a man can persuade a town to surrender and an army to follow him because he has the right words then we don't spill our blood.'

Henry face flushed from the veteran archer's praise. 'Thank you.'

'Merciful Christ, here comes Meulon to tell you how to scratch your arse. God be with you, Master Henry.'

'And you.'

The archers walked back towards their men. Meulon, Renfred and John Jacob were all making their way over to Henry to wish him well. Will knew that would cheer the boy, but he also knew Blackstone was risking much in sending the lad into Avignon. He lifted his own medallion of the Silver Wheel Goddess to his lips. Keep the lad safe, he asked silently.

'He doesn't need any advice from you,' he said as Meulon passed him. 'I've set the lad straight.'

Meulon never broke stride. 'Then he's more fucked than I thought.'

Blackstone glanced towards Cateline and ignored her, instead walking to where Torellini stood waiting by the stables with Henry.

'Father?' said Blackstone. 'You'll travel on with Ashford. I have some ground to cover if I'm to do what you have asked.'

Torellini glanced at Henry.

'Henry, you and John Jacob take the horses to Sir Gilbert,' said Blackstone.

'Yes, Father.'

The moment Henry obeyed his order Torellini took Blackstone's arm and guided him away from the buildings. 'Time is getting short, Thomas. The business at Sarlat has slowed us down. Are your men sufficiently rested?'

'Yes.'

'Good. I thank God for their resilience and Gisbert de Dome's help. If Armagnac has started moving his army, then they could defeat Gaston Phoebus quickly. That would create a threat for the Prince.'

'It's a damned pity he's not here if it's that important, instead of settling his arse on silk cushions in London.'

'Plymouth.'

'What?'

'He settles his arse on silk cushions at his castle in Restormel in Plymouth.'

Blackstone's irritation melted. He grinned. He had never heard the Italian utter any kind of crude remark. 'I'm riding to my Gascon captain, Beyard. He has been recruiting men, and he had scouts following Armagnac's progress. Gaston Phoebus might be young but he's an arrogant nobleman of the old order. He may ignore my offer of help.'

Father Torellini gazed across the broad valley to the cliffs and mountains beyond. The clouds scuttled across the high ground; low clouds would soon smother the heights of Dome. Even the threatening weather seemed to insist Blackstone ride on. 'Thomas, there is nothing more I can say. Find the men you need and convince the Count of Foix he needs your help.'

'And then defeat Armagnac's army.

Torellini smiled and shrugged. 'That too.'

'Do what you can for my son in Avignon,' said Blackstone and strode to where Killbere and the others waited.

Lady Cateline walked across his path. Blackstone could not avoid her. 'You leave us to fight for your Prince?'

'He is not yet here.'

She studied him a moment. 'When does he accept the fealty of those who fought for him and the land your men gave their lives for?'

'The summer.'

'And you will ride at his side?'

'I go where I must.'

'And will I see you again?' she asked.

'That's not in my hands.'

Her hand rested gently on his chest. It was as intimate a gesture as could be tolerated in public. 'And what of you, Thomas? Are you to stay fighting until you are killed or crippled? Your Italian priest has influence. Come to Avignon.'

Blackstone graciously raised her hand to his lips. The scent of rosemary still clung to her skin. 'Goodbye, my lady. A few more days and you'll be safe. I owe you an apology for any harsh words. My heart is not free even for a beautiful woman like you. Forgive me.'

'I would share my domain, Thomas. Two are stronger than one.'

'My duty and my future lie elsewhere.'

Her smile of regret was genuine. There had always been a flicker of hope that Thomas Blackstone would change his mind. 'Then don't abandon your son, Thomas. You send him to a place of learning but he must hide behind his mother's name.'

'It's something he understands. My name draws blood.'

She watched him join Killbere, John Jacob and Will Longdon. He placed a hand on his son's shoulder. The boy nodded at whatever words of encouragement his father said to him. The four men rode down the cobbled yard to the gates.

She willed him to turn in the saddle for a final glance.

Blackstone didn't look back.

She could not know that he never did.

Von Plauen had watched the exchange between Blackstone and Cateline. He swallowed the bile on his tongue. Confusion clouded his thoughts. Was she a common whore sent to ensnare whoever could be drawn into her web? Was she as vulnerable as he thought her to be, and was that why she had once yielded to a common man like Blackstone – if camp gossip was to be believed? He would wait, he decided, until Avignon, and then he would approach her when a suitable moment presented itself. He would offer himself and ask for her hand in marriage. He was poor but could give her the protection she needed. Her lands would be a suitable place for a disgraced Teutonic Knight.

Fearful that his comrades could read his thoughts, he turned to look where they were practising the slow deliberate movements of their sword skills. What he intended meant abandoning the brotherhood and his vows. God would surely punish him. But not before he had supped from the devil's chalice.

CHAPTER FIFTY-TWO

Several days after Blackstone reached Dome, a coach's iron-rimmed wheels jolted across the paved Grand'Rue in Paris. Steam plumed from the brace of horses hauling the carriage bearing a worried Simon Bucy. France was slipping into dangerous times again. The peace treaty with King Edward brought little hope of what was once the greatest country in Christendom ever reclaiming its rightful status in power, learning and culture. The French King had courage but not wisdom. He preferred peace to war and had fought bravely but not skilfully enough. The warrior King Edward had bled France and his son and the wolves who fought for him had ripped out her soul with their savagery. When the Teutonic Knights had sought the Englishman, Bucy thought the Germans with their single-minded desire might succeed where the King, the Dauphin and he had failed to destroy the scourge. News had reached Paris that Sarlat had fallen. He had been pleased when the assertive Gaillard de Miremont had taken matters into his own hands and rooted out the self-serving Gisbert de Dome right under the nose of the English seneschal, William Felton. What had gone wrong? The English had regained the town and reinstated Gisbert de Dome. The French court could not lodge any protest because of the treaty but at least for a moment French defiance and courage had retrieved its honour. So who had killed de Miremont? No one knew. Mercenaries most likely. Gisbert de Dome had sided with them before and it was likely he had sided with them again, but how reliable was the rumour that it was Thomas Blackstone? The nagging doubt lay heavily on Bucy's mind like the mist blanketing the Seine. If it was Blackstone, what was he doing south of Poitiers? The English were still caught up in the Breton war. Thomas Blackstone should be in the Breton marches supporting John de Montfort. South? What was south of Brittany that might draw Blackstone there? Bucy could find no reason to believe it was Blackstone who had released Gisbert de Dome. But unless a traitor behind the walls of Sarlat had opened the gates to mercenaries who else would have dared?

To Bucy's lawyer's mind this was not proof that it was Blackstone, but Bucy's instincts had helped him survive during the uprising in Paris and many years in the French Parlement. And at times instincts were more reliable than logic. He gazed out at the Paris streets, less crowded now that the winter air clung to a man's beard and clothes like moss to a tree. December was almost upon them, heralding a harsh winter and months of biting winds along the Seine. Bucy tugged his cloak tighter around his neck, yet it was not the cold that gnawed at him. His reputation as an authoritarian had marked him to be killed when the insurrection had taken place less than five years before and the chill of fear had never left him. Losing his suburban mansions at Vaugirard, Issy and Viroflay had cost him a fortune and he had never again trusted the population of Paris and the surrounding countryside. Since the terror he had ridden in a coach to and from his new mansion. Inclement weather and court duties were convenient excuses for him both to stop riding openly and to mask his fear. The guards who rode on the carriage were hand-picked. They would protect him should a disgruntled peasant be prepared to throw his life away by attacking the King's trusted senior adviser. That cushion of safety was his daily comfort. Matters of state, however, caused him greater concern.

These days the King was seldom in Paris; since his return from Avignon he spent most days at his country palace at Vincennes. The sharp-witted Dauphin – who had denied the English King a crushing military victory by staying safely behind the city walls when his father was imprisoned in England and had bargained hard when they drew up the treaty – now seemed more interested in his plans for the future of the Louvre as a royal palace. So Bucy had shouldered many state decisions he felt unnecessary to take to the King or the Dauphin, and that was why he had not told either about the Teutonic Knights and their desire to hunt down Blackstone and the Welsh mercenary. He had heard nothing more of the Germans but had prayed fervently that the pagan-slayers had stumbled upon the scar-faced Englishman who had wreaked havoc on the kingdom. He sighed: so much was beyond his control. The exception being the benefits from his influential position at court.

The previous week he had attended a dinner at a wealthy merchant's house and had been fed more than fine food. The Crown needed the support and money of the city's richest, and the wealthy desired patronage. Informality was the key to favours gained and granted. And information. Traders, clerics and pilgrims who travelled the highways across France collected intelligence that was of value. Knowledge could be as powerful as a killer's sword. Or an assassin's dagger. And it was word of an assassination that had been confided to Bucy. A killing planned by a woman. What the merchant had heard from the south confirmed a nagging concern that Bucy had had for some weeks about a noblewoman who had repeatedly tried to gain access to the court. Officials had informed him about a woman who had tried hard to gain favour by selling information. She wanted a hearing, had begged an audience with the King, but officials had turned her away. She had persisted in seeking a meeting with the Dauphin and was denied again. The governance of France had more pressing matters than another aggrieved widow, women who were as common and numerous as roadside weeds. Yet it was her name that had chimed. Bucy knew it, but at the time could not place it and so gave it no more thought. Until now when the merchant had passed on the information.

And as a heavy key turns in a lock until the tumblers mesh it all fell into place. He knew who she was. A frisson of anxiety rippled through him. Whom was she going to assassinate? And where?

CHAPTER FIFTY-THREE

Beyard the Gascon captain watched the four horsemen approach across the open ground. He had waited a week, knowing there was no more he could do to aid Blackstone. Behind the walls of the bastide 376 men were camped. Most were Gascons; others from Navarre and Castile had filtered down from the mountains and sought employment with the promise of booty. He hoped the weather would hold long enough for them to fight before storms swept across the land. Blackstone's reputation for fighting through the winter when others stayed behind city walls was well known but it took its toll on men's strength and if any of these men Beyard had recruited thought it too arduous, then they would desert even Blackstone.

Blackstone rode through the gates with John Jacob and Will Longdon. The bastide's small square was cramped but the gathered men stood when they saw him.

'Beyard, it took me longer to reach you than I thought. Any trouble keeping them here?' said Blackstone, dismounting and tying off the bastard horse whose ears pricked and head reared at the closeness of the crowds of men.

'A few fights. One man dead. I hanged his killer; he wasn't a Gascon so nothing more took hold.'

'You've done well, my friend. Keeping these men behind the walls like rats in a sack was bound to cause violence. Did you find the Welshman?'

'I did. He wouldn't come here, said the place was too easy to breach. He trusts no one.'

'It's what I expected,' said Blackstone. 'Do we know where he is?'

'A few miles from here.'

'Good. We need him. You have news of Armagnac?'

Beyard took out a piece of folded parchment tucked under his belt. It was grubby and ink-stained. 'My scouts have been shadowing him for days. When they reported back I had a scribe write the names of whose pennons they saw. I thought you might need it when you get to Foix. Armagnac's drawn a multitude to his cause, Sir Thomas.'

Blackstone looked at the list of feudal lords who had rallied to the Count d'Armagnac's side. A quick calculation of how many men each knight would have with him made it plain they were outnumbered by a significant number. 'How many archers do we have?'

Beyard grimaced. 'A handful. Welsh mostly. Belligerent bastards. They rode with ap Madoc and didn't like his discipline. They deserted him and joined others on the road. I found them with some Gascon men raiding south. They like the sound of money in a purse as much as their own voices. Whores and wine quieten them down and keep them poor. But I must tell you, Sir Thomas, there's a hard bastard among them who raises his voice and causes trouble.'

'Take me to him after I've spoken to the men.' He strode up a couple of steps that led to the wall and turned to face the crowded square. A murmur rose from the crowd. They quietened.

'You men have fought hard for lords, princes and kings. When the war ended so did your usefulness. Some of you are sworn men to the Captal de Buch and because of it you have answered my call. Others have sold their swords because that is the way a fighting man survives. I fought for Florence against the Visconti: perhaps we faced each other once as enemies. Now we fight the French. Again. This is no skirmish. A battle looms against thousands of men and you will stand shoulder to shoulder with men of Foix, with Gascon, English, Castilian, Navarrese and—'

'You place us Welsh below the standing of Navarrese?' a voice interrupted from the crowd.

Laughter rippled through them; anger blossomed from others.

'A country so insulted should look to where I place Englishmen. Neither above or below but at the core of proud fighters. Have I have eased your sense of offence?'

'A barber-surgeon can heal a wound but an insult, well, I'd say that takes money.'

A cheer of support rose from the men.

Blackstone raised a hand and quietened them. 'I have promised you payment in the King's name. I have his writ. But we can seize a greater wealth. The Count of Armagnac brings his vassals to the fight. Fealty lords, families of great wealth. Monlezun, Frezensaguet, d'Aure, de la Barthe and a dozen more besides. The noble Lords Terride, Falga and Aspet. Every one will have his own men with him. Every one will beat the drum in their attempt to send terror into your heart. Their banners and pennons will fill the sky. They will outnumber us but they do not have the urge to kill us as much as we wish to kill them. Defeat them and the ransoms and booty will send you back to your farms, families or whorehouses with more money than you can spend in a lifetime.'

A roar boomed through the bastide. A flock of crows cawed in alarm and flapped away. Blackstone stepped down to the cheers of the gathered men.

'There's that much plunder?' said Killbere quietly as they followed Beyard through the crowd that parted.

'How would I know? They're noblemen, aren't they? Do you think these men will fight as hard if there's no reward?'

The crowd broke up and by the time Beyard led Blackstone and the others into one of the long buildings the Welsh archers were already inside. Cooking fires burned; blackened iron pots hung suspended over the embers. There were no windows and the only light came from torches hooked into iron holders on the walls. The room stank of sweat and smoke and damp straw used for bedding. The Welshmen's bows were encased in their wax bags and given more care than the scurvy-looking archers. The bags were laid on unused apple racks.

Blackstone picked his way through to where a broken-faced man as big as himself stood. His cloak was almost rags; he had a blanket over his shoulders. He spat through his matted beard when he saw Blackstone walk towards him. He was the man who had jeered in the square. The archer's knife in his hand was ripping open a sack to tie to his worn boots. Its scraped edge showed its razor sharpness.

'The great Lord Blackstone,' said the man sarcastically.

Blackstone punched him square in the face. The blow rocked him off his heels and threw him against the wall. The blow flattened his hooked nose; blood poured into his beard. Dazed, his eyes tried to focus on the man who loomed over him.

'Don't interrupt me when I speak,' said Blackstone. He turned to the men, who had recoiled from the sudden violence. 'Get him up.'

Those men nearest quickly obeyed but the burly archer pushed them away and clambered upright. He stood trembling with rage at the humiliation.

'The next time I'll kill you,' said Blackstone. 'Understood?'

The archer looked confused but then nodded. Thomas Blackstone was not a man to challenge.

'Your name?'

'Meuric Kynith,' he said, and then quickly added, 'my lord.'

Blackstone pointed to Will Longdon. 'This man is my centenar. He is Master Will Longdon. He fought at Morlaix, Sluys, Crécy and Poitiers and every other conflict with me. You will show him respect. He will command all my archers. My ventenar is Jack Halfpenny.'

'And who will command the Welsh among us, my lord?' said Kynith.

'You will be their ventenar even though there are over twenty of you.'

Kynith's chin tilted, the honour not lost on him. 'Aye. We will serve you well, Sir Thomas.'

'You deserted Gruffydd ap Madoc,' said Blackstone. 'I know him. We fought at Crécy together when I was a boy. This man is Sir Gilbert Killbere; he went under a French warhorse fighting at ap Madoc's side. I will have no ill will between you and ap Madoc.'

'The ill will comes from him, my lord. He did not pay us; we live in rags and without a denier to buy nourishing food. An archer needs his strength. He threatened to have his men slaughter us if we complained further.'

Blackstone pulled his purse from his belt and tossed it to the ragged man. 'His debt is now mine.'

Meuric Kynith went down on one knee; the archers followed his example. 'Thank you, Sir Thomas.'

'Don't thank me yet: my archers need more courage than most. I ask much of them. And many of you will die in the battle. If you are too drunk to fight I will flog you. If you kill each other over whores I will hang you. Such men are of no use to me. I value my bowmen and I will not lose one through drunken excess. Understand?'

A murmur of assent rippled through the kneeling men.

'And why have archers not killed for the pot?' said Blackstone.

'There's no game, my lord,' said Kynith. 'The men who swept ahead of us have slaughtered every creature that walks or flies and raided every grain store in every village. Gruffydd ap Madoc hordes supplies.'

Blackstone turned to Beyard. 'What do we have here?'

'Enough for a few days.'

'Distribute it to all the men. Get them fed. We must travel hard and fast.'

'Sir Thomas, what of the journey ahead?' said Beyard.

'Do as I say. I'll get supplies.'

Blackstone and the others turned back through the archers and as he passed each one they dipped their head and spoke his name respectfully.

CHAPTER FIFTY-FOUR

Gruffydd ap Madoc spat out gristle from the meat he was chewing and then wiped the back of his hand across his mouth. Animal fat smeared his beard.

'You are an intensely irritating man, Thomas Blackstone. You come into a man's home and insult him at his table. And you, Killbere, you goat-smelling old bastard, you still stand at his side.'

Blackstone and Killbere, with John Jacob and Will Longdon, had followed Beyard to where the Welshman held court on the high ground in a hilltop town half a day's ride from the bastide.

'A hovel more than a home, you uncouth son of a whore. And your table manners are worse than a wild pig snouting through the forest,' said Killbere.

'Gilbert, I should have left you under that horse in the mud at Crécy. Now, Thomas, you make demands on a man who has settled himself for winter and who is thinking again about the proposition you sent.'

'You have what I need, you knew I was coming, so I ask for it.'

Ap Madoc picked meat from his teeth and grunted. 'Still, I have waited patiently. I was promised money. You have it?'

'Do you think I would carry payment with me?'

The Welshman grinned. 'It should offend me that you don't trust me. Don't forget I was the one who saved your life at

Brignais.' He chewed, ruminating on how best to deal with Blackstone, who was no longer a knight who fought where he chose, but who was now King Edward's Master of War and who carried Edward and the Prince's authority. 'And I gave you back the money I stole from you before the battle at Brignais.'

'To avoid bad blood between us.'

'There was that,' he admitted. 'The thought of us fighting to the death caused my passionate Welsh heart to melt at the prospect of me killing you.' Killbere snorted derisively at the thought of ap Madoc besting Blackstone. The Welshman shrugged. 'Well, I have the men you want. And if you have the King's writ then we can do business.'

'I want supplies for the men who are following me.'

'I've raided all summer to secure winter feed for my horses and men. Why would I share it?'

'Because you made a pledge to the man I sent that you would offer all assistance. For payment.'

'I did, I did. You know, Thomas…' He got off his stool and poured himself more wine into a clay beaker. 'Time is a fickle mistress. Those weeks ago when your men sought me out and you were still wherever it was you were, I made, let's say, an agreement with someone else.'

'You're reneging on your agreement with us?' snorted Killbere. 'If you do, you betray an agreement with the King of England.'

'Now, there you are, Gilbert, jumping to conclusions, casting my character into the shadows. I did not say I was reneging, simply that circumstances have altered my terms of commitment.'

'He's backing out. I told you, Thomas, you cannot trust this whoreson.'

Gruffydd ap Madoc's temper broke and he flung the beaker across the room. 'Damn you, Killbere, I'll not be insulted here in my own stronghold! I will not!'

As Killbere reached for his sword, Blackstone got between the two men. 'Sit down. Both of you. There's a battle to be fought, and it's not in this room.'

The two men quietened.

'Gruffydd, you promised me men.'

'I have them.'

'The six hundred?'

'Almost, Thomas. Some have deserted; others have gone to fight in Spain. The weather is kinder there.'

'How many?'

'Two hundred,' ap Madoc said apologetically.

Blackstone took the bad news stoically. 'Not enough.'

Ap Madoc shrugged. 'Maybe a few more. Another fifty.'

'Four hundred,' said Blackstone. 'That's what I need.'

'No. They are needed elsewhere now. I will give you two hundred and seventy-five men, all equipped and provisioned.'

'Three hundred and fifty, including any more archers you have.'

'Three hundred, but the archers are few now so I cannot spare them.'

'Very well. I'll reduce the agreed payment accordingly.'

'I accept,' said the Welshman. 'I will send them to your captains at the place you choose and as a gesture of my affection and respect for you I will give you the supplies you requested without charge.'

Blackstone looked hard at the man who had changed sides so often. 'There's more you want from me. What is it?'

Gruffydd ap Madoc sat back down and rubbed a finger in spilled wine on the wooden table. 'I ask a great favour of you.'

Killbere quickly glanced at Blackstone. The devious routier was like a winter fever that crept up on an unsuspecting man and brought him down. Ap Madoc's tone was now that of a reasonable man seeking understanding. 'I seek… redemption.'

'I'm no damned priest,' said Blackstone.

'No, no, wait, do not judge me, I beg you.'

'Too late for that, you lying, thieving whoreson,' said Killbere.

Ap Madoc did not raise his voice or a hand in anger. 'I understand you doubt me but only Thomas can help me. I fought for our blessed King Edward, fought as hard as any man. I spoke up for you against my own archers at Crécy when you were a young bowman and you wore the silver goddess at your neck because they thought you had taken her from a dead man. Yes, of course you remember. And you, Gilbert, we bled together. So, when the fighting ended, and we parted – when Thomas hovered close to death – I sold my skills, which set me on a path of violence that continues to this day. We were comrades-in-arms and now… now… I wish to be pardoned by the King and serve him again.'

'God's tears,' said Killbere. 'You waste good breath on a speech fit for a whimpering novice who played with his cock during Holy Communion.'

Gruffydd ap Madoc bowed his head. 'I am not a man who can use words well,' he said and raised his eyes to Blackstone. 'I give you my word. I beg you, speak on my behalf to the King.'

'I have no means of speaking to him,' said Blackstone. 'Even if I believed you.'

Ap Madoc lifted his hands in surrender. 'Then to prove myself I will not accept the payment offered in the King's writ. I cannot join the fight against Armagnac because when you did not arrive in good time I made an agreement to take some of my men and help another. I ride south tomorrow but the men, and the supplies – they are yours. If I cannot serve the King then I will serve the Prince, as do you, Thomas. I will be his vassal. I shall pledge my fealty and my sword to him. I do not wish to be outlawed any longer. I wish to prove myself again as I once did.'

For a ruffian like Gruffydd ap Madoc to refuse a substantial payment for his men was a convincing gesture.

Killbere gazed in disbelief. 'Thomas? You don't believe this scoundrel?'

Blackstone remained silent, giving the proposition thought. 'And if I seek this favour from the Prince you would relinquish the lands and towns you have seized, and return that which has been looted?'

'Gladly,' said the Welshman. 'I was content as a soldier of the King. Come, Thomas, did you not tire of selling your sword to the Italians or any other feudal lord who offered enough money? Was it not a relief to surrender all of that when you were honoured and made his Master of War?'

'Where do you ride tomorrow?'

'To the King of Navarre. He has asked for men.'

'Jean de Grailly is advising him now. Why would you be summoned?'

'An old debt, Thomas. I owe him. I wish to clear my name and reclaim what little of my honour remains. I will do the Prince's bidding. When he receives the fealty of the Lords of Aquitaine I will bend the knee and kiss his hand. I swear it.'

Blackstone hesitated. 'He's not here for some months. Attend to your business with de Grailly and Navarre. I'll speak to the Prince. That's all I can do.'

*

Blackstone and Killbere rode away from the walled town. A dozen levies followed with supply horses and food for the men in the bastide.

'He's a viper that slips beneath a man's blanket for warmth and then sinks his fangs, Thomas.'

'I know. But I have his men and supplies without payment and I can use that money elsewhere for good cause.'

'And you said nothing about von Plauen and his comrades. If they discover where the Welshman is it would remove a potential problem. Why not let them kill him? Who would grieve?'

Blackstone nodded. 'I know but I cannot forget that he and other routiers came to our aid at Brignais. We would all be dead if he had not arrived in good time. If he can be brought to heel and to fight for the Prince, then Aquitaine has gained a man whose presence will help keep the peace. I'm not concerned, Gilbert. It's months until the Prince lands and I would rather have the Welshman away from the field of battle in case he turned and ran when he saw the odds that face us.' The turn of events troubled him but as the bastide hove into view, he couldn't see any reason not to have agreed to ap Madoc's request. Time was against Blackstone. His captains would soon be following on his heels, threading their way across the countryside, forming up their ranks of fighting men. They had arranged a gathering place. Now all he had to do was convince the Count de Foix that he needed them.

CHAPTER FIFTY-FIVE

Gunther von Schwerin rode back into Dome as the chapel bell rang for vespers. His companions were already making their way inside for prayers when he dismounted and handed his reins to a stable lad who had run for the honour of caring for the knight's horse. Sibrand von Ansbach turned around before the doors closed and strode to the mud-splattered knight.

'Gunther, where were you? We searched everywhere. One of the stable hands said you left before we awoke.'

Von Schwerin pulled free his gloves. 'You're missing prayers, my friend.'

'And you have been gone all day. Wolfram is angry.'

'Wolfram is always angry these days. He must have some kind of brain fever. I'll explain everything. I need something to eat and drink – it's been a long ride.'

His fellow knight matched his stride as he made his way towards their tents. Around them the town's soldiers went about their business. Preparations were being made for Father Torellini's departure the next day, and the additional fifty men who were to accompany the King's escort were being harangued by their sergeant.

'Is everything ready for tomorrow?' said von Schwerin. 'Is Wolfram staying true to his pledge of protecting the woman?'

'Gunther, we have no choice. You said yourself we must remain patient. God will lead us to the Welshman in good time.'

Von Schwerin reached his tent and unbuckled his sword belt. He wanted nothing more than to slake his thirst and sluice the sweat from his body. 'I stink. Help me with my mail,' he said, 'and then fetch me that bucket of water.' He bent so that his friend could pull free the weight of the mail from him. Ignoring the cold evening air he stripped off the shirt as von Ansbach placed a wooden bucket at his feet. He splashed the cold water rigorously onto his chest and arms and then soaked his hair. He shook his head like a dog out of water and dried himself with a rough length of sacking. He took out his second shirt from his bag and pulled on the dry linen cloth, then buckled his jerkin on again.

'Well? What have you to say?' said von Ansbach as Gunther drank from a wineskin.

'It's vespers. A time for quiet contemplation on the events of the day that has gone before us,' he said solemnly.

His companion's jaw dropped, and before he could recover sufficiently to reply, Gunther smiled. 'Don't be so serious all the time, Sibrand. We will pray again at compline. By then I will have satisfied the demands of the body with food and drink. My conscience isn't burdened because I left without telling you or the others where I was going. Let's attend to the fire and when Brother Wolfram and Rudi return I'll tell you where I have been.'

He settled himself on the upturned bucket as von Ansbach ignored his own frustration and concentrated on stoking the fire. Gunther watched the activity in the town as he cut a wedge of bread and meat. They could not avoid the journey to Avignon but there was nothing stopping them from riding free of the column as the journey progressed. He watched as Henry Blackstone and the woman's son, Jocard, carried saddlebags towards the stables. The young men worked diligently without supervision: Blackstone's son obeying earlier commands from his now absent father, and acting like a guardian to the younger boy. It was easy to see the lad had leadership qualities. From what von Schwerin had witnessed and heard of Henry Blackstone the boy also had courage and intelligence. The two combined meant he could make a mark in life and he wondered if Blackstone was sending his son to Avignon in the hope that an education would remove him from the bloodshed that stalked his father like death's shadow.

Idle reflections about Blackstone's son left him as thoughts of his own destiny beckoned. When evening prayers ended the two knights watched their companions come out of the chapel. Wolfram von Plauen strode towards him. 'We do not act alone, Gunther. I gave our pledge and we must abide by it. Where did you go?'

'Brother Wolfram, I made no pledge to stay with the Lady Cateline; we only gave our word of honour that we would see you keep yours and act as her guardian. Nothing binds us to you.'

'Except the brotherhood,' said von Burchard.

'Rudi is right, Gunther,' von Ansbach said and stood with his companions. Gunther had not raised himself from where he sat but he knew, as did they all, that their strength lay in the bond between them. They had vowed to travel together until they killed Gruffydd ap Madoc.

'I apologize, Brother. I should have told you but your duties have kept you occupied and away from us.'

Colour crept up von Plauen's neck. Was this mockery? Was his desire so obvious? 'As you said, I swore an oath,' he said coldly. 'Where did you go?'

Gunther von Schwerin looked beyond the three men to where Gisbert de Dome was speaking to one of his captains. A secret could escape without a word being spoken. Men who were given news they were desperate to hear acted differently. Their eagerness would be clear to anyone with a keen eye. He had no choice but to tell them and hope they kept aloof from the others. 'We leave early tomorrow, my friends, with the Italian priest and the Lady Cateline. We ensure that Brother Wolfram stays true to his promises. We will go to Avignon, but along the way we can ride free of the escort without suspicion and attend to our own business. I shadowed Thomas Blackstone. I have found the Welshman.'

CHAPTER FIFTY-SIX

As Blackstone and Killbere, accompanied by John Jacob, rode south towards the Pyrenees, William Ashford led his men out of Dome. Father Niccolò Torellini had Henry and Lady Cateline with her children ride close to him so they had the immediate protection of William Ashford's escort. Gisbert de Dome's additional fifty men rode ahead and the Teutonic Knights brought up the rear. Wolfram von Plauen had attempted to keep Cateline at his side, insisting it was his duty to keep her close. It was a futile suggestion, given the number of men surrounding her but she mollified him by telling him he could camp close to her when they stopped for the night.

Von Plauen's fellow knights remained silent as they watched their leader press his case with her. She was a noblewoman who saw the Teutonic Knight as a vassal monk. His status within the Order meant nothing to her and his companions wondered quietly among themselves whether his behaviour was that of a spurned guardian whose pledge to Blackstone was being rebuffed or of a man unused to being in such proximity to a woman. A beautiful woman.

Gunther von Schwerin rode forward to William Ashford. 'We are leaving the column for a few hours,' he informed the King's sergeant. 'Our horses are used to more a more strenuous pace than this.'

Ashford had no control over the Teutonic Knights; it was Blackstone's decision to make one of them guardian to the Frenchwoman. She seemed self-assured enough to look after herself as far as Ashford was concerned. Von Plauen was no longer a threat now he had been beaten and subjugated to the role of wet nurse and obliged to shadow the woman. And, frankly, William Ashford had seen enough erratic behaviour from wayward priests who lied about visiting whorehouses to have no interest in what the Teutonic Knights wanted to do away from the column.

'As you wish,' he said.

'We will return by morning.'

Ashford shrugged. 'As long as you cause no problems to this escort and the people it protects I don't care.'

The gentle rebuff gave von Schwerin pause and he scowled. These Englishmen had no manners. But then he heeled his horse and returned to his comrades.

Father Torellini had overheard the conversation and turned to watch the four Teutonic Knights gallop away. What was so pressing?

'They're in a hurry,' said Henry, unconsciously echoing the priest's thoughts.

Henry's inquisitiveness was not lost on Torellini. He lowered his voice. 'You're to stay here.'

'My father saved those men. There is a debt of honour. What if they are about to betray us all? We don't know, do we? There is only one way to find out.'

The Italian studied the boy who had been under his care and protection when they were in Florence. He was capable enough of defending himself and had got the better of a knife-wielding assassin when other young men of a similar age would have run for safety. He glanced to where the four horsemen disappeared around the edge of a forest.

'How long would it take to ride back to Dome?' he asked.

Henry looked uncertain. 'I don't know. A fast ride, a few hours.'

'There and back before dark?'

Henry understood. Torellini was giving him an excuse he needed to leave the column. 'By nightfall, yes.'

'Master Ashford,' Torellini called.

The King's sergeant checked his horse and rode to him. 'Father?'

'I have left a document in my chamber. Master Blackstone has offered to ride back and retrieve it for me.'

Ashford looked unhappy. 'I don't know about that, Father. Sir Thomas would skin me alive if anything happened to the lad while under my escort.'

'I will take full responsibility,' said Torellini. 'I think it's important enough for him to go and we are still in safe territory.'

Ashford nodded. The priest's words took the responsibility and authority from him. 'As you wish, Father. But I cannot split the escort and come looking for you,' he told Henry.

'I understand, Master Ashford.'

'Do not push your mount too hard. A skittish horse can put the best of riders under its hooves,' said Ashford.

Henry tugged the reins and heeled the horse.

Henry kept a safe distance from the Teutonic Knights, always staying below the skyline, and when he lost sight of them used his instinct as to what direction they would take. His father had taught him well, and he picked up the trail easily. As skilled as the Germans were they had no expectation of being followed and when they finally saw Gruffydd ap Madoc's bastide they did not spot the lone horseman observing them from the edge of a distant woodland.

'I see no sign of defence,' said von Plauen. 'Are you certain this is where he is?'

'I saw Blackstone ride out with the supplies and the men who stood on the walls were routiers,' Gunther von Schwerin insisted. 'He is here.'

'Gunther, there is no way to assault this bastide,' said von Buchard.

'I have no intention of trying to,' said his comrade. 'We cloak our surcoats and ride in seeking hospitality.' He shrugged at their looks of surprise. 'We are travellers and routiers' greed makes them perfect hosts. They will expect to rob and kill us.'

Von Ansbach pulled his cloak on. 'Gunther is right. Let us get inside and put them to the sword.'

'Without knowing their strength?' said von Plauen.

'It's that or sit here until they move out, and who knows when that might be? They could be behind those walls for winter.'

The argument ended. The four men covered their white surcoats. They spurred their horses into a canter and slowed when they approached the town's gates. Gruffydd ap Madoc's men watched as the four riders drew up their horses outside the walls. Von Plauen called out for hospitality. The routiers on the walls seemed barely able to suppress their delight at welcoming men wearing fine woollen cloaks and riding quality horses. They called down for someone to open the gates and the four knights spurred their horses forward. Gunther von Schwerin looked at the few men who lingered in the courtyard. There were barely a dozen routiers watching their arrival and only six men who lingered on the walls behind them. This was not the force of men that von Schwerin had witnessed.

'Too few,' he said quietly.

They dismounted. Four of the routiers stepped forward to take their reins. The others approached the travellers but stopped when von Plauen looked from one to the other. 'Where is Gruffydd ap Madoc?' he asked.

Their frowns of concern turned into wolverine grins. 'You know our Welshman?' one of them said.

'He has business with the Englishman Thomas Blackstone,' said von Plauen.

The men took a cautious step closer. 'And what business is that of yours?'

'We are riding south with Sir Thomas and he has sent us to speak further with ap Madoc. We are to buy more sacks of grain. We have the money with us.'

One of the routiers spat and placed a hand on the knife at his belt. 'Your Englishman has taken enough supplies, but he didn't pay a damned sou. Ap Madoc left the same day. Blackstone knew that. They struck a deal.' He unsheathed his knife. 'So you don't belong here. But your money does.'

The man stepped purposefully forward as his companions wrenched the horse's reins. The Teutonic Knights showed no sign of fear as the beasts jostled behind them. Rudolph von Burchard was closest to the knife-wielding mercenary and in one swift movement his hand emerged from beneath his cloak. His knife took the routier under the chin, the rapid slash cutting his throat. The sudden action caused the mercenaries to falter for a vital few seconds as the four men cast aside their cloaks, exposing their identity. Gruffydd ap Madoc's men were street fighters and no stranger to using a blade at close quarters but the speed and expertise of the Teutonic Knights caught them flat-footed. Three of the men holding the horses' reins died before they could draw their swords. The sudden rush of men across the square played straight into the knights' hands. With no need for a command they formed a four-man defensive square and let the assault come to them. As they broke the routiers' attack, Gunther von Schwerin stepped clear of the formation and felled two more routiers who had turned to run. Three others retreated to the gate and turned and ran for their lives. Sibrand von Ansbach quickly remounted and spurred his horse after them. Von Plauen held one man beneath his sword point. 'Where is ap Madoc?'

The man shook his head. 'South, is all I know. I swear.'

'Why? Whom does he join?'

'I don't know. They've contracted him.'

The sword point drew a trickle of blood. 'A woman!' the man gasped. 'A noblewoman pays him. He took the men with him. We are to hold this place until he returns.'

'When?' von Plauen demanded.

'My lord, I know nothing more than that.'

'Then you are of no further use,' said von Plauen and killed him.

The other knights had searched the buildings. 'There's no one else,' von Buchard said, stepping around the dead routiers in the yard. 'Ap Madoc's fled.' He looked from von Schwerin and then to their leader. 'Wolfram, it is time we separated. I have spoken to Sibrand. We wish to pursue the Welshman and now we know he rides south then I think we should track him down.'

Gunther listened and glanced at von Plauen, who appeared torn at the suggestion. 'I am obliged to stay,' von Plauen told them.

'And that is why we should go on without you. It is regrettable, Wolfram, but we must act,' said the younger man.

'There's no telling where he's gone,' Gunther said.

'We are closer than we have ever been. We have dogged his trail this far; we will find it again. God willing,' von Buchard insisted.

'God willing,' said von Plauen. 'Gunther? You must go with them.'

Von Schwerin looked about him. 'No, let Rudi and Sibrand go after him. I am still of the opinion we will hear something in Avignon. It's a place of rumour and gossip and the truth sometimes resurrects itself after being buried under the lies. And then we will need the two of us to go after him.'

'Winter is at our throats. Ap Madoc might go into hiding and if we discover where, then we have him,' said von Buchard.

Von Plauen nodded in agreement. 'We will go our separate ways.'

'And the priest's escort, Ashford?' said von Buchard.

'He has no interest in us. If two of us have decided to leave the column he won't care,' von Plauen told him. 'Let's make sure the Welshman has nowhere to return when the time comes. Burn this place down.'

Gunther von Schwerin tipped lantern oil onto straw. 'Blackstone forced a duty upon you, Brother Wolfram, but it might be the hand of the divine that places us in Avignon. The entire world passes through its gates. Word of ap Madoc's whereabouts is bound to reach us there.' He struck his flint, and the spark ignited. Flames quickly took hold.

Von Plauen wiped his blade. He took consolation from his comrade's words. Perhaps it *was* divine intervention that had brought him to the woman. He watched the fire devour the tinder-dry timbers. The flames were as voracious as his desire. To find the Welshman and possess the woman would take patience. It would take Avignon.

From his vantage point Henry Blackstone saw one of the knights pursue three running men who separated in their attempt to escape. He recognized von Ansbach, who methodically killed each man in turn. By the time he had dismounted to ensure each man was dead, smoke plumed from the bastide. Flames took hold and flared into the sky as von Ansbach's companions rode out to rejoin him. Henry could not know how many men they had fought behind the gates that now blazed along with the buildings but they had done it quickly. He watched the four knights embrace and then split up. He turned his horse. Perhaps Father Torellini would know why the Germans had killed these men.

He returned to the column before the Teutonic Knights and reported what he had witnessed to Torellini, who offered no explanation until he had considered the possibilities of recent events.

'Your father needs men to fight and he intended to seek out Gruffydd ap Madoc. These knights are sworn to kill the Welshman for the murder he has committed. One of them must have followed your father. But if you say there were only a handful of men, then ap Madoc was elsewhere. And now two have gone to search him out.'

'Should we warn my father?' said Henry.

The Italian priest shook his head. 'He knows what he's doing, and we must press on to Avignon.'

Henry looked across to where the Teutonic Knights had rejoined the column. 'Those men are indebted to my father but when the Lady Cateline dismisses them their pledge is cancelled. If they believe he has aligned himself with the Welshman then he becomes their enemy as much as ap Madoc.'

'That's possible. But that is in the future and has no bearing on your father's duty now. What you cannot know is that he embarks on a mission of great importance for your King and for your Prince. You must obey his wishes. Your safety under your mother's name in Avignon eases his burden of worry about you.'

Torellini pulled his cloak tighter. The cold wind bit his flesh as sharply as the devil's imps. Thomas Blackstone's task required persuasion, courage and the means to fight an enemy who would gather in greater force than Blackstone could muster even with the help of the likes of Gruffydd ap Madoc. And no matter how often Torellini comforted himself with his belief in Blackstone's skills, he knew, deep in his heart, that the battle soon to take place could overwhelm even the bravest and noblest of fighting men. And if Thomas Blackstone did not survive then it was up to Niccolò Torellini to ensure that his son did. For then he would claim his name and the inheritance of its legend.

CHAPTER FIFTY-SEVEN

Blackstone, Killbere and John Jacob rode towards a broad rocky outcrop that rose hundreds of feet from the valley floor. Its flanks supported crenellated walls protecting the castle's towers. The soaring heights of the snow-buffeted Pyrenees ran like a broken spine down the long valley beyond the stronghold. It was a formidable castle held for centuries by the Counts de Foix.

'I hope he's amenable,' said Killbere. 'Those towers give crossbowmen a clear killing field. So too the loopholes in the walls.'

'He's arrogant enough to swat us like a fly if he so chooses,' said Blackstone. 'John, unfurl my banner. Let them see who approaches.'

John Jacob dismounted and cut a stout low branch from a bare tree and attached Blackstone's blazon.

'If he's belligerent, we could end up in a dungeon in one of those towers and in this cold weather my arse will freeze,' Killbere said. 'He might have blades in his piss if our beloved Prince has upset him.'

'If he agrees to meet me, then we can put the Prince's case to him. He's ripe for persuasion. It's King John who'll turn his piss to ice water,' said Blackstone.

Killbere wiped a hand across his dribbling nose. 'Well, the good thing is he's Jean de Grailly's cousin, and the Captal de Buch spoke for you when we fought the Jacquerie at Meaux. That must count for something.'

'Gilbert, he's a nobleman from one of the most distinguished families in France. He is a feudal Lord of two Pyrenean principalities. It counts for nothing.'

'And you're here on the English King's business and there's no greater nobleman than him. Don't worry, Thomas, I'll keep my mouth shut and my arse clenched and try not to fart when I bow.'

John Jacob remounted and as the wind caught the banner it unfurled, showing the cruciform image of the sword gripped by a gauntlet-clad fist and the declaration *Défiant à la Mort*. They spurred their horses forward. The clear blue sky would not bless them with its glittering light much longer. In the distance the suburbs of Foix had a dusting of snow on their tiled roofs. Smoke fled the chimneys as flurries of snowflakes danced across the rooftops.

The houses clinging to the lower slopes gradually gave way to the winding road that led up to the barbican. Blackstone, Killbere and John Jacob were a hundred yards from the gates when they swung open without challenge.

'They saw us coming,' said John Jacob. 'They know who you are, Sir Thomas. Damned right too.'

'Respect where it's due,' said Killbere. He straightened in the saddle and pushed out his chest. 'Let them see who we are, John. Count Gaston Phoebus of Foix might be a mighty nobleman but he's still a Frenchie. Ride ahead. Lead us in.'

John Jacob spurred his horse forward. Its iron-shod hooves clattered on cobblestones. An outer courtyard and pathways laid in stone denoted wealth. No mud would cling to the sole of this feudal lord's boots. Stable lads appeared as two men strode forward to greet the new arrivals. The sturdier of the two, dressed and armed like any man-at-arms, stood a pace behind his older companion, who wore a dark woollen cloak and tunic. The rich clothing told the world that this was a man of importance in a wealthy man's domain.

'Sir Thomas,' said the elder, dipping his head respectfully. 'I am Alphonse, my Lord Gaston's steward. Master Gregory here serves as his bailiff. He will attend to your horses and arrange food and lodging for your squire,' he said, indicating John Jacob: the assumption borne from years of identifying a lord and those who served them. 'I will escort you and your companion to my master.'

Blackstone and Killbere exchanged glances. It was a mark of respect that the most senior servant in the household had been sent to greet them, someone likely to be from a local noble family. The three men dismounted. 'My squire will attend to my horse; it has a temperament.'

The steward nodded and smiled, perhaps suppressing a tantalizing thought that horse and rider shared common tendencies.

Blackstone and Killbere followed the steward up steps to a guarded portal that opened into a broad passage. The dim light seemed to add to the sudden chill of the stone walls, colder even than outside. He struck his staff of office on the tall doors and without waiting pushed them open into a great hall where a fire blazed in a grate large enough for a dozen armed men to stand shoulder to shoulder. Gaston Phoebus was a renowned hunter, and the walls displayed the stuffed creatures from his sport. Between the richly woven tapestries were the spoils of the hunt: deer and boar heads; mounted wild birds scattered in flight across a wall as if flushed from cover by the mounted wild boar on a plinth. A bear as tall as Blackstone glared with glass eyes as it stood half raised in a cleverly exhibited pose across a fallen log and ferns. Gaston Phoebus's domain offered him sport in mountain, forest and river and he excelled at it.

A pair of live hooded falcons gripped their perch and several hunting dogs of various shapes and sizes stood ready at the knock on the door. The absence of a master of hounds suggested that these dogs were the nobleman's favourites.

A couple of the dogs sauntered forward and sniffed Blackstone and Killbere. The wire-haired wolfhound that snuffled Killbere's clothing sneezed.

Gaston Phoebus remained seated. The men's footfalls across carpets laid on fresh rushes crunched underfoot. Blackstone and Killbere bowed to the nobleman whose tanned features complemented his luxuriant blond hair.

'Sir Thomas and Sir Gilbert, you are welcome. I pray God has blessed you both with good health since we last met?'

'Aye, my lord, and we wish such blessings on you,' said Blackstone.

Gaston Phoebus studied them a moment longer and gave a barely imperceptible flick of his eyes to the steward, who stepped forward quickly with two stools. Blackstone and Killbere sat down.

'Master Alphonse will have food ready for you once we have spoken of matters that concern us.' He nodded to the steward, and they heard the door close behind them. It was to be a private audience. The Count leaned forward. His gentle demeanour from moments before was now tinged with acrimony. 'It is presumptuous for Edward and the Prince to interfere in my affairs. I do not need help. I will not be obliged to offer fealty.'

'No, my lord, that is not the intention of us being here,' Blackstone said.

'You are no politician, Sir Thomas. Your reputation opens doors that would otherwise remain closed. Our chance meeting at Meaux four years ago allowed me to take your measure. Your exploits since then have enhanced your standing further but if negotiations were to take place, an alliance formed, then your King would have sent Sir John Chandos. Not you. You are a fighter not a negotiator. Edward would not have you act as his emissary if there was not a military advantage to be had. Somewhere.' He cocked an eyebrow at Blackstone. 'For either him or me. Which is it?'

Blackstone waited a moment before answering. The Count de Foix and he were of a similar age and Blackstone understood fighting men could be easily insulted. The young Count had fought hard and well at Meaux against the Jacquerie and before the uprising had been on crusade in Prussia. An accomplished, battle-hardened fighter needed no lecture from a mere knight, even if Blackstone was Edward's Master of War. What was said next needed to be spoken with care. The threat of a rancorous dismissal was a breath away.

'My Prince of Wales and Aquitaine has vowed to bring peace and prosperity to southern France. I well know your father and his father's loyalty before him to the French Crown. Before we, the English, fought at Poitiers there was an undertaking between you and my Prince that there would be no harshness expressed between you. During his great *chevauchée* before the battle he made no attack on your domains. Your people went unharmed. His regard for you is beyond doubt. The insult now levied against you by the French King distresses him. We know King John has favoured the Count of Armagnac and that you will fight to restore your honour. I am tasked to serve you.'

Gaston Phoebus listened attentively, one hand draped over the arm of his chair, fingers stroking a dog's head. He remained silent. His hand ceased stroking the hound; it nuzzled him, demanding more attention. An irritated flick of his wrist sent the dog quickly skulking away. Blackstone's heartbeat quickened. He had raised the fact of the de Foix dynasty's loyalty to the French Crown and the previous understanding between the present ruler and the English Prince. Would Gaston Phoebus see it as a taunt followed by an insulting suggestion that he knew whom to side with to protect his principality?

Pulling his fingers through his hair the Count stood and faced the fire. Blackstone and Killbere got to their feet. Finally, de Foix turned and faced them. 'When we met last your brashness was, to say the least, irritating; now you speak in a manner that serves your King and Prince with dignity. You are correct. Family loyalty has counted for nothing. I have known it for years but I have balanced it with the desire of retaining the independence of my principalities. You say your King and Prince have sent you here to serve me. How will you do this?'

'By giving you warning of the Count of Armagnac's move towards you and to commit men against him and stand at your side.'

'I know he has mobilized. My vassal lords have gathered their men. Why would I need English help?'

'How many retained men can you muster?'

The Count twirled a bejewelled ring. 'A thousand… perhaps fifteen hundred. They will serve under my banner. Our backs to the mountains, the forests on our flanks.'

The hunting lord had given himself better odds than were realistic. And Blackstone knew it. 'Too few, my lord. I believe you overestimate your strength.'

'No, you are wrong, Sir Thomas. My informers tell me Armagnac brings his men from the west. He crossed the Dordogne three days ago. No more than a thousand, perhaps twelve hundred. He seeks to root me out in my territory.

'Then you do not know of the two thousand and more men marching south. King John has committed troops and

Marshal of the Army Arnoul d'Audrehem has raised a hundred thousand florins and paid routiers to join your enemy.'

The Count de Foix looked startled. His levies and vassals' troops would not withstand such an assault.

'You have been misinformed, my lord. D'Audrehem's not heading here,' said Blackstone. 'He won't venture into the foothills where he can be outflanked by concealed men. By an army less strong than his own. He'll fight in the open. My Gascons report he has the Count of Comminges with him, the Lords of Albret, Jean de la Barthe, the Lords of Pardhala. He has drawn more to him than even those noblemen bring to the fight. Armagnac's men crossed the Dordogne northward away from you. He'll join up with the others in a place that best suits him. You fight on his terms.'

He handed the Count the folded list of the feudal lords who would fight at the Count d'Armagnac's side. Gaston Phoebus looked at the host that would assault him and felt the crushing knowledge that he had already been outmanoeuvred. 'I have others who will join me—'

'Who? Bertucat d'Albret, Garciot du Châtel? They have deserted you. Armagnac paid them more than you offered,' Blackstone interrupted, taking a step towards de Foix. Under any other circumstances such behaviour would have earned a harsh rebuke but realization dawned on the Count that Blackstone's information was more accurate than his own. The common knight humbled him.

'How many men do you have? Who would follow you?' the Count asked.

'Not enough. Six hundred at best. My own, a few others loyal to the Crown, Gascons mostly and some routiers, men who once came to my aid. They will need payment.'

Gaston Phoebus nodded in agreement.

'I and my men serve you as a gesture of goodwill from my King and Prince.' Blackstone dared a gentle rebuke. 'While you ride at the hunt, my lord, the Count of Armagnac has dug a bear pit and expects you to fall into it.'

The Count let it pass. There was a more pressing concern than any perceived jibe. 'If you were he, where would you fight?'

Blackstone saw the landscape in his mind's eye. He had raided and fought across great swathes of France. He had pursued routiers down the Rhône Valley and faced a French army that besieged Brignais south of Lyons only months before. Troops moving north to meet those marching south would meet somewhere between Lyons and Toulouse. If he led an army at this time of year, he would avoid the eastern borders and keep the snow and wind at his back. Ride further south. Keep the mountains and forests at bay.

'Where, my lord? On the plain north of Toulouse. Reach the place first and choose your deployment. Prepare quickly and keep our archers out of sight. It's open ground with little cover. Array an army there and face your enemy and you would see his strength, or lack of it.'

'Like a boil on a whore's bare arse,' Killbere blurted. And then winced at his crude remark in front of the feudal lord.

The Count showed no sign of approval. But nor was there any expression of censure. 'Then we must lance the boil,' he said.

CHAPTER FIFTY-EIGHT

Blackstone's men had threaded their way eastwards. They hunched into their cloaks as the wind swept down valleys and roared through forests. Jack Halfpenny knew that if the strength of the wind did not ease, then it would make no difference where Blackstone had decided to fight, the bowmen's arrows would be little more than a futile gesture against armoured men. And if they could not be deployed as archers and were asked to fight as infantry then they were too lightly armed for many of them to survive.

'Here,' said Meulon. 'Sir Thomas should be over that ridge.' Blackstone would be waiting in the lee of the low rising ground, little more than a sloping hill. The land had become increasingly flat and Beyard had led them successfully across the country he knew best, riding west of the city of Toulouse that had paid *patis* to a routier horde for protection. Venturing too close to the city walls might alert the mercenaries and jeopardize Blackstone's plans. Meulon turned in the saddle and looked at the column of men. They were rested and fed; some, like Gisbert de Dome's, were fresh. Each of the captains had gone to their designated towns and villages and collected the pockets of men, some as few as thirty strong, others numbering seventy or eighty, and then they had come together and ridden as a column to meet up with Blackstone. It seemed a pitifully small force to deploy in battle but he knew that if Blackstone had convinced the Count de Foix then an army, even though few in number, would be gathered to face the Count d'Armagnac's strength.

They broached the crest and saw the Count de Foix's banner. His feudal lords were camped on the plain below. Pennons fluttered beside pavilions; shields and lances were laid outside every knight's tent; blazons of varying hues caught the light as campfire smoke buffeted the waiting soldiers. Blackstone's tent was next to the Count's, and the blood-red banner, although hoisted respectfully lower than the Count's, beckoned more strongly than any other.

Blackstone watched the column approach the camp. 'Gilbert, they're here.'

Killbere looked up from where he was sharpening his sword. 'Like fleas on a dog's back, Thomas. Too few to cause much more than an irritating itch.'

'We must be grateful that commitments were made, and that they turned up,' said Blackstone. He strode forward and raised a hand. Beyard and Meulon edged their horses through the camp. Will Longdon joined Blackstone. 'Any more archers among them other than our own lads?'

'Not that I can see, Will.'

'Ah, well then, better that way. Less difficult to keep under control.'

'Yes,' said Blackstone. They both knew how desperate they had been for bowmen. 'More arrows for every man this way.'

Will Longdon nodded and frowned. 'I'll make our lads shoot quicker when the time comes.'

Beyard and Meulon reined in their horses. 'Sir Thomas,' said Meulon. 'Are we to fight here?'

'No. A day's ride away. We leave at first light tomorrow. Horses over there with the others and our men together here. Is this everyone?'

'Aye. We didn't wait for anyone who wasn't at the place they should have been.'

Blackstone patted the horse's neck. 'It's enough.'

Meulon grinned. 'That's what I thought.'

'Get them fed and rested.' Blackstone turned back with Killbere. 'We need to get ahead of Armagnac. He's closing on us. We'll abandon the supply horses; they can follow on. We won't need them if we're dead or captured.'

'The Count likes his comfort.'

'He's fought a crusade without home finery – he knows what's at stake. What would he rather have: a full stomach and silver plates to eat from in the field or to lose everything?' He called to his centenar. 'Will?'

The archer ran across from where he was directing Jack Halfpenny and the bowmen where to camp. 'Thomas?'

'Have every archer check his arrows. Make sure each has as many as we carry with us because once the fighting starts there will be no resupply. We need to have you out of sight before Armagnac arrives. Is there trouble with any of the Welsh?'

'A more vicious bunch of bastards I haven't seen for a long time. They're just what I need,' said Will Longdon.

'Have all the archers mounted and ready before first light. No drinking tonight. We'll ride hard.'

Will Longdon nodded and went back to the archers. 'Will?' Blackstone called after him. 'How many do we have?'

'I haven't done a final count. Looks to be about ninety-three, including our own.'

Blackstone walked towards the Count's pavilion. 'We need to find a place where our bowmen will remain unseen until they're needed.'

'He won't like you telling him what to do, Thomas,' said Killbere, stopping short of the tent.

'He has no choice,' said Blackstone. 'We leave first. We'll decide the place. By the time he arrives it will be too late.'

The wind had exhausted itself by the next morning as Blackstone led the bastard horse through the Count's encampment. Cookfires glowed and pottage bubbled in iron pots. The pre-dawn breakfast put warmth into a man's belly for their march to Blackstone's chosen place of deployment where the Count's soldiers would have their last meal until after the battle. High cloud like a newborn's caul stretched across the moonlit sky. Will Longdon and Jack Halfpenny with Meuric Kynith led the archers behind Blackstone and Killbere. Some of Gaston Phoebus's men, readying themselves to follow when the Count ordered, jeered at the archers, declaring they should abandon their war bows and take up sword and shield and fight like men. The antagonists looked to be untried in battle, younger men who followed a feudal lord and lacked the hardened look of those who had fought so close to a man that the stench of his death raised bile and vomit.

'If you're still alive or haven't turned tail and run back to a suckling teat, you mewling whoreson, then I will show you how an archer castrates the likes of you,' said Kynith.

'The likes of him don't have balls,' said Jack Halfpenny. 'These are women from the village dressed in hose and jerkin masquerading as men.'

'Looking for a cock, is it?' Kynith taunted.

The men called after the slow-moving horses and their riders: 'Archers will be the first to die in this fight, you scab-arsed bowman.'

Will Longdon turned in the saddle. 'Enough now, lads. Let's look to the way ahead,' he told them, quietly satisfied that the disparate archers had come together as a fighting force who knew that when battle loomed they were the jewel in any lord's crown.

Meulon and the other captains with their companies followed the archers and as they passed the antagonists he jabbed the end of his spear into one man's chest. 'If you're still alive by the end of the fight, you will say a prayer of thanks to Our Lord Jesus for sparing you and to King Edward of England for these bowmen who slaughtered so many and gave him victory.' He grinned. 'And then you can kiss their arses.'

CHAPTER FIFTY-NINE

It was the coldest winter in years and man and beast felt it in their bones. It froze the rivers and hardened the ground of the great plain north of Toulouse that spread before Blackstone. His memory had guided him as true as a bodkin-tipped arrow towards an enemy. The gently sloping hills to the west showed scattered hamlets where distant clumps of forests huddled against the north wind. A fissure in the ground ahead of where Blackstone studied the landscape opened a narrow jagged tear. It channelled a frozen shallow stream that fed an ancient copse of trees half a mile away. Further north and west the low-roofed houses of the small town of Launac rose from a dormant patchwork of fields.

'This is the place,' said Blackstone.

Killbere grimaced. 'Yes, we'll see and hear the bastards approach.'

Blackstone pointed out the copse. 'Will, your archers will get into those trees. Horses behind our lines. If you're overrun use the ditch to break out – a knight won't risk breaking a horse's leg trying to reach you.'

'Thomas, Armagnac is no fool. He'll stay clear of the trees,' said Longdon.

'Would he think Phoebus has archers under his command? This is an armoured knights' battle, each with their own infantry,' said Meulon, easing his horse alongside.

'Will is right and so are you,' Blackstone told them, 'but we will give Armagnac a juicy bait he cannot resist.'

Killbere leaned on the saddle's pommel and let his horse have a long rein to dip its head and nuzzle frost from the grass. 'That would be us.'

Blackstone smiled. 'We'll make our stand a hundred yards or so in front of the trees. With luck, Armagnac will expect us to be holding our horses in the forest so that when we turn and run – once we've held for a charge or two – Phoebus will press from the front and left flank forcing him onto us.'

The men stayed quiet as they pictured the trap Blackstone planned.

'God's tears, Thomas, we are dead men if Phoebus falters,' said Killbere.

'There's nowhere else we can hide the bowmen, Gilbert.' He turned to Longdon, Halfpenny and Kynith. 'Armagnac outnumbers us. If they trample over us, they will swarm into those trees, so if you see us go down it is already too late. Make your escape as best you can. No one will help you.'

'Some of the lads have never faced a charge, Thomas, and I remember my first time. I was so afraid I pissed myself. When the earth moves under your feet and the war horses thunder towards you it takes grim courage to stand your ground,' said Will Longdon.

The usually robustly spoken Meuric Kynith voiced a quiet agreement. 'I was on the flank at Poitiers when the horses went through our lines.' He faced Longdon and Jack Halfpenny. 'We must get our lads into the trees and tell those who do not understand what they will face.'

'There'll be a hundred men and more of us standing in front of you. We'll hold them,' said Meulon.

'Armagnac and his feudal lords will want more than my blazon offers him,' said Blackstone. 'Jack, you will stand with us in formation. They will see your twenty archers spaced between us and think you are all the bowmen we have. Killing

English archers is a blood sport for the French. They'll come for us.'

Jack Halfpenny nodded his understanding. They all knew Blackstone's plan was the riskiest part of the battle. If the Count d'Armagnac was drawn in seeing Blackstone's flank was the weakest point and the Count de Foix did not falter, then d'Armagnac would be crushed. If, though, Gaston Phoebus did not turn in time, then Blackstone and his men would lie dead.

By that afternoon the Count de Foix et Béarn had led his army to where Blackstone's men waited. They had not been idle. In front of Blackstone's position the men had hacked a series of shallow holes in the hard ground. They were not as deep as was normal practice when faced with charging horses but with luck could make a horse stumble and put an armoured knight on the ground where he would be slain more easily. As the Count rode leisurely forward Blackstone strode to greet him, pulling a hand through his damp hair. Despite the cold December breeze Blackstone and his men sweated from their efforts.

'Here?' said Gaston Phoebus.

'Yes, my lord. Dispose your men in battle order as we discussed. I am there on the flank.'

Gaston Phoebus beckoned one of his feudal lords and instructed him to deploy the men. A squire ran to his side and took his bridle as he dismounted. 'What news of Armagnac?' His enemy's name was sour on his tongue.

'My scouts report he will be here by morning,' said Blackstone.

The Count nodded. 'I understand what you have explained, Sir Thomas, and I can see that you are at the most risk on the exposed flank.'

'Providing you hold the ground and then sweep around and close the trap we will crush him.'

The Count seemed disinterested.

'My lord? Are we in agreement?' said Blackstone, sensing that man's mood had changed. Going into battle demanded a keenness of heart and mind.

The commanders under the feudal lords serving Gaston Phoebus were shouting their orders. Blackstone watched as they drew horses close to where the men-at-arms were taking up positions.

'My lord, we should have the horses to the rear. If we are to encircle Armagnac, we must first stand our ground and defeat his initial waves of attack with infantry and men-at-arms. The ground is too hard for stakes but traps, no matter how shallow, should be dug to make his horses falter. Bring down his knights and, as we kill them, a swift attack by your horsemen from the rear, sweeping his flanks, will trap him. He will have no escape route. He will surrender or die.' He searched the Count's face for a sign of acknowledgement. 'It is what we agreed,' Blackstone added, with a hint of annoyance.

'Your tone of voice is not acceptable. I made the agreement when you insisted on drawing up my battle formation. I have reconsidered. I will attack with my knights mounted, rather than stand in defence like a supplicant. I must show Armagnac our aggression and determination. Standing on cold, hard ground would chill a man in armour.'

'Leave the damned armour. This is no tourney. We do not need a show of peacocks – we need men in mail with no more than arm and leg plate. They need to move freely. Do you not understand? He outnumbers us. Ride directly at him and you will be overcome by sheer weight of numbers. Stand your men on the ground and we will kill at least the first two waves of horsemen who ride at us. We will butcher his knights and lords where they fall.'

Colour flushed the Count's neck and face. He was seething with indignation. 'Do not dare to dictate my conduct. There is no honour in butchering knights lying crushed beneath their horses. I will defeat Armagnac in a full assault.'

'You may as well ride your men at full gallop into a castle's walls. His line will not break. It will suck you in and smother you. He has too many men. Your honour remains intact by winning this battle. Dying destroys the dynasty of the House of Foix and Béarn.'

Blackstone's prediction caused the arrogant nobleman to cast a nervous glance towards the north where the Count d'Armagnac's host would soon appear. He had bickered with his commanders, who insisted that King Edward's Master of War was a common man, granted the honour by the King because of his defiant and troublesome past and kept in France to spare the English King any further aggravation. It was they who insisted that their honour would be tarnished by fighting on foot. And they had swayed Gaston Phoebus.

Blackstone saw doubt furrow the Count's brow. He softened his voice. 'My Lord Phoebus, we destroyed France. We stood our ground. At every battle my King found the best defensive position and let his enemy's arrogance throw them onto our swords. It is the same French arrogance that has brought you to this place. It is their wilful disregard of your family that has caused this. It is their arrogance that makes them believe they will grind you under their horse's hooves.'

The Count de Foix faced him. 'Perhaps you are right, Sir Thomas. I do not doubt your own courage. I saw it when we were at Meaux and I believe that Edward honoured you because you have earned the right, but I have feudal lords whose family honour is as much a burden as any suit of fine armour. My Catalan vassals, the Viscounts of Cardona, Pallars and Castelbou, make demands on me I cannot refuse. If those knights and lords we do not slaughter cry mercy, then we hold them for ransom.'

It was obvious that the Count could not be turned away from what seemed a disastrous course of action. The fight had to be salvaged somehow.

'Very well. Then place your infantry behind your knights. When you ride have them follow on foot. As you gain ground, let them seize it. And hold. Do not let them advance any further than that first line of battle. Cut down your lances so that five infantrymen can attend each one. Three to keep a firm hold so that blood-crazed horses impale themselves, two more to kill its rider. Tell your glory-hungry lords there will be ransom enough for everyone but they have to be alive to claim it. I will hold the right flank and when the time is right use my archers. Then I am spent. If you don't close the circle you will lose this battle and I and my men will die.'

Blackstone's matter-of-fact summation of the coming events had a sobering effect on the Pyrenean prince. 'I will not fail you,' he said, 'I will give my orders so we all know what they must do and when.' He turned away to where his commanders waited and squires burnished their master's armour.

A knot of cold apprehension coiled in Blackstone's stomach. Chaos and slaughter was only hours away and what had been a sound plan of battle was now in tatters.

CHAPTER SIXTY

Blackstone gathered his captains and told them of the Count's intentions. It was not the first time men on the ground had been abandoned to their own fate by fast-moving horsemen or self-serving noblemen. Blackstone half expected that the Dome contingent would desert, but they were men who had fought set battles. Those among them who knew the knights they would be facing spoke to others about the riches that awaited those who killed the noblemen and lived to seize their silk undershirts, bejewelled rings and scabbards encrusted with precious stones. For some, greed would overcome fear.

'Armagnac will try and break our lines before he turns from the main force. We will have a fight on our hands the moment they see our blazon,' said Killbere. They ate salted mutton and washed the sharp taste away with Gascon wine. Hundreds of fires twinkled in the cold night as Phoebus's army bedded down for the night. The smell of cooked food drifted into Blackstone's ranks. None of the arrayed men complained. Like Blackstone's men they lay under their blankets knowing they fought for the one man who would not squander their lives needlessly.

Blackstone walked along the lines. His men slept where they would fight. Will Longdon and his archers were in the trees behind hurdles crudely fashioned from fallen branches, enough to obscure them until horseman broke through Blackstone's ranks. Jack Halfpenny's bowmen curled in the night air, their waxed bow bags tucked close to their bodies.

Blackstone saw his archers' pegs tapped into the ground at fifty-yard intervals. They served as grave markers where a common man's arrow would end a nobleman's life. The frosted air settled on his beard. It made no difference what the weather did the next day. The hard ground would jolt horses' legs, and their iron-shod hooves might find it difficult to gain purchase when urged into the gallop. He cursed a weak man's desire for glory because the Count's own horses would share the same struggle and that put Blackstone's men at greater risk.

He gazed at the moon and raised Arianrhod to his lips. The Silver Wheel Goddess glistened in the veiled moonlight. Memories flooded over him. The great pitched battles of the war echoed in his mind. The fear that gripped a man anticipating the fight and made muscles taut and eyes keen. Lungs filling with bellowing rage that drove a fighting man forward into the fray.

There was no need for prayer. It was not God that such men wanted at their side.

It was Death.

They came three hours after first light. The winter sun was still low in the sky an hour after rising as a distant bell in the village of Launac chimed the terce hour. A rhythmic beat of a hundred drums and a blaring cacophony of trumpets silenced the humble bell. A forest of pennons wavered as massed troops followed the mounted knights. The Count de Foix et Béarn stared in quiet amazement, as did every man under his command. The wall of shimmering steel edged closer, three ranks of knights, one behind the other, followed by infantry. Mercenaries rode on their left flank. Gaston Phoebus knew then that Blackstone had been correct. They were outnumbered three to one. At least. He looked over his shoulder at the sun struggling to rise in the sky. The English Master of War had chosen the place well. The sun would keep its low arc behind the slender hills and be in the Count d'Armagnac's troops' eyes throughout the day. Commanders bellowed orders, breaking his reverie as they brought the knights' war horses forward. Gaston Phoebus wore silver-grey armour, but had not yet donned his bascinet. He mounted his horse, which bore chest armour – added weight for the beast to carry but which offered a chance of survival against lance or spear. The Count de Foix had heard mass at dawn with his priest and his soul and conscience were free of sin and doubt. The battle would determine the future of his family name and if its dynasty were to end this fifth day of December, then it would not be because of trepidation in the face of greater odds. He rode to the front of his men, his blond hair still free of a helm so that all men would know who it was that promised them glory and a share of the spoils.

Blackstone stood with his captains on the most vulnerable flank of the line. Jack Halfpenny's archers were already in position and like those in the woods behind them had been awake before dawn to add extra beeswax to their hemp bow cords, added protection against the brittle air. Now they stood cradling the six-foot bows with their hands tucked beneath their armpits for warmth. Cold, stiff fingers were an added burden when wrapping a fist around the six-inch circumference of a yew bow. Arrows had been carefully assessed and each three-foot-long shaft, an inch thick and tipped with a three-inch-long iron bodkin, had been gathered in a bushel at their feet besides those in arrow bags. Once the arrows were spent they would fight with buckler and bastard sword. Each carried a mercy knife in their belts to pierce the eye slits of a unseated knight's helm, but if the bowmen faced mounted men-at-arms then their lives were soon over.

Killbere, Meulon and Renfred stood at Blackstone's shoulder as they watched the long-haired figure of Gaston Phoebus ride along the ranks and exhort his troops to kill and plunder but insist that if an enemy knight or lord claimed mercy it should be granted and ransom accepted. They should give no mercy to any man of lesser rank.

'If they cut his horse's legs from beneath him I wonder if he would learn sudden respect for the common soldier who had a spear at his throat and blood-lust raging,' said Killbere.

'I care less about him and more about our fate today,' said Renfred, glancing at the gaunt faces of the Dome contingent.

'We keep the men from Dome in the second rank behind us,' said Blackstone. 'A shield wall will not serve any purpose against the first waves of horsemen, but when their infantry fight through that is when they must hold.'

Meulon looked at the gathered arrayed men. 'Spear and shield will hold only for a while. If they break, then Will and his lads behind us will have nowhere to run.'

'They will hold,' said Blackstone, 'because archers will bring down horses before they reach a hundred yards. And then we go forward on my command and claim the ground between us and that first wave because then we deal with those horsemen who will be hampered by the dead and dying in front of them.'

Killbere cleared his throat and spat. He grinned. 'I never thought I would live to see such a battle again. It's how it should be, Thomas. Drums and trumpets and flags.' He laughed aloud. 'It pumps blood into a man's heart and strengthens his sword arm. Let these bastards do their worst; they are no match for those we have killed on greater fields of battle than this puny patch of grass. You chose well, Thomas. The sun will keep their heads tucked down against its low glare. They'll stumble over their own dead and dying and we'll smell their fear and shit when they see our blazon.'

Blackstone strode forward and faced his men. Each of his captains stood paces ahead of their own contingents. Raising his voice so that his words carried along the ranks, he addressed them. 'We are men alone here in this place. We make our stand where no other would dare. When steel and horse thunder forward and the storm of terror threatens then remember this: if our thoughts twist with doubt we turn to the boldness and defiance in our hearts. What stands between us and the fear they inflict is our courage.'

Killbere stepped forward. Raising his sword, he shouted loud enough for his voice to carry along the ranks of waiting men. 'Sir Thomas and defiance!'

Blackstone's captains and men cheered and brandished their weapons. The battle cry rippled along the lines.

'Sir Thomas and defiance!'

The Count de Foix reined in his horse and faced Blackstone's men; then he raised his sword in salute.

When the cry ended the men bellowed in rage, thundering that defiance across the open plain.

'If Armagnac didn't know we were here before, he does now,' said Blackstone. 'All right, take your positions.'

The captains moved to their men as Killbere slipped his sword's blood knot onto his wrist. He pulled on his helm. 'May the angels be with us, Thomas,' he said. He nodded at the cord around Blackstone's neck. 'And your pagan.'

Blackstone pulled on his open-faced bascinet and took his customary strides forward so that his men might see him more clearly. He turned to Halfpenny. 'Start killing them at the two-hundred-and-fifty-yard marker, Jack. Those that live through that mustn't get past a hundred and fifty. The downed horses will slow those that follow on. Will and the others will shoot at a hundred yards. After that, kill them any way you can.'

Jack Halfpenny nodded his understanding. The ground beneath their feet trembled. Gaston Phoebus's and the Count d'Armagnac's knights had spurred their horses from the canter into the charge.

CHAPTER SIXTY-ONE

The two armies hurtled into the centre ground. The clash of steel echoed across the open plain, defeating the sound of trumpet and drum. The shock wave rolled into Blackstone's men, who stood three hundred yards from where the horsemen fought. D'Armagnac's knights yielded slightly from the impact in the centre of their ranks and Blackstone knew if he had led the charge that yielding ground at the first impact would have been intentional. A soft belly in the armour-clad ranks that absorbed the blow and drew in the enemy. D'Armagnac might win this battle in the first hour if they captured or killed Phoebus. Then Blackstone saw, as some horses turned, that he and his men stood in their way as they tried to outflank the Count.

'Jack! Shoot now!'

If the archers could kill those who had yielded and enveloped the Count, then de Foix could fight his way through.

Halfpenny's voice rose up against the roaring passions of the fight. 'Nock! Draw! Loose!'

The flutter of goose fletchings rippled through the still air. No sooner did the first cloud rise into the air than Halfpenny's command called out again. A dozen sharp breaths later another three flights curved into the sky and fell into men already screaming in agony, their cries joined by the pitiful whinnying of wounded horses.

'We've stirred the hornet's nest now, Thomas,' said Killbere. 'They're turning away from the Count towards us.'

Knights yanked reins, raked spurs and fought through the thrashing hooves of the downed horses. Their squires and men-at-arms turned with them; footsoldiers caught in the turmoil followed their master's pennons.

'Two hundred!' Blackstone yelled.

Halfpenny's bowmen loosed again. And then again. But horsemen and infantry in d'Armagnac's ranks had peeled away from the main assault and raced towards Blackstone's thinly held line.

The weight of the charge would trample him and his men underfoot. They needed stopping and Halfpenny's men were too few. Blackstone turned to face the woodland. If Will Longdon did not realize that Gaston Phoebus's attack had caused Blackstone to strike early then there too few archers in Halfpenny's number to slow their attack.

Killbere rolled on the balls of his foot. His eyes locked on the fast-approaching attack. 'Come on, you bastards, come on,' he muttered.

Halfpenny's men were shooting rapidly but a dozen more tireless times of bending into their bows' heavy pull weight would exhaust the arrows at their feet. Twenty-four times they would nock, draw and loose. Men and horses would die, but their arrows would soon be depleted and all that would remain would be what weapons they carried in their belts. The earth shook. At 150 yards three waves of horsemen, forty men wide, had turned towards Blackstone. Horses' nostrils bled, their eyes widened in terror, foam flecked their shoulders and flanks, iron bits tore at their mouths as their riders sawed their reins trying to control their headlong, crazed gallop over those already writhing on the ground.

Will Longdon knew well enough when a battle plan had faltered. A dark cloud of arrows soared through the open spaces between trees bereft of leaves. Blackstone heard his centenar's distant command and turned quickly to Halfpenny. 'Jack! Save what you have. Shoot low when they are halfway closer. Then get back behind the shield wall.' Renfred and Meulon brought their men forward so that Blackstone's first line of defence became an extended line. They would fight forward until they could go further and the men in the shield wall would be at their heels. Ground would be gained, yard by yard, and then held from behind the wall.

Will Longdon's archers held the knights at bay but the arrows had struck more of those on horseback than the footsoldiers who scrambled through the carnage, running forward desperate to kill those who could slaughter from a distance. Jack Halfpenny's archers shot into them. Bodies fell one on top of the other, waist high, another bloody barrier for the attackers to overcome. But still they came.

Time faltered. Gasping, tortured minutes followed every ragged breath. Violence surged and broke again and again onto Blackstone's unyielding ranks. Blackstone's line held. Their dogged resistance saw them give little ground. Some of the attackers gave up the fight and were swallowed by the turmoil behind them as d'Armagnac's men fought in confusion. They were being pressed hard in a great half-circle as Phoebus's men closed behind them, forcing them onto what they thought to be the weak line of archers, but whose men-at-arms were proving to be unbreakable. The fight wore on. An hour passed, and then another. There were moments of respite when those attacking paused, bent over their swords, gasping. Some went down on all fours as exhaustion claimed them, vomiting from effort; others with blood dripping down their faces were too weak to raise their heads and beg for mercy. The line of Englishmen and Gascons seemed tireless. Their killing did not falter. As horses barged and panicked and knights lost control of them another wave from de Foix pushed d'Armagnac's weakening men onto English swords and sudden silent death as arrows ripped into their ranks. By the third hour the weight of men behind them forced them even closer to Blackstone's men. They were pressured from the fighting at the rear and if they could not turn and fight the enemy behind them, then their only chance was to let their fear and rage drive them forward.

'Back now!' Blackstone shouted at the archers and lunged forward to stop d'Armagnac's troops gaining the advantage as they gathered momentum. If they could be held where the horses writhed and the crushed knights slowed the attackers' progress then it gave his men a longer chance to survive the onslaught. Killbere, Meulon and Renfred ran at his heels, their men a few paces behind. It separated John Jacob from the others and he fought alone, with some of Blackstone's men at his side. Small pockets of men fought toe to toe. Blackstone's men were almost overwhelmed. Unseen enemy knights wheeled their mounts behind the fallen. Gaston Phoebus cut his way through the wall of steel, turning the weight of his men in an attempt to tighten the noose. They fought in an ever-smaller arena, jostling for position, but d'Armagnac's knights saw that there was no longer any risk from the archers. If they shot high now, their arrows would fall into allies.

Meulon and his men bravely threw themselves ahead of Blackstone and rammed shortened lances into the ground. Terrified horses clambering over the wall of death impaled themselves. Men leapt onto the knights and killed them underfoot. Thrashing hooves killed more than one man in those frantic moments as Blackstone strode into the fray and blocked a strike against Meulon. Killbere was two paces behind, covering him. Renfred harried the enemy, his men quickly forming a defensive arc around Blackstone because now the enemy were breaking through in force. The balance of the fight was turning against Blackstone's position. A mace swung hard against the side of his head buckled Blackstone's knees. Killbere lunged and caught the man in the throat as Meulon stopped Blackstone from falling. With a shake of his head Blackstone yanked himself free and single-handedly blocked the gap where men clambered through. He fought with furious strength, unassailable, killing with such violent intent that men did all they could to hurtle past him, only to face determined resistance from Killbere and the men fighting with the captains.

Killbere saw it was useless to try and hold their position any longer. The sheer weight of the enemy was pushing aside the dead to reach the scar-faced knight and those at his back. 'Back, Thomas! Back now!' The veteran knight sidestepped a blow, took it on his shield, rammed his sword's hilt beneath the man's chin. His jaw cracked, and he fell back. Killbere leaned forward and pierced his chest with his sword point. He stepped to Blackstone and punched his arm to alert him. Blackstone swung around, sword arcing, ready to decapitate an unseen attacker. Killbere deflected the blow but the force of it nearly broke his stance. Blackstone's blood-splattered face glared at him before recognizing his friend. Nothing more was said. Backing away, they retreated behind the shield wall, which stood firm. A surge of horsemen burst over the dead. They could not be stopped. They would crush the shields. Blackstone and his men stood their ground, lungs heaving, sword arms weary but held ready. Blackstone was suddenly aware of the rush of men behind him. Will Longdon's archers were at their side. Bows creaked and arrows loosed. Blackstone knew they had few arrows left, but they killed and killed again and the horses screamed. Blackstone saw a wounded man rise from amid the fallen bodies. He got to his knees, sword still clutched in a bloodied fist. A rush of fear gripped Blackstone.

It was John Jacob. He must have been bludgeoned to the ground earlier and, recovering consciousness, was now rising from the surrounding dead. He would not survive.

Blackstone pushed through the shields. It was the insane act of a suicidal man but it had the impetus to loose a storm of violence from Blackstone's men. Meuric Kynith tossed aside his bow. His arrow bag was empty. Clutching his buckler and mercy knife he swore in Welsh and went after the Englishman who had once beaten him. His Welsh archers stormed after him. Halfpenny's and Longdon's men were barely a pace behind. Someone grabbed Blackstone's banner and bore it aloft. Blackstone was too far ahead of his men. Someone threw a spear from the enemy ranks. It struck Blackstone's shield; he deflected it but as his shield moved away from his body, a crossbow bolt pierced the top of his shoulder. His shield arm dropped. He protected John Jacob as three men attacked, seizing their chance to kill the wounded knight. Blackstone's strength saved him but then another unseen bowman loosed a second quarrel, piercing Blackstone's leg. He tumbled to one side and fell into the thrashing iron-shod hooves of a gutted horse. A hoof struck his helm and then his unwounded leg. It snapped with the crack of a yew bow broken in two.

His final glimpse of blue sky saw men clambering over him and his banner caught in the sun's rays. The clamour of battle around him faded into silence as he fell into darkness.

CHAPTER SIXTY-TWO

Soon after midday the fighting ceased. Eerie silence settled across the battlefield and the scattered dead. Here and there the dying groaned softly until those who went among them plunged a knife into them and took what they had of value. Pennons lay among the fallen, the honour and glory they had once proclaimed trampled into the blood-soaked grass. Some were still clutched in a dead man's grip and waved gently in the stiffening breeze in macabre farewell.

Gaston Phoebus rode slowly through the carnage. Weariness etched his face beneath his sweat-matted golden hair. The crows and buzzards were already settling, tearing men's flesh and pecking the moist eyes of the dead. Bodies lay in tight knots where they had died, embraced in that final desperate struggle to survive. The Count de Foix eased his horse through the field of death to where the greatest number of dead horses and their riders lay. He had fought many campaigns during his young life but he had never witnessed dead horses sprawled like this, great beasts on top of each other as their riders had bravely sought to jump across those already brought down by lance and arrow. Hundreds of arrows, sown like a sapling forest, smothered the battlefield deep within d'Armagnac's ranks. He knew without a doubt that Blackstone's archers had won the day for him.

Ignoring the stench of gore and excrement that assailed his nostrils, he urged his mount over a horse's entrails and crushed men who bore witness to the ferocity that Blackstone's outnumbered men had inflicted on their enemy. Crows fluttered out of his path and then boldly settled again to feast. He gazed down at the ragged survivors. Blood-splattered archers gripped belts and jewels taken from the dead French knights. He made no objection. Blackstone's men had paid a high price. They deserved their reward. He doubted there was one man among them who did not bear a wound.

He reined in his horse. Meulon sat exhausted with those of his men who had survived. He did not raise himself at the Count's arrival. 'Where is Sir Thomas?' Phoebus asked.

Meulon pointed wearily behind him. Blackstone's men parted their ranks, revealing Killbere cradling Blackstone's broken body.

The Count gazed down at him. There was no sign of life, nor would he expect there to be given the wounds he saw on Blackstone's body. Yet he hoped. 'Does he still live?'

Killbere spat blood. 'Not for long.'

The Count's personal physician and surgeon who accompanied him on that December day were summoned as soon as he knew Blackstone was still alive. The badly wounded knight was carried gently to a pavilion next to de Foix's own where he waited for confirmation that his skilled surgeons had reset Blackstone's leg. The Englishman did not regain consciousness, which all agreed was a blessing, given the intense pain that would have to be endured. Henbane and brandy were mixed and dribbled past Blackstone's lips in a vain attempt to dull his body's agony when they pushed one of the crossbow bolts through his leg muscle and pulled it free. The second was more dangerous and the incision near his shoulder was deep. When the forceps failed to take a firm grip on the quarrel, there was doubt that they could remove it. The shaft broke and was extracted and then the bolt's point was finally dug out.

They could do nothing for Blackstone's head wound other than to bathe and stitch the jagged gash, but when the surgeons expressed concern at Blackstone's shallow breathing, doubting that he would survive, Killbere pushed them aside. 'Stitch him, bathe him and wrap him warm. He's not dead yet, for Christ's sake.'

They left most of the corpses on the field of battle, a winter feast for scavengers. They returned only those of noble rank to their families for burial in their feudal domains. It was a resounding victory for the Count de Foix. D'Armagnac and many of his leading noblemen surrendered and their ransoms ensured that Gaston Phoebus would become one of the richest princes in the west. Never again would he fear being challenged now that his war treasury overflowed. The victorious Count imprisoned d'Armagnac and the other prominent leaders in the castle at Orthez while he returned to the luxury and comfort of his palace.

They carried the unconscious Blackstone onto a wagon to be cared for at the Prince's castle at Foix. Gaston Phoebus promised that the man whose strategy had given him victory would be attended to day and night until he recovered. And Killbere and the men would winter in comfort and warmth. It was a welcome offer and gratefully accepted. Killbere sent the men from Dome back home once the Count had rewarded them. News of the victory would soon reach Paris and Killbere sent word to Gisbert de Dome, warning him to stay true to his pledge of holding Dome and Sarlat in the name of the English King. He was still obliged to pledge his fealty to the Prince of Wales when he arrived in Aquitaine. Killbere knew that once it was known Blackstone lay critically wounded then ambitious men might renege on their agreements, free from their fear of Blackstone's retribution.

And then Killbere and the men waited for Blackstone to survive.

On the third day Blackstone regained consciousness. They had kept his dry lips moist with a wet rag squeezed diligently by Killbere. He ignored the pail of water brought by servants and soaked the cloth in Gascon wine. Blackstone's eyes opened slowly and stared at the grizzled face of the man he had known since he had first gone to war. They had bandaged his arm, and he bore the raw stitches of a head wound. Blackstone said something but it was barely a whisper. Killbere put his ear close to Blackstone's mouth.

'John Jacob?'

Killbere nodded. 'Alive.'

'The others?'

'Wounded. Every man. We lost archers. A lot of the Welshmen. They ran out too far looking for booty and were caught in the open, but Kynith lives. Will Longdon keeps him as ventenar at Halfpenny's side once we get more bowmen. They recalled Beyard to his lord Jean de Grailly to report on the battle. He vows he will return to us as soon as he is able.'

'My horse?'

'The damned beast is stabled – alone as always. It kicks and bites and will never die until the devil comes to reclaim his own.'

Blackstone sighed, his cracked lips creased into a smile. 'Did we win?' he rasped.

Killbere nodded. 'You made the young Count one of the wealthiest men in France. We're his guests and you have physicians nursing you as if you were a damned prince yourself.'

Blackstone raised his bandaged head, the effort nearly defeating him. He attempted to lift his arm but pain shot through him. Killbere put his hand behind Blackstone's neck and supported it back down onto the pillow. 'Steady, Thomas.' He laid a gentle finger next to Blackstone's wounds. 'You took a bolt in this leg and your arm, and a horse kicked your other leg and head. Your leg's broken, ribs as well, but I doubt the blow to your head knocked any sense into you.'

Blackstone sighed. 'I can't lie here.'

'You have no choice. And I need to get the men rested and healed. We are all hurt, Thomas, every last one of us.'

Blackstone turned his head on the pillow. 'They must be rewarded, Gilbert. They fought like lions.'

Killbere dabbed Blackstone's lips. 'The Count treats us well. We are to stay until you are recovered. We'll pass the winter here.'

'Too long,' Blackstone whispered.

'No, my friend, barely long enough for you to heal and regain your strength.'

Blackstone's eyes closed as he drifted into sleep.

'Barely long enough for any of us,' Killbere said to himself.

CHAPTER SIXTY-THREE

Over the months, Gaston Phoebus had watched Blackstone being helped from his bed and using a crutch to force himself around the castle's inner ward. He did it every day no matter how harsh the weather until the day came when he abandoned the support and tested his leg. He fell, got up, fell again until step by painful step he regained the ability to walk unaided. It became a daily ritual that the Count observed without fail. He was watching a man who should have succumbed to his wounds rise like Lazarus. Blackstone's captains kept their distance, fearful of his temper should they try to assist him. By the month of March his leg was sufficiently healed for him to mount his horse; by May he was practising his sword skills. The passing months saw the Englishman regain his strength and as June brought warmth back to the sun Blackstone, still limping from his weakened leg, went beyond the walls and ventured into the foothills, demanding ever more of his body.

After the battle his men's wounds had been debilitating but less severe, and the Count's gratitude secured them treatment from his physician and the healing skills of monks from a nearby monastery. Sir Gilbert Killbere assumed command while Blackstone fought his own determined battle. The men were employed selecting and training the army that Gaston Phoebus recruited with his new-found wealth. Many were poor quality and rejected by Blackstone's captains. But by summer when Blackstone threw off the constant pain of his injuries, the army was as well trained as the Count could hope for. The ransoms from the capture of the Count d'Armagnac, the Lords of Albret and other noblemen meant that the Count de Foix could shower largesse on visitors. His feasts became renowned and Blackstone and Killbere, who kept their distance from the sumptuous gatherings, would hear him regale his guests with tales of the Prussian crusade and of how he rescued the Dauphin's family at Meaux until finally his stories cumulated in the Battle of Launac. Only occasionally was Blackstone's name mentioned in any of his exploits. The Count de Foix's generosity and charm did not extend to deflecting from his own glory.

'He's a nobleman,' said Killbere. 'And now he's a damned rich one, thanks to you.'

'We've all benefited, Gilbert. These past months gave us time for the men to recover and bring them back to strength. You worked them hard. It shows.'

'There was enough booty and putting coins in a man's purse heals many wounds.'

They walked the ramparts gazing across the grandeur of the Pyrenees behind them and the deep, broad valley beyond. 'Having one prince to deal with was difficult enough but our own will be annoyed because you weren't there to meet him at Bordeaux. Bowing as he stepped ashore. He likes ceremony, does Edward.'

Blackstone admired the view. The forests clinging to the foothills had given him the solitude he sought to hide the weakness and pain of his body. He had not wished anyone to see his struggle. 'We must move the men to Bergerac, Gilbert.'

'We're not going to the Prince?'

'No. Not yet.' He smiled. 'Let him come to us.'

Killbere scowled. 'Thomas, he seeks honour and goodwill. There is no point in antagonizing him and earning his displeasure.'

'We brought him the Count's loyalty. He should be thankful for what the men did, Gilbert. They bled for him. Again. And now he arrives with fanfare and a retinue grand enough for a coronation. Sixty knights, three hundred and more archers and two hundred and fifty men-at-arms. He's not the King, Gilbert, he's a prince of the realm who has been rewarded half of France because of what we did. Imagine what we could have done with those men. Will and Jack lost half their archers in the fight at Launac. Meulon, Renfred, all the captains – they all suffered losses. We were too few. The Count is rich and the Prince has Aquitaine. And now he sends word for us to ride to him and present ourselves.'

'Then he means to reward us,' said Killbere.

'He means to bask in our glory. Not this time, Gilbert. I won't ride ahead of an entourage like a damned court jester.'

'God's tears. Listen to you. You're defying him again. We have no excuse.'

Blackstone grinned. 'I am serving him as best as I know how.'

'By turning your back on him. We will undo all the good we have done,' said Killbere, curling a fist in frustration.

'Listen to me. He cannot object if we ride to Bergerac and ensure his safe entry into the city. Gisbert de Dome takes the Bishop of Sarlat to pledge fealty there, as do Breton lords waiting to bend the knee. There's a truce between them but who's to say there isn't one among those miserable northern lords who doesn't hold a grudge against us, the Prince, the King? Eh? It will calm his irritation when he learns that we have showed our consideration for his safety by getting to Bergerac before him.' He put an arm on Killbere's shoulders. 'Besides, we know the city of old and where the best beds are for the men. Taverns and inns will be overrun when his procession chokes the streets. I say we do our duty and look after ourselves.'

Killbere shook his head. 'Thomas, your wounds still trouble you. Let's wait another week. Let him go to Bergerac without us if you insist. We shall send word that we are still healing.'

Blackstone looked at his friend. They had survived together and his heart warmed from the closeness he shared with this man and the others he commanded. 'Gilbert, you worry too much. The King's mother made me swear to look after the Prince. The King made me his Master of War. I have the authority to do just that.'

Killbere sighed in surrender. 'That kick to the head has added to your stubbornness. Very well, we shall defy him again but this time I choose where to go if we are exiled.'

CHAPTER SIXTY-FOUR

Royal authority in France had collapsed. Failure hung over the French King and his ministers as heavily as the persistent black rain-bearing clouds smothering Notre-Dame, drawn in from the sea by the heat in the south. Jean le Bon had expected the Count d'Armagnac and the mighty lords he had gathered with him to defeat the Count de Foix. Arnoul d'Audrehem and Jean d'Armagnac had used a hundred thousand florins from taxes raised in the Languedoc destined for the King's ransom to secure payment for the routiers to fight for him at Launac. Now both the battle and the initiative were lost. The Count de Foix had become rich and powerful and would now swear fealty to the Prince of Wales and Aquitaine. King John had been weakened again. The Breton civil war teetered, a tenuous truce agreement in danger of collapse. Negotiating power now rested more in the hands of the English Prince than his own. Routiers had seized strategic points on the Seine that could threaten trade into Paris. Aquitaine would experience peace but warring factions would plague the rest of the kingdom.

Such affairs of state troubled the counsellor Simon Bucy during his journey back from Vincennes to the Île de la Cité where he had been summoned by the Dauphin. The warm damp weather worsened the Dauphin's constant sniffle and cough. Charles was a man plagued with ill health, less likely to ever lead an army in the field than any of his brothers still held captive in London, yet Bucy had realized months before the Dauphin's lack of physical prowess did not diminish his intellect or his cunning. The future of France and his own status within the court lay with the Dauphin.

He waited obediently in the magnificent room. Despite the layers of carpets and tapestries on the walls the dampness in the royal palace still made his ageing bones ache. No matter how much the fireplace was fed the stone walls retained their chill. Perhaps that was why, Bucy thought idly, the Dauphin planned to create the Louvre as a more welcoming palace. His idle thoughts were quickly dispelled by the Dauphin's snorting into a lace handkerchief and then dropping it without a thought. A servant darted forward, retrieved it and quickly returned to his station against the wall. The Dauphin settled into a padded armchair. Another servant tucked a finely woven blanket across his legs.

'Some months ago a noblewoman sought an audience. Did you know about this?' the Dauphin asked, gazing at the flames. It seemed a casual question but anything the Dauphin asked always had a serious intent. And this question caused Bucy to hesitate, mind racing. His heart felt the squeeze of uncertainly. His own investigation into the woman's intentions had drawn a blank and the unsettled affairs of state had pushed any thoughts of her to the back of his mind. She had simply disappeared from Paris. The threat of an unknown assassination had faded. No one had been injured. No attempt made. It was likely to have been an idle threat from a wronged woman. If every grievance that blossomed into a threat of violence bore fruit the dead would be lying ten deep on the palace steps. But Bucy knew he was just looking for an excuse for not having pursued the warning. Had anyone of importance died?

'Highness, many seek an audience. It is impossible to grant such requests without them being dealt with by your officials. They then pass those with merit to me and your other senior advisers for final assessment,' he said calmly.

The Dauphin's body hunched. 'When Thomas Blackstone killed Lord Mael Babeneaux de Pontivy, it fanned deeply embedded embers of revenge. Those embers now burn brightly.'

Bucy remained silent. The mention of Mael Babeneaux's death struck a chord of deep concern as his lawyer's mind rapidly sifted through connections between that killing and the woman in question. It had not done so when the courtiers had turned the woman away.

'You know that Pope Urban has granted a payment of ninety thousand écus towards our father's ransom?' said the Dauphin, changing emphasis, deflecting Bucy's thoughts.

'Yes, highness.'

The Dauphin sniffed, more in disgust than from his affliction. 'Avignon is a sewer. Turds float in varying hues of ecclesiastical robes. And when the Holy See declares a payment from its treasury, then those with vested interests scurry like sewer rats to thwart such an expenditure.'

Bucy dutifully kept listening, though he had no idea what the Dauphin was alluding to. Turds and priests? Meaning what? 'Highness,' he muttered as if he understood.

'The woman is in Avignon. She arranged shelter there. She plans her schemes in the papal city. When the ransom amount was declared she endeavoured to entice one of the cardinals in the treasury to spill a significant amount from the Holy See's purse for her own purposes. She has already struck a bargain with a mercenary captain to commit murder. The Cardinal does not know his name, but it seems this man is close to Blackstone. And such an additional amount would ensure not only murder but a massacre of noble households. The Cardinal in question seeks favour and passed this information to us through our ambassador in Avignon. Such vile considerations sicken us.'

Bucy's hand trembled. Then the rumours all those months ago had been true. She planned an assassination. That it had not yet occurred meant the woman had taken her time, and planned the killing without haste. Cold logic overcoming the heat of the emotional desire for revenge. He put his arms behind him in case the Dauphin noticed his nervous palsy.

'May I beg to know the name of the woman in question?' he asked, a spark of hope that it might not be the same woman whose name the merchant had given him the night of the dinner.

'Lady de Sagard.'

Merciful God. Bucy's throat tightened. It was the very same. Her name harked back years ago to when he and the King had sent the Savage Priest to ensnare Blackstone. A friend of Blackstone had been used as bait and imprisoned in Sir Rolf de Sagard's castle. Blackstone had stormed the castle and found his friend tortured. Flayed alive. And that had cost Rolf de Sagard his life and cast his widow and children into the insecurity of near poverty. Blackstone would have saved them all the inheritance of revenge if he had slain the whole family, wife, daughter and son. But he had not. Bucy wished Blackstone were more ruthless about considering the future of his actions when he showed such mercy. He had saved Lady de Sagard from the indignity of entering a convent and letting others raise her children. The intervention and financial support of her brother Lord Mael Babeneaux de Pontivy kept her from poverty. A woman who had status and wealth now reduced to a beggar at her brother's door. The final act of humiliation and grief visited on her by Thomas Blackstone.

'My Prince, they had not made Lady de Sagard's grievances known to the court. I had no dealings at all with her, and shall look further in the matter,' he blurted, implying he would deal with the lesser courtiers. 'But now she seems intent on securing routiers to attack and kill Blackstone then surely that plays well for us? Reports that reach us say Blackstone is still weak and injured from Launac. The Count of Foix has him under his care. Does she intend to strike now? Highness, if she has the means to kill him, what better time? His men are few now.' Bucy's hopes rose. He took a couple of steps closer to the Dauphin, his voice rich with the possibility that presented itself. 'Highness, this bodes well. Her intent puts distance between us. If she kills Edward's Master of War, it weakens the English and it rids us of a ravening wolf who has torn the kingdom apart for years. But our hands remain clean. We are not in breach of the peace treaty inflicted upon us.'

The Dauphin averted his eyes from the devouring flames and settled on Bucy's eager face. 'Her son lived with his uncle. Mael Babeneaux was teaching him the skills he would need to become a page and then a squire. He died in Blackstone's attack. Lady de Sagard learnt that Blackstone's son is in Avignon. She intends to kill him.'

Bucy saw the logic in that and his thoughts followed it through. 'Then use an intermediary to get word to Blackstone and draw him into Avignon. They will not permit him to take his men inside the walls. She has him trapped. Sire, it has its merits.'

The Dauphin rose from the chair. Servants ran forward to remove the blanket. Charles, the future King of France, shrugged them away. 'She uses his son as bait to draw Blackstone away from the Prince of Wales. The Prince is her target.'

Bucy's heart thudded more desperately than it had ever done. His jaw dropped in shock.

'Simon,' said the Dauphin gently. 'Send word and warn Thomas Blackstone. He might sacrifice his son, but a prince does not kill a prince.'

PART FIVE

DEATH IN AVIGNON

CHAPTER SIXTY-FIVE

Avignon had changed under the newly elected Pope Urban V. His ambitions lay not in gaining more personal wealth like the cardinals, blinded by the power and influence of their red robes and an insatiable desire to furnish their palaces with exotic animals and tapestries from distant lands. His uncompromising desire was for the papal city to become a place of education and restraint. His first act had been to refuse to lead the mounted procession. Gone were the parades of white horses, silks and jewels with a canopy of woven gold threads above the pontiff when he rode through the streets. The new Pope was an unwavering Benedictine who endowed colleges and universities. He wore a simple monk's robe and slept on hard boards without a mattress. He was a man of contemplation and prayer, a theologian who had already swept corrupt bishops back to their dioceses. He banned priests' illegitimate sons from assisting them at the altar; he condemned debauchery and drunkenness in the clergy and forced the priestly classes to rid themselves of hunting dogs and falcons. And his strictness did not apply only to men of the cloth. He burned all pagan art and sent religious inspectors beyond the walls of Avignon with the whip and thumbscrew to correct infractions. Yet he was only one man, and despite his repressive measures he could not halt the inherent corruption, which was as rife as any plague and reached from the highest to the lowers orders of society. In winter, the bitterly cold Mistral wind kept heads down and shoulders hunched until it abated; now, in high summer, when the citizens raised their eyes once again they were no longer blinded by the dust and detritus but chose instead to close their eyes to venal cardinals and city officials.

This was a world Father Torellini understood. While Henry applied himself to his studies, the priest went about his business of negotiating loans, securing favours and buying information on behalf of the Florentine Bardi banking family whom he served. Some of his informers were beggars on streets; others served in palaces; still others attended cardinals. It made Niccolò Torellini invaluable not only to his patron but also to the English monarch to whom the Bardi bank had loaned vast sums for his war against France. And Torellini had not neglected his role as an unofficial ambassador bearing the goodwill of King Edward towards the Pope and Curia. Alliances were being built for the future.

Torellini's duties in Avignon also allowed him to watch over Henry de Sainteny, who now bore his mother's name. There was never a mention of the name Blackstone and no one knew of Henry's identity except some of those who had travelled with him and they had sworn in God's name, kneeling before a crucifix, never to reveal it. The months had passed quickly, immersed as Henry was in scholastic endeavours, and living in the city had become an unexpected pleasure, even jostling through the weight of people in the overcrowded streets. At first he'd thought the crowds to be a threat, easily concealing anyone who might wish him harm, having discovered his true identity, but as the weeks turned into months he began to feel a sense of security. What fear remained lingered from the year before when close to twenty thousand had died from the plague in an overcrowded Avignon. Henry was not aware that Torellini's network within the city watched over him. The Italian lived in the comfort of the Bardi mansion but Henry de Sainteny was housed in a modest attic room elsewhere in the lower town and fed by the landlord and his family. Unbeknown to Henry, Torellini paid the family to report back on the boy's hours of study and behaviour.

It had been three weeks since Torellini had last spoken to the lad; now he waited for him in the enclosed courtyard of the Bardi house. The priest had taken refuge by the cool fountain for the mid-July heat could be as uncomfortable as the winds in the winter, and here sweet-smelling flowers perfumed the air, their fragrance defeating the odours from the city streets. And the local habit of wine being infused with a slight mixture of fragrant resin helped subdue the unpleasant stench too.

Torellini knew exactly where Henry was and how long it would take for someone to summon the boy. He was in the luxurious new palace that had supplanted the austere old château fort built by one of the earlier Popes, where he spent a few hours a week examining the frescoes in its many chapels. Henry had failed to understand why such study was needed until his mathematics tutor explained the need to balance science with art for a better understanding of geometry and a broader appreciation of the world around him. Henry, however, was less interested in the frescoes than in meeting Lady Cateline's son. In the months since they had left Dome Jocard had grown in strength and despite their age difference the two boys liked nothing more than wrestling in the walled chapel garden thinking they were out of sight from inquisitive eyes.

'Did you think I was unaware of your absence from your studies?' said Torellini when Henry stood before him.

'I don't do it often, Father Torellini, only when I am bored, and looking at frescoes bores me.'

Torellini gestured him to sit at the table with its white cloth, gold cutlery and plates of food. Students ate sparingly in their lodgings and Henry was no exception. A servant had brought him in the back gate of the house from a rear alley so it would appear to a casual onlooker that they had summoned the boy to undertake some kind of service. Henry sat obediently and waited for permission to eat. His stomach growled. Torellini held him in check.

'You see Lady Cateline's son regularly.'

'Yes.'

'And his mother?'

'Sometimes. He takes me back to her house and her servant feeds us.' He glanced at the plate before him. 'Not as good as this, though,' he said.

'His mother meets other noblewomen?' said Torellini, concerned one of them might pose a threat. Women widowed by the war would hate the English, and they might have the means to hire assassins if they discovered by chance that a renowned Englishman's son was here under a different name. A name that would not save him if a slip of the tongue inadvertently revealed his true identity. It was important that Torellini discover whether Blackstone's son knew the circle of noblewomen that Lady Cateline Babeneaux had been drawn into.

Henry nodded. 'I don't know who they are. They're women who meet and gossip, I suppose.'

Torellini gestured to the plate of food. 'Eat,' he told him. He watched as the young man ate hungrily. After a moment he said, 'Do you know whom she meets?'

Henry shook his head, and then swallowed. 'She visits different places in the city. Jocard says she's still waiting for Sir William Felton to declare her domain legal and in her name.'

'And the knight, von Plauen?'

'Stays in servants' quarters. He accompanies her on the streets. Sometimes she almost misses curfew.'

Torellini knew that one Teutonic Knight, Gunther von Schwerin, had sought lodging in the monastery, and that von Plauen was not yet been released from his duty by Cateline. It was like having a bull-baiting dog on a chain so why should she dismiss him? What male protection was available other than a husband or kin? He was the perfect bodyguard, especially if she was careless about curfew. The streets of Avignon were perilous at night but having a highly trained armed man at your side would deter even the most daring Alparuches, gangs that dressed as animals or demons and committed rape, murder and robbery. Avignon's shame was that these gangs were often made up of students and young noblemen as well as the rabble. The municipal marshal and his constables attempted to keep order at night but were fighting a losing battle.

Whispers from the neighbourhood were that von Plauen had become Lady Cateline's lover, but so far they were unproven. If true the lovers were discreet to the point of absolute secrecy. Even servants in nearby properties bribed by Torellini's spies could offer no confirmation. The only possibility was that they went elsewhere for their assignations, and the fact that they risked missing curfew suggested to Torellini that they had a room somewhere in the city. Torellini had hoped that Henry's friendship with Lady Cateline's son might have yielded clues. She would not risk damaging her reputation and possible loss of the right to her domains. Should von Plauen's denial of his vows be discovered, it would result in harsh punishment – possibly even death if his companions learnt of it. In a city of thirty thousand it was easy to remain anonymous, Henry Blackstone was proof of that, but it also meant that Torellini could not have the eyes of his informers everywhere.

'You do not break curfew?'

'I wouldn't,' said Henry. 'Too dangerous.'

Torellini smiled. He believed him. He did not tell him that his spies reported that the second knight, Gunther von Schwerin, followed the boy frequently. The only conclusion Torellini could reach was that von Schwerin believed a connection still existed between Thomas Blackstone and the mercenary Gruffydd ap Madoc and if any secret meeting were to take place then they might use Henry as a contact.

'You've heard from my father again?' said Henry. News of the battle last December had taken days to reach Avignon and it was then more than a month before he and Torellini learnt of Blackstone's wounds. The extent of his injuries remained unknown to the boy. All that Henry had been told was that his father and his men had won the battle at Launac and had wintered at Castle Foix. Torellini decided that telling the boy the truth would have been a mistake. Had he learnt that his father was badly wounded Henry would have left Avignon and gone to him. It was difficult enough to impress on Henry that he must show no sign of celebration of his father's victory, given his anonymity in the city. The battle had been the culmination of bitter rivalry between two aggrieved noblemen and their armies. Now Gaston Phoebus was one of the richest men in France and had recruited and paid for his own army. It was rumoured that nearly four thousand men now enjoyed regular payment under his banner. Torellini thanked God that Blackstone had not only survived, but had secured victory. Now the young Count would pledge his fealty to the Prince of Wales and vast swathes of Aquitaine from west to east were safe from insurrection.

'William Ashford and the King's escort were ordered to Bordeaux. The Prince landed there two weeks ago. Ashford is a good man who hoped to join your father but a King's man has no choice where he serves. There was a great ceremony in the cathedral where many lords pledged their fealty. '

'And you didn't tell me?' said Henry.

'It was a royal occasion but only for the invited guests.'

'I would love to have seen him. Did my father go?'

'No.'

'Surely he would have been invited?'

'Not only invited but expected. He is the King's Master of War. His victory has earned him great praise.'

'Then why didn't he go?'

'I have no idea.'

'I would like to go and see my father. Can you send word and ask him?'

'The Prince is travelling through Aquitaine to receive fealty from all the lords of the region. Sir Thomas has a responsibility to ensure the Prince's journey is unimpeded by protest or violence. He is duty-bound to the Prince. He'll send for you when he's ready. '

'I hope so,' said Henry as he finished eating and pushed his plate away.

'You don't like cabbage?' said Torellini, seeing what remained.

Henry shook his head.

'Your father doesn't care for it either.'

CHAPTER SIXTY-SIX

The city of Bergerac trembled when Thomas Blackstone rode in with his men. The burghers and mayor had expected news of the Prince's arrival, not the sight of rough-hewn men traversing the two-hundred-yard-long narrow causeway across the River Dordogne into the city. Even though few in number, the fact that brigands had ridden ahead of the English vanguard from Bordeaux caused consternation. Were they here to threaten and extort *patis*? Bergerac had been under English protection since its capture several years before but was that enough to dissuade routiers from extortion? Fear rippled through the burghers. But then Blackstone's blazon was unfurled and a squire came forward to declare that the King's Master of War had arrived in the city in advance of the Prince's arrival to ensure lodgings and to review safety for the royals.

The mayor and his council gushed with relief and took more time than was necessary to introduce themselves because they too were to declare their loyalty to their new Prince of Aquitaine. Other guests, Breton noblemen, had already arrived, they told Blackstone, and the Bishop of Sarlat was due to arrive the next day with Gisbert de Dome. The honour bestowed upon the city had cost the city coffers a great deal of money, a comment quickly recanted in case of any misunderstanding. The honour was worth every coin in their treasury.

'That's good information to have,' said Killbere as they settled into their quarters. 'If they have enough money to host the wine-swilling nobility and their wives, then if things go wrong with the Prince we can help ourselves to their treasury and be on our way. I'll take this bed,' he said, testing the mattress. 'Anything softer than a floorboard does not suit you.'

Blackstone looked out of the window at the cobbled streets below. 'We will put men down at the riverbank, Gilbert. The strand is broad and if I was tempted to seize the city I would have barges bring in men from there.'

'Except there will be no attack, Thomas, because the Prince travels with enough men to have covered our flank at Launac. Our presence here is a market-square puppet show and well you know it.'

'All the more reason to make it look genuine. We'll keep the captains with us and the sergeants and their men at strategic places in the city. We are too few to be noticed but it might convince the Prince we are here for his benefit. Let's get down to the tavern and enjoy what time we have before he gets here. Once the royal circus arrives we will be hard pressed to find time for drink and food.'

'And women.' Killbere grinned.

Blackstone dragged a drunken Killbere up the stairs and dropped him onto the floor; then he flopped himself onto the mattress that was too soft but which the heavy Gascon wine helped his aching body ignore. He still felt the effects of his wounds. The steep stairs had tugged at his leg – there was still a weakness that might take more weeks to strengthen. At least the bone had knitted: he was thankful that Will Longdon and John Jacob knew as much as any battlefield surgeon and had set the limb – pressing the broken bone back under the torn skin and binding his leg with two wooden shafts – while he lay unconscious before physicians attended him. The fresh breeze through the window carried the sweet scent of hillside grass from the surrounding fields, which brought memories of Christiana as he drifted into sleep.

The sudden banging on his door moments after he closed his eyes startled him. He had slept for six hours.

'Sir Thomas?' said John Jacob at the door.

Blackstone was wide awake though Killbere still curled asleep on the floorboards. He nodded, swung his feet free and went to the nightstand where there was a washbowl and jug. He sluiced water over his face and neck, then poured the jug of water over his hair, shaking away the grogginess from the night's drinking. 'What is it?'

John Jacob stood back from the door. 'A rider came in. His horse was dead under him. He's been travelling for a week.'

'From where?'

'He won't speak to any of us, Sir Thomas, only you. He's exhausted. I put him at the table and had them feed him.'

Blackstone clattered down the stairs to the tavern below. Men slept on the bottom of the stairs, others under tables. The serving women brushed sawdust around and over them and a dog began defecating and was beaten with the broom. It ran out into the bright sunshine, already hot for that time of the day. John Jacob stepped around the sleeping men. 'I put him in there. The owner didn't like it but I gave him no choice.'

Blackstone stepped through to the tavern owner's room. A bedraggled man, caked in dust and grime, his eyes red from long days in the saddle, bent over a meal of potatoes and mutton. He quaffed wine thirstily. When Blackstone entered he quickly abandoned his breakfast and bent down on one knee. 'Sir Thomas Blackstone?'

Blackstone nodded. 'Get up. Eat. You look as though you need it. Who are you?'

The man glanced past Blackstone to John Jacob.

'You can speak in front of my squire.'

The man chewed rapidly and then wiped his mouth. He pulled aside his jerkin and exposed the French King's fleur-de-lys blazon. 'I am a messenger from the Dauphin Charles in Paris, my lord. '

'You rode from Paris?' said Blackstone, surprised at the sight of the French royal crest and that a messenger had travelled such a distance.

The man nodded. 'Relay horses at towns my King still holds. Twelve, fifteen leagues a day. Two horses died beneath me. First to the Count of Foix where we had been told you were recovering. They told us that you were here awaiting your Prince. There were two of us. One to Bordeaux to reach him and I to find you at Foix. I do not know if the other messenger survived.'

Blackstone sat on the stool opposite the man and poured more wine from the jug for him. 'All right. Drink and know you have succeeded in reaching me.'

'I fear I am close to collapse, my lord, so let me relay the message now. Then do with me what you will.'

'You have served the Dauphin with great determination and courage. You'll be paid for your effort and given a bed and lodging for as long as you need it.'

'God bless you, Sir Thomas. I did not expect such courtesy.'

'From the likes of a man who is your King and Dauphin's sworn enemy?' said Blackstone.

'That was my expectation. I apologize, my lord. Your reputation is fearsome.'

'Your message?'

'There is an assassination plot against the English Prince. My lord the Dauphin does not know where but it might be here. His information is that a mercenary has been paid.'

Blackstone watched the man hesitate. 'Then why send word to me?'

'Your son is in Avignon.'

Blackstone said nothing. The man nodded, emphasizing the point. 'The same person who wishes the Prince's death will also kill your son. It might not be too late. You could save him. It is a choice, Sir Thomas.'

Blackstone pressed his hand on the man's arm. 'Rest. You're safe here. My Prince and I are in your debt.'

'The Dauphin's,' the messenger replied humbly.

'Without your loyalty and courage he would be as mute as a newborn child. You have given voice to his honour.'

Blackstone left the exhausted man and went out into the street. His men were lodged in rooms and inns in the immediate vicinity of where the royal party would be housed and where the ceremony would take place. 'Bring the captains, John. We must have a tight noose around here. The Prince is due today and tomorrow he takes the pledges of fealty.'

'Sir Thomas, what can we do to help Henry?'

Blackstone imagined his son caught in the confines of the city. An assassin's knife was easily wielded in crowded streets. A paid urchin could deliver the killing blow. If there was a chance of warning him, then he might seek refuge with Father Torellini. Even so, a determined assassin would find a way to kill. But there was no time.

'Whoever threatens the Prince is trying to draw me away. Henry must face his own danger, John. He has the courage; he needs good fortune. He's on his own.'

CHAPTER SIXTY-SEVEN

Avignon was second only to Paris now that they had rebuilt the walls. Defensively it would be difficult for any of those routiers who passed along the banks of the Rhône to attack the papal city. Though who would wish to even think of attack in the sweltering summer temperatures? The clamour of tradesmen and merchants thronged the thoroughfares. Wine, spices, herbs and freshly baked bread and sweet biscuits fought in the stifling air to overpower each other and the stench of the streets. Poultry trapped in cages squawked and fruit sold quickly before it ruined. Raised voices from stallholders tried to outsell each other. Urchins ran between the jostling crowds offering to carry packages or loads of wood and kindling for the cooking fires that added to the increasing heat. Tempers flared. Fights were common but the marshal was only summoned if someone was killed.

It was late in the day and Henry was behind in his studies, but he had promised to meet Jocard. He shouldered his way through to one of the squares. There were few open spaces in the city. Citizens, Henry had discovered, held meetings that were both sacred and profane in the cemeteries, much-prized land for those wishing to develop more housing. Those were not places that held an audience for long. Scavenging pigs often rooted up the recently buried dead from their shallow graves. But here in the square there was room to buy a sweet cake and watch the jugglers and the armless woman who could sew and spin with her feet and play dice with her toes.

Jocard was not at their meeting place. Henry waited. It was not unusual for the boy to be late for their meetings: trying to negotiate the confined streets in good time was difficult. He watched the entertainers for a while, ate his cake and then went off to find the younger man.

There was no sign of him at his lodgings: Henry ran upstairs to the attic room, knocked, but had no reply. Pushing open the door, he saw the unmade bedding on the cot and a set of books on a small table. The wooden floor creaked and the small open window let in the noise and smells of the city. It would soon be dark and the watchman would blow his trumpet from the Tour de la Gâche on the Pope's Palace to announce the start of the night watch's vigil. The city byways would empty and where there had been life death would soon lurk. He hesitated. If there was anything wrong Jocard would go to his mother's rented house, but that was across the city and he would not make it back to his own room in time. He asked the landlord if he knew where Jocard might be. The toothless man shrugged and continued to pluck the dead chicken on his lap.

'He said a friend might come looking,' said the landlord, concentrating on pulling tufts off the chicken.

'And what? Did he leave a message for me?'

'Left a message for a friend. How do I know you're that friend?'

'My name is Henry de Sainteny.'

The man sneezed. 'Bless me. Bless this house. Oh yeah? Not Henry Blackstone?'

Henry swallowed hard. The man didn't seem to know the name. The chicken was more important.

'No, de Sainteny,' Henry repeated.

'Uh-huh. Sounds right. The lad said if his friend Henry came calling to tell him someone approached him. Don't ask me who: he never said. But the man asked if he was this Henry Blackstone.'

'That's the message?'

The man looked up. 'I'm not a damned scribe. Anything more than that he should have written it down himself.'

Henry realized Jocard must be running scared. How had his name surfaced? The boy had obviously not gone to their meeting on the square, fearful of being followed and leading the stranger to him.

He abandoned the risk of the city at night and, turning away from the old house, headed for the safety of Torellini's mansion. He did not see the cloaked Gunther von Schwerin standing in the distance watching him.

The boy's hesitation interested the knight. He stepped across the street. 'You know that boy?' he asked the landlord.

The man looked him up and down. The cloak and the scuffed leather boots peeping below it suggested a man of insufficient means to offer a coin for information and the shaved hair above his ears told him he was some kind of monk, one of those hospitallers, and everyone knew they didn't have two deniers to rub together. 'Who wants to know?'

'The merciful Lord would cast His benevolence on you and this house if you tell me.'

'The merciful Lord saw fit to take my wife and daughter in the plague last year. Why do you think I am doing a woman's work and plucking the damned chicken? Be off with you.'

Von Schwerin eased aside his cloak enough to show his sword hilt and the knife in his belt. The black cross surcoat loomed ominously. The landlord had a decision to make. The gesture impressed on him that this was a holy warrior asking, who would slit his throat without a moment's hesitation. He wanted to eat his chicken that night. He recounted what he had told Henry.

Von Schwerin turned away, striding rapidly to the Lady Cateline's quarters. This might be the contact from the Welshman he had hoped for. To ask for Blackstone by name meant someone had been sent into the city to seek him out; Lady Cateline's son might have more information and it was possible he had run to his mother. But the German knight knew he would not reach the house before curfew and it was doubtful even he could defeat a determined gang of ten or more if they attacked him. He would go as far as he could and then find a church to wait in. Once the night eased into the early hours of the morning, the danger on the streets would filter away.

It was a good time to pray and offer thanks for what might be a chance to track down Gruffydd ap Madoc.

The night's heat clawed into the skin and inflamed passions. In overcrowded buildings short-tempered fights broke out between men and their wives. Wolfram von Plauen felt the heat suck the life out of him. For the past few days the only coolness came from Lady Cateline. He had watched the overtures from the rich merchants. He knew the day would come when someone would ask for her hand. She had touched something more in him than the fear of the devil, unlocking an overwhelming tenderness he never knew existed. It was destroying him. And now he was facing her final rejection. Nothing in any battle had brought him to his knees as had these feelings: a turbulence more violent than the crashing cross-currents of the River Rhône that only three years before had surged and torn down part of the city walls. For months von Plauen had been her shadow and now his protection was no longer required. She was releasing him from his pledge. It crushed him. He begged, implored and debased himself, expressing his love, promising her his life, vowing to keep her… but she had no need of him. She had recently been granted legal rights to her domain. And that had brought a proposal of marriage from a wealthy merchant. Her status was assured, as was the well-being of her children.

She gazed at him. Pity swept over her. She was not cold-hearted and tried to calm his distress, understanding the man's wounded pride.

Thunder rumbled as the pressure built in the night sky. A great storm was gathering. Tears stung his eyes as he trembled. She backed away from him. He reached for her, murmuring his impassioned pleas, embracing her too tightly. She struggled. His hand held her face as he forced his lips on hers. She squirmed, struck him. Blood seeped not from his split lip but from somewhere behind his eyes. It flooded his thoughts, blinding him. He did not remember striking her. He remembered a startled scream and then silence. The roof shook from a thunderclap, which snapped him back to his violent act. She lay sprawled on the floor. The window shutters rattled, banging repeatedly; rain splattered into the room as the rolling storm struck. He knew she was dead. The neck he had pressed his lips to, a place he breathed her perfume, was twisted. Her eyes stared at him.

A sound startled him. The servant, Melita, stood in the doorway in her nightdress, clutching Cateline's daughter, who was terrified by the storm. Melita gazed at her dead mistress. Von Plauen stepped towards her, not in anger but wishing in that desperate moment to explain. Before he could find the words she turned and ran down the corridor. He went after her and as she turned for the stairs he heard her scream. From the landing he saw the two crumpled bodies at the bottom of the stone-hard chestnut stairs.

Von Plauen took the steps three at a time and bent to find a heartbeat but Melita's broken skull and the crushed child beneath her told him both were dead. He stumbled to the door that had been blown open. Somewhere through the noise of the heavy rain and the insistent thunder he heard a lone church bell calling him to prayer. He stepped into the storm.

CHAPTER SIXTY-EIGHT

Henry found Lady Cateline's son at Torellini's house. Jocard had run, confused and frightened, not knowing what to do. Once there, he confessed that it was he who had revealed Henry's name by pretending to be him when he fought an older bully a couple of weeks before and compounded the lie by threatening to send his father Thomas Blackstone to confront the aggressive student. Somehow that slip of the tongue had found its way into the hands of those who sought a reward for such information. Father Torellini confined the two boys to his house.

He questioned Jocard relentlessly until tears spilled down the boy's face, swearing he had told no one except his mother what he had done. That was the link that Torellini sought. Now he would reach into the heart of Avignon's society. Further investigation among Lady Cateline's circle of pampered women acquaintances would reveal which of them would benefit from knowing Henry Blackstone's real identity. His enquiries had already discovered that a Lady de Sagard was in the city. The name was familiar to him but he could not recall a link between the woman and Thomas Blackstone. If the connection was something to do with Blackstone's past then, like him, she might be gathering information in this city of whispers. The servants took the boys to the guest bedrooms.

It was unlikely that an enemy would dare to attack the Bardi mansion but until he learnt more Torellini would increase the guards on the house. The storm thundered as his staff ran from window to window locking the shutters and Torellini watched the dancing rain leap from the marble-paved courtyard. No matter how hard the summer rains scourged the city it would never wash away its intrigue and violence.

Gunther von Schwerin spent the hours in an empty chapel drawing its dim light and stillness to him until the storm gave him the cover he needed to make his way to Lady Cateline's house. He was impervious to the soaking rain and relished the relief from the oppressive heat. He was soaked when he reached the house and when he stepped into the open entrance he immediately saw the servant and child. He checked their still warm bodies, drew his knife and ran up the stairs. At the top of the first step he saw the servant's shoe and the raised threshold between stair and landing – the wooden slat had lifted, tripping the servant, plummeting her and the child to their deaths. The bedroom door was open, revealing Lady Cateline's sprawled body. Someone had broken her neck. Von Plauen's cloak, surcoat and weapons were on a chair. The scene confirmed his suspicion that the months confined in Avignon had corrupted his devout friend and comrade. Gathering up the weapons, he wrapped them in the cloak, quickly checked the other rooms and, seeing there was no sign of her son, made his way back into the swirling rain. Water gushed down the gutters, ridding the city of its detritus as the pounding rain also kept the citizens off the streets. Von Schwerin pulled up his hood and stood looking around the nearby buildings. His comrade had run, but to where? A crackle of lightning illuminated the tower of a small suburban church. From murder to penitence was only a few hundred yards.

The heavy wooden door was ajar. The Teutonic Knight pressed his shoulder against it and slipped into the darkness. He waited, listening in the silence that surrounded him now that the beating rain was kept at bay. A lone candle burned near the altar and as the shuddering light from a crash of lightning reached through the high window, he saw von Plauen's kneeling figure. His shirt was plastered to his skin halfway down his back. The upper part and shoulders streamed with blood from a self-inflicted whipping. A knotted rope lay at his side.

Gunther walked quietly behind his tormented friend. 'Wolfram,' he called gently. There was no reply; the man was deep in prayer and despair. He stepped around him so that the candlelight illuminated his comrade's tear-filled face. Mucus trickled from his nose into his beard above tightly clasped hands pressed into his chest. Von Schwerin reached out and covered the clenched fists with his own. Von Plauen's lips stopped reciting the prayer of contrition. His eyes opened as if awakening from a deep sleep. He recognized von Schwerin, and bowed his head in shame. 'Leave me, Gunther. I am lost. I am beyond saving now.' Realization struck him. 'You have been to her house?'

Von Schwerin nodded.

'It was an accident. I had no intent to kill her. I struck out blindly. God forgive me but I… I loved her. You can never know what that does to you.'

'We are brothers-in-arms, Wolfram. The Order binds us. I understand love.'

Von Plauen wiped a hand across his face and shook his head. 'No, my friend, the power of what I felt did nothing but destroy. I did not kill the servant and child.'

'I saw what happened. She tripped,' said von Schwerin.

The once devoted Teutonic Knight still seemed dazed at the turn of events. 'What must I do?'

Gunther studied the man with whom he had served from when they first knelt before the Grand Master in their youth and swore their act of obedience. His heart ached for the downfall of a great knight and champion. 'You have to leave the city. You have money in your purse? Enough to buy food?'

Wolfram's hand instinctively touched his belt. 'Enough.'

'Then we must get you to the stables before the dawn breaks.' He extended his hand, and the defeated man allowed his comrade to pull him to his feet. Von Schwerin tugged the rain and blood-soaked shirt over the lacerations. Wolfram made no complaint as the rough shirt snagged his wounds, and then his friend eased his cloak over him. 'I'll keep your sword and knife until we get there.'

Von Plauen nodded and then heaved a great sigh. 'Gunther,' he whispered, 'I have betrayed the Brotherhood. I have shamed it forever.'

His friend put his arm around the man's waist and guided him towards the door. 'We will think of a way to obscure what has been done,' he said.

Once back in the streets von Schwerin guided his friend towards the city walls where the narrow alleys entwined into a labyrinth. 'I should join the brigands. That is all I can do now,' said von Plauen.

'Then your guilt will be obvious,' said von Schwerin. 'They will find the bodies at dawn and they will search for you. You will not get through the gates unless you leave now. They will seize you, Wolfram, and they will hold you for murder.'

The stark truth penetrated von Plauen's mind. He stared at his friend as if hearing him for the first time. There could be no escape.

'You will not be beheaded like a common criminal. They will sew you into a sack and throw you in the river.'

'Then there is no redemption and the shame will stain the Order forever.'

'Not if it is thought that a gang invaded her house and that you gave chase. Then your honour is restored and the Order unblemished.'

'Gave chase beyond the walls?' said von Plauen. He studied his friend. 'An act of cowardice and untruth.' His panic calmed. 'I cannot. And we both know it.'

They stopped, the rain soaking their beards, von Schwerin's tears mingling with the droplets. His friend understood.

'I gave chase and I was robbed and killed when I found them.'

The two men stood silently. Von Plauen pulled on his surcoat and then tugged free the purse from his belt and pressed it into von Schwerin's hand. He cupped his friend's face and kissed each cheek. 'Find Blackstone. He will lead you to the Welshman. I thank God for our friendship.'

'I too, dear friend,' said Gunther von Schwerin and plunged his knife into his comrade's heart.

CHAPTER SIXTY-NINE

The rain eased in Avignon, the glistening sheen of the pavements and cobbled streets reflecting a new day and the illusion that the storm had swept the city of its sins. Torellini sent a servant to Jocard's mother's house to assure her that her son was safe. The news of her death on the servant's return shocked the household. Giving the servants strict instructions not to discuss the tragedy, he drew Henry to one side and shared the news. What concerned Torellini was the cause of the three deaths in Lady Cateline's house. Had the assassin thought Jocard to be Henry Blackstone and at some point followed him to Lady Cateline's lodgings? It was unclear what had occurred. The Teutonic Knight von Plauen had been found dead in the streets. It appeared he had pursued the attackers and met his own death. His purse and weapons were missing. Was that a robbery committed by Alparuches which had turned to murder? That would be the more acceptable explanation: a gang on the rampage. Such scum were known to invade houses if there were fewer people on the streets to assault at night. If that were not the case it meant assassins were still at large, perhaps aware that they had still not found Thomas Blackstone's son.

Father Torellini decided to seek out the woman he suspected of having the connection to Blackstone. He would contact the Marshal of the Court. He was highly placed and the most corrupt of officials, and he would know about the socializing the noblewomen undertook.

'You and young Jocard are to stay here in the safety of the Bardi house,' he instructed Henry. 'The servants will not mention the death of his mother and sister on pain of dismissal but a slip of the tongue or an overheard whisper cannot always be avoided. I shall tell the boy before I leave, but…' His words drifted away. His hesitation was easy to understand.

'I'll tell him,' said Henry.

'I am grateful,' Torellini told him, relieved. 'Remember, do not leave here under any circumstances. I do not know who has been alerted by your name being mentioned.'

He left the house accompanied by two servants. Strong men who would cut a swathe through the crowded streets.

Henry took Jocard to his room. 'We need to talk,' he told the boy.

Lady Cateline's son hunched his shoulders as he sat on the edge of the bed. 'If I am to be chastised for what I did, I understand. I am sorry, Henry. I tried to keep whoever was asking about you away from our meeting place.'

'I know that. This is about something else.'

Jocard raised his head, uncertain.

'I have known the pain of losing my mother and my baby sister,' said Henry. 'They are wounds that never heal.'

'I don't understand. Mother and Jehanne are close by.' He suddenly looked startled. 'Are you sending me away from here? Is that my punishment? Henry, I beg you, do not. I will make amends to you, I swear.'

Henry knew the stark reality of what had happened the previous night was best dealt with the way barber-surgeons cauterized a wound. The pain was sharp, but the injury healed more quickly. 'Someone went into the house last night. Your mother was attacked and killed and her servant died with your sister,' he said gently.

Jocard's mouth opened and closed, a look of wild disbelief in his eyes. His lip trembled until he could no longer hold back the tears. He fell weeping to his knees, hands covering his face. Henry let him sink into his agony until he was exhausted. When Jocard slumped back on his haunches, Henry soaked a cloth and bathed the boy's face. 'It's all right, Jocard. Let the pain take you: it will strip you of your grief soon enough. The tear in your heart will burn for years to come but you will live with it and accept what has happened.' He brushed his hand through the boy's hair, lifting it from his forehead. 'From this moment on, you will grow stronger.'

Jocard looked blankly at the older boy. 'Were they looking for you? Did they think I was you? Did they die because of what I said?'

'No. Father Torellini thinks a gang attacked the house and that von Plauen went after them but they killed him as well.' He helped the boy to his feet. 'It was nothing to do with you,' he said. He knew where the truth lay but was unwilling to add guilt to the lad's grief.

Jocard began to fasten his tunic. 'I must go to them, Henry.'

'No, you can't. We must be careful.'

Jocard looked up, his trembling fingers struggling with the buttons. Henry reached forward and did them up it for him. 'If we must be careful,' said Jocard, 'then it might have something to do with them thinking I am you. A man was looking for you. So…' He blinked, his thoughts attempting to unravel what might have happened. 'So… there could be a connection.'

'Perhaps,' Henry admitted.

'I must still go to her. My mother's locket. It was all she had from my father. Gravediggers will strip her body of her jewellery.' He tried to push past Henry, but he gripped Jocard's arm.

'You will stay here. You will be master of your mother's estates now. You must embrace that responsibility. Father Torellini will help you and my father will extend his protection until you are of age. Do you understand?'

Jocard nodded and sat down again. 'Forgive me, Henry, I have brought a great threat to your life.' He smiled bravely. 'I will do as you say. Do you think the servants would give me some wine?'

'Of course. I'll get it.' He went to the door and looked back. 'We must wait until Father Torellini returns and he will arrange an escort for you. I'll come with you. We'll go together.'

Henry instructed the servants to take two beakers of wine and some bread to his room. He led the servant upstairs but when he opened the door, the window was open and the boy was gone. Henry ran and looked to the street below. A drainpipe descended close enough for a lithe boy to clamber down. Henry turned and ran down the stairs, pushing past the house staff and out through the small rear gate he had entered hours before. Jocard couldn't be more than a few minutes away and heading for his mother's house. Henry barged people aside, earning curses, feet skidding on the slippery wet cobbles and pavements as he pounded through the streets. Where was he? There was no sign ahead of anyone being jostled aside. He skirted down a less choked side alley, knowing it would loop around to Lady Cateline's house. The city walls loomed close by, the stench of urine telling him he was where beggars and thieves congregated at night. Now, though, there was only the sound of shouts of alarm. Two women appeared, followed by a handful of men running in panic. At first he thought the men were chasing the women but then saw that others were also running towards him. Away from a commotion at the next corner. Screams echoed around him. He saw a hooded figure bent double, swinging his arm back and forth. Blood spilling from a ragged body as loose and lifeless as a child's rag doll.

The assassin had found the boy he thought to be Blackstone's son.

Henry bellowed. A raw animal sound. The killer turned. A pockmarked face snarled at him. A face without fear. It was a man he had never seen before. A killer who could be lost in a crowd. Henry slowed. The assassin braced himself, the bloodied knife in his hand wet with slime. Henry was in a daze, uncertain what was happening, and then realized he had drawn his own knife. He faced the crouching man. He knew it was already too late to save Jocard.

He felt the surge of violence rise in him. His eyes blurred. His hand trembled with rage. And fear. Then it calmed. He entered the world his father had spoken of and gathered its power. Striding forward, he feinted; the killer tried to stop a strike that had already curved away and slashed his free arm. Shock creased his face. Henry sidestepped and parried the man's rapid response. His blade cut low, its tip catching Henry's thigh, a flesh wound that threatened to slow him down, but the stinging pain had no effect on his attack. The man was thrown off balance and raised his wounded arm to halt the blade that jabbed at his throat but Henry grabbed his wrist and yanked the arm down. It pulled the killer onto his toes. Henry rammed his knife up below the man's sternum. He was close enough to smell the stench of the man's breath as he exhaled. Henry clasped him close.

'I am Henry Blackstone,' he spat.

The man's eyes widened. He choked, but had the dying strength to ram his knife into the back of Henry's shoulder. The pain shot through him, forcing him to drop the man's weight. Henry staggered back against the wall, his strength slipping away. Using the wall for support, he tried to reach Jocard's savaged body but his legs no longer supported him. He slid down the wall and settled into pools of blood. He thought of his father. And the inheritance that was now his.

CHAPTER SEVENTY

Sir John Chandos escorted Blackstone to the Prince's dressing room. He dismissed the various servants. There was no sign of Joan, the Princess of Wales. Edward was dressed for the impending ceremony. He wore long robes, his circular cloak held at the shoulder with four large jewelled buttons. His fair hair was trimmed to below his neck and Blackstone was as impressed as any onlooker at his striking figure.

'Our barber says my beard better suits my face this way. What do you think, Thomas?'

Blackstone had expected admonishment, not to be asked to give an opinion on the finer points of the Prince's looks. They had denied him an audience until Edward was settled in his quarters and the dignitaries had paid their respects before the planned reception. Blackstone had to bend on one knee, his recent injury tugging at the muscles. He gazed up at the imperious man whose life had been so intricately woven with his own. The long fair beard was shaped below the chin into a point. The comparison between the two men could not be more stark. Both were of similar height and age but Blackstone's battle-worn clothes, despite the best attempts of the washerwomen, made him look like a pauper compared to Edward's grandeur.

'The beard is fine, highness,' said Blackstone.

'Get to your feet, Thomas. The ability to flatter still escapes you.'

'You have enough people around you to do that, my Prince.'

Edward fussed the cuffs on his gown. 'And we have you as our tormentor.'

Blackstone remained silent.

'We ordered you to Bordeaux and you disobeyed us.'

'My men were recovering from their wounds. The Count of Foix gave us time to heal. Beyond that, there was no time to reach you. I wanted to ensure that Bergerac was secure for your arrival.'

'And they tell us you too were injured.'

'I am recovered.'

The Prince glanced at Chandos. 'Are they ready below?'

'Yes, highness.'

'Then we will discuss the matter further after the ceremony, Thomas.'

'I gave Sir John information, my lord. There is an assassin on the loose. You cannot walk the streets without an escort.'

'Cannot?'

Blackstone ignored the reprimand. 'We do not know who the assassins are. All manner of men cram the city.'

'Sir John has lined the streets with our escort. He has everything under control. We suggest you confine your own men to their quarters should their roughly dressed demeanour lead them to be mistaken for brigands.'

The Prince stepped towards the door but Blackstone had the temerity to move in his way.

John Chandos came forward quickly but the Prince raised a hand.

'There are rival factions from Brittany down in that hall,' Blackstone insisted. 'Their hatred for us will not be eased by the truce. Who knows how many routiers are out there in the streets? A Breton lord bends the knee and strikes with a knife and the city burns, your wife is a widow and the King lays waste to France. Caution, I beg you. Let me stand close to you.'

The Prince's eyes blazed with anger but he refrained from castigating his father's Master of War. Blackstone always had more leeway than most. The scar-faced knight's defiance had often delivered victory and had once saved his life. He relented. 'I take the Dauphin's warning seriously. He sent word to you – even your most bitter enemy trusted you to protect us, although no messenger survived the journey to us at Bordeaux. Very well. Stand in the wings. Put yourself among the Bretons. Move through the crowds as you wish. Do not disrupt the proceedings.'

Blackstone lowered his head and stepped aside. Chandos scowled at him as he opened the door; the retinue of courtiers bowed as the Prince made his way briskly down the passage to where his wife stood. She looked even more alluring than her reputation. Her tight-fitting dress and low-cut neckline trimmed with silk and ermine was daring. Precious stones and pearls laced into her hair sparkled and glowed. The staid wives of feudal lords could not hope to follow her fashionable trend. And any woman other than the sensuous Princess would not have the style and charm to carry it off. Blackstone waited as the finely dressed entourage descended to the lower landings and then through the doors that would lead to the ornate rooms where the Prince and Princess would receive the lords and dignitaries. He looked to one side where Killbere leaned against the balustrade, watching the procession snake away.

'Are we still free men?'

'He thinks he's safe.'

Killbere pulled a face. 'Not with his wife dressed like a routier's whore,' he said quietly.

'God's tears, Gilbert, keep those thoughts to yourself. Secure the entrance and the side passages. Chandos has enough men on the street. We'll guard the hallways down there and make sure there's no one in the shadows. If I was going to kill him I wouldn't do it out there. The confines of a building give him nowhere to run.'

'Beyard arrived two hours ago with ten Gascon men-at-arms. I had them fed and put them at the entrance in the street. It was the Gascon lords who wanted the Prince in Aquitaine so their presence bearing Jean de Grailly's blazon made sense.'

Blackstone and Killbere went down the stairs and past the guard on the first landing's door. Beyond that the stairs descended to the main entrance hall. A familiar face smiled up at them.

'Sir Thomas,' said William Ashford.

Blackstone welcomed the King's sergeant-at-arms. 'William, we missed you at Launac.'

'And that was my misfortune. My men and I wished nothing more than to stand at your side but they summoned us to the Prince instead. My men are under Sir John's command.'

'Did you see my son before you left Avignon?'

'Yes. By all accounts his studies go well.'

It was small comfort. William Ashford had left Avignon weeks ago and anything could have happened since then. 'We'll talk later, William. Keep your men alert. There's a threat against the Prince.'

'He knows about this?'

'He does but he will change nothing. He leaves for Périgueux tomorrow and there can be no delay.'

'All well and good,' said Ashford, 'but if they carry out the threat then we'll have a war on our hands.' He nodded and turned to rejoin his men.

Blackstone and Killbere made their way to the hall where the Prince and Princess would be received. The room was full. Men and women jostled for a look at the legendary Prince but perhaps too the opportunity to see the renowned beauty of the Fair Maid of Kent, whose reputation was as scandalous as her husband's taste in luxury. The room stank of sweat from the pressed bodies. Open windows above where the royal couple were seated afforded some air on one side of the room. On other side an enclosed balcony allowed those not important enough to be invited into the great hall to view the proceedings.

'We'll circle the room. You go left; I'll go right. Chandos has a cordon of men around the Prince. See what's being said. If there are whispers of trouble, we get them out of the room.'

They separated. Speeches were being made. The Mayor of Bergerac's voice urged the gathered lords and dignitaries to bless the day that the Prince now ruled Aquitaine. The praise went on long enough for Blackstone to circle half the room, stopping and listening to the muttered comments by those who no longer had any choice but to swear fealty. A knot of Breton lords stood together. Men who had fought for Charles de Blois against the English favourite, de Montfort. Their faces were sour with bitterness that a truce had been declared between the warring parties for the succession of Brittany. That they had been summoned to attend and put their seals to the document was to them little more than public humiliation. The men craned their necks over the crowd to see the Prince and Princess as Blackstone eased behind them. One of the lords, Jean de Beaumanoir, led the faction of Charles de Blois and a man at his side was whispering loud enough for Blackstone to overhear.

'So, Jean, now we have seen the Princess, will you dress your wife differently and have her cast aside those drab clothes of hers?'

De Beaumanoir grimaced and Blackstone thought if the room had not been so crowded he would have spat in disgust. The Breton turned his face to his friend so his words could not be heard too clearly by those straining to listen to the Mayor's droning speech. 'The Prince shows no embarrassment at his wife's shameful display. Is the court of Aquitaine to take on the appearance of a brothel? My wife is an honest woman. Dignity and self-respect would allow none of our wives to dress so scandalously.'

Blackstone stepped to his shoulder. 'Take care, my lord,' he said quietly. 'There is a pledge to be signed. Insulting the Princess might cause the ink to take longer to dry.'

Jean de Beaumanoir and his fellow Breton lords glared at the tall man who intruded on their group but the faded blazon on his chest identified him and forced them to restrain any desire to argue.

'I see what I see,' de Beaumanoir muttered.

'Then let such observations remain unspoken,' said Blackstone. He moved away through the crowd, satisfied the disgruntled Bretons posed no threat. He rejoined Killbere at the door.

'I heard nothing more than a desire to be a part of the new court,' said Killbere. 'If there is any killing to be done it's between those courtiers wanting the Prince's favour.'

'Then let's be thankful we face a more honest enemy when we fight.'

Blackstone pushed open the doors into the entrance and the steps that led down into the street. Crowds thronged in the sunlight. Jean de Grailly's blazon caught Blackstone's eye.

'Beyard!' he called to his Gascon captain, who stood vigilantly with his ten men-at-arms on the steps leading into the building.

Beyard smiled when he saw Blackstone and stepped quickly to him. 'Have we ever seen such a day? It does the people good to have a royal prince and his wife visit. I'm pleased to see you are recovered.'

'It took time but we are all well. I thought Lord de Grailly would have sent you north with the King of Navarre? That man will never learn his lesson. The French will defeat him again. It's good to have you back with us.'

'It is indeed, Sir Thomas. Lord de Grailly extends his good wishes to you. I and my men's return is a gesture of his friendship.'

'I hope he doesn't get caught up with the political ambitions of Navarre. Did the Welshman make amends with him?'

'Ap Madoc? He wasn't there.'

'He went to make his peace with your master,' said Blackstone.

'He was never there. I saw him less than an hour ago.' Beyard turned and pointed to one of the side streets. 'Down there with some of his men. I thought you had him guarding the side streets.'

The Welshman's lie betrayed him. He had asked Blackstone to get him close to the Prince. Now Blackstone knew the assassin's identity.

CHAPTER SEVENTY-ONE

The stifling heat cooled as Blackstone and the others entered the broad corridor. The smooth limestone slabs beneath their feet bore witness to the centuries of men and women passing this way to attend great occasions in the palatial hall, a fitting place for a prince to receive oaths of fealty. The corridor's arched roof channelled whispers and muted silken rustling across the stone as distant voices paid homage. Passageways went left and right, swallowed by darkness. There were too many to search but without knowing if they led back to where the Prince would leave the great hall Blackstone had to try. He gestured to three of them. 'John, there. Meulon, take that one, Beyard, the other. Gilbert, with me.'

'Sir Thomas, an assassin would strike where the Prince is least guarded,' said John Jacob. 'His entourage will take the main stairs to his rooms. That's where his courtiers will leave him. When I served the King as his sergeant-at-arms at Windsor, his bodyguard stood at the end of the corridor that led to his chamber. He demanded privacy with the Queen. Would the Prince not do the same with his lady?'

'We would catch the killer like a rat in a trap. A narrow corridor serves no purpose for an assassin – he can kill but he cannot escape,' said Killbere.

Blackstone nodded. 'Gruffydd ap Madoc will not act alone. They would make more than one attempt in case the first failed. There are guards on every floor. Who would get past them without the alarm being raised?'

'Unless the killer was already in the Prince's chamber,' said John Jacob.

'John, search the passage. Gilbert, guard this route from the great hall. I'll go up.' Blackstone ran for the stairs.

Killbere ordered the men into position. Blackstone's footsteps receded into the heights of the palace. He took the stairs two at a time. He reached the vaulted verandah on the next floor and saw the first of the prince's guards at the studded oak door that led to the main rooms and staircase beyond. 'Has anyone passed this way? Any servant? Any man-at-arms?'

'None, Sir Thomas,' said the sentry.

Blackstone looked down into the floor below. Some of the local merchants gathered at the balcony window that opened onto the ceremony. They were jostling to hear what was being said in the great hall as the civic dignitaries finished proclaiming the Prince's letters of commission, followed by the regional lords and eventually the bishop confirming their oath of loyalty. There were too many gathered at the lower windows. 'Where is the next sentry?'

'A floor above and another on the other side of this door,' the man answered.

Blackstone studied the throng of people below him. It would not be impossible for a crossbow to be used through the open window. 'Get below and clear the area. There are too many people there. Close the windows. Guard the entrance. No one is to enter.'

The soldier didn't hesitate and ran for the stairs. A bronze lion's-head door handle, the size of a dinner plate, glared at Blackstone. He turned the iron ring clamped in its jaws and heard the latch lift. As he pulled the door open the man-at-arms on the other side spun around, his sword already half drawn. He stayed his hand when he saw who it was.

Blackstone took in the broad half-landing. The staircase was lit by glass lanterns; the balustraded steps dog-legged down to where another man stood guard in the flickering light. 'Has anyone come up those stairs and gone up to the Prince's rooms?' he asked the guard at the door.

'Only a girl with fresh bed linen.'

'No one else? No manservant or anyone from the Prince's entourage?'

'No, Sir Thomas.'

'And there is no other way to his rooms? No servant's staircase?'

'None. The guard commander checked. Anyone who needs to reach the Prince's floor must pass by on this staircase.'

'Were his quarters checked after he went down to the ceremony? Could anyone have stayed behind?'

A puzzled look crossed the man's face. 'One of his courtiers or attendants, you mean? I don't know. Maybe a house servant.'

'Bolt the door. No one enters from the outside.' Blackstone was already striding to the next flight of stairs when he heard the thud of the latch being driven home. On the top floor three rooms led off from the broad landing. Of the three doors, two were on opposite sides while the third, the Prince and Princess's quarters, was at the end of a corridor twenty paces long. Blackstone checked each of the rooms on the landing. They were not furnished for a nobleman but were comfortable and clean, kept for those in high office who accompanied the Prince. A woven carpet covered much of the planked floor; there was a soft mattress on a bed base and a washbowl stand and jug in the corner. The window opened onto the street three floors below. Satisfied that no one could scale the heights and gain entry, he strode quickly towards the Prince's rooms. As he pushed open the door, a startled servant girl jerked upright from fussing with the bed. She bent her knee in deference but Blackstone ignored her as he checked the room. These quarters were more sumptuous than the others. Tapestries hung on the walls and richly coloured silk cloths adorned the dark wood-carved furniture. Blackstone checked the two similarly well-furnished anterooms where the Prince and Princess would be attended to. He pulled back the curtain covering the garderobe. There was no threat in the room and no access other than what the sentries had explained.

Blackstone studied the room. The maidservant stood unmoving, frozen in the presence of the tall scar-faced knight. She trembled. Blackstone saw nothing unusual in the room and had turned to leave, when the sunlight streaming through the window onto the bolstered bed caught his eye. The slanting rays showed barely noticeable damp spots on the two pillows. He hovered his hand across them, touched his palm onto the feather-filled covers and raised his hand to his nose. There was no smell. He glared at the servant, who bowed her head and stepped towards the door. Her hands were sweating, and she dropped a small glass bottle. As it clattered to the floor, she ran. Blackstone snatched at her, caught her wrist but what had been a demure servant girl was now a snarling wildcat whose free hand slashed at Blackstone with a short-bladed dagger. As he parried the blow, he saw that her hands were soft and unblemished. She was no servant. He cuffed her behind her head with the flat of his hand. It knocked the fight out of her.

'Poison?' Blackstone said, easily forcing the knife from her hand.

'Leave me! Leave me!' she spat.

Blackstone twisted her arms; pain creased her face, tears filled her eyes, she gulped air like a drowning woman.

'Who are you?'

'Kill me or let me go. I beg you. Do not give me over to torture.'

Her cowl fell free, loosening fair hair. Blackstone eased his grip on her wrists. She had succumbed quickly to fear and spent what violence she had.

'You sprinkle poison on the pillows. Why kill the Prince? Who paid you?'

She shook her head and slumped further onto the floor. Blackstone released his grip. There was no escape for her. She wiped an arm across her face to clean her tears. 'I beg you. Do not let them put hot irons on me,' she said, raising her face to him.

'You tried to kill a prince of the realm. I cannot save you. Answer my questions and I will ask they give you a quick death.'

'Garrotted in the main square tied to a stake? Or beheaded?' She shook her head. 'I don't have the courage to face that.'

Blackstone went down on one knee and gently lifted her chin. 'Listen to me, child, whoever paid you to do this threw your life away the moment they pressed gold into your hand,' he said tenderly. 'You are no servant. Your hands are soft. Are you the daughter of a gentlewoman who has fallen on hard times?'

She pushed back the hair that had fallen across her face. She couldn't have been much older than his son. 'I did not do this for payment. My family are your sworn enemies. We vowed to seek revenge against you and the English Prince who honours you.'

Blackstone had never seen the girl before. Even so, there were many families who would wish Blackstone dead. 'Then why not kill me?'

Her face became a picture of calm innocence. What he imagined an unsullied angel might look like. 'You must live so you may suffer.'

'You make no sense, girl.'

'I was in Paris when you invaded my father's castle and killed him. My mother swore she would see you suffer and dishonoured. You cast her and my young brother and sister into poverty. My sister died in the plague and were it not for the kindness of my uncle I would have had to serve a noblewoman as little more than a servant. I would have been shamed. My brother was raised by my uncle and died with him when you attacked him.' She smiled again. 'You cannot protect your Prince. He will die. I have failed, but the others will not.'

Blackstone realized it was not the look of an angel but of someone possessed with an unswerving desire to cause him harm.

'Where does the Welshman intend to strike?' he demanded.

She shook her head. 'If my poison did not kill the Prince, then a blade will. Remember who it is who brings you down. Let your heart ache forever to know we dishonoured you because you did not protect your Prince and we revenged ourselves with the death of your son.'

Blackstone wrenched her to her feet. 'Who are you?'

'Sir Rolf de Sagard was my father. Lord Mael Babeneaux de Pontivy was my uncle.'

The girl sprawled as Blackstone threw her back down. The family who had helped the Savage Priest flay alive Blackstone's friend. The friend he had killed in mercy. The sneering creature in the shadows of a man's mind was Fate. Ever present. Waiting for the moment to bring retribution for Blackstone having killed the girl's father. And this was only one attempt on the Prince's life in case a more direct assault failed. Blackstone grabbed her. 'Where will the assassins strike?'

Blackstone had not seen her retrieve the small bottle from the floor. She threw back her head and tipped it to her lips. She choked and then shuddered. Her eyes rolled back. She fell as gently as a silk scarf being dropped to the floor.

The cathedral bells rang out. Others joined in from across the city. A joyous celebration of the English Prince being honoured.

Blackstone knew it could also herald the Prince's death.

CHAPTER SEVENTY-TWO

Blackstone hurtled down the stairs; his leg protested but he ignored its demand for him to slow down. If the Welshman was going to strike it would be when everyone was celebrating, when all eyes would be turned to the Prince. Cheering crowds would flatter a prince's vanity, erasing any thoughts of danger. The Prince's sense of occasion, the grandeur that was a reflection of the English Crown, was a deliberate show to lift the spirits of the populace plagued so long by war and pestilence. One hundred paces. Slow-moving. His entourage behind him, soldiers either side keeping back the throng. Soldiers who would stop at the entrance and block the cheering crowds from entering. The assassins would not make an attempt on his life in the street when he left the great hall and turned to walk the short route towards the palace entrance: the risk of failure was too great. But once inside, it would be only the Prince and his bride and the courtiers. Sir John Chandos would follow a respectful ten paces behind the Prince. That's where they would try to kill him. In the confines of the entrance hall before he reached the stairs.

Blackstone heard voices and laughter rise from below. Now the formalities were over the joyous occasion had raised everyone's spirits. Blackstone made the final turn and saw the Prince step into view. If an attack was imminent, it was time to gamble. If his instincts were wrong, they would laugh him out of court. Blackstone trusted his instincts.

'To arms!' Blackstone bellowed.

His sudden cry and appearance, pounding down the stairs, Wolf Sword in hand, momentarily stunned the Prince. Alarmed at the fleeting thought it was Blackstone trying to kill him, the Prince shielded the Princess. Blackstone gestured him away from the stairs. 'Get back!' By the time his words echoed across the cold stone walls he was in front of the Prince, putting himself between the royals and the men who loomed out of the depths of the building. Men's voices roared as a sudden and furious clash of steel spilled from the side passages into the hallway. Three men lunged from the shadows towards Blackstone, big men wielding falchions and swords. Blackstone rushed at them as Killbere and the captains blocked more attacks from the side passages. The entourage scattered, crouching against the walls as Chandos and his armed escort of four men threw themselves to support Blackstone, who killed the first assassin and blocked another. A knife slashed his left arm. He ignored it. Blackstone turned, saw the bloodletting behind him as some of the entourage were struck down. He ignored the blurred image of half-lit death in the shadows.

'Get them out!' Chandos bellowed as Blackstone killed another assailant.

Blackstone seized the Prince's arm. 'With me!' Blackstone commanded the heir to the English throne.

Prince Edward made no complaint. He grabbed his wife's arm and pulled her up the stairs behind Blackstone. The studded door swung open at his hammering. The wide-eyed sentry jumped back, already armed, alerted by the commotion below.

'Guard the stairs,' said Blackstone. 'Go!' he ordered the Prince, who tugged his wife with him. Too late. Cries of alarm echoed up from the floor below as the guard there was killed. Footfalls pounded upwards. 'Come on!' Blackstone ordered the sentry. They reached the top floor. The Prince rushed towards his quarters.

'No,' Blackstone yelled. 'The bedding is poisoned. In here.' He shouldered open one of the other doors. The Prince pushed his uncomplaining wife inside. 'Block the door,' Blackstone told him.

Their eyes met. 'Thomas, I am unarmed.'

Without a second thought Blackstone pressed Wolf Sword into the Prince's outstretched hand. 'God save you, my lord,' said Blackstone. The door slammed. He turned to face the attackers swarming up the stairs. A dozen or more men. Sword blades slaked with blood. It was a well-sprung trap – the first assault below had forced the Prince into the only escape route open to him: the staircase. The sentry killed the first two men as they struggled up the steep stairs. Blackstone seized a fallen sword. He and the man stood shoulder to shoulder, holding the high ground as the surging attackers crammed up the stairwell, hampering each other's strikes. The unnamed soldier fought well but then sword thrust and grabbing hands yanked him down into the wolf pit. Blackstone stood alone, the dead at the top of the stairs slowing the attack. He peered into the throng of men and saw the unmistakable burly figure of Gruffydd ap Madoc, silver mane and beard sluiced with sweat and stained with blood. A wild man shouldering his men aside as he stormed up the staircase to engage with Blackstone. So it was true. Lady de Sagard had bought the Welshman off.

Ap Madoc bellowed: 'Thomas! Give him up and I'll spare you. In God's name I swear it!'

Blackstone rammed his blade into a man's stomach and then booted the body free of its grip. He cut and thrust and parried, using his fist to beat the men forging through what was now a narrow gap as they stumbled over their fallen comrades. A slashing knife blade cut into his injured leg's thigh. He staggered momentarily and then braced against the searing pain as he jabbed the sword into the snarling man's throat. Sweat stung his eyes.

'God has disowned you,' he shouted over the grunting roars of the men determined to kill him and the Prince. It was only a matter of time now before they overwhelmed him. He could hold them back for a short while longer. Their sheer numbers would push him back. Heartbeats pounded away the minutes of life that remained.

And then that unfaithful bitch Fate blessed him with the kiss of life.

The assault faltered as Meulon's strength forced open the door on the half-landing below, pushing aside the tide of men. Chandos and Killbere, with John Jacob and Beyard at their back, cut a swathe into the attackers with their men. Blackstone saw the look on ap Madoc's face. The attack had failed and he knew it. He raised his face to Blackstone and, baring his teeth with a grin, turned and escaped down the stairs. Chandos, Killbere and John Jacob fought their way up to Blackstone. Meulon, Beyard and the others made quick work of the surviving routiers. The men's splattered faces and jupons bore witness to the hard and bitter fight it had taken to reach Blackstone. As Chandos reached the top step John Jacob bent and hauled aside the bodies to give them free passage.

'The Prince?' said Chandos.

'In there. Take care in his chamber – poison was used on his bed. There's a dead girl.'

Chandos nodded and pushed past Blackstone. This was no time for more questions.

'Bastards fought hard, Thomas. They were determined,' said Killbere.

'And here,' Blackstone replied, binding his leg with a dead man's belt.

'Aye, I see that. Who led these men?'

'The Welshman.'

Killbere scowled. 'He's not among the dead,' he said, glancing down the body-strewn stairs. 'What next?'

'He escaped. You and the others stay and guard the Prince. Take nothing for granted now, Gilbert. We are in the heart of the whore.' Blackstone stepped over the dead and went as quickly as he could down the stairs.

'No, Thomas! Wait for us,' Killbere called.

Blackstone turned. 'Gilbert, protect him. Do as Chandos commands.' He smiled. 'Do as I ask, my friend. I have to finish this.'

CHAPTER SEVENTY-THREE

Blackstone pursued Gruffydd ap Madoc into the cellars. Wine barrels lay along one wall, racks of wine bottles on the other. Light seeped down a narrow stone staircase at the end of the room. It was the only way out. Gripping the sword hilt tighter, he stepped warily onto the narrow steps that curved up to the right. Shifting the borrowed sword into his left hand, he edged around the corner. Light spilled down. Ap Madoc was running for his life but there was no sign of him. Blackstone pressed his weight into his wounded leg, ignored its protest and pushed up further into the room above. Pig, sheep and game carcasses, skinned and cured, hung from hooks. A servant lay slumped against a wall in a pool of blood; what had been a tray of wine bottles lay shattered at his feet. An open arch revealed a kitchen: meat on a spit, signs of food being prepared on a vast table, steam rising from a cauldron. The servants had fled, no doubt terrified by the fleeing Welshman and the violent death of one of their own. An open, arched wooden door led into another passage from where sounds of a busy city reached him. He turned into a narrow alley that led into the street. An overturned handcart, baskets of fruit and vegetables scattered, the carter thrown off-balance on the sloping cobbled street. The lumbering Welshman was as strong as an ox and had collided with him. There was still no sign of ap Madoc as burghers stooped to help the man right his cart while others gathered his wares and ran off with them. When he saw Blackstone, one of those helping the fallen man pointed towards a narrow alley across the street. Behind him to the right Blackstone saw soldiers blocking the main entrance to the palace. There was no time or need to warn them of the narrow entrance at the rear that gave access to the cellars. The attack had failed and there would be no further attempt on the Prince's life that day. Not when the assassin's leader had escaped.

Blackstone ran hard, his injured leg throwing him into an awkward gait. The narrow street was blocked halfway down. Men and women cowered, pressing themselves back against the shopkeepers' stalls. A man lay sprawled, the back of his head caved in, his blood on the cobbles not yet congealed. A child cried uncontrollably, pressed close to the skirts of a woman in the crowd. The dead man wore a blacksmith's apron and an iron bar lay close to his outstretched hand. Perhaps he had tried to stop ap Madoc and paid the price.

'There!' said a man, pointing at the sunken watercourse that ran under the city. The Canal du Caudeau had been dug over fifty years to divert water from the River Caudeau north of the city; it powered water mills to grind wheat for the city's bakers and flowed beneath the streets, eventually to spill out into the broad expanse of the fast-flowing River Dordogne beyond the city. Blackstone clambered over the low stone wall to see the shallow water gushing into a tunnel. He glanced up at the sky trying to gauge where he was in the city. The sun was behind his shoulder; the Dordogne was south of the walls. The canal offered the chance of escaping beneath the city walls and if ap Madoc reached the river he would be gone on one of the many barges plying their trade.

'The river?' Blackstone called.

'Five hundred paces,' the man shouted, pointing behind him. 'Four men!' he warned.

Blackstone slithered down into the water. Ap Madoc must have escaped with survivors from the attack. He crouched, peering into the gloomy tunnel; the reflected light from the water gave only so much illumination along the curved walls and roof. He waded in, the knee-deep water pushing behind his legs. His free hand guided him along the walls, eyes adjusting to the near darkness. He edged around a corner into complete darkness. He paused, attempting to hear a man's laboured breathing or footfalls splashing through the water. There was only the echo of the gurgling stream.

Blackstone pressed ahead and as he turned another corner firelight flickered across the ceiling twenty paces ahead. The spluttering sound of water droplets hitting flames sizzled in the dank air. The light grew brighter. It came from a side passage. He increased his pace. If more routiers had escaped and found another route beneath the city, he wanted to kill them before they turned into the main tunnel. An arm extended forward, the burning torch guiding its bearer. Blackstone snatched the man's wrist, his blade angled low, ready to plunge beneath the man's armpit. The torchbearer cried out, terror widening mouth and eyes; were it not for Blackstone's strength he would have fallen back into the stream. Blackstone felt the old man's body tremble beneath his grip as he kept the torch raised.

'Who are you?' said Blackstone.

'Lord, don't hurt me, I beg you. I am the tunnel keeper. I am charged with keeping the water free of obstruction… I beg you…' the man stuttered.

Blackstone lowered his sword. 'How far does this passage take me until I see light again?'

'I have a torch burning in each chamber where another passage joins this one.'

'No daylight? I thought the canal revealed itself to the streets above.'

'It does, it does,' said the keeper, 'but not here, not until it runs into the river.'

'Darkness the whole way?'

'Aye, lord. The whole way. Except for my torches. A man can get lost down here and drown. The nearer the river, the stronger the flow and depth. And there are no torches burning once you are past the final chamber. Only darkness. And then the drop into the river.'

'Take me to the next chamber,' said Blackstone.

Shadows cast the man's face into a contorted grimace. He shook his head. 'I am fearful, Lord, of what you seek.'

'Men who tried to kill the English Prince.'

The man shuddered, crossing himself. 'Assassins? They could wait in any of the side tunnels. We would never see them before they struck at us. Even the Almighty cannot see us down here.'

'Then ask His forgiveness for your blasphemy and thank Him I am here instead.'

Blackstone kept one hand on the nervous man's shoulder, pushing him ahead. Blackstone sweated in the fetid air and his lungs laboured from the heat. He ignored the pain in his leg that demanded he stop and attend to it. He could not gauge how far they had travelled but when the tunnel widened the tunnel keeper hesitated, bracing against Blackstone's grip. With quickening breath, he whispered, 'Someone's ahead.' His voice was barely audible over the splashing of the water, which had increased in strength, making Blackstone think they must be closer to one of the chambers and soon after the plunge down to the river.

'Where?'

The man trembled as he nodded: forward. Although Blackstone could see no one, he trusted the keeper's instincts. He put his ear close to the man's mouth, ignoring the stench of someone working in sweating darkness day in, day out. 'A passage. To the right,' the man whispered.

Blackstone pushed him onward. The man's head shook from side to side in dread. 'Keep moving,' said Blackstone, eyes searching the hewn-stone walls. And then the flickering light exposed a darker patch in the wall, not yet discernible as anything more than deeper shadow. Three paces from the side passage was a narrow tunnel. Blackstone forced the man's arm forward, the torch now level with the side entrance. A shadow loomed; steel glinted. Blackstone hauled the tunnel keeper aside; the attacker's blade struck stone instead of flesh. The torchlight flickered behind Blackstone as the tunnel keeper turned and ran, splashing through the water. Blackstone rammed the sword at the half-turned man but he twisted, parried the blow and in the diminished light Blackstone did not see that in his free hand he held a sharp-pointed dagger. Blackstone felt it pierce his mail into his side; the barely healed old wound tore. Ignoring the raw pain, he grasped the man's wrist, keeping the blade in his side, smothering the man with his own body, stopping him from bringing his sword to bear. Blackstone head-butted him. Felt and heard bone, cartilage and teeth break; forced the man to step back with a spluttered gasp. Blackstone released his wrist and rammed the sword into the man's stomach and then kicked him down into the swirling water. The darkness had, by now, engulfed them, but Blackstone knew his attacker would have no fight left in him. He knelt on one knee in the water, grappled for the man's head and hauled it above the surface, pressing his other knee into the man's stomach wound.

'The Welshman. Gruffydd ap Madoc. Where? Where is he? Ahead or in a side tunnel?'

He felt rather than saw the man shake his head. He was gasping for breath, fighting for the life that would soon desert him.

'Where?' Blackstone asked again.

'Ahead. Waiting... I tried to escape... but the tunnel was... too narrow...'

Blackstone let the wounded man's head drop back into the water and pressed his weight onto his throat until his struggle ceased. He stepped over him, felt the wound in his side and knew that loss of blood and his injured leg would disadvantage him against the Welshman's strength. There were still three more men ahead waiting to kill him. He stumbled forward, confident they would not attack him in the darkness. It would serve no purpose. Three men against one would get in each other's way and might cause more injury to themselves than to him. He reasoned that if they were waiting to ambush him together rather than one man at a time, then they would be in one of the far chambers and would use the tunnel keeper's torches to attack him. That would give them enough room and light to overpower him.

A distant glimmer of light on water forewarned him of the hidden chamber. Tumbling water reflected tongues of flame. The strength of the current behind his legs pushed him on. Beyond the chamber the sound of cascading water echoed along the tunnel. Pressing himself against the wall, he edged forward. When he reached the chamber's mouth he would have no choice but to step into plain sight and expose himself to immediate attack. Torchlight danced across the roof, showing the tunnel widened left and right. Straight ahead was darkness as the cave-like canal tumbled the water away towards the river.

Where would the killers be? Left or right? If he laid such a trap, he would have men on both sides to overwhelm him. Two on one side, the third on the other. The curving wall led into the chamber. Men wielding swords with their right hand would want room to throw their arms back and strike. The chamber wall to the left would restrict their movement. It was clear to him that they would attack from the right-hand side of the chamber. He tightened his grip on the inferior sword and took a determined stride into the open space. A rapid glance to his left showed the chamber empty but as he turned he saw ap Madoc standing behind a second man. Where was the third? It made no difference. And it was too late. The shadows concealed what the man held.

There was the sudden twang of a bow cord and then searing pain as a crossbow bolt pierced his chest. The impact forced him back against the wall. His sword arm went slack and he forced his left hand across his body to grasp the sword before it fell into the water. He gasped for air. Ap Madoc remained motionless as the bowman threw aside the crossbow and lunged forward. Blackstone parried the sword strike but the man's strength easily blocked it and then he swung his fist into Blackstone's face, splitting the skin on his forehead. Blood blinded one eye. His knees sagged. He brought his head up sharply and connected beneath the man's chin. The routier staggered back, spat out what remained of his teeth and rammed his sword towards Blackstone's exposed midriff. Blackstone twisted onto his injured leg, which gave way, dropping his hip; the blade edge ripped across his jupon, scraping against the mail beneath. The man's impetus took him past Blackstone, who backhanded the sword pommel into his temple. Dazed, he fell back, stumbled in the water and fell. Blackstone threw his weight down onto him, pushing the blade into his chest. He squirmed, his contortions so fierce that Blackstone's sword blade snapped.

Blackstone's injuries from the battlefield at Launac and the newly inflicted wounds weakened him. He pushed his back against the wall to keep himself upright. There was still half a blade left on his sword. He tightened his grip and turned his head to one side so that the blood trickled away from his one good eye. His blurred vision showed the big man step closer, a look of regret creasing his brow.

'I'm sorry, Thomas. I have no desire to kill you. Better the others did that for me. I have no choice now. I am paid to see your son and the Prince dead. By now your boy is slain by one of my men in Avignon. You stopped me from ending the Prince's life but my reward will be as great for ending yours. The Lady de Sagard nurses a vendetta against you and the Prince you serve.' He took another step. He was no fool. He knew Blackstone could still strike at him. 'If I do not kill you then you will spend your life hunting me down. I'll finish it quickly,' he said.

Death beckoned. Blackstone knew that even if he could wound the Welshman the fourth man waited somewhere in the shadows.

'You'll die first,' he vowed. 'I'll see your body swept away before mine.'

Gruffydd ap Madoc hesitated. 'Thomas, you are the most defiant bastard I have ever known. No different from when you were a boy at Crécy. By Christ, I swear I thought you dead that day.' He laughed. 'And now you are moments from death and you threaten me. Look at you, man. Lame, wounded, barely upright. Drop that useless blade and let's be done with this.'

Crécy. The terror and noise of that first great battle lurked in Blackstone's memory, always ready to be summoned. The mutilation and death of his brother, the sprawling fight across fallen bodies trying to reach him and then the final moments of his own life beneath the Bohemian knight's sword. Death a heartbeat away. A desperate final breath that gave the young Blackstone the will and strength to kill the aggressor.

Gruffydd ap Madoc half-turned, swinging back his sword arm. Blackstone pushed himself off the wall, threw himself forward, smothered the strike, jabbed upward with the broken shard, felt it strike mail and then the agonizing surge of pain as his own body weight snapped the crossbow bolt. The burly Welshman brushed him aside. Blackstone stumbled, striking his head against the wall. Instinct made him twist. He sat in the water, back once more against the wall, the current tugging at him. He lifted his head. Ap Madoc's raised sword would not be blocked again.

'Enough, Thomas,' he grunted.

Suddenly the Welshman saw something on the other side of the chamber. His mouth gaped; his sword arm faltered. Blackstone heard someone moving. He turned his head. A figure stepped from the darkness. Blackstone shook his head, trying to clear his mind. Once again he was lying on the field at Crécy, the priest giving him the last sacrament. Beyond his shattered body a great cross of fire emblazoned the sky as a windmill burned. He stared hard. Torchlight blazed brightly against a black cross. The flaming symbol came closer. Ap Madoc cursed, turning to face the apparition. Steel clanged. The burning cross swayed before Blackstone's eyes. A cry echoed. Two, three, perhaps more sword strikes and then a final blow. Gruffydd ap Madoc dropped to his knees and fell face down, dead, into the water.

Blackstone fought the darkness that reached for him. He extended his hand towards the blurred fiery cross. It came closer but Blackstone fell sideways into the water and felt it tear him away. It was a comfort from the persistent pain. The current rolled him onto his back as the water swept him away into the black tunnel.

They found Thomas Blackstone's body later that day, washed up on the river's muddy banks.

CHAPTER SEVENTY-FOUR

Killbere, John Jacob and the captains stood silently in the room. Sun streamed through the window, bringing warmth to the stone walls. Blackstone lay on a bed covered in a linen sheet.

Killbere's sigh was a curse. 'He was always so damned pig-headed. He should have taken some of us with him.'

'He cared more for the safety of the Prince than his own life,' said John Jacob.

'Better to die on the field of battle than down a damned sewer,' said Meulon.

Before anyone else shared their thoughts on Blackstone's courage a hubbub of excited voices reached them from the corridor beyond the closed door.

'See who's making such an undignified noise when he's lying here like this,' said Killbere.

Renfred opened the door and saw a flurry of activity as Sir John Chandos led the Earl of Warwick, the Prince and members of his retinue towards the room. John Chandos carried Blackstone's sword. He reached the door.

'Everyone out,' he barked.

Killbere and the others stepped quickly into the corridor and pressed themselves against the wall. Thomas de Beauchamp, Earl of Warwick, made a sweeping gesture and the retinue parted, following Killbere's example. Heads bowed from both sides of the corridor as the Prince strode forward. He looked neither left nor right. When he reached the door Chandos presented him with Blackstone's sword. The Prince stepped inside. Chandos closed the door behind him.

Edward, Prince of Wales and Aquitaine, stood for a moment looking at the man whose path had crossed his own on numerous occasions. They had fought in war and argued in private and he had despaired often at Blackstone's defiance. Alone in the room without servants he ceased for a moment to be a prince of the realm and pulled a stool forward to sit next to Blackstone.

A pigeon cooed and fluttered against the window's stippled glass. The Prince saw the shadow disappear and when he turned back Blackstone's eyes were watching him. Blackstone tried to rise but the Prince gently pressed a hand against his chest, easing him back onto the pillow. 'There is no need for that, Thomas. Not today.'

'You're safe,' said Blackstone.

The Prince nodded. 'Yet again you save our life. Yet again we are in your debt,' he said.

'There is no such debt, sire.'

The Prince lifted Blackstone's belt and scabbard from the chair and slid the hardened steel home. 'If Wolf Sword had been in your hand instead of an inferior blade, you would have suffered less injury.'

'I'll heal.'

'We would have it no other way. Our personal physician cares for you. One of your archers had the impertinence to raise his voice and demand an apothecary trained in the use of herbs to also attend you.'

'That would be Will Longdon.'

'We believe that to be his name. He was thrown into the cells. A few days of stale bread and water will serve as sufficient punishment. Don't worry – we will release him without charge. We are familiar with insubordination from you and those who follow you.'

'All good men. All would die for you.'

'And some did during the attempt on our life. Were it not for you, Thomas, the Lady Joan and I would be dead. You readily gave up your sword when the enemy was at our door.'

'My duty has always been clear. But you would have saved her. You forget, I've seen you fight.'

The Prince smiled. Two soldiers sharing a common heritage of war.

'How long have I been here?' Blackstone asked.

'Two days. You stank like a sewer rat when you were found and no doubt you fought like one. You were bathed and your wounds attended to.'

Blackstone fell silent. The Prince shared his silence. He knew how far their journey had been together.

'When I lay in the darkness facing death, my mind took me to the field at Crécy. I saw the burning cross again and heard the whisper of angels. My mind played tricks but I know the torchlight down there showed me a cross of fire.'

'We fight our battles over and over, Thomas. When they dragged your body from the riverbank we once again saw the boy lying wounded at our feet at Crécy. I too was young and that burning windmill lit up the sky for miles. It heralded our victory louder than any trumpet or drum. It was a sign we would one day win our father's war.' The Prince smiled. 'You were not mistaken, Thomas. The man who saved you was a Teutonic Knight. His name is Gunther von Schwerin.'

Blackstone smiled. 'The fourth man.'

The Prince's expression showed he did not understand.

'When I went after the Welshman I thought four men had gone down into the canal,' Blackstone explained. 'He must have been shadowing us and finally saw his chance for revenge when ap Madoc ran from the attack. It was the torchlight on his blazon I saw. Where is he now?'

'Gone. He warned your men that the water had swept you away. He told us he owed you a debt, that you had saved him and his fellow knights. And when you were found alive on the riverbank, he rode on.'

The Prince laid a hand on Blackstone's arm. 'You could have gone to Avignon to save your son,' he said, his voice unusually tender. 'You chose to stay. We are humbled, Thomas. And grateful. We had news that your son is safe. Wounded, but safe.'

A tear formed in the corner of Blackstone's eye.

The Prince nodded and smiled in understanding. 'When you are healed we will send for you.' He stood ready to leave and placed a hand across Blackstone's. 'We desire peace, but it is the nature of these times that there will always be conflict. We begin a new journey together, Thomas. We will have need of you to fight again.'

AUTHOR'S NOTES

Medieval manuscripts and maps refer to the hilltop town of Domme, in the region now commonly known as the Dordogne, as Dome. Gilbert de Dome, Lord of Vitrac and one time Seneschal of the Périgord, was also known by a different spelling to his name. The names Gilbert, Gisbert, Gilibert and Guibert de Dome are recorded. I chose Gisbert to differentiate between him and the series' more familiar character Gilbert Killbere.

I thought it worth mentioning some background detail on a recurring character, Simon Bucy, who throughout the series is Thomas Blackstone's enemy. He was an influential adviser to both the King of France and his son, the Dauphin. The loss of his estates during the (earlier) Jacquerie uprising and the threat to those in power at the time must have been as terrifying as the revolution that was to be inflicted on France four hundred years later, but his political sense of survival was keenly honed. His career began as a procurator in the French Parlement in 1326 and he became its first president for the years 1345–50 and he was ennobled in 1339 for service to the Crown and State.

When Thomas Blackstone fought the Teutonic Knight, I referred to the medieval method of sword fighting. The Royal Armoury at Leeds holds one of the earliest dated manuscripts in Latin, with drawings of fencers without armour showing techniques of sword and buckler fighting. Many of the technical terms are in German, which implies that the author was a German cleric. The text suggests that rather than relying on strength alone, skill and manoeuvrability were the key to success. In the first book of the *Master of War* series, Jean de Harcourt, Blackstone's French mentor and friend, taught him various sword skills. In this book I did not wish to dwell too long on theoretical texts so I barely touched on the subject, but the schooling of knights, in this case the Teutonic Knights, fitted neatly with my characters.

By way of a very brief introduction to a complex subject here are a few of the named attacks: *Schiltslac* (shield strike), *Stichslac* (thrust strike) and *Durchtritt* (step through). Blackstone and von Plauen were not wearing suited armour, so I had Killbere refer to the type of combat as *Kampffechten* (armoured combat on foot) rather than *Blossfechten* (unarmoured combat). By having a third party, Killbere, recount the type of combat I gave myself some leeway in case any purists insisted that because they were not wearing full armour when they fought then it should be referred to as the latter rather than the former. However, the five *Meisterhauwen* (mastercuts) are well documented. One reference by medieval German fencing masters is to the *Funff Haue* (the five hidden or secret strikes). This was what Killbere warned Blackstone about. *Zornhau* (strike of wrath): the diagonal descending stroke from the right shoulder. *Krumphau* (crooked strike), which breaks any attacking high thrust and is aimed at the opponent's hands. *Zwerchhau* (crosswise strike) is a multi-faceted strike aimed at head, hands or body. *Schielhau* (squinting strike): this unusual term might refer to the fighter glancing away from an opponent to make him believe that a feint is coming. The downward diagonal strike descends in a sliding motion towards the head and shoulder. And, finally, *Scheitelhau* (crown strike), a vertical strike targeting the top of the head.

It is historically accurate that at the Battle of Launac Gaston Phoebus was outnumbered by Count Jean d'Armagnac, and also that the broad flat plain offered no cover except for a copse of trees, which is where the Count de Foix positioned his bowmen. D'Armagnac did not expect his arch-rival to have longbow archers under his command and it was this tactical error that lost him the battle. I was uncertain if the cold December conditions would affect the draw of the archers' longbows so I turned once again to the expertise of Captain David Whitmore of the Shire Bowmen Longbow Roving Marks, who explained that when shooting in winter he would add an extra coating of beeswax to his bow's hemp cord. I am, as always, grateful for his insight.

I visited the various locations during the research for this novel but when I was in Bergerac, I could find no record of where the Bishop of Sarlat, Austence de Saint-Colombe, rendered homage to the Prince of Wales. I am grateful to the historian and author Michael Jones whose book *The Black Prince* gave me additional insights into the Prince of Wales and his journey throughout Aquitaine at that time. He advised me that the ceremony was unlikely to have been in the city's medieval church of Saint Jacques as it was being rebuilt and only completed in 1377.

Tourists who visit Sarlat, one of the best preserved medieval cities in France, and who are familiar with that city, know the cathedral does not sit in the main square, which is how I have presented it in *Cross of Fire*. I studied medieval maps of Sarlat and discovered the buildings that surround the cathedral were constructed in the fifteenth and sixteenth centuries onwards, so at the time of Blackstone's fight in the main square I took the view that the city was far more open and that the cathedral would have formed the focal point of the city. I am grateful to Laurène and Kelsey, knowledgeable tourist advisers at the Office de Tourisme, Sarlat Périgord Noir (info@sarlat-tourisme.com) for confirming the probable length of the medieval city walls at the time of the action taking place in this book, and also in confirming the date that the church of Saint Sacerdos was declared a cathedral – 1317.

Finally, I extend my thanks to my readers, who wait patiently every year for Thomas Blackstone to once again enter their reading lives and who share their enthusiasm for the Master of War series. My thanks to you all.

David Gilman
Devonshire
2019

www.davidgilman.com
www.facebook.com/davidgilman.author
https://twitter.com/davidgilmanuk